Us

The Shape of Us

DREW DAVIES

bookouture

Published by Bookouture in 2018

An imprint of StoryFire Ltd.

Carmelite House
50 Victoria Embankment
London EC4Y 0DZ

www.bookouture.com

ISBN: 978-1-78681-709-9
eBook ISBN: 978-1-78681-708-2

To Peter Farmer,
in fond memory of his warmth & wit.

CHAPTER ONE

'London,' they say, eyes twinkling. 'London is a city for lovers!'

Look down the sweeping avenues of Shaftesbury or Sloane and you'll find them, hands entwined, cheeks pink and dimpled with joy, *loving* at each other. On the Tube they'll self-consciously flirt (though not self-consciously enough, you'll sniff, ruffling the *Evening Standard*). He'll make a grand gesture of offering her the empty seat or perhaps she'll perch coquettishly on his lap – while the rest of the carriage tries desperately to ignore them.

Yes, London is for the young and in love, but loathed are they by all good Londoners. Like tourists and pigeons, lovers are a blight on this great city – a fact they are completely (and conveniently) blind to. That is, until one day, when a lover finds themselves standing behind a couple so amorously entwined it's a wonder the cheap bottle of Spanish red they're holding doesn't smash to the floor – in fact, they *want* it to smash – and suddenly our lover finds themselves under stark fluorescents, unable to wait for the self-service checkouts after all and quite out of love with the idea of love. But until then, my friend (twinkle, twinkle), until then!

*

Here come Chris and Daisy – two soon-to-be lovers – now, both hurrying towards their meeting point near Embankment station, both in their early thirties, both thinking they are the only one who is twelve minutes late for their first date. She is quite lovely – her

hair in brown curls that took two attempts and a navy dress she
'borrowed' from work that floats in all the right cleavage-type
places and none of the thigh-revealing wrong ones. He is holding
a copy of *The Big Issue* that he hopes will make him seem more
edgy and less posh than he is, and is wearing jeans that do good
things for his rather square buttocks. Chris looks younger than
he has a right to and, all things considered, fairly handsome.

A few paces from the meeting point, they finally see each
other and realise they are not the only one late, and oh the relief,
and how funny to arrive at exactly the same moment, and they
take in the smells of each other (him: soap and sandalwood,
her: jasmine and the slight zest of something – deodorant?) and
talk and laugh like this for some time before realising they have
successfully side-stepped the awkward 'Do I kiss you on one
cheek or two?' routine and cut straight to 'Can I hold the cuff
of your jacket while I adjust my shoe?' Once Daisy's heel strap
is fastened in place, they walk down the steps to the riverside
entrance to Gordon's Wine Bar, a popular drinking grotto (and
the capital's oldest), still chatting breathlessly, until the gloom
and the heat of the cave-like bar stifles them. *Why did I suggest
this place?* Chris thinks. It's one of those bars he's always meaning
to go to, but never does – in his mind it is full of dripping
candles and romantic hideaways – in reality it's cramped and
dark and full of overbearing men, who are yelling at someone
called Smithee to get three bottles, not two. With a conspiratorial
nod, the couple head back up into the daylight to the long row
of tables and chairs outside the bar instead. It's busy here too,
though – they nab one seat, which Daisy guards with Chris's
jacket, while he walks the length of the terrace, seeing if any
more are free. As he hustles the tables, she watches his style:
charming, direct, not too flirty with the ladies, not too 'alright,
mate?' with the guys. His first three attempts are thwarted as
the empty seats are being held for people, but he pushes on

and finally returns to her, eyebrows wiggling in victory, with the prize of another chair.

It is only now, after Chris positions the chair beside Daisy and sits, that they really look at each other.

He's less goofy than she remembers, or maybe less goofy than the mental image of him she's been turning around in her mind the past week. Could she kiss him? The answer comes immediately: *Yes.* Good. Daisy could do with a drink, though. She hopes he's not going to be one of those men who barely touches his glass, forcing her to sneak sips when he's not paying attention. She had six months off the booze last year, mostly just to prove she could, and yes, her skin was better and she barely missed a yoga class, but she felt too good, too chaste, and restless, with so much extra time. When she caught herself ironing bed sheets one Saturday morning, she knew it was either start drinking again or join a nunnery.

Chris decides Daisy looks different too, better. What is it? She's softer around the eyes than when they first met. This is probably not surprising considering he cycled up to her from nowhere and brazenly asked her out. He wasn't usually so impulsive, but the Boris bike he'd rented had given him such a wonderful sense of freedom, whizzing around the West End with the spokes humming, that he'd felt intoxicated with possibility and found himself compelled to ask for her number, this beautiful woman walking along Carnaby Street, carrying a miniature palm tree, safe in the knowledge that he could whizz away again if she spurned him. She'd peered at him, through the leaves of the palm, with a cool blankness as if this happened all the time, strange man-boys on bikes being so forward, and said that she wouldn't give him her number but she would take his. He'd assumed this was a deflection and so was surprised when Daisy called the next day to ask him out. He'd said yes, and that was that. There was no other correspondence in the days running up to the date. In fact, they had both wondered if the other would show up at all. But here they were now, in the late September sun, together in one of the most exciting cities in the— and with no drinks, he realises now. He stands up. White? Red? A bottle, yes? She smiles, a broad grin he hasn't seen before, and there's a zip of energy in his solar plexus, a tenderness in his lungs, and he walks back down into the gloom again to order drinks, feeling oddly light.

*

On the other side of London, Adam Jiggins walks from Moorgate station through the Barbican Centre – a large, imposing arts venue – and towards his gym. Adam walks with purpose, or more accurately, does his best to imitate a person who has a purposeful walk. Until four months ago he would have hurried quite naturally: power-walking from his flat in east London's Hackney to the small digital advertising agency in Farringdon where he worked; jogging to buy lunch before all the good sandwiches were taken, and running/sprinting/diving to catch the bus at the end of the day. But now that he is unemployed (no, between jobs), he has to remind himself to quicken his stride.

The gym is his salvation, an oasis in uncertain times. When his agency began to lose clients, Adam considered joining a cheaper gym – one without the fat white towels rolled up in their cubbyholes, or the pretty blonde girls at the reception desk. He knew he should be downsizing to save money in case – God forbid – anything happened at work, but he had become too used to certain standards, and anyway, it was false economy to join the YMCA, with its questionable showers and rancid mats, because he'd never go. This way Adam had justified shelling out the crazy-a-month membership fee even after his bosses had called him into the small meeting room/breakout space to explain 'the situation'.

'You're f-firing me?' he'd cried, his stammer always worse under stress, taking a grip of one of the handles on the foosball table beside him for support.

'We have to make some bloody difficult decisions, and it's killing us. You must know that.'

Adam looked out of the window across to Smithfield Market, where they'd once held public executions, feeling the proverbial rope tighten around his own neck.

'What if I went p-part-time? I could do three days a week until…?'

'We just don't have the work in the pipeline. It's this climate, everyone in the industry is feeling the pinch.'

'But we're *d-d-digital*!' he'd almost shouted, letting go of the handle and causing three wooden footballers to spin on their axis.

It didn't make sense. He'd watched a webinar on it only the other week – digital marketing was the new rock and roll. Companies were moving away from old-world advertising in newspapers and on TV, and spending money on search engines instead. Every movement was tracked, every click counted. Adam had felt a surge of pride, knowing the online adverts he created for pet insurance and wound glue were part of the revolution. *How could this be happening?* And then it had dawned on him – there was a revolution, yes, and advertisers *were* spending more online, but only with the good agencies. And to be honest, their agency was not very good. It wasn't that they were lazy – it was just that before you didn't have to work so hard to seem competent. You could sprinkle the conversation with 'social network' this, and 'augmented reality' that, and walk away with a six-figure contract. But now, every university grad was a self-certified social media guru, the market was flooded. And Adam had been washed away.

The memory gives him a stabbing pain in the sternum. He tries to walk taller, puff up his chest. By now he's worked his way through the Barbican Centre and out the other side into the setting sun, following the pavement that will spit him out near the doorstep of his gym. He checks his watch, still on schedule.

After the shock of unemployment settled, Adam had felt briefly liberated by all the spare time. He could go to the supermarket and spend a whole afternoon browsing the foreign cheese section, or head to a midnight screening of a cult film. Quickly, however, the rush of freedom had faded, and he sensed something else instead: ennui and a familiar depression. It was at the gym he felt it most keenly. If he went at peak times he was acutely aware of a countdown to nine o'clock or the end of lunchtime; a frenetic energy he was no longer able to tap into. Mornings or afternoons were the reverse – languid stretches of emptiness broken only by the retired or infirm padding around the exercise equipment like ghouls, or a damp grey mass, looming in the back of the steam room like some silverbacked gorilla, grunting occasionally. Adam had settled on late in the evening, long after the post-work rush, imagining it made him appear hardworking and driven. He could almost feel a wave of respect from the towel attendant when he arrived close to ten o'clock. Though weekends were more oblique time-wise, he had kept to his new gym routine and visited as late as he could. Routines were good; all the therapists and self-help books agreed on that. So here he was on a sunny Saturday evening – shoulders back, eyes fixed on the middle distance, looking to all the world like your average employed and employable Joe.

His foot gives way under him, causing him to wobble comically, and Adam bends down to see what has made him slip. It's a corporate identity card in a plastic case belonging to one Mark J. Smith. Adam knows the company, Mercer and Daggen, well – it's one of those big finance-y investment-y places a few streets over, with its intimidating glass foyer and scowling security guards. Carrying on his way, Adam inspects the photo more closely: Mark J. Smith is an unexceptional-looking man in his mid-thirties, a clone of a million other city workers – cropped brown hair, pink shirt, slightly overweight and with sallow skin from too much alcohol and time spent indoors. If you were playing Guess Who, you'd be stymied – the only distinguishable feature is perhaps that one earlobe seems slightly bigger than the other. Still, Adam feels a pang of jealousy. Even though his old agency had been too small to need such security, the pass feels like a talisman of his past. It annoys him that he covets this pasty man's job, a job the man himself most likely resents. Sighing, Adam tucks the security card into his wallet, reminding himself to return it to Mercer and Daggen after his workout, and enters the gym to a chorus of pretty blonde girls welcoming him in happy unison.

*

Dinner is not going well. In an attempt to avoid the 'zombie monologue' Chris has experienced so often on dates (dead-eyed regurgitations of family, study, career and relationship history), he has led Daisy on a twisting free-form conversation which has taken in current affairs (avoiding anything too mobilising), film, music, best sick day excuses (they both agree, the more graphically scatological, the better), travel and strangest place names (having visited Tasmania, he has an unfair advantage – Lovely Bottom, Mouldy Hole and Misery Knob are just a few he can list off). To begin with, Daisy takes to the challenge, enjoying the great sweeps in topic (noticing that whenever she raises the subject of work, he steers her onto another topic. Not a red flag, she thinks, but possibly an amber one?), meeting his jokes with riffs of her own, and thinking how nice it is not to be talked at for a change. At one point she places her hand on his, squeezing it to emphasise a punchline, and notes the jolt of electricity that seems to pass through his body.

It's only when the main courses arrive that things take a turn.

'And how do you feel about pets?' she asks, as the waiter grinds pepper over Chris's Cornish lamb.

'I'm all for them, as a rule,' he says, removing the sprig of garnish daintily with his knife and fork. 'I love dogs,' (this is no surprise to her, he even looks part Labrador with his big brown eyes and floppy blonde hair), 'but I am allergic to cats.'

Her heart drops. She knows it's silly – she doesn't even own a cat – but Daisy always imagined that one day her dream family would include a kitten. As a child, she had a much-loved mog called Hazel, who had run away when they'd moved house, and she had never gotten over the guilt (she'd walked around the neighbourhood with her mum, looking under every car for weeks). She still has dreams where she puts up 'Missing' posters and hears a far-off plaintive mew.

'What about one of those hypoallergenic ones?' Daisy says brightly, trying not to make it sound like an interrogation. 'Or taking a normal cat and shaving it?'

Inside she cringes at the thought of Hazel, shaved and shivering in some abandoned alleyway, but he laughs and she feels she has successfully negotiated herself away from crazy cat lady territory.

'Doesn't work, I still swell up,' he says and puffs out his cheeks.

'Can you take antihistamines?' she asks as casually as she can, picking at a mushroom in her risotto.

He stops, a pink slither of meat wobbling on his fork.

'You're not one of those crazy cat women, are you? Newspaper all over the floor, bathtubs full of mince?'

She feels her cheeks starting to redden.

'You are, aren't you?'

Daisy smiles and rolls her eyes, but he's enjoying teasing her and won't let go.

'How many do you have? Ten? Fifty? I bet you dress them up as Hollywood movie stars and post pictures of them online. Catalie Portman. Tony Purrtis,' Chris pauses, thinking, 'George Claw-ny!' She knows she needs to join in if she's to save face, but she feels the froth of anger and disappointment bubbling up in her throat, suppressing her sense of humour. 'Ginger Rogers – that one you don't even need to change if you get the right colour!'

She feels an impulse to grab the copy of *The Big Issue* he's laid carefully beside him and swat him, very hard, around the side of the head.

This is going very well, he thinks.

*

Adam emerges into the cool evening air with damp hair and a full-body glow of wellbeing. He's given up on building muscle (his biceps stubbornly refuse to grow; his arms remain defiantly spindly) or shedding his (slight) beer belly – it's the endorphins he craves. Although he was no longer so vexed by his stutter, he still enjoyed any activity that put him in close proximity to others, without the obligation to speak.

Remembering the security card in his bag, Adam crosses the road away from the station and walks towards the Museum of London. The City is dead on the weekends – all the eateries closed and most of the pubs too. Adam takes a left at St Anne's and then down Wood Street onto Cheapside. Mercer and Daggen looms in front of him, the glass windows lit from inside giving it an eerie blue glow. As he draws closer, he's surprised to find it empty. The reception is fitted out in the usual combination of silver turnstiles, large orb lights dangling from the ceiling and the obligatory massive abstract canvas, a token appeasement for the regular balls-out capitalism ('look, we buy art – we're not evil!'). He considers knocking on the glass, but tries the door instead and it pushes open.

'Yes, please?' comes a voice, and the head of a black security guard pokes over the reception desk. The guard is in his sixties, and a world away from the neckless bruisers Adam usually sees here during the week. His suit seems too big, as if he's borrowed it from his dad, and his eyes are bloodshot and tired. Adam wonders if he was sleeping.

'Ah, hello,' says Adam, putting down his sports bag on the floor and searching inside it. 'I, um, I've g-got… Oh, I just had it.'

The security guard looks down impassively as Adam pulls out his sweaty gym gear (he hopes the guard can't smell his shoes) until finally he finds the photo card and holds it up with a triumphant 'Aha!' The guard nods and his head disappears again behind the desk, and Adam hears a click at the silver turnstiles as a small red light turns to green.

Adam takes a step towards the desk. 'I think you've...'

'It's okay, it's okay,' says the security guard, who's now seated, and gives Adam a wave of his hand in the direction beyond the turnstiles as if he has better things to do than sit here chatting (go back to sleep, perhaps?). Adam places the ID card on the reception counter and the security guard stares at it for a moment and then (was that a sigh he heard?) dutifully picks it up to examine it. Adam is about to explain he found it at The Barbican when the security guard grunts and nods again, and hands the card back with another quick wave towards the turnstile. 'Yes, yes, Mr Smith,' he says, sitting back down in his chair.

Adam is stunned. How can he have been mistaken for the grey-skinned schlub in the photo? He is not even thirty yet and he's *thin*! Perhaps the guard's eyes are rheumy? Adam is about to turn around and go, when he picks up the ID card instead and takes another look at the dark circles under Mark J. Smith's eyes. Feeling a sudden surge of energy, he pockets it, picks up his bag, walks through the turnstile – they make a satisfying 'tink-tink-tink' sound – and he is on the other side, heading into the depths of Mercer and Daggen like a man with purpose, a man who belongs, and for the first time in nearly four months, he believes it.

*

She has decided the date must end. Chris seems sweet – *too* sweet, Daisy thinks now, but he is not her type after all. The cat thing is not the deal breaker – she's not that petty, for the right guy she would forgo all furry animals. But only for the right guy, which clearly, he's not (he's a bit too posh anyway, someone her dad might call 'Port Side' on his radio to the taxi controller, a code that his passenger was firmly of the Upper Crust). However, Daisy isn't about to make a fuss. The last thing she wants is for him to realise he's ruined the evening and will never see her again. The date might be over, but she doesn't want to ruin the illusion of the date – she hasn't stolen the dress from work for nothing. To this end, Daisy smiles through dessert, but turns down coffee. Chris doesn't seem to have noticed she is now completely closed off to him, and this is both pleasing and worrying to her. It's pleasing, because she's glad she can give the semblance of an interested party even during an aberration of an evening like this, but worrying because she wonders if her days are running out to find a suitor who will not only see through the facade, but call her on it.

On a scale of one to ten, Chris is seven drunk and eight point five randy. Each time Daisy glances down to her lap (he thinks she is being demure, in reality she is checking the time on her phone), he takes a mental photograph of her plunging neckline. He then returns his focus to her face to examine the image – the summer tanned skin on her neck and chest, and that wonderful crevice that leads to two perfectly ample breasts. When the mental image fades he simply waits for her to glance down again to renew it.

After the bill is paid (Daisy makes certain they split it), they find themselves on the street again and she is about to make her excuses when Chris suggests one last drink at this great place he knows, just over the bridge. She scrunches up her nose and starts to say how late it is, and she should really get going, and he wonders: *should I kiss her?* As his brain processes this thought, Chris stares awkwardly at her, mouth slack, eyes wide. *Like a puppy*, she thinks, *a big goofy puppy*. And there's something so harmless about him now – definitely not sexy, but cute – that Daisy doesn't have the heart to crush his feelings, and so she lets him take her by the hand and lead them into the night. They walk towards Embankment Pier and over the Hungerford footbridge, taking in the River Thames and all the lights around it, looking to all the world like young, happy lovers.

One drink, Daisy thinks, *one drink and I'm gone*.

The bar is tucked beneath the next bridge and he orders two large mojitos – she's forgotten how much she likes them – and they sit on tall barstools and feel that giddy feeling brought about by strong drinks and dangling legs. As they are officially dutching this date now, Daisy buys the next and final round, but then they need a shot for the road (her shout), and it tastes so delicious, like toffees, that they must have another one (his shout) and a chaser of something the barman calls a Wet Nurse, which is so silky and throat-warming they have one more, and somehow they are out of the bar now and have met people on the street, a short Italian in a leather jacket and his cigarette-smoking girlfriend – they have made friends! Where are they going? Can they come too? Of course! And they laugh at their good fortune and hail a cab, bundling together inside, and when they arrive at the new bar in Vauxhall (or is it a club? The Italians' English isn't great), the pair feel connected to their new friends in a way rarely felt in London and when asked how long they've been a couple, Chris replies, 'What time is it?' and Daisy laughs, although the Italians don't seem to get the joke. The line for the club (it must be a club – they can hear a thumping bass) is long, and aren't there a lot of men in the queue? And it is time for the Italians to laugh now because it's a gay club, and Chris runs a hand through his floppy blonde hair and tries not to ogle as two women in front of them kiss.

A breeze has picked up – Daisy shivers, pulling Chris's jacket around her tighter, and wonders if he's really gay after all and engineered this whole 'accidental' expedition on purpose. She decides it doesn't matter – maybe it's better this way? – but feels a twinge of disappointment, which surprises her.

After bouncers pat down their pockets and search his wallet (no condom, Chris thinks, thankfully), they skip up a small flight of steps and into the belly of the club. It's warm in here, almost radiantly hot, and seems to be heated by the naked, gyrating bodies of hundreds of attractive young men. Chris bows formally and takes Daisy's hand (*cor, he is posh*, she thinks), twirling her once, twice. Someone claps and whoops, and they don't know if it's for them or not, but cheered by the music and the happy crowd, they dance together, arms in the air, unselfconsciously. And now the Italians are back with drinks for all of them – hooray! – and the music really kicks in, and it's a song Daisy thinks she knows, and everything is spinning, spinning.

Several cocktails later, the couple find themselves quite seriously drunk. At some point, the male Italian leads them, like two stumbling, doe-eyed children, towards the toilets and into the women's loos. This is not so strange as it might ordinarily have been – the room is full of men: muscled ones with huge chunks of meat for arms, skinny vested boys checking their shoulders for acne in the mirrors, and drag queens cackling together by the hand dryers. Women are definitely in the minority in these, the women's toilets.

The Italian enters a stall and beckons the other two in. Giggling bemusedly, they join him, but this takes some choreography, the Italian sliding behind the toilet door to allow Daisy and Chris to squeeze in and squash up either side of the cistern so he can close the door again and lock it. Taking out his wallet, he removes a small plastic bag full of white powder.

'What is it?' they ask in unison, both apprehensive.

The Italian taps the bag with his finger.

'K,' he says, his teeth chattering.

'What does it do?'

The Italian smiles. 'Make you feel good, feel floaty.'

Daisy remembers listening to a segment about ketamine on *Woman's Hour* – what had been the risks? Her mind draws a blank, but she remembers they tranquilised horses with it. Fortunately, Chris looks as nervous as she is.

'You try?' the Italian asks.

'Not for me,' Chris replies. 'I don't want to commandeer your supply.'

'Supply? You want?'

'No, no, it's fine.'

'It's okay, I get,' says the Italian, and he opens the door and shuts it again behind him. It happens so quickly – poof and he's gone – that they laugh in confusion. Should they leave too? Alone, they are instantly shy. Daisy's hand is on the door handle when Chris finally takes his moment and, touching the back of her head, turns her face to meet his mouth.

He's kissing me, she thinks. *I'm kissing him*. She closes her eyes, feeling a wonderful bubbly sensation rise through her body. *I hope my lips aren't sweaty.*

Daisy touches Chris's shoulder, and he flinches.

'I'm sorry,' she says, startled by his reaction.

'Don't be,' he replies, shaking his head. 'It's just an old war wound.'

'What war was that?'

Chris kisses her again. 'Life,' he says, between kisses, and Daisy tactfully slips her hands down to his arm, away from his shoulder.

They're still kissing when the cubicle door opens and they're joined again by another person. Imagining it to be their friend, the sound of a cockney accent makes them jump.

'Your Italian mate said you wanted to buy some K?'

They turn to find a bulldog of a man inside the cubicle with them. If everything didn't feel so warm and wonderful from the kiss, Daisy might have screamed.

'I'm sorry, what?' Chris says, sounding painfully clipped and upper class.

'Do you want to buy some K?' the man repeats slowly. He has a boxer's squashed nose and cauliflower ears, a shaved head and tattoos up the side of his neck. In a building full of Brazilian go-go boys, he must stand out like a glow stick.

'Er, sure,' Chris replies. *Just buy the stuff*, he thinks, *keep him happy and we can escape.*

The drug dealer sniffs and takes a manila parcel out of his jacket pocket and opens it. Inside is an array of small paper envelopes and plastic bags full of coloured pills. He takes out one of the envelopes, and opens the top flap, peering inside. They watch him together, transfixed. Unsatisfied with the contents, the dealer closes the flap again and chucks it back in the big manila parcel.

'My mother died recently,' he says casually, taking out another small envelope.

'Oh, I'm so sorry,' Daisy replies automatically.

The drug dealer nods gravely but says nothing, focusing on the contents of the envelope instead.

'Were you very close?' she offers, because it seems like the polite thing to say.

'Not really,' he says, taking his cue, 'not to begin with, anyway. She wasn't always there for me, my mum. Didn't always agree with my choices. But over the past few years we started to bond again.' He holds up the small origami envelope. 'She'd help me out, make these paper wraps to put the K and coke in, and I'd give her pocket money in return. The doctor told her she had only a few weeks left and when we were clearing out her house, I found this stack of wraps she'd been working on, hidden beside a bookshelf. She was stock-piling them because she knew she wasn't going to be around for much longer and didn't want me to run out.' The couple look at each other, not knowing what to say, or if it's even appropriate to speak. 'Couldn't use them. Her eyesight was so bad towards the end she couldn't fold properly, so I'm stuck with thousands of these badly-made wraps. I can't use them, and I can't throw them away because, you know, they're the final thing my mum gave to me before she died.'

The dealer has found the envelope he's searching for and hands it over.

'Funny, life. Right, that's forty quid.'

*

Adam wakes at dawn in the makeshift bed he's created out of three cushions, a coat and an old copy of the *Financial Times*. He's aware of a nagging concern that perhaps it wasn't the best decision to set up camp in this spacious corner office with its leather furniture and view of St Paul's Cathedral – being discovered here might increase the severity of recrimination – but the rows of computer cubicles outside felt too exposed. No, tucked under this desk he is practically invisible, even if someone were to come into the room – if they wanted to sit at the desk though, then he'd have problems.

Pulling a pink sheet of the newspaper around his shoulders, he feels snug. The bed – *a nest*, Adam thinks sleepily, *I'm like an animal curled up in its nest* – is surprisingly comfortable and he's slept better than he has for weeks. He knows he must leave before he's found in the morning, but he's lulled by the hum of the fluorescent lights and his eyes start to close again.

'One more hour,' he murmurs. 'One more hour and I'll go.'

CHAPTER TWO

JoJo, Joan to her late mother, is sixty-three years old and should know better. She scans the other customers in the Primrose Hill café and is greeted by the approving faces of at least six yummy mummies. JoJo can guess what they're thinking: *how sweet to be so in love still, I hope we're like that at their age*! A few of the mothers turn back to their friends and say these very words as if JoJo can't hear them, as if she and Frank are animals in a zoo, a couple of ancient pandas, unthreatening as a greeting card image. She smiles to herself, and Frank, seeing the smile, squeezes her hand. They have been sitting like this for nearly half an hour, neither of them speaking, alternatively staring down at the table or out towards the park. Their lattes have gone cold and formed thick milky skins.

JoJo and Frank are sixty-three and sixty-five respectively and have just agreed to begin an affair. Although, JoJo ponders, is it an affair if you're already married to the man? If there's a third person involved, and *she* doesn't know, then yes. Yes, it is. JoJo didn't like the term 'affair', though. Rather, it was a 'reclamation'– she was reclaiming Frank back from his pretty, young, devious mistress. It was not a complete transaction yet, but that was only a matter of time (and will, which JoJo had to spare).

She looks around the café. Yummy mummies, JoJo thinks, they don't seem so yummy to me. They're too athletic and angular; they'd catch in your throat and choke you (it never ceased to amaze her – after leaving her family's struggling farm on the outskirts of Johannesburg as a teenager – that status and style for women in the West would be predominated by the ability *not* to eat). And yet, with all their gaunt athleticism, the children still seem to run free, spilling things or banging the things that can't be spilled and, as a general rule, crying. The mothers are either too busy breastfeeding to do anything, or seem bemused, as if their child is delighting them in some way: 'Look at little Gregory, smashing his cup against that woman's leg, how clever.'

The café, an old DIY shop, has kept some of the original features: a cupboard behind the counter full of small drawers once used to sort nails is now home to organic teabags with names like Earth Mother Cleansing Broth, and the walls are dotted with antique signs for metal polishes and lubrications. It's an odd mix, the industrial and the maternal, but it helps highlight to JoJo what she is really looking at: baby machines.

JoJo turns her attention back to Frank, who has closed his eyes and is humming to himself. It's the opening of Bach's 'Brandenburg Concerto No. 4' if she's not mistaken, the bit before it gets too fast and unhummable. She joins in too, best she can – she's never had a natural ear – and Frank opens his eyes and smiles fondly at her.

But it won't all be hand holding and humming. There will be sex. *Comforting*, her mother used to call it back in South Africa euphemistically, they will comfort each other. It's been months of abstinence and JoJo is looking forward to it, not in the skin-tingling way she did in her twenties, or the dread of her teens, but in the way one looks forward to a good meal. There are details they have to sort out first, though. Yes, *details*. Now who's speaking in code? she thinks wryly.

She lets go of Frank's hand and starts to get up. Chivalrously, he stands too, or tries to: the tables beside them wedge them both in. JoJo has to sit again and pull the table towards her to let Frank out first – it presses into her stomach in a very unflattering way – and then he pulls the table back to release her.

'I won't be long,' she says matter-of-factly and moves to go, but he pulls her back and kisses her tenderly on the cheek.

He really must love me, she thinks, stepping over a small child as she goes again – *the old fool*. She checks herself. She's not going to let cynicism seep into today. Today is a cynic-free zone. Today she is happy. She has everything she wants, has wanted, for months now. She has Frank. Again. She, JoJo, has Frank again.

JoJo is surprised to find the toilet unoccupied, but takes this as another sign the world is aligning in her favour. She closes the door, remembering to lock it (the shame of being sprung in a public loo!), shuffles up her dress, pulls down her underwear, and sits. Her new medication is doing strange things to her bladder and recently, she's been peeing like an ox. It smells slightly metallic too, as if it's been left overnight in a rusty can. *That's what I've become*, she thinks, *a rusty old can*. At least she's continent. JoJo's heard the horror stories, ripped this, nappy that, and counts herself lucky. As she waits, she adjusts her wedding band, the one Frank gave her all those years ago. Well, not that one exactly. She lost that one down the sink in the late eighties and this is a replacement. JoJo never told him, but she feels she could now – perhaps she will – and is impressed with the change in herself. Also impressive: she's *still* peeing like a burst dam. She checks the loo roll. Sufficient. She prepares a few sheets and her mind slips back to the wedding day itself.

They were married at the registry office in Wimbledon. The church wedding had to wait another twelve months because although Frank had been divorced for well over two years, they were both officially Catholic, and the Church liked to make things as difficult as they could. JoJo had worn a dress Frank liked to call her 'smart little number' – dark blue satin that stopped just above the knees with a very fetching silken braid around the waist. As always, Frank was in a suit, but had pimped his outfit ('pimped' was the right expression, wasn't it?) with a trilby, which made him look like the lesser-known Kray triplet. How they laughed that day! Everything seemed to go wrong. As they signed the marriage licence, the pen had snapped under the pressure of Frank's heavy signature and blue ink exploded everywhere. On the way back to the hotel, the cab had almost run out of petrol and Frank had to lend the driver five pounds to buy some more, because for some unknown and impractical reason, the cabby wasn't carrying any cash. And the hotel itself! Clean, which was a blessing, but almost too sterile: reeking of ammonia, it felt like a hospital ward. But after messing it up the best they could during the day, they spent the night locked in each other's embrace, more than making up for it.

JoJo wipes, pulls up her clothes again and flushes. She confronts the mirror – it's streaky, which helps. She's no longer vain, but it's useful to remember to be kind to oneself and only look in mirrors that flatter. She risks a peek, and regrets it instantly. In the eighties, she'd reminded people of the dark-haired actress in an American cop show about two female detectives – they'd shared the same arched eyebrows, dimples in their cheeks and a similar heart-shaped face. JoJo had quite liked the comparison. Now the face staring back at her is long and grey. She had considered cosmetic surgery, once visiting a Harley Street clinic, but the consultant had turned her off the idea by saying 'incision' one too many times. It was probably for the best. Most of the women in the magazines looked like they had the palsy.

JoJo turns on the tap at the sink, washes her hands, and then moves to the dryer. She groans. It's one of those machines where you need to wave your hands through a grill to activate the heating sensor. If she'd been asked when she was a child what the future would hold, she would never have guessed that the greatest leaps in technology would have been in hand drying. Teleportation, hover cars, food in pill form – none of these had materialised – but here was a device that could blow warm air at your hands at Mach 3 speeds. JoJo lowers her hands into the grill and the device jumps to life, noisily huffing air and making the loose skin on her hands quiver and dance. She slowly lowers and raises her hands, a very unnatural motion, she finds (only a man would come up with it), until they are both bone dry.

A yummy mummy is standing outside the toilet door when JoJo opens it, jiggling a small child on her hip and frowning impatiently. On seeing JoJo, however, the woman's face transforms into a radiant smile.

'I think it's so lovely,' she says, beaming.

JoJo is unsure what the woman means at first – perhaps she's talking about the toilet – and she glances back behind her (*It's clean, I suppose, but nothing to…*)

'Your husband,' the yummy mummy continues, 'the two of you.'

'Yes, well…' starts JoJo.

'To still be so in love, at your age. You're such an inspiration. We all say "till death do us part", don't we, but no one stops to think what that really means. But you make it look so easy. I can't even imagine what life will be like when *I'm* seventy!'

JoJo gives a tight-lipped smile. *Not today*, the voice in her head pleads, *not today!*

'How old are you, my dear?'

The yummy mummy becomes sheepish – she doesn't want the other mothers to know her real age, but now she's caught in JoJo's radiant faux grandmother beam, there's no escape.

She lowers her voice: 'Thirty-five next month, can you believe it?'

'I can believe it,' JoJo replies in her warmest, most sugared tones. 'And this one here,' she strokes the girl's cheek with her finger, 'any brothers or sisters?'

'We're trying,' the yummy mummy says, her eyes flicking to the floor in embarrassment.

'Yes, you must try. Before it's too late. It goes so quickly, you know.'

JoJo has scored a direct hit. The yummy mummy starts mumbling about IVF, so she goes in for the kill: 'I was like you when I was your age, full of dreams, but at forty, everything changes.' It's her turn to lower her voice: 'They don't tell you what it's like. Perhaps because no one can prepare you for what happens…'

The yummy mummy leans forward: 'The menopause?' she whispers.

JoJo laughs: 'Oh there are worse things than that, my dear. That's the tip of the iceberg. Menopause!'

'What then?'

JoJo takes a deep breath, pausing for effect.

'It shrivels,' she says finally.

The yummy mummy stares back, wide-eyed.

'Not your…?'

JoJo nods kindly.

'Until it's totally unrecognisable. Like a small dead hedgehog.'

And with that she takes leave of the yummy mummy, who stands, in stunned disbelief, until the young girl starts to whimper.

Frank is no longer at their table. JoJo feels a stab of panic, but tries not to let it take hold further. *Instant karma*, she thinks. She walks over to the table. The cups are still there, but his wallet is gone. It's alright; he'll be on his phone, shouting away at someone. Frank has learnt that he's far too loud, and now heads outside whenever it rings to stop the angry glares. Her handbag is still here on her chair, so she throws it over her shoulder and exits the café. Part of her, because she's never been more fragmented than over these past few months, part of her is gloating: 'You see, we knew this would happen.' With the wave of a hand, she brushes the thought away and turns left towards the station. She stops, remembering her phone: it's in her handbag and she snatches it out. There's a text message – it's from a pizza delivery place, offering her two for one with toppings of her choice. '*To opt out text STOP*'. *Stop*, she thinks, *Stop? When did I tell you to bloody start?*

JoJo is about to call Frank when she sees the right-sized shape of a suited man on the other side of the street, about thirty yards away. He's walking slowly towards her, one hand to his ear, the other drawing circles in the air. *Thank Occam's Razor*, she thinks – and now she can hear him, his big booming voice. It'll be work stuff, punishment for leaving the office in the afternoon – the shares have plummeted, the secretaries are all on fire – anything to make sure his absence from the investment bank he'd helped set up in the early nineties is not a regular occurrence. She waves at him, but he doesn't see and turns away. He's finished his phone call now and starts walking. JoJo is about to shout to him, but she can't find her voice. *Why is he walking off?* part of her thinks. But JoJo knows why. It's *her*. She's here. Belinda Rose Davidson – the other woman, the one that stole Frank away. Sure enough, the sleek black car is gliding along the street to meet him. JoJo takes a step back towards the café door (not quite the alley leap the situation might warrant on *Midsomer Murders*) and the car stops just beside him. Frank walks to the driver's seat and opens the door to allow her out – he never did like being the passenger – and the girl skips around the front of the Mercedes and towards the passenger seat. Massive sunglasses, heels too, and her hair is even shorter this time, like the hair on a Ken doll. A pixie cut. She opens the car door but takes some time to sit, as if she's deciding on the most attractive angle to make her descent into the seat, but finally she glides into the car and is gone. They are already driving towards JoJo before she realises she will be seen. It's too late to dive into the café, so she stands where she is, letting the Universe decide the outcome, and the Mercedes cruises past noiselessly, both Frank and Belinda gazing straight ahead. Of course he doesn't look, Frank wouldn't be so obvious. He's cleverer than that. An old pro. And JoJo feels a sadness, dormant inside her for days, start to stir.

*

It is three days after their date officially ended, and he is trying to compose her a text message:

Hi!

He deletes this.

Hey!

Still too much.

Hey,

Better.

Hey, I've been thinking about you a lot.

He deletes this quickly.

Hey,

He sighs.

Hey, hope your week's going well.

No. This puts too much emphasis on the fact the week is well under way and he has not yet texted her. He knows he should have sent a message on Monday to thank her for a great weekend, said something – said *anything* – to keep the momentum going. But he didn't because… why? Because his brain was still muddled from all the booze – and something else. He was embarrassed. They didn't have sex – not really: it was too late and they were still woozy from the club – just a playful fumble. But he'd found it so intense kissing her, emotional, you could say, and he'd said words, *those* words, the ones you're not supposed to say to anyone, save a lucky few. She was lying next to him, partially clothed on her floral duvet, and out it tumbled: 'I love you.'

Hey, had a really great time Saturday. You're one special girl.

'You're one special girl'? Oh God, he hates himself. Delete.

Why had he said 'I love you'? He'd ruined a perfectly good first date. She had laughed, not in a nasty way, more in – what? Bemusement? Shock? When she'd finished laughing, she stroked his face, running a finger along his eyebrow and down his cheekbone. Her finger felt deliciously cool and smooth, and he'd closed his eyes. She traced her way to his lower lip and he was about to kiss her finger when he felt a tap on his nose and heard her make a sound not unlike a pressed button at a cash machine. He kept his eyes shut. Did she just boop his nose? Maybe he misheard her. Perhaps she said 'You too'? He replays the sound in his head. No, it didn't sound like 'You too'. It sounded like 'boop!' His cheeks flush with embarrassment at the memory.

Hey, had a really great time Saturday!

Come on, what next? Momentum. Next steps. You want to see this girl again, don't you? *Don't you?* Of course, he thinks. But – and he knows this is his pride speaking and it doesn't make sense – *why does she get 'I love you' and I get booped?*

Impulsively, Daisy takes out her phone. Her best work friend Samira peers over her shoulder (she has full screen observing permissions).

'Hasn't he texted yet?' she asks.

Daisy shakes her head. 'What should I write? I'm no good at this.'

'Just be yourself. But a more chilled-out version. Like when all the models turn up on time, and no one asks for anything stupid, and we finish ahead of schedule. That kind of you.'

'A completely improbable and made-up me then?'

'Exactly.' Samira squeezes Daisy's shoulder. 'Good luck!' she says, dashing off.

'Thanks!'

Frowning, Daisy starts to type:

So how about that weekend, huh? Bit of a mad one!

Why is she talking like some deranged Ibiza club promoter? Delete.

Hi Chris,

More formal, better.

Hi Chris, had such a lovely time

She hesitates, adding:

Hi Chris, had such a lovely time with you

Too intense? She leaves it, she can always change it later.

Hi Chris, had such a lovely time with you this weekend.

Now it sounds like a Jane Austen letter: 'Dearest Christopher, had such a wonderful time with you at the cottage this weekend. The twins speak so fondly of you.' Delete.

Hi Chris, it's me, Daisy, you know, that girl you went out with on Saturday night? Hello!

She looks at this message as if it's a grenade in her hand, but pushes on:

Hi Chris, it's me, Daisy, you know, that girl you went out with on Saturday night? Hello! Hope you're still alive! I've made it through the week (barely) but it was worth it. Really, I haven't enjoyed myself like that for a very long time. So that's me, just checking in to make sure you're okay and to say hi. So, hi!

She counts the exclamation points. Three. Like an unhinged teenager.

Why hasn't he texted her yet? Daisy isn't against taking the initiative, but she'd been the one to call and ask him out in the first place (okay fine, Chris didn't even have her number initially – but now he does), and she doesn't want to seem pushy or desperate. *Maybe he doesn't like me as much as I thought?* she wonders. Sure, Chris had inexplicably said he loved her, but he was under the influence – it didn't count. And now the radio silence. Theoretically, Daisy knows she should be fluid when it comes to dating, flowing around the knockbacks and dead ends, but matters of the heart have never flowed for her. They have fizzed, exploded, collapsed, but never flowed.

Hi Chris, it's Daisy. Had a lovely time on Saturday. Really, I haven't enjoyed myself so much in ages. Would be great to see you again (I have to give your coat back too!)

And she's still got my coat, he thinks.

It's this image that saves it really: Daisy, after the club, wrapped up in his coat, her big eyes staring out at him from the footpath as he attempted to hail a taxi. He's never met a Daisy with brown hair. Weren't they usually blonde? Daisy the Milkmaid? Daisy. He remembers the curve of her neck, the way she squints when she laughs, her ridiculously tiny feet.

Hey, had a great time this weekend. Sorry about delayed contact. Taken three days just to tie my shoes! Not used to boozing anymore, clearly. What are you doing Friday? I thought we could check out which DJ is playing at Ministry of Sound? Kidding! But a drink would be nice…

He reads the message back to himself. Yes, it's light, breezy. It proposes a date but allows for negotiation if she's busy. But how to sign off? After his recent faux pas, he doesn't want to appear too keen. Usually he'd go for a kiss, but he feels a kiss here might be too much. He tries it:

x

Yes, way too much. He might as well just drive over to her house and start masturbating into her letterbox.

:)

That could work. Everyone likes a smiley face. He might give it a nose, though.

:-)

Perfect.

Daisy is still agonising over her message. It now reads:

Hi Chris, it's Daisy. Had a lovely time on Saturday. Just remembered I still have your coat! Not to worry, I've put it somewhere safe. One thing – I did just list it on eBay, so technically you have 5 days to claim it or it goes to the highest bidder ;) You could bid for it, I suppose, but some guy in Ipswich seems pretty taken with it! Anyhow, let me know.

She looks at the message in utter horror. *This is what it takes to get a second date in this city*, she thinks. *Blackmail.*

Stop writing, she commands herself, *put down the phone*!

Daisy deletes the message, stares at the blank screen for a moment and then switches it off completely.

*

Adam spends the next few days waiting to be arrested. He's not sure how it will happen – if the police will burst into his flat or whether it will be a more subdued affair, an email asking him into the station for questioning, perhaps – but what's certain is that it's only a matter of time. As well as trespassing on private property, Adam had helped himself to three muesli bars in the kitchenette and, to cap it off, he still had the ID security card in his bedroom, hidden under a pile of old magazines. Someone this very moment was probably reviewing the weekend's security camera footage and doing a spit take at the sight of Adam, tiptoeing towards the elevator, having woken, finally, at the sound of aggressive vacuuming. The cleaner had barely looked at him, but that didn't mean she wouldn't pick him in a line-up. His fingerprints were all over the place too. They had everyone on a database now, didn't they?

'What's up with you?' asks his flatmate Patrick. Patrick is tall, lean and still incredibly brown for an Australian who has lived in London for two years (Adam suspects spray tans but has yet to find evidence on any of the white towels).

Adam shrugs and tries to act as casually as he can, which isn't easy around Patrick, who is so laid-back, he makes Adam seem like a jumped-up meth addict at the best of times. They're sharing a massive doughy pizza covered in the occasional slice of salami, the cardboard box is dark with oil, and Adam already feels sluggish after two slices, but he takes another and bites nonchalantly.

Patrick watches him closely. 'How's the job hunting going?'

'Oh, you know, the usual. Everyone wants to do phone interviews now. You only get a face to face if they're pretty sure they want to hire you,' (to keep the failures off their property, is what it feels like to Adam), 'and it's t-tough working your magic on a Skype call.'

'How many phone interviews have you had?' There's nothing confrontational in Patrick's question, but Adam still wishes he'd mind his own bloody business. Patrick has a lack of emotional empathy when it came to asking personal questions, which Adam blames on him being from such a geographically large country. Unsolicited talk like this might be fine when you have your own part of a continent and don't see another person for weeks at a time, but it's jarring in the confines of a cramped two-bedroom flat in Hackney.

'Three or four. There's something at this one agency that's pretty exciting.'

'Yeah? Which one?'

Damn. Adam hoped he wouldn't be asked this. Patrick works at a big advertising conglomerate near Carnaby Street and has an annoying habit of seeming to know every professional person in London and the status of any agency, big or small.

Adam takes a stab in the dark: 'P-Proctor M-Media?'

Patrick nods, 'I heard they were hiring. But I thought they were focusing on digital displays?'

'They're diversifying,' Adam replies. It's one of his interview go-to words. That and 'extrapolate'.

Patrick mulls over this new piece of information.

'You'd tell me if anything was wrong, wouldn't you, mate?'

If I couldn't pay the rent, you mean, thinks Adam, but he mumbles something in the affirmative and takes a swig of beer.

Adam misses the good old days when Patrick was fresh off the boat and finding his feet in London. When Patrick first moved in, replacing Adam's old flatmate Tori, who had eloped to America with her boyfriend, Adam had felt a sense of brotherly protection towards him. He'd guided Patrick through the red tape of setting up his first British bank account, patiently explained the pronunciations of Leicester Square, Marylebone and Southwark, and given him a detailed profile on English women (get them drunk, but not *too* drunk – there was a fine line). But as the weeks and months went by, Adam was surprised to see how well Patrick took to everything. He excelled at his job, made friends with ease, and seemed to be getting *browner*. Adam's minor bouts of depression hadn't helped either. The cycle had begun years ago: Adam's brothers bullied him mercilessly, he developed a stutter (causation or correlation, no one could say), he was teased even more for visiting a 'retard therapist', his speech impediment grew worse, and by thirteen he was diagnosed as clinically depressed (personally, he just felt fed up). A prescription for antidepressants followed, which only made him drowsy, and his stammer worse – rinse and repeat until university, where Adam decided enough was enough, and he went cold turkey. His studies and his career would be his salvation, he decided. Only, every year since graduating, there was always a *dark month*, and some kindly doctor, reading Adam's notes, would suggest a return to medication. Adam would resist, but that was seen as just another symptom, and before long he was in a groggy fug, until he summoned enough energy to detoxify again. Patrick had been through one such cycle with him nine months ago, and the status in their relationship had irrevocably flipped – so now it felt like Patrick had been sent to monitor *his* wellbeing, especially after Adam lost his job too.

And now jail, thinks Adam. Probably. He might get community service. But he'd definitely get a criminal record, which he'd be legally obliged to reveal at every job interview – as if they weren't difficult enough. Breaking and entering. Well, not really breaking. Entering and staying then.

There had been no sign of the security guard at the front desk when Adam crept out in the morning, but he had spied a steaming cup of coffee behind the reception counter. It had been cold outside and Adam was ravenously hungry after his meagre muesli bar dinner, but there was another sensation too, something that took him a few minutes, walking to St Paul's Tube station, to identify. And it was this: now he was back in the real world (which seemed oddly less real to him), Adam felt surprisingly calm. Serene even. He mentally rattled off his usual list of fears and worries, most to do with money, and not one of them gave him that familiar pain in his gut.

Huh? he'd thought.

Patrick picks up the last slice of pizza, folds the dripping tongue of cheese back onto itself and takes a huge bite. He's polished off two thirds of the pizza already and there's a small barrel of ice cream waiting in the freezer for dessert, but Patrick never seems to gain any weight. Hollow legs and a fast metabolism, he says by way of explanation, but Adam suspects it's the twelve cups of Italian coffee Patrick drinks a day. A sleek, grey coffee machine sits on the kitchen counter like a metallic lozenge. Adam can never get it to work – he's more of a tea man anyway. Tea with a dash of soy, as milk upsets his stomach.

Adam had brewed himself several cups of tea at Mercer and Daggen, and it had felt strange, making something so comforting as tea in such an illicit situation, like one of those stories you hear of a burglar breaking into a house and cooking a roast dinner before making off with the silverware. He had opened all the cupboards in the office kitchenette to find the one containing cups, discovering a shelf with the usual motley selection of crockery – chipped 'I Love My Dad' mugs and client freebies ('Systemax – Leaders in Fiscal Tech Procurement!'), all with blotchy stains inside. He'd chosen a plain green cup at the back of the cupboard, imagining it to be the least used – it was a bit dusty, so he rinsed it out and tossed in a teabag from the bulk box he'd found next to the sink. There were six plastic cartons of milk in the fridge, at various stages of fermentation, but no soy, so he scooped the teabag out with a teaspoon, flicked it into the sink, and filled the cup with some cold water from the tap. He was about to head back into the corner office (*'his' corner office*, he'd thought automatically), when he hesitated, and put his cup down again. Adam picked up the hot teabag with his thumb and finger and, with his other hand poised underneath to collect drips, moved it to the bin and dropped it in. Best not to leave a trace, he'd thought, taking his cup from the bench and walking through the channel of cubicles, unknowingly dripping tea onto the cable-strewn carpet as he went.

'You know,' says Patrick, reaching for the TV remote and flipping the channel, 'we might have something going in my office again. The role would be a bit more junior, so the money isn't great, but we'd get to work in the same building?'

Adam gets up to fetch another beer and buys himself some time. They've gone down this path already – Patrick offering to help Adam with work in his office, but somehow the good intentions have never paid off, leaving Adam feeling even more deflated.

'Actually,' he says, opening the fridge, the door shielding his face, 'I didn't want to jinx it, but I had a job offer today. It's in-house at a financial services company. Nothing's set in stone, but they're p-pretty keen.'

'Mate! You kept that under your hat! No wonder you've been on tenterhooks. Where is it?'

Adam takes two beers out of the fridge and shuts the door again.

'Mercer and Daggen. Do you know them?'

Patrick raises his eyebrows.

'Know them? They're the big boys. How did you land that?'

'Nailed the interview,' says Adam, throwing a beer to Patrick. 'They made me an offer right there in the room.'

'I heard Mercer and Daggen were monsters in their interviews. Did they give you a psychometric test?'

'Yeah. Aced it. Said I was exactly what they want. Even gave me a cup.'

Patrick cocks his head. 'They… what?'

Adam takes a big gulp of his beer and then wipes his mouth with the back of his hand.

'They gave me a c-cup. That green cup.'

He nods in the direction of the drying rack, where the green cup is sitting.

'I wondered where that came from,' says Patrick, frowning. 'They gave you a cup in the interview?'

Adam starts to rip the label off his beer.

'Yeah. Not just a cup, it was a whole goody bag. They gave one to everyone they interviewed. There was a notepad, a pencil, a c-c-calculator…' he trails off.

Patrick nods slowly.

'When do you start?' he asks.

'Monday,' replies Adam, and takes such a long swig on his beer he almost drains the bottle.

CHAPTER THREE

The mythical second date! What greater prize exists for the cosmopolitan singleton? First dates come and go, most like a bad dream, but a few – a very few – stick. It might be the promise of sex (or the result of promising sex), or the recognition of some sort of 'connection' that shoots, beam-like, into the sky: a beacon of potential compatibility. Now the singleton runs to their window, throws it open and shouts: 'We have something in common!', 'I don't hate him (or her)!' and more quietly, 'I might not die alone.'

Unlike their New York counterparts, Londoners are never really sure of the rules of dating. Dating isn't really a thing, is it, except in romantic comedies? Did they date in *Notting Hill*? In *Four Weddings*, he just kept showing up at events until it finally wore her down. And here the gold standard is revealed: Londoners aren't direct in their romantic relationships, they sidle up to them. They'll organise to be at the same bar as that girl they like, but if they do finally talk to her, it'll only be to ask her out for another drink. Drinks beget drinks, but a date is too formal, too exact. A date implies being picked up at eight, buying flowers, organising a fancy restaurant, standing when she leaves for the bathroom, and that's not really in their blood. A drink is less commitment, which is exactly the problem. A drink is not much to pin your future on.

For our lovers, though, the countdown begins.

*

On Wednesday, Daisy makes two appointments – one for a waxing (with her favourite beautician Trina, who wears adult braces and barely speaks) and another for a haircut. The trim will be almost unnoticeable, not even an inch off the length – anything too dramatic now will show over-keenness. Subtle embellishments: new and expensive makeup carefully applied or a more structured bra can raise the stakes just enough without setting off alarm bells. Even though she understands the rules, Daisy doesn't particularly like living by them. She's never considered herself a 'girly-girl'. Yes, technically, she does work in the fashion industry, creating backdrops and props for editorial shoots, but she's always the one in the basement, wearing a pair of beat-up overalls and hot-gluing feathers to a punch bag, and has never let herself feel 'fashionable'. Fashion for Daisy is like artillery to the army: it helps get your point across, but only in extreme circumstances – such as war… or a second date.

The week slips by for Chris, but on Friday, he manages a visit to the barber. Returning to his flat afterwards for a shower, he takes in his new hairstyle in the full-length bathroom mirror. He likes it, much tidier, but does it make him appear rather woolly *down there*?

After hunting around his apartment for an old newspaper, Chris lays the sheets on the bathroom floor and sets about taking to his pubic region with the electric trimmer he usually keeps for his sideburns. Things go well for a few swipes, but then the confident hum of the motor turns to a whine and soon stops altogether. Cursing in several different languages for good measure, Chris brushes the hair off his feet and goes back into his bedroom to search for the charger. One of the joys of living by oneself is being able to walk around naked from the waist down with no one any the wiser, but Chris hasn't factored in the ability of newly severed pubes, always the wiliest of hair, to disperse. Three weeks later, he will still be finding curly hairs, but never, unfortunately, the charger. After ransacking his bedroom and coming up empty-handed, he returns to the bathroom to assess the situation in the mirror. In his haste, he has somehow carved out two distinct patches of hair, like two separate crops on a farm. *Or eyes*, he thinks, *it's like I've shaved eyes above my penis*.

He has an idea and heads into the kitchen, returning with a pair of scissors. Holding something sharp so close to his genitals makes his eyes water, but Chris carefully snips away at the pubic hair until it's a uniform length. He steps back and takes a look in the mirror again. Terrible. Not only is it patchy but it somehow makes his testicles seem exceptionally hairy. He'd always thought of them as averagely fuzzy, but now they are like two strange furry gourds hanging there. Carefully, *carefully*, he takes a few snips at the surrounding hair with the scissors, but only succeeds in making them look even more like the Gallagher brothers.

Chris sits down on the edge of the bathtub, the ceramic cold under his buttocks, and hangs his head. He's completely ruined his crotch now. He will become one of those anecdotes Daisy will tell for years: 'My date with Mr No-Pubes Hairy Balls.' Unless… he spies his wet razor on the cabinet shelf and stands to pick it up. This blade is rather grubby but he has spares. *Is it better to use a slightly blunt blade that might take longer, or a new one that could accidentally slice*, he wonders? Slightly blunt, comes the answer quickly as Chris feels the blood drain from his extremities, slightly blunt. He scoops warm water onto his groin and then squirts a palmful of foam onto his hand, applying it liberally (*this isn't so bad*, he thinks). With the razor poised, he considers where he should start. He has to meet Daisy in twenty-five minutes, but he can't rush the job now. *Flat sections first*, he decides, and makes short work of the pubic hair stubble before moving on to the more technical areas. Carefully, *carefully*, he glides the blade over the skin. *It's like shaving a walnut*, he thinks. *A very important walnut.*

Daisy is walking briskly up Central London's Tottenham Court Road exactly one week to the minute that she met Chris at Embankment last Saturday. She is moisturised, plucked and preened – even the cramps from her protein diet seem to have calmed down. All she needs to do now is break up with her boyfriend. *Not my boyfriend*, she chides herself mentally as she hurries along the footpath. *Just… someone. Someone I was seeing, sometimes.*

She's left it to the last minute, but Daisy has fashioned herself a dating code of conduct over the years, which states you should always let a person know if you stop seeing them. No ghosting. It's only polite.

She takes out her phone and selects Warren's number. Daisy hopes he won't pick up so she can leave a message, but his familiar Manchester brogue answers on the second ring.

'Hello?'

Daisy's face blooms with a reactive smile. She's read somewhere that people can hear a smile in your voice, and has trained herself to grin on difficult calls.

'Warren, hi, it's me,' she says, and yes, her voice does sound bright and smiley.

There's a pause.

'Who's this?'

Confused, Daisy quickly checks the phone display to make sure she's dialled the right Mancunian Warren (she has).

'It's Daisy.'

'Of course, Daisy!' (She can hear the exclamation mark in his voice.) 'How are you?'

'Good, thanks, good.' She weaves her way through the oncoming pedestrians, mostly commuters who haven't been lured into a post-work drink. 'Did you get a new phone?'

'What?'

Daisy's cheeks are hurting now from the rigour of smiling.

'Did your phone get stolen or something?'

'No, why?'

'Oh, I just thought... No reason. How are you?'

'I'm good, our kid. Yeah, I'm good. Sorry I haven't been in touch, I've just had a lot of stuff on.'

It was true, she knew. Warren was very much in demand, being a whizz at lighting anorexic models in a way that didn't make them appear too translucent or veiny. They'd met on a shoot nearly a year ago and Daisy had liked the way he called himself 'the electrician' in a self-deprecating way, unusual in a room filled with wall-to-wall ego. After the shoot, they'd sat chatting in the corner of the pub together, knees touching, till closing.

'I've been busy as well,' she says. 'It's no problem.'

'Yeah, but I never replied to your last text message. Bit shitty of me, to be honest.'

'Really, Warren, it's fine.'

'But I can make it up to you. Actually, I'm free tonight. Any plans?'

Daisy doesn't want to be drawn into what she's doing tonight. She spots the cinema further up the street and reminds herself to take the next left.

'Warren, I just wanted to say how much I've enjoyed spending time with you these past few months. You're a really great guy, I hope you know that.'

He snorts.

'Sounds like you're breaking up with me.'

Daisy changes the phone to her other hand.

'Yes, I guess I am,' she replies. The line goes quiet. 'Are you there?'

Warren makes a huffing noise. 'I don't believe this.'

Daisy thinks of all the clichés she could use here: it's not you, it's me, I'm just not in 'that' place now – anything but the real reason: I think I've found someone better. But before she can reply, Warren speaks again:

'I don't need your charity, Daisy. And anyway, why call me up just to tell me that? You've never phoned any other time.'

'Sure I have,' says Daisy, but there's doubt in her voice. 'I just thought you deserved to hear it from me. After all, we were dating for a while.'

'Dating?' Warren splutters. 'We were never dating.'

'Alright,' she says, through gritted teeth, 'what would you call it then?'

'We had dinner twice. After that, we'd just hook up. You know, booty calls.'

'*Booty calls*? You can't be serious?'

'You tell me,' replies Warren. 'You were the one calling the shots.'

Daisy opens her mouth to refute this, but the words don't come.

'You'd go out and get drunk,' he continues, 'and then message me to come over – always after midnight so I'd have to pay for a taxi. Occasionally, if I was lucky, I'd get breakfast in the morning but afterwards I'd be sent on my way, job done.'

Daisy winces, but it's true. The last few times she's seen Warren, she's woken up beside him in her bed, head pounding. When he leaves (after the sloppy fry-up she cooks – yes – out of guilt), she has to check the drunken messages on her phone to piece together the events of the previous night. She does keep meaning to meet Warren for a nice grown-up drink because she likes him (and she'd always suspected he liked her quite a bit). He's tall and has good hair and he's easy to be with. She just never got around to calling him – and now, frankly, she's regretting she did.

'Whatever we had,' Daisy says, trying to keep her tone light, 'isn't it better we end it like this, rather than just never speaking to each other again?'

'No, I would have preferred that,' replies Warren curtly.

'Fine, I thought we could be grown-ups, but obviously…'

'There. I've deleted you from Facebook. That's how you break up with someone.'

Daisy sighs.

'This isn't like you, Warren, so I'm going to give you the benefit of the doubt and…'

'Instagram too.'

She hangs up, and just in time – Chris is on the other side of the street, holding a big bunch of flowers and smiling from ear to ear.

*

In Croydon, south London, Dylan Moon is having a writing crisis. He stares at the screen. What has he done today? The cursor blinks expectantly.

I walked my dog, types Dylan.

He screws up his face. This week he's written about Otis once already, an observational piece about how owners look like their pets (Otis is chocolate brown, and sleek and handsome like a seal pup, so not a terrible comparison), which means dog-related ideas are out. Otis, sprawled out under his chair, seems to sense this decision and whimpers.

Dylan stares out of the window. The weather is grey, unexceptional. The house is quiet. His dad won't be home for another hour. Dylan recalls the old proverb they half-heartedly debated once at school: when nothing happens in a silent forest, does anyone write about it?

If the blog was supposed to motivate him to live a more interesting life, it had failed. Dylan had started with such energy too. After much deliberation, he'd named his blog 'Moon over Croydon' and with aspirations of becoming a travel writer, filled it with reviews of local attractions. He'd started with the museum ('a stunning collection of old and semi-old relics') and moved on to icons such as the Croydon Clock Tower ('a must for anyone who enjoys tall clocks'). His passion for reviewing ended one day, however, after an anonymous reader left the comment 'Ha ha, mate, hilarious!!' on his very detailed report of the local IKEA. 'Ha ha, mate, hilarious!!'? Dylan couldn't work it out. How was an 800-word blog post on the merits of Swedish cooking in Croydon hilarious?

Without the travel essays to fall back on, his life was revealed to be repetitive and dull. Take tonight, for example. The highlights would include making his dad dinner (meat and three veg, nothing revolutionary there), watching telly and playing Xbox. There were only so many times you could fall back on writing a jolly, tongue-in-cheek meta-post about not having anything to write about, and Dylan felt he'd reached his limit weeks ago. That left social commentary (his recent post 'On the Other Side of the Glass' had examined the sometimes turbulent relationship between bus driver and passenger), his reactions to new music and things he'd read online… and Otis. Dylan nudges the dog with his foot, and Otis peers up expectantly.

Dog lies on floor, he types, *Crowds go wild.*

There are other things he could write about – growing up with a white father and an absentee black mother being one, his illness another, but he feels coy about starting anything too personal. Anyway, who would want to read about that?

Janelle might, of course. Janelle, Janelle, *Janelle*. Even thinking her name makes Dylan feel light-headed. Obviously, with his chronic fatigue syndrome (also known as M.E.), Dylan felt light-headed quite often, but this was the *nice* sort, not the gasping, dizzy kind – and it meant only one thing. *He was in love.*

Being in love with Janelle was beneficial for several reasons. Firstly, it gave him something to do. Because of his illness, Dylan wasn't able to leave the house much – even now he was technically a lot better – and boredom was his greatest enemy. Secondly, he worried less about his sexuality (Dylan had questioned if he even liked girls at all, and what that might mean *bigger picture*, but now he loved Janelle, so that put matters to rest). And to top it off, Janelle was an exceptional human being – someone he could look up to, a person who had helped him – *healed* him, even.

Dylan was amazed at how much they shared in common. Janelle (who was twenty-one, a mere five years older than him) had mixed-heritage parents too: a Welsh mother and a British-Nigerian father. She'd also been unwell in her teens, with the double whammy of a rare form of ovarian cancer *and* M.E. She'd beaten the cancer, of course, and overcome her chronic fatigue using a technique called The Firebolt Process. Afterwards, she'd even trained to be a practitioner of the neurolinguistics programming course, becoming the youngest certified person in the country.

Before meeting Janelle, Dylan and his father had tried everything – beta blockers, cortisol tablets, strict wheat- and lactose-free diets, painful vitamin B12 injections in the butt cheek – but nothing had worked. Someone online had suggested the three-day Firebolt Process course, which had apparently helped a lot of M.E. sufferers, but by then, Dylan was too ill to leave his bed. Janelle had gallantly come to them instead, teaching Dylan everything he needed to begin his recovery.

Janelle also loved French films – just like Dylan. Well, that wasn't completely true. Dylan was attempting to love French films, but liking them did not come as naturally as loving Janelle. Dylan had sat through five now, all recommended by Janelle, and it had been a challenge, to say the least. The first film, *Boyfriends and Girlfriends*, was shot in front of several white buildings, and because the subtitles were in white too, they'd completely disappear for long stretches until someone walked past the screen in a contrasting colour. Dylan had freeze-framed the movie, but even when he did catch the dialogue, he was none the wiser. He wasn't sure if the film even had an actual plot – the characters only seemed to smoke cigarettes. Was he missing something? Probably, but he'd reported back to Janelle that he'd found the film 'intriguing'.

Dylan now remembers that Janelle had suggested a new movie to watch, so he logs into his email. As well as knowing her email address, they were friends on Facebook, but he was still building up the courage to ask for her phone number. Dylan wasn't sure if that would be overstepping some kind of mark. There were lots of grey areas when you were in love with your health professional. He was of legal age now, which helped, but Dylan wasn't sure what his dad might think about his feelings for Janelle, so he'd kept them under wraps, in case they got her into trouble. In many ways, it made Dylan's feelings stronger – theirs was a forbidden love. It was like a Jean-Luc Godard movie (probably – he really hadn't been paying attention).

Scrolling through his inbox, he finds Janelle's latest email, dated a day ago:

Dylan!

Her emails always started with an exclamation mark,

Hope you're feeling strong, and you're committing to the visualisations and the meditation we set. So glad you're enjoying our little film club. I was thinking you should suggest the next film to watch?
    Lots of love sweetie, Janelle

Lots of love. He lingers on the words, resting the cursor over them as if to touch them, ignoring the tacked-on 'sweetie'. Janelle sent him love. Dylan considers visiting another type of website on a private browser (a trick which has saved him many sleepless nights since his dad brought home a magazine from WH Smith called *Getting to Know Your PC*) but he tells himself to focus instead. Janelle deserved a gentleman. She'd once confided in Dylan that her previous boyfriend – a barber with an Instagram account full of his bulging biceps and tattoos – was violent during an argument, rolling up her sleeves to show the bruises on her wrists. Dylan would be different. Her knight in shining armour.

Bringing up the search browser, Dylan feels the burden of having to choose a film that will impress Janelle. He wants to suggest something grown-up and sophisticated, so he types: 'Adult French movie' into the search box and clicks on the first result, which sounds suitably classy: *Celestine, Maid at your Service*. A French version of *Downton Abbey* perhaps? There's a video embedded on the webpage, a trailer possibly, so Dylan clicks on it, but it's the whole film – from the seventies, by the looks of it. He skips ahead. *Whoa!* – it was definitely not like *Downton Abbey*, unless Dylan had missed the scene where Maggie Smith played with her exposed nipples, as another woman watched, eating a lemon...?

There's a jingling of keys from the front door and Otis shoots out of the room, barking. Dylan jumps up too, knocking his chair backwards, and as he bends down to right it, he can feel his eyesight starting to swim, his head spinning, the world turning into a familiar blur. *The computer!* he thinks, but he can already hear his father coming down the hallway, Otis's barks turning into ecstatic yaps of pleasure, and Dylan has to steady himself against the doorway. He decides to turn the power off at the socket, it will be easier than shutting the computer down and, using the wall, slides beside the desk and fumbles at the nest of cables. There are deep blue spots in his vision now as well as the crescendo of hazy movement, and groping so blindly at the cables, he's afraid he'll electrocute himself. The socket is just out of reach behind the desk – he could give it a yank to try to unplug the extension lead, but it might bring the computer crashing down on him too. He eases himself back up to sitting – he'll have to go under the desk instead – but flinches as something warm and wet starts lapping at his face. Dylan tries to push Otis away, but the dog retaliates by nipping at his chin. 'That's enough,' Dylan commands the brown blur, and the assault stops, but he knows if he heads under the desk now, Otis will think it's a game and attack again.

'Dylan? You there?' his dad calls, and there's a clunk as something heavy hits a table top, probably leftover parts from a boiler he's fixing.

Just get out of the room, thinks Dylan, crawling towards the door now (Otis licks his ear). *Don't be found with the incriminating evidence.* Using the chair and the door handle to lever himself upright again, Dylan stands swaying for a few seconds, willing the blurriness to go.

This is his first attack for weeks. The dizziness and the blurred vision are a side effect, a reminder from his body, Janelle called it, that he needed to 'sit down and take stock!' He desperately doesn't want to get ill again.

'Don't say desperate!' he hears Janelle's voice in his mind. 'You're programming, remember? Choose a more positive word.'

Positive then, Dylan is positive he doesn't want to get sick again.

'Cheat!' Janelle shouts good-naturedly in his head.

Taking a few cautious steps forward – Dylan can see the doorway but its dimensions keep shifting – he staggers into the living room, where the sound of a running tap from the kitchen gives away his father's location. Dylan holds onto the back of the couch, riding the waves of dizziness like a surfer. He tries to steer his body into the sensation, something else Janelle taught him. A surge from his core almost makes him fall backwards, but he grasps the couch in time and holds on as the feeling spirals through him. He doesn't feel nauseous though, and at least he's at home. School was always the worst: his teachers assuming he was faking the dizziness to get out of work. 'Just put your head between your legs,' one maths teacher had yelled at him, causing the room to erupt with laughter. From then on, Dylan's nickname had been Auto, as in Autofellator, and not, as he'd mistakenly first thought, *The Simpsons'* character Otto (this error was quickly cleared up by one of his classmates, who helpfully explained: 'It's because you suck your own dick, fag nuts.' Nope, he really did not miss school one bit).

The swaying subsides for a second and, in the hiatus, Dylan manages to manoeuvre around to the front of the couch, walking sideways like a crab, steadying himself with both hands. When he reaches the cushions, he sits. Otis jumps up too: he's not allowed on the furniture usually, but Dylan hasn't got time to enforce this rule. If he can just compose himself, if he can bring into practice what Janelle has taught him, maybe he can turn this around. He sees Janelle now, as if she's being backlit by a very bright light, her beautiful round face, the immaculate makeup bringing out the rich tones of her skin while trying to hide the smattering of acne scars, her expertly pencilled-in eyebrows, the combination of false eyelashes and thick eyeliner giving her a doe-like appearance, her wide dazzling smile, lower teeth ever so slightly crooked, and a halo of curly hair, parted straight down the middle. Janelle winks at him roguishly, and everything goes bright…

He opens his eyes. Dylan is lying on the sofa, wrapped in a blanket. Next to him sits his father, eating a plate of fish fingers, chips and mushy peas, and watching the news. Otis is beside him too, lying in the gap between Dylan and the couch, spread out lengthways, making the most of the evening's relaxed stance on animals and furniture.

'Had a spell then?' asks his dad, biting into a fish finger.

Dylan nods groggily.

'Want some dinner?'

He nods again.

Still chewing, his father gets up from the couch and heads into the kitchen. Dylan sits up quickly, pushing back the blanket, and cranes his neck towards the box room. The door is open and he can see the computer screen is in darkness, but he can't tell if it's turned off or just sleeping. He considers running over – he doesn't feel dizzy at all now – but before he can make a move, his father returns, holding a plate with a tea towel in one hand, and a knife and fork in the other.

'It's hot,' he warns. 'Use a cushion.'

The news has finished, so after his dad sits back down, he sets about flicking through the channels.

'Any requests?'

'I don't mind.'

'How about something from the seventies?'

Dylan shrugs, not really listening, and starts on his food.

'Hungry, huh?' his dad asks.

Dylan grunts, mouth full.

'There aren't any fish fingers or French fries left, but there's plenty of *petit pois* if you want some more.'

Dylan freezes.

'What did you say?'

'If you're still hungry. Plenty of peas.'

And finding a repeat of *Only Fools and Horses*, Dylan's father settles back to watch with barely a perceptible smile.

*

The second date is over and it's gone very well, they can both feel it. Something has changed in their alchemy tonight, and it's significant and exciting.

Chris walks Daisy down to Tottenham Court Road station (they have become shy at the prospect of sleeping together and deferred it to another night by mutual unspoken agreement), and here they kiss extravagantly, a 'my train is leaving the station and perhaps I'll never see you again' kiss, arms wrapped around each other, Daisy standing on her tiptoes, oblivious to the occasional bump from a passer-by, and unconcerned that she's still none the wiser about what Chris does for a living. When they can kiss no more, Daisy waves goodbye to him over her shoulder and heads down into the Underground. It's busy in the station, but she barely notices and glides down the escalator. The train is crowded too, but she stands happily and is so caught up in her own thoughts, she almost misses her stop at Queensway.

Once outside again, Daisy has a sudden impulse to text Chris, but she fights it until she's nearly home. Only after she stops to buy milk for the morning does she cave and under the relative safety of the shop's awning, takes out her phone. The screen is empty – no message from Chris – and she feels a wobble of uncertainty. But after placing the milk and the bunch of roses by her feet, she's about to text when a very funny thing happens: she calls him instead. Daisy calls Chris. The phone is ringing before she fully realises what she's done.

Chris picks up almost immediately.

'I was just texting you!' he says, sounding genuinely pleased, and she feels a rush of relief.

'Yes…' her mind races, 'I was actually ringing to tell you I'm psychic.'

He laughs.

'So, what am I thinking now?' he asks mischievously and it's her turn to laugh.

'I had a great night.'

'Me too.'

There's a pause, but it doesn't feel awkward. *If there's such a thing as a comfortable silence, this is it*, thinks Daisy. *But he's waiting*, she realises, *he's waiting for me to say something*.

'Well, goodnight.'

'That's it?' He chuckles.

'Yes…' she says meekly, knowing she must sound like an imbecile.

'Then this is the nicest phone call I've ever had.'

Oh God, she thinks, *I'm blushing*.

'Goodnight then.'

'Goodnight.'

And then another funny thing happens: Daisy starts to speak again.

'Let's not use the Internet or text messages unless we have to. I mean, I don't think they're very good for this, for getting to know someone. They dilute things and turn things around, and well, I know I sound like a crazy person, and I'll completely understand if you hang up and never speak to me again, but I don't want our…' (She can't bring herself to say 'relationship'), '…whatever this becomes, to happen through status updates.' There's another pause. 'Unless you want to and then I'm totally cool with it.'

When Chris finally speaks, his voice sounds measured.

'Yes, I can work with that, I think. It'll be like 2002 again. That's the year I got my first mobile phone by the way and not just a random year – my mother bought it in case my Swedish nanny decided to abduct me. I think I still have the phone somewhere, propping open a door…'

He's rambling now, but she appreciates it. (Also, a Swedish nanny, huh? Fancy. Daisy's babysitter had been a girl called Tracey, who made seven-year-old Daisy light her cigarettes because 'you can get cancer off them butane fumes'.) Chris's ramble is a ramble to make her own ramble seem less crazy. She wants to kiss him all over.

They say their goodbyes again and Daisy picks up her carton of semi-skimmed milk and the flowers, and walks the six minutes home, humming all the way.

*

JoJo and Frank are drifting off to sleep in their matrimonial bed at the end of their second evening (she can't bring herself to call it a 'liaison', or worse still, a 'date'). The bed was a wedding present from Frank's best friend Denny, as a punishment, JoJo always thought, for doing him the inconvenience of getting hitched. It's a massive thing, solid oak with four hand-carved pillars. Denny did the detailing himself, stopping just short of carving a Grotesque on the headboard. JoJo hated it on sight. 'How will we get in the front door?' she'd cried, but Denny had thought of that and the bed frame came apart like a jigsaw. And so it had become part of their household and part of them. Frank and JoJo had literally grown into it: the older and fatter they became, the more it seemed that Denny hadn't been spiteful at all, but somehow clairvoyant.

JoJo opens her eyes. There's a crescent moon tonight, it keeps slipping behind the clouds, but she can see it now through the large bay windows of their Battersea townhouse (they've never closed the curtains, the angle of the bedroom and a few well-placed trees affording them privacy).

She looks at him now. He's turned away from her, the sheets pulled protectively under his arm. Apart from the sound of his breathing, Frank is not making any discernible noise, which is unusual – he can snore, grind his teeth, talk and mumble in his sleep if the fancy takes him. Break wind too. The nuns never prepared JoJo for the likes of that.

It's what she missed most, not the farting, that's for certain, but having another living breathing human beside her at the end of the day. He had travelled on business, of course, but she always knew he was coming home. When Frank left her that bright spring morning, it didn't really sink in until she was lying in bed, and found herself all off-balance, like one person on a see-saw.

Is Belinda feeling that sense of aloneness now? JoJo pushes away the thought, but it slips behind her and round the other side. Belinda, with her close-cropped hair. Belinda, the writer for *The Economist* magazine who'd met Frank at a gala dinner and asked him outright for an interview – Frank who didn't court the media ('Court them? Won't fucking put up with their shit more like!') – it was quite the coup. JoJo had read the article at a train station. There was nothing flirtatious in it, nothing that would hint at the eighteen months to come, and anyhow, why should JoJo suspect? She and Frank had an agreement. They had been through many things: her hysterectomy, the death of his brother in a skiing accident, his cancer scare. But the rule stayed the same: be with me if you want to be. The moment you don't, the moment it gets too much, or the urge for the unknown gets too strong, they would tell the other and move on. They even shook hands on it – a gentleman's agreement. She'd meant it too. It wasn't some feminist dogma motivating her or an attempt to call his bluff, but a strange sense of entitlement. JoJo had never been the most beautiful woman in the world, but she kept a good figure and people still found her face pleasant enough – the bridge of her nose wrinkling when she smiled. She ignored every faddish hairstyle: strictly no tapering, no texturing, no layering, no nape undercut, no feathering, no bangs, nothing choppy, something simple yet sophisticated – what the wife of a disgraced French politician might wear – a naturally grey imperceptibly tousled bob. She had wit and charm (when she chose to), and felt a keen sense of her own worth and – something deeper – a knowledge that she deserved to be loved. JoJo had met many glamorous and wealthy women in her life, but very few seemed to share this power. And that's what hurt the most, that Frank had betrayed her in such a conventional way. He had lied to her, slept with a woman half his age – it was all so boring and hurtful. Hadn't they agreed they would save each other the embarrassment? Hadn't they shaken on it?

JoJo takes a deep breath – she's wound herself up now. She considers getting up to make a hot drink, but just then Frank rolls over onto his back. Isn't it strange, she thinks, how you can tell in a darkened room if a person's eyes are open? You'd say it was the moonlight catching them, but she checks, the moon is hidden behind the clouds again.

Frank reaches out and takes her hand, stroking it with his thumb. It's not suggestive – neither of them wants any more sex tonight – merely reassuring, and for some reason it makes JoJo's eyes well up. Stop this, she thinks. What do you have to cry about? He's here, isn't he? You could have taken him for everything he was worth or gone potty and cut up his clothes. But you didn't. You bided your time and when the moment came, you brought him back, like a ship that had veered off course. That took nerve. Your pride was on the line. But you did it. *You won.* How many wives can say that?

The old war cry is tiring, and thankfully, she lets it fade. JoJo stares out of the window in that comfortable place of no thought for some time and the trivialities of the day begin drifting back to her. She recalls an article she'd read in the morning – one of those 'isn't the world funny?' pieces *The Telegraph* seemed full of these days. Apparently – all these articles needed to be prefixed with 'apparently' – we each carry an average of nine keys, but can only identify what six of them are for. JoJo had taken out her own set then and counted them. Ten. Close. She'd inspected them one by one. There were the house keys, two of them, and the retractable car key, a heavy one for the shed, and a slighter key for the small greenhouse where she tried (and mostly failed) to grow hothouse tomatoes. One for her wardrobe – though she never locked it, she should really take it off – and another for the cottage. That left three. The first was small and silver – it might open a music box of some kind, the sort where a ballerina twirls to chintzy music – but it was probably for an ancient piece of luggage that had been thrown away years ago. The second was a lever key, not quite silver, not quite brass, with a simple flat top head. It was cold in her hand and seemed to be made of denser metal than the others – perhaps it opened a gate, although JoJo couldn't imagine where. The final key appeared to be a copy – it had the local locksmith's name stamped into it – and seemed out of place among the other keys, too, shiny and unmarked, as if it had been cut only yesterday. How had she not noticed it?

Lying in the darkness, JoJo turns the mystery keys around in her mind again. She has a sense that they are definitely *hers*; there *is* a certain familiarity to them, but this only makes it more annoying. Not only has she been proven statistically average by *The Telegraph*, but she feels that somewhere, something is waiting for her, unopened and therefore, by some means, unfinished…

Frank clears his throat. She was almost asleep, JoJo realises now, in that strange mental place where we forget which room we're in, our names, where the bed seems to float in the ether.

He speaks then; JoJo hears the words, but for a second they don't register, like a key she can't quite make fit.

'She's pregnant, you know.'

And just like that, the lock clicks open.

CHAPTER FOUR

On Monday morning – the first Monday in October – Adam wakes with his alarm at six o'clock to shower, shave and get dressed. He eats a hurried breakfast of brown toast and marmalade (trying not to get crumbs on his suit) and leaves the house just before Patrick is due to get up at half past six. It's drizzling outside, and although Adam is a fervent defender of Hackney's very rough-around-the-edges east London charm, even he has to admit it's especially grim and sodden this morning. A rubbish bag has been torn apart by foxes – vegetable peelings, cigarette butts and one bloated disposable nappy, strewn across the footpath – and despite the rain, the air is heavy with car fumes. He opens his umbrella, picks his way through the peelings and sets off along the road.

Half an hour later, Adam has joined the stream of people walking west – it's like stepping onto a conveyor belt, one that winds itself along towards the City. There, their paths begin to diverge: the secretaries and paralegals in white trainers, the coffee runners and office goons, the bonus chasers, the hotshots in pinstripes, the secret millionaires and atop them all, those masters of the Universe.

As Adam walks, he lists his options, like a soldier about to go over the top. He could turn and run. He could distract himself, maybe head to the gym – he might feel differently after a good long steam? But despite these alternatives, he stays on course. It's almost out of his control now anyway. Something bigger is in operation. Mercer and Daggen is calling.

Arriving at the building, Adam stands on the opposite side of the street, shielding his face with the umbrella. It looks warm inside. Warm and dry. A tall security guard – no sleepy hound-dog today – is standing to attention beside the doors, inspecting each new person as they walk in, watching as they swipe their card and push through the turnstile (*tink-tink-tink*, thinks Adam). The security guard can't remember all their faces though, can he? Adam keeps count – four people arrive within ten seconds. That's – he takes his mobile out of his pocket and selects the calculator app – twenty-four people a minute or 1,440 an hour. There are peaks too, moments when a group appears, five or six people arriving in the foyer together, holding the door open for the others or shaking the water from their brollies. If he times his arrival with one of these flash mobs, he'll be just another face in the crowd. Simple.

'Insane,' Adam mutters under his breath.

His phone vibrates. It's a text message from Patrick:

Mate! You left before I could say good luck! Congrats on being a wage slave again! Gonna miss having a house bitch to fold my washing though… Beers later to celebrate?

Adam clicks his phone to sleep mode, slips it back in his pocket and crosses the road. His heart is thumping in his chest and his legs feel too springy, as if he's bouncing towards Mercer and Daggen. 'Walk normally!' he commands his legs – he must look like Tigger from *Winnie the Pooh*, bounding up to the front doors.

Adam gets a better view of the security guard now. He's tall and broad, with olive skin, and sports a buzz cut that accentuates the strong angles of his skull. He's chewing gum slowly and his jaw bulges menacingly each time he masticates – he's probably not supposed to chew gum on the job, thinks Adam, but he does anyway. That's the kind of man this security guard is. He'll enforce the rules, but he won't live by them.

Adam remembers to push, not pull the door handle (only a complete rookie would pull it, thank God he didn't stumble at the first hurdle!) and collapses his umbrella as he whisks through the doors. His heart is beating so hard now, he's sure it must be audible. A queue has formed behind the two turnstiles and he walks up to the one on the right, furthest away from the security guard.

Sitting behind the reception desk, he sees today, is an alarmingly pretty brunette with bright red lips: she's cradling a phone between her shoulder and ear, perfectly manicured hands flipping through a folder of papers.

'No, it's not here,' she says down the phone, with a slight twang to her voice. American? Canadian maybe? 'I'm telling you, it's not. I can fax it to you if you want? Fine.' She hangs up the phone and huffs. 'He won't find it,' she says to no one in particular.

Adam reluctantly pulls his gaze away from the beautiful receptionist and risks a peek at the security guard. Mr Mastication is staring out through the glass doors so Adam slips his hand into his left pocket and removes the security card, holding it photo side down. He's taken precautions with his appearance today – blow-drying the kink out of his hair to make it as straight as possible, and wearing a similar shirt to the one Mark J. Smith has in the photo – but he's not sure if it's helped or hindered. Is he a believable doppelgänger or a game of 'spot the difference'? – Adam can't decide.

One thing is almost certain: the security card he found two days ago is likely deactivated – the card reported missing or stolen by Mark the moment he realised it was gone from his wallet. Adam is under no illusion about the square of plastic he's holding.

There's someone behind him now: Adam is locked into the queue. A bead of sweat runs down his back.

Focus, he thinks.

There are just two people in front of Adam now – a stout older gentleman in pole position, and behind him, a man in wet cycling gear. The older gent is having trouble with his card, he keeps swiping it through the reader but the light on the turnstile stays obstinately red. Stubbornly, he swipes it again and again, cursing and increasingly flustered.

'Can I help?' the receptionist asks, one slender hand resting on the counter. 'Let me see.' She takes the card from the man and rubs it on her sleeve. 'It's the static,' she explains, still rubbing, 'I don't know why it works, but it does. Try it now.' The receptionist hands the card back to him, and this time when he swipes, the light clicks green.

'Hey presto!' she says with a smile, but the stout man shoves his way through the turnstile without a thank you or even a backwards glance. Adam is about to tut and roll his eyes – let the receptionist know not everyone accepts such bad manners – but he pulls himself up sharply. He can't start flirting with the receptionist, he has to keep his head down and concentrate. The consequences of failing are too great for him to even consider, and he only gets one chance at this. One chance.

Adam takes a quick look of the security guard before he—

The guard turns to meet his gaze.

Shit, buggery, bugger. Adam turns back. The man in cycling gear has misplaced his card – this delay, added to the kerfuffle with the gentleman, is making the people behind Adam defect to the other queue. He feels exposed now and the sweat down his back is slicking his shirt against his skin in a very uncomfortable way.

Is the security guard still staring at him?

Adam turns again. Yes, yes, he is.

'Mondays, huh?' says Adam, rolling his eyes.

The security guard nods – he knows all about Mondays (sardonic chew, sardonic chew) – until a new arrival in the foyer draws the guard's attention.

The cycling man has found his card now so Adam quickly extends the shaft of his collapsible umbrella, the head of the brolly on its longest pole, and readies himself. He spent the previous day in the Underground trying to master the exact timing, but managed to get it right only half the time – more often than not the turnstile would snap closed. The trick was to fully cover the sensor panel on the turnstile without the person in front realising they were being tailgated, but it was a real art, and much harder than the dodgy website Adam had researched made it sound.

Cycling man swipes his card – it takes only one attempt for the light to click green this time – and as he walks through the turnstile, lifting his cycle helmet and bag over the metal arms, Adam extends the umbrella head so it slides along the side of the turnstile. He's purposefully left the umbrella canopy unfastened so it hangs down and covers more space allowing greater room for error, but if he doesn't cover the motion sensor in time, the man will pass through the turnstile, it will click back to red and all will be lost. 'Tink-tink-tink' – Adam holds his breath – 'click'. Red.

As a last attempt, Adam swipes his card – maybe he has been overly pessimistic, perhaps it would still work? But the light stays red. Mark must have already called it in.

Game over.

*

It was game on. Chris called the following night, which was charming, and then the night after, which was cute, and then they had a ritual to follow, and Daisy began surreptitiously clearing her evening schedule to make sure she wouldn't miss his calls. There was something about talking on the telephone, how intimate it was. Yes, Daisy spoke to her mother almost every day, but there was no new information there, save a few details, and Daisy was usually on her laptop, on the Internet, half listening anyway – except the other night, when she told her parents about him. 'What's he like?' her mum had asked. 'Tall and posh,' Daisy had answered. 'Literally or comparatively?' Dad had yelled at the phone, once her mother had relayed this information. 'Both!' Daisy yelled back.

Phone calls with Chris were different. Daisy would prepare the space – moving the washing off the comfortable chair so she could sit, dimming the lights, making sure her flatmate wasn't in hearing distance, and pre-boiling the noisy kettle so she could have a hottish drink if she wanted, without having to yell. She'd even brush her teeth. Although she was expecting it, the ringing phone always startled Daisy, making her yelp. And then they'd talk about nothing really, nothing of substance – the people they'd seen that day (a woman so swollen she looked as if she was about to pop – 'How does she get her shoes on?' Chris had asked, 'pregnancy truly is a miracle.'), the mishaps (a sheepish man on the Jubilee line platform with his foot stuck between the train doors) and near misses. Or they would choose a random TV channel or a show to stream, the kookier the better, and try to orientate themselves in an old Western or a Japanese cooking programme, building surreal character motivations into a narrative all their own. These moments seemed the most intimate, when there were long stretches of silence between them, and Daisy wanted to ask, 'are you still there, Chris?', feeling the tension of this question building in her throat – but of course, he always was.

*

Adam retracts the umbrella quickly, palms the card and moves out of the queue, resting his backpack against the reception desk. Here, he pretends to search for his ID to buy himself some time while he figures out what the hell to do next. The receptionist glances up and Adam smiles, remembering to engage with his eyes (he'd practised earlier that morning while shaving) and she returns it with a clinical 'I get paid to be nice to people' smile of her own.

He should leave this very second. Chalk this up to experience, one that – mercifully – didn't get him arrested. If he goes right now, he might even catch the end of his favourite daytime TV show, *Cash in the Attic*.

Adam wonders if things would be different – scientifically speaking – if his penis were bigger. In the same way that children with vocational surnames (Baker, Pilot) have a greater chance of joining the profession when they grow up (according to the theory of nominative determinism), surely added swagger in the trouser department would have incrementally boosted his confidence over the years? Adam would probably be one of those guys who could talk his way into the building and bed the receptionist to boot – Jason Bourne by way of James Bond. Instead, he's a sweating, nervous wreck, emptying his pockets (which mostly contain used tissues) in front of a very pretty woman for a third time.

As he fills his pockets with his possessions again, Adam turns his body so he can better see the turnstile and watches as the next few people file through. From this angle, he can spot that the motion sensor is much lower on these turnstiles than at the Underground, at knee height rather than thigh level. He would have had to aim the umbrella lower, but then he'd never get through the metal arms because the pole would be wedged through, stopping them from rotating. They are clever, these turnstile makers, he thinks. It's almost as if they've designed them to be difficult to cheat. Unless…

Making a show of finding his card ('In my jacket p-pocket all along, tsk'), Adam slings his bag over his shoulders, throws his coat over his right arm and picks up the umbrella in his right hand. Both lines are flowing again, so he joins his original queue. As the woman in front of him swipes her card, Adam extends the umbrella. He waits for her to walk a few steps and at the last 'tink', pushes the umbrella through the turnstile (his coat shields this action from onlookers behind) and rests it on the metal arms.

This time, as the woman moves off, the light stays green. Adam swipes his card as he rests his thigh against the metal arms, but before he pushes through, he dangles his coat down the side of the sensor and unthreads the umbrella from its resting place with his other hand. Carefully, he walks through the turnstile, making sure to keep the dangling coat in place to cover the sensor. He can't believe it, he's made it. Adam expects at any moment to hear 'Hey, you, come back!' but he turns the corner of the foyer into the hallway behind without any intervention.

It's the elevators next, but they're easy. *Even babies can do elevators!* Adam thinks giddily. A doorway beside the two lifts is marked as a stairwell, but only an interloper would take the stairs unnecessarily, so he waits with the small crowd until the elevator on the left dings and the doors slide open. There's a bit of interactive public theatre as people shuffle on, balancing their coffee cups and calling out their desired floor (there are seven all up, including a basement) while the person closest to the panel obligingly pushes the buttons. The doors shut and the lift starts its ascent to the first floor. On his previous visit, Adam instinctively travelled to the fourth floor – it was a halfway point after all, and four felt like a good round number – but today he has a loftier destination in mind. As the doors open and people exit the elevator, he is afforded a quick glimpse of the layout on each level. The first floor seems to be a warren of small offices: accountancy and IT probably (best to keep them locked away), while two and three are similar to four in that they are large open spaces filled with cubicles and dual screen monitors, two large offices in the far corners (his heart gives a leap when he sees 'his' corner office. It seems unoccupied this morning, its owner no early bird, sniffs Adam). The doors shut on four and the elevator resumes its climb with only two people left: Adam and a severe-looking woman in an expensive dress-suit and a statement brooch. She gives him a sideways glance and Adam worries she might challenge him on why he's heading to the upper echelons of Mercer and Daggen, but as they reach the fifth floor he realises it smells 'musky' in the confines of the elevator and perhaps his deodorant hasn't lived up to its promise of twenty-four-hour protection after all. As the lift doors open, the woman hurries out into the hallway and through glass doors that divide another reception area, this one smaller and swankier than the one downstairs, obviously for higher-ups and VIPs.

Adam steps out of the lift gingerly, turns left and keeps on walking until he finds the men's toilet. Pushing open the door, he is met by the scent of lilac, the sound of panpipe music and the soft, amber lighting of a superior executive bathroom. Lucky bamboo twists sit in terracotta pots behind the basins and everything is neat and spotlessly clean.

He checks himself in the mirror. Adam needn't have worried about appearing like Mark J. Smith's doppelgänger – with the bags under his eyes, his pasty complexion, and hair wet, stringy and matted to his forehead, the similarity is uncanny.

Adam's shirt is properly soggy, so he removes his suit jacket and stands, back hunched to the hairdryer, blasting himself with hot air. Next, he takes a handful of paper towels, wets a wedge of them and moves to a toilet cubicle, where he removes his shirt and gives himself a pirate bath, patting himself dry afterwards with the remaining towels. Dressed again, he exits the cubicle, washes his face at the sink, tidies his hair, sprays on more deodorant (which he's brought with him in his bag), and steps back to take in the effect. Much better: less 'drowned rat' and more Michael J. Fox in *The Secret of My Success*.

Back in the hallway, Adam nips to the door leading to the stairwell and walks up the flight of steps slowly, listening for any noise above him. The online press release had said the refurbishment of the 'empty space' would start in December (the top floor had been leased to a celebrity chef, who was opening a seafood restaurant), but better not take any chances. If he's discovered, he'll just say he was going for a cigarette – everyone knows how smokers love to flout trespassing rules.

At the top of the stairs, he pauses, listening intently. There's no sound. In fact, there's *no* sound. It's strangely quiet, except for a few intermittent clicks and the faint background hum of elevators. A small brown spider wanders over to his shoe, taps it cautiously with one of its eight legs and ambles on its way again. Adam rests one hand on the stairwell door and takes out his phone with the other, touching the screen to make it spring to life. He types in the password and, selecting Patrick's message, hits reply:

Dude! Defo drinks tonight. It's mad here. Going to lay low, get my bearings before they realise they've made a terrible mistake! Cheers for standing by me these past few months. Don't want to get all soppy, but I really appreciate it. Will rip it up here – you see if I don't… A

The text sent, he pauses – listening intently for one more moment – then pushes open the door.

*

In south London, Dylan has barely logged on to the computer when a Skype video call pops up from Chris. He considers ignoring it, but feels guilty instantly. They've been linked in the Big Brother programme for almost five months, and although it was rocky to start with, Dylan really does enjoy Chris's fortnightly visits. It's just… No, he's being uncharitable. It's nothing. He clicks accept, and a box pops up in the screen, filled mostly with Chris's forehead.

'Moonster!'

'Hey, Chris.'

'Moonamundo!'

Chris can go on like this for some time, so Dylan starts signing into his blog.

'Moonarelli!'

'How's it going?'

'Great, perfect. Peachy even.'

'What's up?'

'Just wanted to check in with my favourite amigo.'

In their first few weeks, Chris had experimented with the bro-banter (as Dylan secretly thought of it), trialling a series of hip-hop influenced takes until settling on a (only slightly less racist) Latino-inspired persona. Dylan didn't mind really. He couldn't get angry with Chris for misjudging his tone in the same way he could never stay annoyed if Otis chewed his Nikes.

'How's the old grey matter?'

'Better, thanks. I haven't had an episode since the other day.'

'Good to hear.'

'Might be able to go back to school in a few weeks too.'

'Excellento! That's great news! The girls don't know what's about to hit them!'

Yeah, thinks Dylan, *an invalid with skinny legs, who can't sit up too fast for fear of passing out. I'll be fighting them off.*

'How are things with you?' he says, changing the subject before Chris can start giving him advice on chat-up lines.

'Never better. This girl I've been seeing – Daisy – she's kind of fantastic. You'll love her.'

'Does she like dogs?'

'Mate, animals adore her. She's like Eliza Doolittle. Every morning, small birds fly through her window and help get her dressed. A rabbit makes her coffee.'

'She might get disappointed when Otis can't make hot drinks.'

'No one could ever be disappointed with Otis. How is the Beast?'

'He was attacked by a pug the other day.'

'Those things can be mean.'

'It was tiny. It couldn't even see properly with its big googly eyes.'

'Otis is risk averse. It's a sign of intelligence.'

'It's a sign he—'

Dylan stops dead in his tracks. There was a comment on his latest blog post. It might be spam, though. He shouldn't get too excited, he told himself, as he clicked on the post.

Chris, who has been speaking, realises he's being ignored and taps the microphone.

'Is this thing on?'

'Sorry, what were you saying?'

'Do you mind if we postpone our next catch up until the following weekend? I was hoping to take Daisy away for a couple of days on Saturday. You know, surprise her.'

'Yeah, sure,' Dylan replies, scrolling down to the comment section. And yes! There it was, from AquariusRising07. Janelle's handle! The comment read simply:

Love this.

She loved it!

'Great, I'll make it up to you. We can go tenpin bowling.'

Dylan has a new thought – a comment from Janelle often meant a follow-up email. He loads up his inbox, and sure enough, there's one waiting.

'Okay, maybe not tenpin bowling,' says Chris. 'Tough crowd. You choose. As long as it's not one of those soppy teenage wizard vampire movies, I'm in.'

Dylan bites his tongue. Chris loves to tease him about 'youth culture', but he won't take the bait today (and so what if he likes *Harry Potter*?). Instead, he clicks on the email:

Dylan!

I'm afraid I'm going to have to pause our little film club. I'm really sorry, but life is getting complicated, I hope you understand. I can't get into it now, but there are forces at play, and I need all my energy to deal with them.

Keep doing your exercises, and stick to the programme, and you'll be fine. Know what a great guy you are. Who knows, if you were a few years older, I might have snapped you up myself!

Chris is still talking.

'…and George Clooney slapped me round the face with a French baguette.'

'Great,' Dylan says distractedly.

'Aha! I knew you weren't listening. George Clooney is a gentleman – the Cary Grant of our generation – he would never waste food like that. What's going on, kiddo? You seem, preoccupied. Is it a girl?'

'No.'

Chris knew about Janelle of course, but he'd always acted jealous at any mention of her (sensing that he was in her shadow), so Dylan had learned to keep her out of the conversation.

'It *is* a girl, I can see it in your face. You sly dog, Moonshine. You're chatting to her now, aren't you? I feel dirty, like I'm being digitally cheated on. Can she hear me? Hullo, lady friend, nice to meet you! Be good to Dylan, or you'll have me to deal with. None of your wily womanly charms and if you break his heart, I'll…'

Dylan considers closing the chat box and saying the computer crashed. Instead, he reads the email again. What can Janelle have meant by 'forces at play'? Maybe it was her abusive ex-boyfriend again? Or the domineering father she'd mentioned, during one of their heart-to-hearts? Dylan feels like rushing to her side – Janelle lived in Archway, he remembered, he didn't know where exactly… Maybe he could offer to go visit? He hadn't travelled out of Croydon for a very long time, but this would be worth the risk, times a million.

At the bottom of the email, Dylan notices a p.s. There was a p.s.!

p.s. I'm sending you something, a surprise – it should arrive in the next couple of weeks. You'll have to sign for it, so keep an eye out.

'Right,' says Chris, 'I can tell you're riveted by my company. I'll let you get back to your girlfriend. Call me next week.'

'Good luck with Eliza,' Dylan says to Chris.

'Her name's Daisy.'

'Daisy, sorry – good luck.'

'Thanks, pal. Don't go changing, Moonskies.'

'I won't.'

'Adios!'

But Dylan is too distracted to say goodbye. A surprise? he thinks, his brain ticking over wildly – what could it possibly be? He understood the symbolism though. In some way, Janelle loved him too. She loved him! And Dylan was going to do everything in his power to help her…

CHAPTER FIVE

'Be prepared!' goes the old Scout motto, but for a romantic weekend away a more accurate aphorism might read: always *come* prepared.

Pack your toothbrush. Pack a comb. Take Viagra, condoms, tampons, crampons (and climbing rope). Remember breath mints. Mouthwash. Femfresh™ and wipes! Your antidepressants in a multivitamin bottle. Real vitamins. That bit of weed you've been saving. Bring a copy of *Zen in the Art of Archery*. Pack floss, contact lens solution, cigars, poppers and something to keep the kids busy (at least for an hour). Don't forget a hip flask of brandy or your Korean anti-aging cream. A waterproof camera. Coal tar soap. Hormone replacement medication. Pack your goggles! Take baby oil, your night brace and the printout with the doctor's latest findings. Don't leave without the instructions on how to turn off the alarm. Remember sun lotion. The dog-eared photo of your brother's ex-wife. *Tantra for Dummies* and extra toilet paper. Tiger balm. Your new piercings. Bring ear plugs, gaffer tape and the final dose of penicillin. Protein shakes – vanilla, cherry and pecan brownie. Pack your therapist's notes. The concert tickets. The signed divorce papers and moisturiser for the stubble rash. Buy Odor-Eaters. A fake ID. A briefcase for Monday. Bring a bottle of supermarket own-brand bubbly and a crate of energy drinks. Kosher jam for the morning. Pack your knitting – pack clothes if you must – if we have to leave London, why can't we be a little prepared for once?

*

Daisy is having trouble zipping up her suitcase when a car horn toots outside. From her first-floor bedroom window, she watches as a cherry red Alfa Romeo – surrounded by a small but appreciative crowd of onlookers – pulls into a parking space below. Emerging from the leathered interior of the two-seater, Chris seems like he expects a round of applause, but the crowd disperses silently instead. Glancing up, he sees Daisy and raises a hand in greeting. She feels it then, the delicious flutter of her good fortune – a life flowing with spontaneous easy pleasures – but she pulls herself together, afraid she might jinx it. Chris is handsome today, though. What is it? Definitely not the cheesy rented sportscar. He's wearing his usual look of posh-Brit-meets-American-casual – a periwinkle linen shirt rolled up at the sleeves, tan chinos with a brown belt and grey espadrilles – so nothing especially titillating there. Perhaps it's because she knows the body beneath the fabric now: the red devil tattoo on his left thigh, the solid legs built up from years of rowing, the surprisingly hairless groin. She considers him some more but comes to no definitive conclusion – maybe it is the new wheels after all?

Downstairs, Chris is pointing at something, first casually and then more emphatically, and so engrossed is Daisy that it takes her a few moments to understand he wants, quite reasonably, to be let in.

Chris is leaning across the doorframe in a mock-Lothario pose as she opens the front door.

'What do you think?' he asks, waggling his eyebrows towards the car.

'They'll love that in the Lake District,' Daisy replies with a grin, widening her eyes for effect. She's beautiful today, Chris decides, quite stunning in a low-cut turquoise top, flicky black eye makeup and a gold snake necklace (the head curled around her clavicle to grasp its own tail) – like some Egyptian queen.

'Nice try,' he says, leaning in for a kiss and feeling a thrill at the casual intimacy he's allowed now.

'Cornwall?'

'I'm not telling.'

'So, it might be Cornwall?'

'I'm not ruling it out.'

'It's Cornwall then,' she says, planting her mouth on his.

'No,' he says, when their lips part again, 'it's not.'

'That could be misdirection.'

'Misinformation, you mean?'

'You admit it?'

He laughs and chances another kiss.

They successfully fasten her suitcase and load it into the boot of the car.

'Wherever we're going,' says Daisy, drawing the seat belt across her chest, 'it must be a bit of a distance to justify this bad boy. I can't imagine we'll head to Brighton, or you'll have to do laps around Hove just to get your money's worth.'

'It's not the length of the ride,' says Chris, turning the key in the ignition, the engine starting with a muffled growl, 'but how you enjoy it that counts.'

'Said the actress to the bishop!' they both say in unison.

'Now, Scotland,' says Daisy as he pulls out from the kerb, 'might be too far. We'd have left London earlier. By my calculations,' she licks a finger and holds it up, 'we are heading… north. Or west. I'm not very good with directions. I know! We're heading to Wales, aren't we? Leek country!'

'You don't give up, do you?' says Chris, squeezing her knee. 'You're in a mischievous mood today.'

'Am I?' Daisy doesn't *feel* particularly mischievous – excited maybe. She clears her throat. 'Joking aside, I really do have to let Mum know where I'm going this weekend. She's worried you might molest me or something.'

Chris looks at her horrified, the colour draining from his face.

'Of course, I didn't think – we're going to…'

'No – hey!' Daisy says quickly, 'I was kidding. She doesn't care what you do with me, honestly. Molest me all you want. I'll stop now, I want to be surprised. Don't tell me where we're going. That was mean, I'm sorry.'

Chris smiles weakly.

I am being mischievous, Daisy thinks. *Cut it out.*

They sit for a few moments, both thinking of something to say.

'How was the rest of your week?' Daisy asks finally.

'Good, thanks.'

'Get up to anything much?'

'No, a regular old week. Just the Barnardo's stuff – the Big Brother programme.'

'I wish I did something charitable. What made you start?'

'I'm an only child, like you – and I always wanted brothers to play with. But mostly, it's a blatant attempt at altruism to right some of my former wrongs.'

'What ones are those?'

'Wouldn't you like to know…'

Daisy *would* actually. She was very nearly over Chris's constant mysterious withholding.

'The Barnardo's stuff is only one day a fortnight though, isn't it? What do you do the rest of the time?'

She waits for him to reply, but he doesn't.

They approach a roundabout and Chris accelerates to nip in front of an oncoming van – Daisy gasps and steadies a hand against the glove department. *Oh, great*, she thinks, *he's going to be one of* those *drivers*.

'How was your week?' Chris asks after he's sped into the left turn.

Deflection, she thinks, *he doesn't want to answer me so he's asked the same question.*

'I had to wangle a few things to get time off,' she says. 'I've been on a shoot for a line of swanky jewellery and the art director wanted me to make all these miniature Edwardian-style armchairs for the hand models to sit their hands in – so the hands are like people sitting in chairs, their fingers as legs – it's all very high concept! What will they come up with next? Anyway, I'm quite proud of these chairs, but they're very delicate and the hand models keep busting them. It's heartbreaking. Hand models are the worst, by the way, they're evil.'

'Why's that?'

'I don't know. They're usually older than regular models and they never have very nice faces – they don't have to, I guess – so maybe they compensate by being horrible. They make bucket loads too, so there's no need. One particular model really has it in for me. I think she was putting too much pressure on the chair and trying to break it on purpose.'

'What did you do?'

'I waited until we were alone and told her she should be careful of splinters.'

'You threatened her?' Chris says, laughing.

'Not really. I just said it would be a shame if anything happened to those lovely fingers of hers and she should maybe not press down too hard, as there might be something sharp concealed inside – like a rusty nail. And had she had her tetanus shots?'

'It's like *On the Waterfront*,' says Chris, still laughing.

'Is that the one with Kevin Costner set in the future, where they all live in the water?'

'That's *Waterworld*. *On the Waterfront* has Marlon Brando taking on the mob and corruption.'

'Ah, I see. Makes more sense. Honestly, though, they're paranoid these hand models. Some of them wear leather gloves eating lunch.'

'It's their livelihood, I suppose.'

'Exactly. I made my position clear with the model and we came to an understanding. I don't think any of the chairs will break while I'm away, let's just say that.'

'You're ruthless. I like it.'

'It's a ruthless industry,' shrugs Daisy.

'I once thought about hand modelling. I even went for a manicure for research, but it was so uncomfortable, I gave up on the whole idea.'

'Show me your hands?' Chris raises his left one for inspection. The fingers are long, the nails glossy. 'Nice cuticles. You've never done a day's hard work, have you?'

'Guilty. Unless you count digging ditches as a kid. I went through a stage of burying things: time capsules, biscuit tins full of messages in secret code, or the reverse – searching for pirate treasure—'

'So, when you're not at Barnardo's,' interrupts Daisy, 'what's a typical week for Chris?' She wants to ask: how do you pay your rent? Hire a car like this? Buy all those *chinos*? But the taboo of asking another Englishman directly about money is too great. Daisy thinks back on other dates, he must have talked about a job? No, she realises, he's always been evasive, saying something like 'What don't I do?' and waggling those lovely eyebrows of his. He's talked about his travels but nothing concerning university or a career. And come to think of it, didn't he say he was an *unpaid volunteer* at Barnardo's?

'A typical week?'

'While I'm slaving away over miniature furniture.'

'I work as a singing telegram. In a gorilla suit.'

Chris starts to make grunting noises and scratches his armpit.

'Joking aside...'

'I sit waiting for you, of course.'

'Aw, sweet – creepy, but sweet. Seriously, how do you keep the wolf from the door?'

Chris fixes his eyes on the road.

'I get by.'

Shit, Daisy thinks, *he's unemployed. I should never have asked. I've embarrassed him. It's none of my business.* Except, it is – if they are to have a relationship together. Isn't it?

'It's complicated,' he says, after a pause.

'You don't have to tell me anything...'

'No, I want to.'

Daisy is silent. The car is heading up Kilburn High Road now, she notes peripherally – they are travelling north after all.

'When I was ten, my grandmother died and left me an inheritance, which came to me when I was twenty-one.'

'I'm sorry,' Daisy says automatically, 'about your grandmother.'

'It was a long time ago, she was very old,' he says, shrugging it off.

She waits for him to go on.

'So, you're a trust fund kid?' she says eventually when he doesn't. He winces.

'All it meant is I didn't have to work. That I was comfortable – if I was careful.'

'You've *never* had a job?'

Chris shakes his head and Daisy mulls this over for a second. She's always had a complicated relationship with money. Daisy was lucky enough to get into a prestigious all-girls' school on part scholarship, but it meant her parents had to work incredibly hard to pay the outstanding balance. The guilt and responsibility weighed heavily on Daisy during her teens – they never went on family holidays, her dad was always in his cab, working extra hours, especially on public holidays to get time and a half, and she knew her mum hated the temperamental boiler, but never suggested replacing it. To make matters worse, Daisy was teased by the richer girls for not having the 'it' piece of jewellery or the 'in' hairstyle, or for her battered old schoolbag. The irony of ending up in the fashion industry hadn't escaped her – but she was able to compartmentalise; other people had infinity pools, and ocelot furs and handbags that cost as much as a house. Daisy didn't, and that was fine. Wealth, in her experience, was basically a character flaw. Fleeting trends, must-have exclusives, limited editions – they were all designed to extract money from the wealthiest. She wanted no part in the con.

'I travelled overseas when I left school,' Chris says. 'I only planned to go for a year, but it ended up being four. And when I came back… I'd known about the inheritance since I was ten. I'd been waiting for it, I had all these plans.'

'And what happened?'

He sighs.

'Money changes things.'

He stares at the road again. Viewed in profile, his eyes are hard set, colder. His face seems to have tightened.

'So, you're thirty-one now and turned out alright?' says Daisy. 'You're not sitting in a wedding dress somewhere with all the clocks stopped at least. But didn't you want to study? Or have a career?'

Daisy thinks back on her own childhood – she was always coming up with a new scheme to become a horse wrangler or a marine biologist, fantasising about honour and glory in some exotic profession.

'No, I just wanted the money and to be left alone.'

Chris says this so dispassionately it surprises her. It's so unlike him, this person sitting in the driving seat, that it's shocking.

'Left alone? By whom?'

Daisy knows she shouldn't keep pressing him, but she can't help herself.

He hesitates.

'You become a target. People always want something from you. And the ones with money are just as bad. Worse even. It becomes like an addiction, you keep wanting more.' Chris turns to her. 'I'm being very frank with you.'

'I'm being very nosey. But I won't tell anyone, I promise. I don't know anyone to tell it to anyway.'

'You know hand models.'

'True. But they won't say anything if they know what's good for them.'

Chris smiles faintly. 'It's just so meaningless, this money stuff.'

'Only if you have it. If you don't, money is a very interesting topic.'

'That's what I mean, everyone is so *interested* in it.'

'You can't blame people really. We've been programmed all our lives to think it's the most important stuff in the world.'

'Yes, but it's all so, I don't know, common.'

Daisy shakes her head in stunned disbelief. He didn't just say *common*, did he? *Jesus Franklin Christ*, she thinks, *I'm sitting here, imagining Chris has gone through some terrible trauma, and the only thing he's inflicted with is spoilt rich kid syndrome. Boo fucking hoo! My heart bleeds. Some of us commoners would like to not work.* She recounts all the favours she had to promise to secure a long weekend off. The hand model would take her revenge one day too, that was for certain. Add to this the almost daily financial humiliations – overpriced food, the silly money spent on travel only to suffer delays and overcrowding and, to top it all off, after years of scrimping and pinching, Daisy is still no closer to owning even the most derelict of homes. There are many people worse off, of course, but the whole point of living in a dangerously overpopulated city in the first place was so she could meet someone to partner up with and take on London together. Daisy can't be a team with Chris. It's too uneven – it made her feel inadequate. He's from old money; her parents cut out coupons and shop at Aldi. Chris would never be able to understand Daisy, and eventually, he'd grow to resent her – just like the posh girls who'd terrorised her at school.

And just like that the spell is broken. Daisy finds herself in a car (still going much too fast) with a complete stranger. She only met Chris *three weeks* ago! What made her think she was ready to go away for a whole weekend with him? His revelation proves he could be anyone. What else hasn't he told her? That he likes to lure women away, under the pretence of a long weekend, only to murder them in some secluded woods? That she is, this very moment, speeding towards a grisly death at the hands of a homicidal maniac?

She's gone very quiet, thinks Chris.

He presses his foot down on the accelerator, and as he does so, his right shoulder throbs in response. *It's psychosomatic*, he tells himself, gritting his jaw and trying to ignore the pain. It's been a long time since he's allowed himself in the driving seat of a car, and a sportscar at that. This was progress – he was getting back on the horse. A very fast horse. All he wants is to arrive at the hotel in good time and get to their room. Chris has organised an ice bucket with champagne to be waiting – they can lock the door, change into terrycloth robes and dive into the king-sized bed. From the moment they slip between those sheets their feet shall not touch the ground again until Sunday – they'll eat room service all weekend if they have to; build a bridge to the bathroom out of cushions, like he did when he was a child, pretending the floor was molten lava.

They stop at the lights outside Kilburn Tube station.

He knows he should have let Daisy in on his situation sooner, but he didn't have a high success rate with girls once he told them about the inheritance. Expectation crept in. It started with a trend towards more elaborate restaurants (one girl would quite unashamedly trace a line down the right side of the menu until she found the most expensive dish) and casual interrogation about the cost of his flat. Gradually, the curiosity became more pressing – Chris had to be careful where he left his mail after he caught one of his ex-girlfriends steaming open his bank statements. At birthdays, or the flimsiest excuse for an anniversary, gifts would become mandatory, with hints dropped weeks in advance about some gold bracelet at Tiffany's, or a charming boutique hotel in Prague. It made him feel used – as if he was a walking money bag.

A car behind them beeps – the light has changed to green – and Chris floors the pedal to make it across in time.

Although it's clear Daisy is no gold digger, he'll still have to deal with her friends. Chris will be labelled 'that rich guy' – her male friends will be particularly difficult, dropping passive aggressive remarks disguised as good-natured banter in an attempt to knock him down a peg or two. Chris will buy the lion's share of drinks to curry favour, but at the end of the night, one of the drunker ones will stop him on his way back from the toilets and grill him over every last detail – what sort of tax does he pay? Is the money kept in a Swiss bank account? Does he swim in it, like Scrooge McDuck? – and if Chris doesn't comply completely, he'll soon get a new nickname: that rich *wanker*.

There was a darker side too. A few years back, one of Chris's good friends had asked for a loan to start a new business – to provide executive services for time-poor bankers. It seemed like a robust idea, and after he'd gone through the business plan, Chris agreed to loan the money in full. It was a no-brainer really, he trusted Duncan – they'd travelled around India together, Chris had even dated Duncan's cousin – and it would be a blast to be part of his mate's endeavour. But the company never materialised, and

Duncan had disappeared – even his cousin didn't know where he was (sitting on a beach in Thailand, drinking cocktails was Chris's guess). Now he can't walk down a busy street without imagining he sees Duncan's face somewhere in the crowd.

There were things that were unrelated with his inheritance that Chris wanted to open up about too, bad choices he'd made – one especially, that even now he can't bring himself to think of – but money always took precedent. It was a curse. It stopped people relating to each other. Stopped them relating to him. Chris wasn't sure if a woman would be able to love him – *really* love him – if she knew about his family's wealth. And then he'd met wonderful Daisy…

There was the little matter of his parents too. They'd want to meet Daisy soon enough, God help her – with his father's 'sense of humour', and his mother's icy interrogations – if money wasn't an issue now, it certainly would be after that.

He glances at Daisy again. She's really being exceptionally quiet. Chris tries to think of something to break the silence – a rollicking game of I Spy for some good retro fun, perhaps? They're fast approaching the M1 – an open stretch of road will lighten the mood. The world seems better when you're cruising along a motorway.

Daisy sits bolt upright as if she's been struck by lightning.

'Is everything okay?' asks Chris.

'No,' she says, shaking her head. 'No, it's not.'

They are gaining on the turn off to join the M1.

'Is there anything I can do?'

'You can stop the car.'

Chris does a double take.

'What? Why?'

'I want to get out.'

'There'll be a motorway services in about ten minutes if you'd like?' But even as Chris says this, he knows this won't be enough to appease her. There's something resolute in Daisy's voice, an edge of panic too. When he looks at her again, he's shocked to find her eyes are filled with tears. 'We can absolutely stop,' he says, slowing down. 'Let me just find a place where I can pull over.'

This is easier said than done. They are already on the underpass speeding towards the roundabout, but Chris spots an entrance to a tile warehouse on his left. He indicates and quickly makes the turn. There are a few angry honks behind them, but they arrive in the car park in one piece.

As soon as he pulls on the handbrake, Daisy opens her door and scurries out. Chris does the same and when he joins her, she's already lifting her suitcase out of the trunk.

'Can we talk about this?' Chris is no longer thinking about getting to the hotel now, he just wants to salvage whatever he can. 'I'll take you home at least?'

Daisy's eyes are smudged with black. He's never seen her cry before, it's only been three weeks after all. Chris has a sense that everything has fallen apart, right under his eyes. He feels like crying himself. Or howling.

'I'm sorry,' is all Daisy says as she turns to go (*Where?* thinks Chris. *Into the tile warehouse?*).

'Just tell me what I've done wrong,' he calls after her.

She doesn't turn back. He stands, dumbfounded, watching Daisy as she walks away, pulling her suitcase behind her. At one point, the case loses balance and topples over so Daisy has to right it again. It seems to Chris the most wretched thing he's ever seen.

How could this have happened? he thinks. *We were happy a moment ago.*

As she reaches the entrance to the warehouse, she does pause briefly to look at him.

'You were right the first time,' he calls, his voice hoarse. 'About where we were going. It was the Lake District.'

Daisy turns and disappears through the doors.

*

Janelle always smelt sweet. The sweetest of sweet smells. Like boiled sweets. Or fresh strawberries. Or candyfloss.

They first met during Dylan's worst days: he was bedridden, couldn't even bear to listen to music so he lay in silence. When he'd stirred (it wasn't really sleep, all he ever managed was a waking doze), he'd smelt the sweetness of her perfume first (Angel by Mugler, he learnt later), and felt the mattress move as she sat down beside him. As he opened his eyes, her smiling features greeted him. This new face seemed so *foreign* – Dylan's father had been his only visitor for days – and so beautiful.

'There you are,' she'd said. 'My name's Janelle. I've brought you something.'

For a moment, Dylan really did think he'd passed away and was receiving a gift on The Other Side from an Angel – Birkenstocks maybe. Or perhaps this was his mother, a younger version, sent to welcome him to The Pearly Gates? Technically, his mother *was* still alive, although Dylan hadn't seen her for many years. He could still remember what she looked like though (vaguely) and on closer inspection, the face in front of him did seem structurally different. As he puzzled over this, he felt something touch his hand, and realised she'd given him a pack of cards.

'Before we start working together, I'm going to give you a reading,' she said, 'and then we'll get you well again. Can you sit up to see better?'

Janelle had helped him up, moving his pillows so his back was supported.

No, Dylan decided, he was still in his bedroom. The Pokémon poster over his chest of drawers was definitely his.

Sitting back, the pretty young woman shuffled the pack of cards – her hands moved very professionally, the speed of them made Dylan's head spin so he turned away.

'I want you to choose six cards,' she said when she'd finished, fanning them out in front of him. 'Just point at the ones you like.'

With considerable effort, Dylan had moved his finger towards the sweep of cards, tapping six different places.

'Good, let's see what we have.'

The reading itself is foggy – Dylan wasn't used to so much information all in one go (although he does remember he was relieved not to have picked the Death card). Janelle had laughed a lot, he did too – it was the first time he'd found anything funny in months. She described dark clouds, paths with forked roads and a woman that sounded very much like his mother, but Dylan was more transfixed by Janelle's hands, the rattle of her silver bangles on her wrists, the healthy crescent shaped cuticles on her fingernails.

'That's one way it can go,' she'd said at the end, leaning forward and staring him straight in the eye. 'But you get to decide what happens next, alright?' Janelle took the cards, putting them back in their packet. 'You'll have to work hard, but no one can shape your future, except you. Not me, not these cards, not your father, or the doctors.' The mattress moved again as she stood up. 'I'll be back tomorrow.' She blew him a kiss and was gone.

When his dad came in later with a bowl of soup, Dylan asked, 'Who was that girl?'

'The people from the Firebolt Process I was telling you about sent her. She's helped a lot of teenagers like you.'

Dylan couldn't recall. He'd closed his eyes, too tired to eat, Janelle's bright smiling face seeping into all his dreams.

Over the next six months, Janelle had visited him every week. Gradually, Dylan started to get better, moving from his bedroom to the sofa when she arrived for each session. Together, they'd go through the exercises and anything that had come up for Dylan during the past seven days, but there was always time to chat, and gossip, and swap stories, Janelle often staying much longer than her allotted forty-five minutes. She told him about her mother, whom she loved, and her father, whom she didn't because he was traditional and overbearing and wouldn't allow pets when she was a child (Janelle liked dogs, but she was more of a bird person – a fact she only revealed while covering Otis's ears).

As Dylan emerged from the illness, he embraced his new-found love for Janelle. It was the small things – the way she laughed at his jokes, how animated she became about the film *Amélie*, or how she organised his pillows so he was extra comfortable. Dylan was also aware he didn't want to be an invalid anymore so that they were closer to being equals, to give their love more weight. In this way too, Janelle spurred on his recovery.

Once he'd graduated to sessions at the kitchen table, Janelle invited Dylan to a support group for young people with illnesses. Dylan had been resistant – he didn't like the idea of being around other sick people – but he agreed to go because she would be there. It wasn't a success. Dylan didn't like competing for Janelle's attention, and loathed being grouped together with other boys (some as young as ten) – it was humiliating, and seemed to create a chasm between them. There was an attitude with the other organisers too; Dylan was quite the catch, a mixed-race kid from a broken family – he would tick a lot of boxes in the diversity requirements report. Embarrassed by the whole episode, he'd stopped seeing Janelle for a few weeks, and then Chris had started coming. Almost at once, Dylan regretted pausing the sessions with Janelle. Perhaps his feelings would fade? he'd wondered. Well, they hadn't – he loved her more than ever. And now she was in danger. Her life might be in jeopardy! It was up to him—

A knock at his bedroom door snaps Dylan to attention.

'Yeah?' he yells, and the door opens.

'Can we talk?' asks his father. He's holding a folded piece of paper and a very full glass of rosé.

'What about?' replies Dylan, suspiciously.

'We've never had a proper chat about, you know, the birds and the bees…'

Dylan starts to protest.

'You weren't well enough before,' continues his dad, speaking over him, 'but now you're almost back on your feet. And what with your French fancies on the computer the other day, I think it's about time we have the conversation.'

Dad sits on the chair next to the bed and rests his wine glass carefully on the bedside table. Putting on his reading glasses from his shirt pocket, he unfolds the piece of paper, and clears his throat.

'Now,' he says, 'there's intercourse obviously. Who you do it with. Always wear a condom. Have you rolled one on a banana yet?'

'Dad, this is embarrassing.'

'Not as embarrassing as an unplanned pregnancy, believe me.'

He takes a massive swig of the rosé.

'There's heterosexual, that's a man and a woman, and then there's homosexual, that's gays and lesbians, but there's also bisexuals – they like a bit of both. And they're invisible in our society, the bisexuals, so it's important to recognise them. Any questions so far?'

'No, Dad—'

'That's your sex bit out of the way, but then there's also gendered identity. You might feel like a girl in a boy's body, or the other way around. That's when you're trans identified. Or there's another one, hold on,' he scans the sheet of paper. 'Yes – intersex.'

'You've already done that one. Bananas. Condoms. I got it.'

'Not "into" sex. Intersex. It means you might be a bit of a boy and a bit of a girl. Down there. Physically.'

'Dad, where did you get this information from?'

'The Internet – now quiet, don't ruin my flow.' He squints at the writing on the paper. 'There are also people who don't want to have sex with anyone ever. They're called asexuals. And there are those who want to have sex dressed up in animal costumes. They are called furries.'

'What about people who like dressing up in animal costumes but don't want to have sex with anyone?'

'You'd have to ask them, don't be smart. What I'm trying to say is, as long as you don't hurt anyone, and you get consent, and it's legal, it's fine – there should be no shame in it.'

'Are we done?'

His dad screws up his face, which is as bright pink as the wine.

'I know you haven't had normal teenage years,' he says, his voice wavering slightly, 'but I just wanted you to know I'm supportive of you, whoever you end up being. You're my only son... And your mum is proud of you too.' Dylan flinches at the mention of his mum. 'I know you don't like me bringing her up, and she and I have had our differences in the past, that's true. I might not have been very good at keeping those grievances to myself, but I don't want to think I've poisoned the well. You only get one mother, and she's not perfect – God knows, neither am I. She did what she had to do, and I know how hard that must have been for her. Your mum loves you and misses you, she does...'

'Don't cry,' Dylan says to his dad, trying to mask his own discomfort.

'It's the truth,' and with that, his dad gives him a crushing bear hug, drains the rest of the wine in his glass, and leaves.

Once the mortification of the talk is over, Dylan turns his attention back to Janelle. He had to be prepared to help her, and that meant being well enough to travel. There was only one thing for it...

*

Yes. The *details*.

Eight months after their initial separation, they would start to see each other again. JoJo had played her cards absolutely right, leveraging everything she knew of Frank from their long marriage. First, there was the anniversary of his father's death. JoJo had sent him a letter; brief, sincere. Then she organised the leak in the roof to be fixed – Frank could never keep his hands out of a DIY project, and it had meant greater communication, more time together, the forging of a new path. Finally, she'd visited him at his office after hours, and told him straight: *I want you.* They had made love right there on his desk, and afterwards, Frank had declared his undying love for her. JoJo's mission was a success.

In the first few days of their reunion, they agreed to meet only in west London – neutral territory – to stop Belinda becoming suspicious. JoJo had initially rallied against the idea. Why should she care what Belinda thought? But Frank had calmed her down, he needed time to end it with her, find a way of extracting himself that was mutually beneficial in the circumstances – Belinda was high profile, she could make things difficult.

'Difficult for you, you mean,' JoJo had spluttered.

'For us,' Frank said calmly. 'She's very well connected.'

And I'm not, thought JoJo. *That's why she's so alluring to you, all those sinewy* connections.

There were other caveats too, some imposed by JoJo, others forced upon her. Timings. Sleeping arrangements. What was and wasn't acceptable in terms of last-minute cancellations. They negotiated. When Frank had his diplomat hat on, he was composed and direct, using his hands to carve up his conversation. 'I'll come here Tuesdays,' he'd said, cutting Tuesday with his rigid left hand, thumb in the air. 'The rest of the week,' Frank's other hand shifted the invisible chips of Wednesday, Thursday, Friday to his right, 'I'll be there. But we can have Sundays too. Belinda sees her mother.'

In another situation, at an earlier time, JoJo would have guffawed at this. Seeing her mother? How conveniently charitable of her – two old birds with one stone – but she holds her tongue. JoJo doesn't want to scare Frank off just when she's getting him back. She felt neutered and it was an unusual sensation. She used to think Frank loved her for her caustic sense of humour, her knack of pithily cutting things down to the quick, but since his affair she was never sure if Belinda was a younger model – flattery of a sort – or a reprieve. Although their marriage, for the most part, had always seemed a well-matched and untroubled one, JoJo fought a nagging suspicion that she had somehow worn Frank down, like a weak acid, slowly eroding him over their years together, until all that remained was his teeth in a pool of human pulp.

JoJo sits in her kitchen, stirring a cup of tea with a teaspoon. The house has taken on an ethereal quality since she found out about the baby – the light plays differently, night and day take on less significance. She finds herself watching television until the early morning, managing to sleep only a few hours before waking, feeling no more refreshed. Her appetite has gone too.

It is not depression, JoJo tells herself. I do not feel depressed. What is it then? Her mind shutting down? A walking coma? JoJo's worst nightmare is to become a conscious vegetable, slowly blinking out messages from a hospital bed – 'Turn on the fan, please', 'The nurse keeps stealing my chocolates' – that sort of thing. This sensation doesn't terrify her though (it reminds her of her Diazepam days, except there's no lethargy, she's quite spritely going up stairs). And when she thinks 'baby', her blood does not boil. Baby. Nothing. Belinda and Frank's bundle of joy. Quite calm.

JoJo drops the teaspoon, the metal rattling on the brushed granite counter top.

I'm in shock, she thinks. JoJo considers this revelation with the same languidness of her other minimal thoughts. Standing, she walks over to the bookshelf and takes the medical dictionary off the shelf. The entry is not helpful, however – medical shock is all blue lips and chest pain – so JoJo pads through the kitchen to the hallway and into the downstairs study. It is officially Frank's, although he rarely used it – his contribution, a wall of books on locomotives and Second World War aeroplanes, anything loud or chugging black smoke from one end.

Frank. When JoJo imagines him now, it's not his face she pictures, but the sense of everything he left in his wake: the groups of sycophants and networkers and hangers-on at the few parties they'd attend, which he'd muscle through, so they could find an empty room to finish their drinks in peace, or get their coats and escape early; the women who'd smile and laugh and flirt, especially when Frank was younger, and then later, especially when he was wealthier, which he must see (how could he not? They weren't exactly subtle about it), but always ignored; and the shoes, and the socks, and other items of clothing JoJo would find the next morning – scattered along the staircase or hung up on door handles – haphazardly discarded in his impatience to join her in bed.

On weekends, their dynamic shifted, and Frank, shrugging off his corporate identity, took much pleasure in trailing after JoJo as she weeded or hacked away at the hedges (he knew better than to offer help, the garden was her domain), repositioning his chair in the closest shade or under a protective branch to start a crossword, sort out papers from work, or – more often than not – doze. And on holidays, it was strictly JoJo who called the shots, from the places they stayed to the cafés and restaurants where they'd play Shithead, Spite and their infamously raucous games of Six Card Cribbage.

She knew all of Frank's weaknesses too, of course, identified and mentally catalogued over the years: the history of suicide that ran in his family, the slight curve to his penis, his worry it was not thick enough to please her; now, the arthritis. The death of his favourite cousin when he was a child. His brother gone. Whether or not his father had ever really loved him. In turn, Frank had met JoJo's family. After that first fateful trip back to South Africa, the one in which her mother had raged with accusations of abandonment and perceived wrongs – leaving the farm, marrying an Englishman, their lack of offspring – he'd held JoJo and told her: *I understand who you are now.*

They'd rarely argued for two such strong personalities. If JoJo was cross, Frank would soften. When he would get worked up, she would gently tease him back to normalcy. It always worked. Or at least, it had.

JoJo walks to the far bookshelf. It's dimly lit in the study, so she has to squint at the book spines, but she can't seem to make any sense of them. It's mostly her gardening books here anyway, something might be upstairs in her office, but she can't face going up to hunt for it. A new thought occurs: perhaps Belinda will know about shock? She's Oxbridge trained, isn't she? Hadn't Frank let slip how smart she was? Let's see, where would Belinda be…? JoJo's recent hobby seemed to be obsessing over the girl's likely schedule. She had read practically everything Belinda had ever written (even going to the British Library to look through old newspapers and periodicals), educating herself enough about Twitter to monitor her tweets, and following all the recent gossip. This consisted of Belinda's connection to the twelfth Duke of Buckinghamshire – relatively handsome (by Duke standards), young too, in his early forties and 'hip' as the kids would have once said (but no doubt no longer did), being a music producer jet setter. Belinda had been spotted with him at a big event and the tabloids and broadsheets all perked up, writing scurrilous things and making her the talk of the town. *Tart of the town, more like*, JoJo had scoffed. There were photos of them leaving clubs hand in hand, looking harassed, and others arriving at film premieres, looking smug, and even one at a Royal Garden Party, with Belinda in demure gloves, standing perilously close to the Queen. JoJo wondered if Frank knew about the Duke? She'd tucked the information away as useful ammunition.

JoJo tries to bring her wandering mind back to Belinda's whereabouts.

Today is a weekday, she's almost certain of it – Thursday, maybe Friday. The offices at the *Financial Times* then.

JoJo walks back into the hallway and takes her coat from the stand. She pats her pocket – yes, she has her keys. Her purse is somewhere – she can't be bothered to find it now, so she raids the hall cupboard, where she keeps a jar with coins and a small stash of notes. Outside, it's overcast and chilly, but JoJo feels energised by the cold. She can't remember the last time she left the house. A week? How funny. A net curtain stirs across the street – Mrs Hartridge at number twenty-eight – and JoJo quickens her pace in case she's accosted. The woman is a busybody and she's in no mood for it. She's in no mood at all, really.

JoJo finds a black cab near Battersea Park and remembers it's *The Economist* Belinda works for, not the *FT*. The Knowledge obviously doesn't spread to private business locations, so the cabby taps at his phone until he finds the address (JoJo realises that, in her haste, she's not brought her phone with her either).

'St James,' he calls through the glass.

Onwards! – she thinks hazily. She's glad she got a taxi; she might have wandered into the Thames by herself.

The mid-October sky is mushy with grey clouds as they pass over Chelsea Bridge. She's reminded of cotton wool balls, and then, her mind cycling back, of babies. It's not that she and Frank never tried – they were good at the trying – it was the conceiving they found so difficult. And then she had her trouble and, shortly after, the operation. Then it was impossible. They'd half-heartedly considered adoption, but the people were so intrusive, she knew it would never work. Babies! Such strange things. She'd never found one she was attracted to. To her they all seemed like queer Martians, or geriatrics, or both. The smell wasn't unappealing – she'd grown up on a dairy farm outside of Johannesburg after all and it was very similar: creamy, sweet, with an undertone of shit. But the hats and booties and the *bibs*, it makes her shudder.

JoJo comes back to the journey at hand as they reach their destination. The cabby drops her outside *The Economist* building – the fare is twenty-one pounds but when he sees the scrunched-up ball of twenties, he lets her off the pound coin.

Inside, JoJo asks for Belinda but when the receptionist asks what it's regarding, JoJo's mind draws a blank. What *was* it for? She starts to feel foolish, but before she can say anything, the receptionist smiles at someone beside her.

'Ah, Belinda, perfect timing – this woman is here to see you.'

'Yes, hello?' says Belinda, turning towards JoJo, 'can I help?'

She knows me, thinks JoJo in her faraway mind, she must recognise me from a photo or have seen me from the car, and then she's cognisant of something else. A hand – *her* hand – whizzing past her right ear and hitting Belinda square on the jaw with a deliciously satisfying smacking noise.

CHAPTER SIX

Let's pause, briefly, to talk about the weather. Oh yes, the weather, the weather, the odious weather! Sluggish jet streams are the culprit, we're told, water vapour in the atmosphere. While rain in Paris or snow in Moscow might be romantic, the people of London take their meteorological shortcomings personally. Londoners worry that *they* are grey, damp, predictable and disappointing. They take refuge in dank pubs and darker pints, and behind their famous grumblings.

But lo! 'Tis a front! Yes, London is wet, but wetter still are Rome, Brisbane, New York, Tokyo and Rio de Janeiro. London might be cool, but its climes are warmer than Seattle, Toronto and (less convincingly, perhaps) Dublin. And those relentless blue Californian skies bring only wild fires. Your tropical heat? – malaria. Indeed, blank out the cities not afflicted with earthquakes and volcanoes or ten months of snow and you'll discover something curious, something known by rich Arabs and students from the Gulf. London can be quite pleasant. Quietly, its citizens know this too, but look what happened when people discovered Spain's agreeable weather, the place was overrun by sun-seeking holidaymakers and retirees... As a buffer then, Londoners spin climatic bleakness with the same diligence they once built defensive walls against the Romans.

That being said, October is particularly depressing, with a dissatisfying summer yielding to the beginnings of a long cold winter, and only the countdown to Christmas any less appealing.

*

Adam, though, is in an unseasonably good mood. He was always happier when he had a routine. There was the issue of the early starts, which he'd set as a precedent that first morning, but they were easily overcome. To begin with, he hid at a local greasy spoon, but he worried Patrick might see him (and the smell of cooked fat began to linger in his suit) so he devised a better solution. Each morning, while Patrick was still asleep, Adam threw on a robe, made a cup of tea in the kitchen and – checking twice he had his keys – exited the flat. After shutting the door with a healthy slam, he opened the hatch to the hallway cupboard under the stairs, sitting inside quite happily – sipping tea and reading *The 7 Habits of Highly Effective People* by candlelight – until Patrick finished his ablutions and left for work. Adam could then return to his (still cosily warm) bed for an extra few hours of contented sleep before heading to the gym, buying supplies at the supermarket and arriving at Mercer and Daggen to coincide with the post-lunch rush. The turnstiles were child's play now – the security guard even acknowledged him with a nod. Once on the fifth floor, Adam would make his usual pit stop at the men's bathroom and leg it up the stairs.

The top floor of the building was smaller than the ones below – about two thirds the size – owing to an area of roof space Adam imagined was once used by executives to smoke cigars, but was now strictly no access. Although its square footage was smaller, the sixth floor felt more cavernous as it was empty save for a few haphazard piles of broken furniture, old filing cabinets and shabby room dividers. The open-plan arrangement had presented a challenge to Adam, but his office – well, his *day* office – was a construction he was proud of. He had created a hideaway in the shape of a lean-to against the far western wall using three large desktops, layered so he could see movement from the door without being detected himself. The trick was to give the structure the appearance of a random collection of furniture rather than an organised entity (Adam would have preferred to shield himself further with filing cabinets, but this made it appear too much like a hut). After completing his new working quarters, he'd cleared the carpet of glass, nails, and mean little chips of metal, before settling inside – and just in time…

The frequency of visitors had surprised Adam: electricians testing the lights, security guards on late afternoon rounds (he now thought of them as sleepy night-time 'Jekylls' or brutish daytime 'Hydes'), and most annoyingly, workers from the lower floors on their mobile phones. Imagining they were alone, these employees shouted conversations into their handsets and roamed the space, pulling at dangling wires, picking holes in the walls or perching awkwardly on bits of furniture. And what had happened to manners? Even Dian Fossey would have recoiled at the bogey wiping, bollocks scratching and crotch groping Adam was now witness to. The conversations were no less graphic: calls to drug dealers, mistresses, recruitment agents and a whole host of other seedy underworld types.

Mostly, however, Adam was left in peace. When he arrived for the day, he took off his shoes (he left his jacket on – there was no central heating on the sixth floor) and scooted inside the hideaway. He no longer felt claustrophobic in the slightest. The only issue was how to get comfortable: the angle of the lean-to meant he couldn't sit upright, and his feet poked out if he lay on his stomach, so he had to sit slightly hunched to one side against the wall, swapping position every half hour to avoid neck pain. Sometimes he worried all the time spent in enclosed spaces might be affecting him psychologically (would he develop into some type of mole-person, for example, and become sensitive to light?), but his afternoons were busy, what with all the documents to read for his master plan, and he felt cheerful enough.

At roughly seven o'clock – as the sun was setting – Adam would pack up his things and begin the journey downstairs. Once on the stairwell, he would crouch on the third step, listening. He had discovered he could tell how many people were in the building by the frequency of the elevator cars. If both lifts were motionless, the left one would respond to a call first, making a slightly different sound (a raspier whirring). Using this aural cue, Adam was able to keep a mental running narrative as the building emptied out: 'Lefty on two, Righty on three. Long delay on two [the accountants were chronic door holders]. Righty on ground, now on four for a quick pick-up [the doors shutting almost as soon as they opened meant a single passenger, entering quickly and jabbing the 'close' button].' When the lifts had all but stopped for the day, Adam would amble down the stairwell, giving the elevator shaft one final pat for luck and feeling quite proud of his new skill, until he realised that being an 'elevator whisperer' was never going to win him a girlfriend, and perhaps explained why he didn't already have one.

*

17:41 Daisy has logged on
17:47 Daisy has logged off
21:52 Daisy has logged on
21:54 Daisy: hi
21:54 Daisy: :)
21:55 Daisy: Could we talk?
22:16 Daisy has logged off
22:30 Daisy has logged on
22:33 Daisy: *waves*
22:33 Daisy: ok how about a joke?
22:33 Daisy: Why did the scarecrow win a Nobel Prize?
22:34 Daisy: He was out standing in his field
22:38 Daisy: ?

23:04 Daisy: tough crowd 😕
23:38 Daisy: So
23:39 Daisy: Night
23:51 Daisy has logged off

*

The daytime occupant of the corner office – the one Adam slept in on the night he found the security card – exhibited three agreeable habits. First, he regularly travelled overseas (Adam found the boarding stubs in the wastepaper basket). Secondly, when he was in London, he liked to vacate the office by seven, and finally, before departing for the day, he closed the blinds *and left the door unlocked*. That meant Adam only had the stragglers working at their cubicles to get past, but so cocooned were they behind headphones and monitors, he could've cartwheeled naked down the aisles without attracting much attention.

The smell of well-worn leather, furniture polish and aftershave greeted Adam as he entered the corner office. Keeping the lights off, he would adjust the blinds to allow him to see movement from the workstations outside, before taking his place behind the desk. He was vigilant not to disturb anything as he settled himself – even a stapler pointing in the wrong direction could alert someone to his presence. There was another reason he was so careful: he felt a connection to the daytime occupant – a kinship even. Out of respect, Adam left the drawers of the desk unopened; the cupboard next to the windows untouched.

He couldn't resist a little snooping, but he kept it to a minimum: only personal effects on public display. Of these, there were few. Except for a passport-sized photo of a smiling blonde girl of about ten tucked into a framed letter above the desk, the walls were bare. On the desk sat a giant screen attached to a bulky system unit by a clutch of cables (someone had helpfully written 'Push this too' on a white sticker above the monitor button) and next to it, a pen holder containing a small battery powered fan with a hot pink propeller and sixteen pencils, all ferociously sharp.

The only discovery of any intrigue was a box of Hawaiian girl figurines, tucked away on the shelf like a dirty (hip-swaying) secret. The hula girls were different shapes and sizes – a few brazenly bare breasted – but all were engraved on their base with a date in six-digit form, ranging the past twenty years. Adam wondered what the dates signified – promotions perhaps, or to mark some office tomfoolery? – as one of the figurines sprang to life, gyrating and singing 'Rock-a-hula Baby', prompting a girly cry from Adam and ten minutes under the desk in case anyone came to investigate.

Each night, at nine o'clock, after he'd snooped and studied sufficiently (Adam tried to go home as late as possible so that he wouldn't have to spend the evening making up lies to Patrick), he'd wander around the cubicles, or if he was feeling bold, he might visit one of the lower floors.

It was on one of these expeditions, while making a cup of tea in the first-floor kitchenette, that Adam happened upon someone he recognised.

'Hello,' said the pretty woman, as Adam's panicked brain scrambled to remember how he knew her. The woman casually filled the kettle, switched it on and leant her hip against the counter, examining the red painted nails on her left hand.

'I'm Cara, I work downstairs,' she said, glancing up when she noticed Adam staring at her. 'On reception.'

'Yes, of course! I didn't recognise you out of c-context. Of the r-reception.'

'And I've dyed my hair blonde.'

'So you have,' Adam said. 'It's very nice.'

'I'm not sure,' Cara replied. 'Everyone keeps giving me funny looks.'

'They probably think you're the evil twin.' At that, Cara gave Adam a funny look, but not the usual one people gave him when they noticed his stutter, which was refreshing. 'You know – on the soaps,' he elaborated, feeling less confident as he went on, 'the evil twin is always identical except for something like an eye patch or different coloured hair… Or a g-goatee…'

'I just thought blonde is maybe not my colour – makes me look washed out.'

'Or it could be that.'

The kettle boiled – it was still hot from Adam's tea – and Cara poured water into her cup.

'You're Canadian?'

'What gave it away?'

'Well, er, um… The accent m-mostly.'

'Most people think I'm American.'

'I'm not, um… I mean, I'm not… most p-people,' Adam replied, fluffing the line completely. 'You're working late tonight?' he said, trying to cover, taking a sip from his own cup and instantly burning his mouth.

'One of the night staff is sick, so I'm covering until they find someone.'

Adam nodded, and sucked air into his mouth to try and cool down his burning tongue. Soon, Cara would finish making her coffee and the interaction would be over. That was always how it seemed to play out with girls – Adam just couldn't keep up the momentum. He'd had two girlfriends in his life – one called Paige at university, a tall, serious molecular biology student to whom he'd lost his virginity on a bar crawl; and Elle, a girl he'd met at a networking event, who drank four litres of diet coke every day and talked a lot – but both relationships had petered out after a couple of months. Adam had lasered the tufts of hair on his shoulders, bleached his teeth white, even bought some Viagra off the Internet, but nothing seemed to tip the scales when it came to him finding and keeping a girlfriend.

The receptionist picked up her cup.

'Bye then,' she said. 'Guess I'll see you about' (the 'about' a drawn-out 'aboot' sound).

'B-bye,' Adam replied, lamely. She'd be gone in three seconds, two…

'I guess I should go check my twin is still tied up.'

Adam thought he'd misheard, so he replayed the sentence over in his head. '*My twin is still tied up.*' My twin! Cara had lobbed a ball back to him! She'd thrown him a bone!

'Ha, yes!' he'd called after her jubilantly, much too loud for someone who was supposed to be keeping a very low profile.

*

The letter arrived on 20 October:

Hi Chris,

It's me again. I know you're angry and not replying to my calls or emails – and you've a right to be. I just want a chance to explain. I went slightly crazy, I'm sorry. I blew things out of proportion in my head. It all made sense at the time, but two weeks later, it makes no sense at all. Usually I'd bow out ungracefully, but I'd feel terrible if I never had a chance to see you again, even if it's only to apologise. Sorry about my stupid handwriting too. I hadn't realised how messy it'd become. I can't even do cursive anymore! And my Ss are like 8s. I'm rambling. This is my third attempt, so I'm just going to plow (spelling?) on.

Where was I? Yes, I'm sorry and I'm stupid, and I just want to see you again. I miss you, I really do. Crap, now I've cried on the paper. That wasn't intentional, by the way, my tears are not designed to tug at your heart strings. Ugh, it's making the ink run! I don't think I can do another version. Each time it makes me sadder and sadder. This is ridiculous. I'm going to end now before I self-combust with my own miserableness.

Please call me, or email me, or stand on a hill and fire off a flare or something. Anything. Text me even. I know we said we shouldn't use text messages, but I think I would overlook the rule just this once.

Love,

Daisy xox

*

Patrick was always in bed when Adam arrived back, so it came as a surprise the night he opened the door to find his flatmate still wide awake on the sofa.

'Yo stranger!' bellowed Patrick, yawning and stretching his arms out into a 'V' shape. 'Long time, no see!'

'You're up late,' said Adam, shutting the door again and glancing up at the kitchen clock – it was half past midnight. 'What are you w-watching?'

'A *Predator* marathon. I have a seven thirty meeting,' Patrick said with another yawn, 'but what can you do? How's it all going, anyway? Haven't seen you in for ever!'

Adam moved to the toaster, picking up the small stack of mail beside it.

'I don't want to interrupt your movie marathon.'

'Not to worry, mate, it's only *Alien vs. Predator*. Diminishing returns. I should be in bed anyway.'

Yes, why aren't you? thought Adam.

Patrick waited expectantly.

'Not m-much to tell,' Adam said as he sorted through the letters – junk mail and a packet addressed to an old tenant. 'You know how it is, the first few weeks are sink or swim. I'm p-picking things up, but it's a much bigger job than I realised.'

'You've been putting in the hours.'

Adam didn't know if it was a statement or a question – sometimes Patrick's inflection was hard to read.

'I'm the newbie,' shrugged Adam. 'It p-pays to be k-keen. I'm making some inroads, but I'm still in my probation period – one slip up and it could all be over.'

'Sounds brutal, mate.'

'In a strange way, it's reassuring.'

'How's that?'

'Everything is performance based. No one cares what I had for lunch, or which football team I support, I'm left alone to get on with things. It's sort of c-comforting.'

Patrick frowned. 'They're not pushing you too hard, are they?' Adam shook his head. 'But you're working weekends…?'

'Only for the short term,' Adam replied quickly. 'I'm on a big project, which should be finished in a month or two.'

'What is it?'

'What's what?'

'The big project?'

'I can't say,' said Adam, adding, 'It's c-con-confidential.'

'Alright, mate, I'm glad you're settling in. I hadn't seen you for so long, I was worried they'd locked you away in there.'

Adam gave what he hoped was a jovial chuckle: 'No, I'm still let out for good b-behaviour!'

Patrick nodded. There was something odd about the way he was staring at Adam, as if he was trying to peer inside him.

'Any girls on the go?'

'Chance would be a fine thing!'

'Must be lots of new ladies in the office?'

'A few.'

Patrick furrowed his brow.

'How many people in your building?'

'Nine hundred and twenty-six,' said Adam without hesitation.

'And what about in your team?'

'It varies. And depends. On factors.'

'No women though?'

'Not c-currently,' said Adam, eyeing the sanctuary of his bedroom. 'There's a receptionist who's kind of interesting. Her name's Cara.'

'What's she like?'

'She's twenty-eight, grew up in Canada and moved here when she was twelve. She's been with the company for thirteen months, and she's never taken a sick day.'

Patrick raised an eyebrow, and Adam began to feel paranoid that he'd given too much away.

'I should be getting to bed myself,' said Adam as he moved towards his room.

'One thing I've meant to ask,' said Patrick, 'and this might sound like a stupid question, so excuse my ignorance, but what do you actually do? I mean, don't give away any trade secrets, but what's your actual job?'

Adam blinked at Patrick.

'Digital marketing,' he replied. 'Search.'

'Yeah, but why does a financial institution like M.D. want to do online stuff? Aren't they a big enough name to get clients through reputation and word of mouth alone?'

Adam blinked.

'Well…'

'And surely,' continued Patrick, 'if you're someone who's about to invest millions of dollars in hedge funds, say, you're not just going to *Google* it, are you?'

'No, you're right, Patrick.' Adam rubbed his eyes, fatigue washing over him. 'You g-got me. Everything you've said is spot on.' He tries to rouse what little energy he has left. 'Traditionally, investment banks haven't been early adopters of the Web, it's t-true. But last year, the industry saw a six per cent increase in new business from online brokers. It's not huge, but the number's set to grow. And it's a misnomer to think investors don't use G-Google. They might not be searching "where should I invest my millions?" but they're harnessing it as a research tool, like everyone else. There's a whole new generation of investors who have grown up with the Internet, and if they're not catered for, they'll go somewhere else. Which is why I've come along, I suppose. I'm going to bring Mercer and Daggen into the twenty-first century.'

It was Patrick's turn to be speechless.

'Right, I'm off to bed,' said Adam.

'You around this weekend?' Patrick called after him.

'I'll be at the office.'

'Hey?'

Adam turned.

'Yeah?'

Patrick switched off the TV with the remote.

'One thing I had to learn the hard way, mate – don't give any company your soul, they don't deserve it.'

Adam felt a surge of brotherly love towards Patrick. He remembered all the months they had hung out together, how close they had been when he'd first arrived in the country, how understanding Patrick had been when Adam, his brain foggy from the last batch of antidepressants, had overwatered the pot plants and drowned them all.

'No chance of that!' replied Adam, giving Patrick a manic thumbs up and closing his bedroom door with a bang.

*

It arrived at 1.26 p.m. on 22 October:

DAISY AGAIN (-STOP-) WHO KNEW TELEGRAMS WERE
STILL A THING HUH (-STOP-) NOW I'VE DEFINITELY
ARRIVED AT DESPERATE-VILLE BUT I JUST WANTED TO
TRY ONE LAST TIME (-STOP-) SO HERE I AM (-STOP-)
TRYING (-STOP-) DON'T (-STOP-) BELIEVING (-STOP-)
SORRY MUST (-STOP-) ANYWAY I JUST WANTED TO SAY

GOODBYE I SUPPOSE (–STOP–) GOODBYE AND THANK YOU
FOR EVERYTHING (–STOP–) GOODBYE CHRIS

*

After drawing the curtains and kicking off his shoes, Adam sat down on the bed. He could hear the water running in the bathroom – Patrick was brushing his teeth.

Adam hated lying to him. In a way, however, the ambush had brought out a kind of truth. He *was* working on a big project, and it *would* hopefully be finished in a few weeks.

Getting on the Wi-Fi at Mercer and Daggen had been surprisingly easy – Adam had discovered the login and password on a Post-it during one of his evening reconnaissance missions. What he also needed, though, was access to the company intranet and department sensitive folders – sales documentation, website data and communications from Human Resources. Hacking into these private files would take more technical wizardry than he was capable of, but again, the Universe provided.

In the corner office, two days after his Wi-Fi discovery, Adam had accidentally nudged the mouse on the desk, making the computer screen jump to life. For the briefest of seconds, he debated the moral implications of accessing another person's desktop, until he realised the computer wasn't even password protected. In his books, that was basically an invitation. A quick scan of the hard drive revealed it was connected to every department of Mercer and Daggen, with a staggering level of access – the owner must be very high up in the company, Adam had realised.

Through this central hub, he could follow the entire life cycle of new positions from hiring to firing, and bring up individual files on all current employees (such as, say, Cara the receptionist). The notes on potential candidates were particularly revealing: 'Arrived without a tie' read one sniffily, 'Obviously uneducated,' read another, 'Thought "market cap" was a something a butcher wears'.

The toilet flushed. Patrick had finished in the bathroom. Adam should really brush his teeth, but he felt too tired to move. He realised he was still holding the pile of mail he'd picked up from the kitchen. Taking out the packet addressed to the ex-tenant, he ripped it open. It was a reminder from the electoral role – nothing exciting – and Adam frisbeed it across the room.

His goal was simple: Adam would explore the company from the inside, learn everything about Mercer and Daggen, and if a position became available – *when* one became available – it would be his for the taking. He was practically an employee already ('contracts' and 'payment' aside) and he was definitely putting in more hours than anyone else. The greatest part of his plan – it was in their best interest too: Adam's research was throwing up genuine opportunities the company would be mad not to explore, such as implementing Baidu search ads to recruit Chinese investors, running LinkedIn ads to target high-earning CEOs, and leveraging the profiles of their wealth managers using promoted tweets.

So convinced was he these strategies would work, Adam had given up searching for other jobs. Although his savings were dwindling and he wasn't sure how he was going to pay next month's rent, the logic felt flawless. Why go for a job in another company he knew nothing about? More effective than visualisation or manifestation or any of the buzzwords from the self-help books – he was practicing *actualisation*. Do the job you want, in the place you want to work – and eventually, you'd find yourself a slot. Adam seriously wondered why more people hadn't tried it.

*

An email was waiting on the morning of 25 October:

I know I ended my last correspondence with great finality, but it's 4.25 a.m. and I can't sleep (plus I've just searched: 'stages of grief' and I think I'm stuck in denial).

Yesterday, I was having a terrible day (long story, but it included accidentally giving a Hollywood wax to a model with some industrial-strength sticky back plastic – you won't see that on Blue Peter) but afterwards I walked along Carnaby Street, where we first met. Do you remember – I was lugging a palm tree on the way to a shoot? It was so blinking heavy and the leaves kept scratching me. Then along you come and almost knock me over. I didn't know whether to laugh or cry. Here I was – drenched in sweat, late for the shoot, with some lunatic on a bicycle asking me out. I was about to give you some lie about having a boyfriend, like any sane girl should, but then I noticed something in your eye. Not the Disney romantic 'something in your eyes,' I mean literally. An eyelash, I think. And I remember wanting to wipe it away for you. In fact, the whole time you were writing down your number, I was thinking: 'I should tell him he has an eyelash in his eye.' But it was too late – you were gone.

I don't want to make light of what happened. Leaving the way I did without explanation (especially after all the time, money and effort you spent organising the trip) was horrible, unforgiveable even. But if you're the person I think you are, this will be killing you. You're not the type to go cold, things matter to you. That's why I liked you so much: you care.

So, I'm asking for an eyelash. Here's my idea (we're entering the 'bartering' stage, I think) – if you really never want to see me again, send a blank message. Just hit reply right now and press send. And I'll stop. No more letters, or telegrams or messages in Morse code, I promise. We'll have communicated one last time, which is probably once more than I deserve. I just want to know it's really over. I'll sleep easier, hopefully you will too. And even a blank message would be better than nothing at all.

I miss you.
X D

CHAPTER SEVEN

For once, Dylan Moon arrives at the station first. He waits beside the ticket machines feeling naked without Otis to fuss over. Bereft of the dog, he fiddles with a can of INsanity energy drink – his third of the morning – pinging the pull-tab to the tune of 'Call Me Maybe' and memorising the ingredients: glucuronolactone, L-theanine and, his personal favourite, ginkgo biloba. The can label promises 'Heightened awareness, brain capacity and *PEAK PHYSICAL PERFORMANCE!*' but the only effect so far is a twitch in Dylan's left eye.

East Croydon station is bustling with Saturday shoppers arriving to take the tramlink to IKEA or heading into central London to clog up the West End. Officially, Chris was supposed to pick up Dylan from his house, but after their first session the two had agreed to meet at the station instead. This was partly so Chris didn't have to take an extra bus ride, but it also helped to know he wouldn't get lost in south London wearing expensive designer loafers.

Dylan spots Chris at the ticket barriers, but there's something strange about his face today: Chris has let his stubble grow, Dylan realises. No, not stubble – his face is covered in the first blonde wisps of what can only kindly be described as a beard.

'Where's the pooch?' asks Chris, scanning the station and failing to hide his disappointment when he can't find Otis.

'I thought we could go into town today?' Dylan says, trying not to stare at the gentle curl of fluff either side of his mouth.

Chris's ears prick up at this.

'Really? You sure?'

They'd exhausted Croydon's list of attractions weeks ago, but Dylan had always felt nervous venturing further from home, so Chris wastes no time in buying tickets and hurrying them through the barriers, seemingly before Dylan can get cold feet. They walk along the platform towards the front of the train, stopping at the last carriage because it's quietest, although once inside they find it smells very strongly of oranges.

'So why the change of heart?' asks Chris once they've chosen seats, Chris facing forward, Dylan opposite him.

Dylan shrugs. 'You can't stay at home for ever. Life's too short.'

Chris strokes the patchy hair around his jaw thoughtfully.

'Wise words,' he says finally, still stroking his chin.

Dylan narrows his eyes. *Wise words?* Usually, Chris would have insisted on a fist bump at the very least (luckily, the complicated secret handshake had been abandoned after their third attempt).

'How've you been?' asks Dylan, taking the last swig of his energy drink.

'Yeah, fine,' Chris replies. 'Sorry for cancelling our session the other week.'

Fine, notes Dylan. Not *bodacious* or *excellent* or *gnarly*? Something is definitely up.

'Did Daisy enjoy your surprise trip?'

Chris makes a tutting sound. 'Not exactly.'

'Where did you go?'

Chris replies, but Dylan must have misheard – it sounded like he said, 'Up shit creek'. Perhaps it was somewhere in Scotland? 'Was the weather nice?' he asks. Chris snorts, but leaves the question dangling, so Dylan tries again. 'Maybe Daisy could come and meet Otis next time?'

Chris sighs. 'I don't think that'll be happening.'

'Otis doesn't jump up into people's groins anymore.'

'It's a nice offer, but…'

'He's too big – he reaches their stomachs.'

'Moon, Daisy and I broke up.'

The train chooses this exact moment to begin its journey, lurching slightly.

Ah, thinks Dylan.

'Oh,' he says, steadying a hand against the window. 'What happened?'

Chris takes a deep breath.

'I know it's been a bit low on the oestrogen at Chez Moon since your mum flew the coop. How much do you know about women?'

Dylan shrugs again, trying to be nonchalant in the face of an unexpected mention of his mum. 'A bit,' he says.

'Then trust me,' says Chris, 'it's a minefield out there. You can forget all that *Men are from Mars, Women from Venus* crap too. The problem is we're not only on different planets, we're in *alternate dimensions*. Men are from Earth, Women are from – I don't know – Epsilon *BlooBlahBleeBlah*. Hands for feet, butts for noses and the Nazis never lost the war…'

Dylan is only half listening – he's trained himself to tune out whenever Chris gets into one of his rants. He starts to wonder – and not for the first time – if Chris has many friends. It would explain why he usually arrived at their sessions so charged up: maybe he didn't have anyone else to talk to? When Dylan asked about his career, Chris always seemed to be doing something different – 'angel investing' when they first met, then 'property development', 'art collecting' and most recently, something called 'lifestyle design'. Lacking a real job, Chris probably didn't have many work friends: he lived alone, he was an only child and he never mentioned his parents. Without Otis or his dad to keep him company (the Internet coming a close third), Dylan felt sure he'd be *completely* mental by now.

Chris is still speaking so Dylan tries to pay attention.

'... a different language. No, not different, it's deceptively similar, like the Scandinavian languages. The Swedes kind of understand the Danes, but if you ask for a fork in Swedish, you're not sure if the Danish waiter will bring back cutlery, or a jar of spiders. So, when you ask a woman does she want to go away for a romantic weekend? and she replies: "Yes, sure," what this means in – let's call it *wimglish* – is radically different to how you or I would interpret it, Moon. We process this sentence at face value, without comprehending its potential hidden meaning, which is: "Yes, unless I freak out on the M1 and leave without saying a bloody word." You and I can sit here quite happily, having a perfectly reasonable conversation – why? Because *we* both speak the same language.'

'Manglish?' offers Dylan.

'Exactly. But have the same conversation with a woman and all you get is...'

'A jar of spiders?'

'Precisely. Why do we even bother? We should just build our own island and go around shirtless, and grow our beards and burp and fart and kill our food with our *hands*, because that's *our* culture, Moon, our God-given right, and we'd never have any problems ever again. You with me, Moonraker?'

Dylan nods politely, but this Man Island idea sounds kind of gross. He'd never actually finished *Lord of the Flies*, but he knew from Wikipedia it didn't end well.

'Maybe we could learn wimglish?'

'You can't learn wimglish, Moon. It's like trying to learn Mandarin or something.'

'People learn Mandarin.'

'Not normal people. Sanskrit then.'

Dylan rests his empty can on the seat next to him.

'Why did Daisy freak out?'

'Who knows? It could have been the moon's gravitational pull. Or the Freemasons? Or maybe it was global warming?'

'She might've been car sick? Or maybe she left the oven on?'

'It doesn't matter anyway,' says Chris. 'I have a date with someone else next week, so it's fine.'

Dylan can't keep up. 'Who with?'

'A girl I met a few months ago called Celeste. Blonde, very pretty, works as a buyer for Harrods. I'm taking her to the opera.'

Dylan sits bolt upright.

'*Phantom of the Opera*?' It's been on his wish list for ever. *Mamma Mia!* too.

'No – fat women singing, Viking helmets, everyone dies.'

'Oh.'

'Celeste, she's nice. She's, you know, she seems a lovely girl.'

'I thought you liked Daisy?'

'I did,' Chris says, rubbing his eye, 'but sometimes that's not enough.'

Dylan doesn't know what to say. He's never seen Chris like this – sadder, less brash – it makes him a lot easier to like. What had Janelle told him once? 'We are rarely moved by people's success, we only relate through each other's failure.'

There was another mystery Dylan often pondered: why had Chris become a Befriender in the first place? Travelling all the way to Croydon, even with Otis as a reward, was a big commitment – especially when Chris grew noticeably restless an hour into their sessions. When Dylan quizzed him on it once, Chris explained that without a younger brother of his own, he needed some way to pass on his badass ninja skills (Chris's words), but Dylan never bought this explanation, or not completely. To him it felt as if Chris was doing *penance* for something. Or perhaps he was just lonely after all?

'I think you should see Daisy again.'

Chris squints at Dylan. 'What did you say?'

'Daisy, I think you should give her another chance.'

'It's not as easy as that.'

'Why not? Just call her.'

'One day you'll understand about these sorts of things, Moon.'

'I know about people. And all people are stupid sometimes.'

'It's more complicated.'

'I think you're making it complicated.'

'You don't know the full story. Things don't work out – it's part of the game.'

'Not if you like someone.' Dylan was going to add, 'like Ron and Hermione,' but thought better of it.

'Mate, it's kind of you – but I'm not going to take advice from someone who hasn't even hit puberty yet.'

Dylan scowls.

'Sorry,' says Chris, 'I didn't mean to…'

Dylan clenches his jaw. 'I know some stuff about women.'

'Of course you do, I was being a…'

'I'm not a stupid kid.'

'I know you're not…'

'In fact, I know more than you think.'

'Moon, I was only…'

'Because I'm sort of seeing someone right now *actually*.' The caffeine was really rushing around Dylan's circulatory system. 'And she's not a girl, she's a woman. A twenty-one-year-old woman.'

*

JoJo is furious. Of all the idiotic things to do! She dabs at the white stain with a tissue, but it's no use – the toothpaste has set. After all the time she'd spent getting dressed this morning too! – standing in front of the mirror like some teenage girl before a date, holding the hangers to her chest, one by one, and despairing. Everything seemed either too dour or frou-frou. Ditzy florals at her age – what had she been thinking? Her usual choice of black shift dress made her arms look saggy, and when she'd tried it with a long-sleeved cream top, it made her appear less like Catherine Deneuve and more like Edina Monsoon from *Ab Fab*. No, worse – the doddery grandmother playing dress up in her daughter's wardrobe. And now, toothpaste on her blouse. She tries to arrange her scarf so it's not so noticeable – people on the bus must have thought a bird shat on her breast!

'Something wrong?' asks a voice.

JoJo looks up to find Belinda dressed in a knee-length grey fur coat (fake, although a very good fake), which makes her appear tall and slim and not in the least bit pregnant.

'Just the dementia setting in,' replies JoJo, quickly finishing her arrangements.

'I like your scarf.'

'When you're my age, you'll have a whole retinue of props to hide the drooping flesh,' gripes JoJo, but she's pleased at the compliment, and then annoyed at herself for being so pleased.

'It suits you.'

'Kill me with kindness,' mutters JoJo under her breath. 'I'm on to you, lady.'

'After you,' says Belinda.

JoJo pushes open the door to Hogarth, the fancy steakhouse near London Bridge – Belinda's choice. The restaurant is dim inside and seems to be dressed up like a traditional gentlemen's club – coats of armour, upholstered leather furniture and polished oak balustrades on the stairs – although from JoJo's limited experience, it doesn't smell quite enough of cigars and piss to be truly authentic.

A smartly dressed woman, more like a patron than a member of staff, takes their coats and leads them down the stairs into a subterranean dining area. Only a few people are eating – JoJo wonders if Belinda chose the restaurant knowing it would be this quiet on a Saturday afternoon.

They've barely sat down when a waitress, brandishing a silver tray covered in raw pieces of meat, starts to give them a very detailed account of the different cuts, their country of origin and what the animal fed on.

Pretending to pay attention, JoJo sizes up Belinda instead. There is definitely something sphinx-like about the girl. Poised, one might say – calculated, if you were less charitable. Belinda's pixie fringe is so straight it looks as if it's been cut this morning using a precision ruler, and although she's wearing pearls (which say demure), she's countered them with cleavage (which shouts sexpot). Yes, well put together, JoJo concedes. Pretty, fine features, good teeth. A bit pale perhaps. And remarkably strong for such a slender frame…

The grip, with which Belinda pulled JoJo through the foyer post-slap, was so tight, it had left a bruise on her wrist and three crescent shaped cuts where her nails had broken the skin. Once outside, and still without saying a word, Belinda had whisked them around the back of *The Economist* building and into a café on the street behind – JoJo struggling to keep up. The café was closing for the day, but the owner had taken down the chairs from a table, making them each a strong black coffee before he continued with mopping the floors.

Sipping from her cup, JoJo had begun to feel a sliver of clarity again – the adrenaline seemed to be pumping away the cobwebs, her wits returning.

Belinda sat silently, watching JoJo – her cheek a mottled pink.

'Joan,' she said at last, 'I have to go next door and explain what happened. But I don't think we should mention this to Frank. Not yet. We should talk first.' Belinda gave JoJo her card, before carefully stepping over the wet linoleum towards the door.

The waitress comes to the end of her beef monologue and finally leaves for another table, the silver tray balanced on her shoulder.

'The ceviche is lovely,' Belinda says, as she opens her menu. 'They marinate the raw tuna in lime juice instead of cooking it.'

'Does the salmonella come on the side?' scoffs JoJo. She tries not to squint, but her reading glasses are in her handbag, and without them she can barely make out a word. 'Fine,' she says, closing the menu. 'We'll play Russian roulette – I'll have whatever you're having. Although I expect it will be much harder to get a verdict of accidental death if you order for both of us.'

'Oh, I don't know,' says Belinda without taking her eyes from her menu. 'With friends in high places, you can make almost anything stick.'

So, she does have a sense of humour, thinks JoJo.

'Two fillet steaks, please,' Belinda says to a hovering waiter. 'Well done for me, I'm afraid.'

'The bloodier mine is, the better.'

After the waiter takes their orders for sides and clears the menus, Belinda settles back in her chair.

'Yes, I can definitely hear an accent now,' she says. 'It's subtle though.'

'It's been a long time since I left South Africa.'

'What made you come to England?'

'The Beatles splitting up.'

'Really?'

'The year 1970 was the end of my innocence. I hated farm life and being down at the arse end of the world, but the Beatles made it bearable. When they broke up, I knew I couldn't wait any longer. Two years later, when I was seventeen, I bought a one-way ticket. And here we are.'

'Here we are indeed.' Belinda smiles, taking JoJo in. 'You seem... better today.'

'Full of beans,' replies JoJo. She takes a bread roll out of the basket and saws it down the middle with her knife. 'How did you explain our little scene to your colleagues the other day?'

Belinda bats the question away with her hand.

'I told them it was all a hilarious misunderstanding.'

'And did they believe you?'

A smile flickers across her face.

'I don't think so. But I was able to play the pregnancy card.'

'Ah yes,' says JoJo, cutting the cube of butter, 'the pregnancy card. You've got quite a lot of mileage with that one already.'

The smile flashes across Belinda's face again.

'Joan, I'm really pleased we managed to meet today. If I'm honest, I wasn't sure you'd come.'

'I never turn down a free meal. And enough of this Joan nonsense – it's JoJo. The only person who calls me Joan is my accountant.'

'JoJo then. I wanted us to have an opportunity to talk. Get to know each other.'

'Do each other's nails?'

'In a perfect world, we might become friends.'

'I'd be friendlier if you stopped fucking my husband.'

Belinda laughs. 'Frank said you were funny.'

'I'm hysterical, just you wait.'

'Fine, becoming friends might not be realistic. But we're two intelligent women, we should be able to…'

'Work something out?' JoJo scoffs. 'If you're planning on wasting my time, I'll ask the kitchen to wrap up my steak to go.'

She takes a large bite of her buttered roll, and Belinda seizes the opportunity while JoJo has her mouth full.

'Nobody wants to be the other woman, believe me, JoJo. It takes far too much energy to live in someone else's shadow. Frank thinks of you so highly, it's as if I can never do anything right.'

'I'm sure you can do *some* things right,' says JoJo, spitting crumbs.

'Some things, perhaps.' Belinda sits back in her chair, placing both hands on her stomach. 'I'm an economist by trade, so I hope you'll excuse this lazy attempt at metaphor… But what I'm experiencing,' she pats her belly, 'is a *redistribution of resources*. Not only has it taken over my body, but with all the progesterone and oestrogen flooding my brain, it's changing how I think. Last week, I asked the Governor at the Bank of England if he was losing much sleep over the next erection. I'm lucky if I can leave the house with matching shoes. And I don't seem to care about things in the same way.' She leans forward. 'Even before our little "introduction" at my office the other day, your feelings were clear. The guilt weighed heavily on Frank – he tried not to let it show, so of course it did. But since this happened,' Belinda nods at her stomach, 'I don't have the energy to worry about culpability, or Frank's remorse, or your animosity – any of it really. This Cronenbergian body horror show is making its own demands. I don't want to sound blasé, I take full responsibility for my actions, but it all feels so *unproductive* to worry anymore.'

'Our food will here in a minute, why don't you just tell me what you've come to peddle?'

'I understand why you're upset,' Belinda says, after a breath, 'I do, but it's not the best use of our resources. I know it sounds hokey, but I felt if we could meet, we might be able to give up the roles of jilted wife and wicked mistress and find some common ground.'

'Wicked mistress?' mutters JoJo. 'Try evil husband-stealing succubus.'

Belinda leans back in her chair again.

'An amnesty, perhaps? No,' she grimaces, 'it sounded better in my head. I don't know. At the very least, I'd like to be sure you're not plotting to knock my block off again next week.'

JoJo, her mouth full of bread again, tries to laugh, but breaks into a coughing fit instead, spraying more crumbs across the tablecloth.

'You have moxie, I'll give you that,' she says when she's recovered slightly, her voice still hoarse from coughing, 'holding up the olive branch and making yourself out to be so damn reasonable.

And what if I say no? You run back to Frank and tell him how unfair I've been – even after you bought us both a nice steak dinner – how you pleaded for me to be civil, for the sake of an unborn child, no less!' JoJo thrusts a finger at Belinda. 'I'm not going to give up my marriage just because you bat your eyelids. I have a hard time believing a baby wasn't a convenient pawn in your scheme all along.'

'I think we might have different ideas about what's convenient,' Belinda replies archly.

'Poppycock! Frank is a frustratingly honourable man, you must have known he'd do the right thing. Feed me some bullshit story about restructuring your resources or whatever, and you get to skip off to play happy parents with my husband!

'And here's some economics lingo for you,' JoJo says, gaining steam, 'Try *competitive advantage*. You're not married to someone for almost half a century without learning a few things. Frank likes to think he enjoys a puzzle, but he's never once finished a crossword or even a Sudoku. You must have presented him with a very captivating challenge, a real brainteaser, I'm sure, but he'll tire of you, he always does, and then all the bonnie wee babies in Purgatory won't help you!'

Belinda gives a wan smile. 'I think I preferred it when we were coming to blows,' she says.

The waiter returns with two large white plates. JoJo's steak is massive and so pink, it's almost iridescent.

'How lovely,' says Belinda, although she seems even paler.

JoJo stabs at the steak with her fork, roughly hewing a chunk of the meat and chomping at it angrily.

'What I've never understood,' JoJo says, chewing, 'is why a girl like you would want to slum it with a geriatric old fool like Frank. Sure, he's made a bit of money for himself, but couldn't you have set your sights higher?'

'That almost sounds like a compliment.'

'My apologies,' says JoJo. 'I must be losing my touch.'

Belinda considers the question as she seasons her steak – JoJo notices her hand is trembling as she picks up the salt.

'I don't know how much you've dated recently,' she says, cutting a piece of her meat and dabbing it in the gravy, 'but men like Frank don't come around every day.'

'Humph!' says JoJo, her mouth full.

Belinda puts down her knife and fork.

'I know, by the way,' she says calmly, 'about you and Frank seeing each other again.'

JoJo is speechless – she's forgotten about her own clandestine arrangements.

'He's still my husband,' she manages to say at last. This woman couldn't expect to take the high road after everything she'd done, could she? The initial betrayal had almost broken JoJo – she'd found a message from Belinda in Frank's wallet while filing away his ever-burgeoning wad of receipts. 'Thank you for tonight x B' it read, written on the back of a taxi receipt. Then there were the unscheduled business trips, the smell of perfume on his clothes, the abrupt end to phone calls – all so clichéd. The searing sting of betrayal is never clichéd though – it's always white hot from the furnace.

JoJo recalls something she'd been storing in the recess of her mind.

'And I know all about you and this Duke business!' she says, still reeling.

'What?' Belinda says, with a giggle. 'No, Teddy's gay. I did an interview with him, we hit it off, and he invited me to a couple of premieres. Apparently, Teddy does this every six months to some young woman, it's all publicity for his DJing. He's actually dating one of the Sheik's sons. They just bought an island together in the Caribbean.'

JoJo feels as if she's been knocked off balance.

'An observation about Frank,' continues Belinda, picking up her knife and fork again. 'Deep down, he really wants to please everyone. He'll deny it until he's blue in the face – it doesn't quite fit his image as a business behemoth – but it's true. A child though, that has to come first. It's how we're designed. Believe me, it's running the show already. Things will change, JoJo, and when they do, it will be better if we're on the same side. Because soon, there's only going to be one side.'

JoJo shakes her head.

'Frank is nearly sixty-six years old. He wants to retire and buy a stupidly big boat. You've forced fatherhood on him and when he…'

'No, you have it all wrong,' interrupts Belinda. 'I didn't force anything – he wouldn't even consider the other options. It was *Frank* who wanted to keep the baby.'

JoJo feels the air knocked out of her. *Frank*, she thinks. *You idiot.* She can see it all now: Frank cradling a swathed bundle, his progeny wriggling in his arms – a final triumph of his aging loins, the unexpected heir apparent. Her chest feels as if it's being crushed by an invisible force.

Belinda excuses herself to use the bathroom and JoJo fights the impulse to run up the stairs, collect her coat and leave the restaurant – the only thing stopping her is giving Belinda the satisfaction of seeing her flee.

How can she have been so stupid? Trusting Frank, agreeing to this lunch – was she really so naive?

There's nothing else for it. JoJo flags down a waiter.

'Bring me the drinks list again,' she barks, when he nears the table. 'And quick!'

*

'How old?' asks Chris incredulously.

Dylan squirms in his seat.

'Twenty-one.'

Chris stares open-mouthed.

'What? How is that possible? You never leave the house! Where do you know her from?'

'She reads my blog,' Dylan says, truthfully.

'Oh, Moon, if you met her online, that could be a whole mess of trouble…'

'It's not what you think…'

'She could weigh three hundred pounds – or be a hundred years old.' Chris leans in, lowering his voice: 'She could be a dude.'

'You're not…'

'And if it was one of those emails from a sexy Russian model – *believe me* – they're fakes.'

Dylan lets out a long, frustrated sigh.

'She's real,' he says emphatically.

'Okay, what's her name then?' Chris asks.

'I don't want to say,' says Dylan eventually, 'because you'll tell Dad.'

'Why don't you want him to know, huh?'

Dylan scowls.

'Do you tell your parents everything?' he asks. 'I'm allowed to have my privacy, aren't I? When you're sick, everyone knows your business – what you had for breakfast, how many white blood cells you have, when you went to the toilet last, they even try to get in your head. I deserve something of my own I don't have to share with anyone else.'

'Moon, that's all fine in principle, and I don't mean to cock block you, but this is not a good idea. She's five years older than you. Does she know you're still at school?'

'I'm not a child – I've been sixteen for weeks now. I can get married and drive a moped and… other stuff.'

'It's the other stuff I'm worried about,' says Chris. 'You're only just back on your feet. Does this mystery woman know about your condition?'

'Of course she does. Anyway, I'm better now.'

'Yes, but you don't want to go from zero to ninety overnight.'

Chris rubs his forehead. The Barnardo's training hadn't prepared him for this. He looks at Dylan, who's wearing an oversized grey hoodie and baggy track pants in an attempt to disguise his natural gangliness while accessorising the outfit with a rainbow striped scarf and fluorescent green bobble socks. He's officially the least coolly dressed kid Chris has ever seen (and this coming from Chris, who spent his teens wearing oversized rugby tops – collar turned up – with his hair in severe bleached curtains). Dylan's smooth face and oversized head gave him a baby-like quality – he didn't look fourteen, let alone sixteen. Was it really possible that they lived in a world where skinny, bedridden virgins were picking up older girlfriends, and Chris had struck out again?

'What does she do for a job?'

'She's a professional,' Dylan says eventually.

'That better not be a euphemism,' Chris replies.

'I don't know what one of those is.'

'What type of profession is she in?'

'She's a specialist… practitioner. She helped me and now I'm going to help her.'

'And what exactly are you helping her with?'

Dylan shrugs defiantly.

'If you don't spill,' continues Chris, 'I'll have to tell your dad everything. Bros before hoes.'

'Okay!' huffs Dylan. 'I think her ex-boyfriend is being violent again. Maybe he's threatening her and she had to go into hiding. Or it could be something to do with her dad. He was never around when she needed him…'

Dylan was speaking so fast, it was difficult for Chris to keep up.

'Her dad – wait? What?'

Chris runs both hands through his hair.

'First, you need to slow down and start from the top,' he says. 'And secondly, why do you keep winking at me...?'

Dylan makes a gagging sound – Chris raises both hands in the air.

'Dude, are you alright?'

'The train... and the oranges...' Dylan manages to say, covering his mouth.

'Do you want to swap seats so you're facing the right direction?'

Dylan nods and they both stand, but before they can change over, Dylan starts to dry-heave.

Frantically, Chris searches for a container to catch the impending vomit. Like many trains, this one doesn't seem have a rubbish bin – there aren't even any old newspapers lying around. The only part of the window that slides open is too high. He could lift Dylan up to puke? No, impractical. And if Chris pulled the emergency alarm, it would only stop the train, which won't help them either.

'Does anyone have a bag or something they don't need?' he calls along the carriage to the other passengers. 'Anything?'

No one answers, but someone, somewhere, tuts.

'Thanks a bunch,' Chris says, emptying his pockets. He finds a small plastic bag holding a packet of new razors he still hasn't got around to using (the blades remind him of his pube shaving disaster, and then of Daisy, but he shoves the thought of her aside). It will have to do.

'Here,' he says, taking the razors and holding the bag open.

Dylan sticks his face inside the bag and begins to puke noisily (the gushing sound almost makes Chris follow suit).

When Dylan comes up for air, Chris nearly drops the bag. 'Dude, I think we should get you to a hospital!'

'Why?' Dylan asks between spits.

'Your vomit... It's radioactive!'

'It's [spit] *INsanity*.'

'You're telling me. You should really see a doctor – it could be serious.'

Dylan reaches beside him and picks up the empty can of energy drink.

'Ah,' Chris says, the penny dropping, 'What the hell do they put in those things?'

'L-theanine and ginkgo biloba,' replies Dylan weakly, still spitting.

'How are you feeling?'

'Better,' says Dylan, wiping his mouth. 'I hope I didn't get any on your face.'

Chris grins: 'Said the bishop to the actress.'

'What?'

'Just something Daisy and I used to say,' says Chris. 'It doesn't matter.' But he has an especially wistful look in his eye for someone balancing a bag full of blue sick.

*

In the restaurant even the few remaining diners are beginning to thin out. JoJo raises her eyebrows as Belinda arrives back at the table.

'You took your sweet time.'

'My apologies,' Belinda says as she approaches the table.

'Your phone was ringing.'

Taking her seat again, Belinda checks her messages.

'Another journo wanting something juicy about the Duke. Honestly, if I'd known what I was signing up for…'

'Why did you go along with his story?'

Belinda shrugs, putting the phone away in her purse.

'I'd just met Frank,' she replies, 'and I thought it might make him slightly jealous, but he couldn't care less. Anyway, Teddy's a sweetheart. Who doesn't like putting on a lovely dress and being treated like a princess, especially when nothing's expected in return at the end of the night? Doesn't hurt my image either. Editors are always banging on about raising one's profile.'

JoJo nods grimly, her suspicions confirmed.

'Your food's probably gone cold too,' JoJo says.

'I'm sure they can…' Belinda points to the glass sitting beside her plate. 'What's this?'

'It's for you,' JoJo says.

'I didn't order a drink.'

'No, but I did.'

The highball is filled with a brownish, yellowish liquid. JoJo has to admit it doesn't appear very appetising – a bubbly scum has formed at the top of the glass and a few indiscriminate leaves are floating in the murky brine.

'What is it?' asks Belinda.

'Try it. I asked them to make it especially.'

Belinda glances around the restaurant as if checking there are one or two witnesses left.

'I need to know what I'm drinking first.'

'Don't you trust me?' JoJo asks, enjoying herself. 'I thought you wanted us to be friends?'

Tentatively, Belinda picks up the tumbler and sniffs it.

'My mother used to swear by it,' JoJo says, 'two parts ginger beer, one part lemon juice, fresh peppermint and a dash of bitters. Fixes up any dodgy tummy. Even morning sickness.' JoJo thinks about her hysterectomy twenty years ago when she'd used this very drink to settle her own stomach, how Frank lay awake with her all night after the operation, how hard he'd tried to mask his disappointment and neutralise hers.

Belinda shoots her a look, before resignedly taking a sip.

'It doesn't taste too bad.'

'Oh well, you can't have everything.' JoJo lifts her own glass, this one containing red wine. 'Look at us, swapping old family recipes,' she says, through gritted teeth. 'Seems we're going to be friends after all. Drink up!'

CHAPTER EIGHT

Not all of us can be Joy Ride Jessies or Ladies who Lunch – some of us must earn our crust.

Work, that most taxing of occupations, has lured lovers into cities for generations. Since the Industrial Revolution, Londoners have sacrificed their lives (and often their limbs) to keep the cogs of industry turning, and all for pennies apiece.

Money, in its abstract form, isn't gold bars at the Bank of England or zeros and ones in a trading room server, it's energy, pure and simple. At its most basic, money represents the power of the sun (used to grow crops or trapped underground as coal and oil). Further along the line it becomes *human* energy, the collective toil of all our fellow comrades (harvesting those crops and barrelling that oil), and each time we head down the proverbial coalmine, it's only so we can collect enough of this stored human energy for ourselves, so we can make others do our bidding in turn.

The British have always honoured this arrangement, creating a society based on divisions of labour, while inventing the 'working class' to boot.

So, let's raise a glass to the matchstick maker! The cocktail shaker! The amphetamine baker! Money might make the world go round, but it's our sweat that mints the dosh in the first place – hoorah!

*

A frazzled Samira appears in the doorway of the workshop. Her typically flyaway hair is launched in new and daring directions, her shoulders hunched, fingers splayed – as if a glass has smashed at her feet.

Daisy stops sawing.

'You're not going to like this,' says Samira, wide-eyed.

Daisy pulls the dust mask off her mouth, sawdust swirling under the fluorescents, and puffs the air angrily.

'What do they want now?'

Samira, glancing at the hacksaw in Daisy's hand, hesitates – so Daisy places the saw on the bench beside her.

'You know I'm a big fan of yours.'

'Samira…'

'Only last week I told my therapist we're like sisters.'

'Just tell me what happened.'

Samira completes a squirmy dance on the spot, transferring what little weight she has from one leg to the other as if struggling with a full bladder.

'They wanted to try a few things…'

'Who did?'

Samira bites her lip.

'You promise not to get angry?'

'Absolutely,' Daisy replies, giving her most reassuring smile.

Samira still doesn't seem convinced, so Daisy delivers her *coup de grâce*.

'Don't sisters tell each other everything?'

Samira beams sweetly and clasps her hands to her chest.

'Flair was testing some new shots and he thought it would be a good idea to see what the birds would look like under the green lighting gels…'

'That chimping rat-faced shit!' shouts Daisy as she storms towards the doorway, a squealing Samira leaping out of the way and trailing behind as Daisy stomps through the catacomb of hallways and darkened spaces, erupting into the brightly lit main studio.

Flair is chatting up a harem of interns by the fire exit, as his two assistants struggle with a massive bank of lights; the models, ever the opportunists when it comes to cigarette breaks, are outside the main doors smoking (but, tellingly, Paula the animal wrangler is nowhere to be seen).

Scanning the set, Daisy sees the damage immediately. *Those feathered bastards*, she thinks. *I'll roast the buggers!*

'Ah, Daisy,' says Flair, pulling himself away from the giggling interns, 'you've seen our technical glitch? Animals and children, eh?' He brushes sawdust off her shoulder. 'What happened to you? Have a fight with a bag of flour?' The interns titter obediently, but when Daisy doesn't respond, Flair pulls the mask away from her throat mischievously and starts to sing: 'Daisy, Daisy, give me your answer…'

'Don't,' she growls, snatching it back.

Flair chuckles and crosses his arms.

'So, what are we going to do?'

'We?' asks Daisy. '*We* were still cutting those branches you asked for twenty minutes ago.'

'Good, good. Are they ready yet?'

Daisy shakes her head in disbelief.

'The branches were supposed to stop *this* from happening.' She gesticulates towards the set. In front of the backdrop sits a table laden with food – tropical fruit, loaves of bread, plates overflowing with meats – a gorgeous banquet now liberally splattered with bird crap.

Flair smooths the sides of his quiff.

'We must have backups, no?'

The models saunter in from their smoke, sensing some new kind of drama unfolding.

'Backups?' asks Daisy, her eyes narrowing.

Flair waves a hand in the air. 'Extra pomegranates and things…'

Samira whimpers.

'I don't know how many times you've woken up before dawn on a freezing winter morning to head to the markets,' Daisy says through clenched teeth, 'but having personally trawled every stall this morning, I can confidently tell you there are no *extra* pomegranates, Flair. There are no *extra* pomegranates north of the English Channel, *because we have every last one here.*'

'So, let's clean them up and get back to it.'

Daisy lets out a frustrated cry, making the assistants glance up from their bulb work.

'Couldn't you have waited *five minutes* for me to prepare the branches you just asked for?'

Flair, fiddling with the grubby string bracelet on his wrist, shrugs.

'We had to get the shot.'

'Which is exactly why I was hacking up a cypress tree in the first place!'

'I don't see what the problem is, Daisy. Let's get a cloth and sort it out.'

'Bird shit is acidic. It'll mark everything, especially under the lights. Paula and I had a long conversation this morning…'

'Paula thought if we sat the birds on the…'

'I'll tell you where she can stick her bloody birds!'

There's a gasp behind the backdrop – so Paula is still in the studio, notes Daisy with satisfaction.

'Where does this leave us?' asks Flair, checking his watch.

'Everything's ruined. We'll have to start over.'

'We can't. That's not an option – we have to push on.'

'Not my problem. Talk to Paula and see if she can wrangle some birds that shit mineral water next time.'

The models glide closer: they can smell fresh blood now.

'The team's waiting,' Flair says, his brow creasing. 'I don't want to pull rank, but unless you want to pay everyone's overtime…'

'Unless you want a picnic dripping in faeces…'

'It's not a *picnic*,' Flair says, his voice straining. 'It's an ancient Zoroastrian feast.'

'But if it's an ancient religion,' replies Daisy, coyly, 'why is Jesus having afternoon tea with Marie Antoinette?'

'*It's not afternoon tea!*' shouts Flair. 'It's a modern representation of… It's about…' he pauses. 'It's about icons, they're icons.'

And there it is. By making him spell out the theme, Daisy has broken the photo shoot. Any artistic magic evaporates instantly.

Flair seems to realise he's made a fatal error.

'Listen, Daisy, I'm sorry if you think you're too good for this. If you'd rather be selling handmade pincushions on fucking Etsy. But we came to do a job today and when I asked for a feast, I meant a feast. It's supposed to be Paradise, not a stocktake at the bloody Co-op, so why don't you take this opportunity to reassess your designs, yeah? (*Stick it up your Zoroastrian*, thinks Daisy, but has the sense to stay silent.) Now, I'm going to have a cigarette and when I come back, this mess better be cleaned up, or I'll really lose my rag!'

Flair marches off towards the main doors, assistants and interns scrambling in his wake.

When he's gone, Samira taps Daisy on the shoulder.

'I'll help you,' she says in a conspiratorial whisper.

Daisy smiles at her appreciatively.

'What sort of a bullshit name is Flair anyway?' Daisy says.

Samira tucks a wisp of rebellious hair behind her ear.

'It's short for Flavio, I think. He's named after a grandfather who was a war hero or something.'

'Of course he is,' sighs Daisy, rolling up her sleeves.

*

Scratch the surface, and Mercer and Daggen was a veritable quagmire of vice and petty criminality. Adam had uncovered eBay addicts and secret novel writers, chronic timesheet fiddlers and an employee outsourcing all his highly sensitive work to Bangladesh. Almost every computer contained pornography, either stashed in amusingly inappropriate folders ('Research', 'Summer Holiday', 'Family Pics') or extensively logged in web browser histories. Schoolboy pranks were rife – especially in the week preceding a stag party; workstations wrapped in foil, tampered chairs and hacked spell check programmes autocorrecting the word 'client' into 'wanker'.

More covert were the office dalliances, but even these were laid bare by not-so-cryptic emails and the occasional Human Resources report. Team building away-days seemed to be the most lascivious (apart from one exceptionally debauched conference in Copenhagen), but as the ratio of men to woman was 15:1, the odds of an indiscretion skyrocketed whenever a female moved to a new department – or simply changed desks.

Darkest of all were the retaliations. One suspected adulterer found his mobile phone at the bottom of a water cooler, a scathing text sent to all his contacts moments before it was drowned. And when a member of the Commodities team became violently sick one afternoon, gossipy emails suggested it was no accident, and strongly recommended against eating the Hobnobs doing the rounds on the second floor.

All this left a bad taste in Adam's mouth. If he was going to invest his considerable energies into M&D, he wanted the company to be fit for purpose, not mired in filth and shenanigans. Adam wasn't a moraliser but he did have standards, and as he was volunteering his services *free of charge*, he felt he had a right to be judgemental.

Nevertheless, Adam's revelations didn't stop him monitoring the pretty receptionist's computer. Initially, he only wanted to see if Cara had a boyfriend (she did, but they hadn't been together long – although he was Northern and worked as an electrician, so was probably rugged and handsome and knew instinctively where all the fuse boxes were kept), but soon Adam was obsessing over every last detail: her favourite websites, the music she played, her friends in the office, what she liked to eat for lunch. Then, while flicking through Cara's inbox one evening, he noticed a receipt for a pair of gloves. Sensible, he thought, the weather was definitely getting colder – maybe he would buy a pair too? When he clicked the link, however, he was directed to an online fetish shop, where he found himself staring at the black, elbow-length PVC gloves for half an hour, the phrase 'high performance, extra durable' somehow more troubling than the large-breasted woman in eighties eye-makeup modelling them. Adam had always been afraid of kinks: they seemed so *decisive*. Most days, he couldn't choose between white or brown toast, let alone if he wanted to be tied up or spanked. He wondered which Cara might prefer and his trousers twitched reactively. The excitement soon dissipated. If he ever saw Cara wearing the PVC gloves, he'd probably give himself a hernia. Or wet himself. Or both.

There was only one place Adam felt safe from all unwelcome surprises. His corner-office compatriot avoided email altogether and gave the Web a wide berth (leaving it to his PA). His computer desktop, though, was littered with Excel spreadsheets, with documents stacked on top of each other in haphazard piles, each containing long lists of numbers with short notes in the margins. Adam made a habit of skimming through these notes, trying to decipher their meaning: 'Short on 2, ER is 3.8', 'arobridge, langley, until the end of the week', 'Countermand NOT proxy' – but, like the *Shipping Forecast* or Prime Minister's Question Time, it was the very incomprehensibleness he found reassuring and calming. Adam would make only the smallest of changes: correcting the more obvious spelling mistakes, standardising the font size or deleting extra spaces, but it felt good to keep a tiny corner of Mercer and Daggen in order; a bastion for all that was right and decent.

*

Monday, 1 November
Sorry I haven't written a post for a while, apologies to all my fans (joke).

One thing that's always been hard for me is letting stuff go. Everyone is always telling me it's not healthy to bottle stuff up, and I get it. My M.E. was probably made worse because I hold onto things. I'm not saying that M.E. is all in the mind though, it's definitely a physical disease. I know there are people who disagree with that, but I'll bet a hundred pounds they've never had it. But we experience everything in our own way. Like, if you go on a roller coaster ride, for some people it's the most fun thing they can do, and they'll wait all day in a queue for the fastest rides, but for other people, it's their worst nightmare. The same ride – you either love it or hate it. And with some things, I go all the way to the front of the queue, but then I can't get on the ride. I know I should, I've waited all this time, everyone else is going on, they're all being encouraging, but it's like my legs are stuck. Something inside me keeps saying 'no!'. Janelle says that voice is just trying to keep me safe. It's valuable out in the wild, where there are bears and tigers and stuff (well, not in Croydon maybe), but it's no longer helpful in the modern world, where it's only a roller coaster, and I can't really get hurt. Part of evolving is unlearning that warning, so I can get on the ride. I've been sitting on the sidelines so long. Maybe there's something wrong with me? I have so many people trying to help. If I can't do it for me, why don't I just do it for them? And what if, hypothetically, you liked someone? Like liked them? They were in trouble. You worried about them fifty times a day, at least. Shouldn't your survival instinct kick in and be useful then?

I don't know, I'm so tired of feeling stuck.

Anyway, pretty gloomy. Here's a gif of a cat falling off a table.

D

*

With Samira's help, Daisy manages to rescue the banquet, turning over fruit to reveal unblemished skin, slicing off the tops of the afflicted loaves and replacing the ruined meat with rolled-up slices of turkey luncheon. With the table arranged, she takes the cypress branches from the workshop, fixing them around the base of the bird stand, using hot glue and cable ties to provide a shield over the food.

Disaster averted, the shoot resumes.

Daisy has to fight the impulse to hide in her workshop – she'd like nothing more than to disappear for the afternoon, but she knows the gossipmongers will work themselves into a frenzy if left alone. Instead, she diligently spritzes the food with hairspray (careful not to squirt the birds) – replacing items as they sag and wilt under the lights – and busies herself making a crown of thorns for Jesus to wear in the final shot.

As punishment for her earlier outburst, Flair refuses to speak to Daisy for the rest of the day, and Paula is even more frosty and uncooperative, but fortunately the birds have emptied themselves of excrement and are mostly well-behaved. By mid-afternoon, Flair gets the wide shot and wraps the birds (Paula makes a great show of giving effusive goodbyes to everyone except Daisy), but there's no time to relax: the banquet needs to be cleared and new props set, the collective energy in the studio frantic now the finishing line is in sight.

Daisy is hurriedly binning the second platter of now rather whiffy turkey luncheon when a thought stops her cold. *Why am I doing this*, she thinks, *why am I rushing?* It's not as if she has anything planned for the evening. She'll avoid the after-work drink and head straight home, but to what? Hours spent mindlessly trawling the Internet in front of the TV. A string of missed calls from her mother. One glass of wine that turns into five. *Rush all you like*, comes the needling voice in her mind, *but you're only making the void approach faster…*

Scraping the last of the processed meat into the bin with a splat and putting the plate to one side, Daisy sees Samira chatting to a gorilla. She blinks and wipes her brow with the back of her wrist – she must have hairspray sweat in her eyes – but when Daisy looks again, Samira is still nodding politely as the creature taps its chest and pats the top of its head, Samira – it appears – completely unfazed by a six-foot gorilla in their midst. When it stops gesticulating, Samira scans the studio and seeing Daisy, points directly at her. The gorilla turns, and Daisy feels her stomach somersault as she locks eyes with the animal, the jolt of adrenaline dislodging a bubble of sadness that has been growing in her chest all day. Daisy is acutely aware she's in serious danger of bursting into tears if she doesn't find somewhere private to compose herself, but the gorilla is already loping towards her, arms swinging by its sides, and Daisy can only stand watching, transfixed. As the creature draws nearer, she starts to see the limitations of the suit: there's an obvious line around the neck, and the eyes aren't quite right, but it's very realistic, the hair thick and full, and the hands and feet are wonderful.

When the gorilla is a few steps away, it stops and grunts: 'Ah-uh-de-eh?'

'I'm sorry… I don't…?' Daisy wants to say, 'I don't understand gorilla', but knows this is ridiculous, so shakes her head instead.

'Ah uh, Aisy?'

Daisy catches the muffled sound of her name this time.

'Yes, I'm her. I'm Daisy.'

'Eh-oo elp-ee.'

She leans closer, still not understanding, and the gorilla starts to point at its left ear.

'Eh ip is uh,' it says, jabbing at the side of its head.

Daisy looks helplessly in the direction of Samira, but she's no longer there. The lump in Daisy's chest has travelled up to her throat now, an acidic burning sensation at the back of her mouth.

The gorilla hangs its head in defeat, but perks up again – making the sign for a pen with one hand and paper with the other. Daisy rummages in her pockets and finds a pencil and an old receipt, welcoming the distraction of playing Pictionary with a gorilla, but of course it can do more than draw pictures, this beast is literate:

The zip is stuck. The costume lady wants you to take it off without damaging it.

Please. [It adds as an afterthought.]

This is another of Flair's icons for tomorrow's shoot, realises Daisy: King Kong or Donkey Kong – one of the Kongs at least – probably tap dancing with Gandhi if today was anything to go by.

Daisy takes a pair of tweezers out of her tool belt and walks behind the gorilla to find the zip. Locating it at the base of its neck, she pats the gorilla's shoulder and it crouches obediently.

'I've figured out why you gave me such a fright,' she says, parting the hair along the seam of the zipper.

'Eh-oh?' says the gorilla over its shoulder.

Daisy starts to pick away the fur caught between the zip's teeth.

'I was dating this guy recently, you see, who was a bit of a romantic. Chronically romantic, really. We were at a bar once, and one of those flower sellers came round with the roses wrapped in cellophane? Well, Chris – his name was Chris – he decided he wanted to buy me the lot. Hold still.' Daisy tugs at a particularly stubborn clump of hair. 'Except he didn't have enough cash for them all,' she continues, 'so we had to leave the bar and trudge around South Kensington to find an ATM. The flower seller came with us, complaining in Romani the whole time. Chris said she was putting a curse on us, which – come to think of it – would explain a lot…' The gorilla shakes its head and taps its ear again, but Daisy is too busy fishing out a lip balm from her pocket to notice. 'So anyway,' she says, applying balm to the zipper, 'when I first saw you, I guess I thought Chris had hired a singing telegram or something. I know it sounds stupid, but it's the sort of grand gesture he'd make. In fact, I think he joked about it once. He's an absolute, utter cheese ball. I mean, there were at least thirty roses in that bunch and they weren't even very nice. But the look on his stupid goofy face when he…' Daisy's eyes begin to well up with tears. She gives the zipper a good tug to try and divert attention from her sniffing. 'Wow,' she says, still sniffing and wiggling the zip, 'this thing is really jammed tight.'

Daisy feels a tap on her shoulder and turns to find Samira holding out a powder blue envelope.

'Sorry to interrupt,' she says, 'but this arrived for you yesterday. It's my fault, I forgot about it until now – whoops!'

Daisy takes the envelope from Samira. Her name is written on it in small, neat letters, underscored with a curly line.

'Eh-ha-to-go-son.'

'Hold on,' she tells the gorilla.

Opening the envelope, Daisy takes out a card with a picture of a ginger cat on the front, the cat wearing what appears to be Scarlett O'Hara's green curtain dress, complete with bonnet and drapery cord belt.

Inside, the card reads:

I've been a fool. Forgive me? Chris.

'What's wrong?' asks Samira, but Daisy can't speak, she's sobbing so hard. Samira drops her voice to a whisper: 'Are you scared of gorillas too?' She strokes Daisy's shoulder. 'My aunt's an absolute phobic.'

*

The misdeeds weren't only happening during office hours.

The Mercer and Daggen cleaning staff, dressed in soul-crushing uniforms of grey on grey, arrived each evening at nine o'clock to mop the floors, restock cupboards, empty bins and hoover the carpets. When they'd finished for the night, Adam would emerge from the corner office to make himself a final cup of tea before heading home and it was here, standing alone on the fourth floor with his teabag steeping, that he made his first puzzling discovery.

Having used the last of the sugar cubes for his tea, Adam opened a fresh box from the cupboard and found it was missing a row. This in itself might not have been very peculiar, but he noticed the same quirk in different kitchenettes – unopened boxes of sugar, when opened, were missing exactly one line of sugar cubes: ten cubes in total, no more, no less. Adding it to his list (of things to raise with management once he was given an official job), Adam rang the customer support hotline, but no, they'd never ship a faulty product – a missing row of cubes would be picked up before distribution. Which company did he work for, and what was his name? Adam had hung up immediately.

The following night he tried an experiment. Prior to the cleaners arriving, Adam collected every unopened box of sugar on the second floor and replaced the missing sugar cubes (it was possible, he learnt, to open and close the top flaps without ripping the cardboard), marking each box, before returning them to their cupboards. When he opened the same boxes after the cleaners had finished, the cubes were gone!

His initial sting operation a total success, Adam ramped up surveillance and made his second startling discovery.

Peeking through the corner office blinds one Tuesday, he watched a cleaner stop her dusting, check to see if anyone was watching, and make a beeline for one of the desk phones. Removing a folded sheet of paper from her pocket, the cleaner carefully dialled a number and, after waiting a few seconds, began to read aloud from the page (Adam was too far away to hear what she was saying). The cleaner repeated the process several times until she was disturbed by an approaching security guard, forcing her to hang up abruptly and resume her dusting.

Adam was fascinated. What could she possibly be doing? But of course, it was obvious – she must be a *spy*. The cleaner was collecting sensitive material during her rounds and reading them over the phone, to be transcribed by a rival company – probably those swines at The 800 Group. Forget sugar cubes, Adam thought, this was corporate espionage and Mercer and Daggen would make him Employee of the Year when he brought it to light. Despite his initial excitement, Adam decided the best course of action was to lay low while he collected more evidence – there were a few things that didn't add up (for example, why did the cleaner make multiple calls?) and he wanted to make sure he had all the answers before officially blowing the whistle. He was pleased he waited: only a few nights later, he spotted two different cleaners make calls *simultaneously*, both reading from pages and taking turns to watch out for security. This was not the work of a lone gunman, he realised, it was a crime *syndicate*!

The constant adrenaline rush of discovery left Adam either hyperactive or drained. He considered switching to decaf, but cups of tea were the only thing keeping him going as he zipped between floors, checking in cupboards or finding vantage points to spy on the cleaners. It was on one of these trips, not long after he'd uncovered the goings-on with the cleaners, that Adam heard the whistle.

There are generally two types of whistle humans use to get attention: the salacious wolf-call, and the friendlier, ascending 'hey, you!' This was definitely the latter and as loud noises were uncommon in the offices (apart from the drone of a vacuum), the sound startled Adam. It was late though – the cleaners had all gone home and the desks were empty. Confused, he was about to continue on his way when he heard the whistle again. This time when he turned, he saw the man from Maintenance, in his black uniform, sitting on a chair by the windows with his legs stretched out, hands behind his head, ever-present Bluetooth in his left ear.

Adam had two thoughts, one after the other in quick succession. The first had been bugging him for a while now: *where exactly is this guy from?* Although Adam spoke only English, he prided himself on being able to guess a person's accent (or make a reasonable stab at it), but the snippets of Mr Maintenance's phone conversations had always been unplaceable. Azerbaijan perhaps? Or one of the nations that ended in 'stan'? Uzbekistan – was that a country?

Adam's second thought was new, having sparked into life that very millisecond: *why is he wearing the cleaners' uniform?* Adam hadn't noticed, maybe because all the cleaners were female, but the maintenance man's uniform was very similar in design. In fact, now he was really paying attention, it even had the same grey stripe around the sleeves and the colour was dark grey, not black. Grey on grey…

Still reclining on his chair, the man who may or may not be from the Maintenance department did something which sent a chill down Adam's spine: he *winked* at him.

*

Wednesday, 3 November

I deleted that last post, sorry if you hadn't read it. You missed out on a pretty bad metaphor about a roller coaster (I've been learning about metaphors, euphemisms and similes recently – they're all sort of confusing. I think it was a metaphor). I was disappointed about a trip that failed. Badly. When I re-read the blog post, I felt it was a bit too personal, but mostly, it made me angry – I was, like, stop complaining and do something then. That's the cycle I go in – I just go round and round in circles until I get sick. No more circles. Even if I don't know if it's the right decision to make, I'm just going to make one. I am going to do something. I should think of a new catchphrase. Just make it happen! I'll work on it. Oh yeah, 'Just do it'. Duh. Nike. Stupid. Maybe that's what Nike means? I always thought it meant just buy the shoes, but maybe it can be applied to lots of things? Nike might sue me if I use their catchphrase. Mine can be 'Just do something' then. I don't think anyone will have copyrighted it, because it's not very good.

JUST DO SOMETHING

Yeah, it's kind of bad.

But it's something.

CHAPTER NINE

Retail. Therapy. Together, these words are oxymoronic. JoJo finds no part of the process therapeutic: not the changing rooms, nor the long queues, and definitely not the gormless staff, but as her mother used to say in Johannesburg all those years ago: *needs must when the devil drives.*

JoJo begins at Selfridges, arriving when the store opens and scurrying past the perfume hawkers, already wafting around their tester cards, and down the escalator to the basement (there are already Christmas decorations up, in early November! she notes exasperatedly). At Wine & Spirits, next to the Harry Gordon bar (not yet open), she's met by a tall, drawn-looking man in his forties, who's finishing a mouthful of something – his breakfast perhaps? – and seems, at first glance, to be rather pompous. But maybe this is unfair – it might be his suit or the surroundings; either way, JoJo puffs out her chest, standing as erect as she dares around so many glass bottle phalluses.

'Whisky,' she says to the man, forgoing any pleasantries.

The assistant – he has a name tag: Barry, the assistant Barry – nods and walks to the middle of three alcoves lined with glass cabinets, unlocking one of them and taking out a dark green bottle reverently.

'This has just come in,' Barry says, holding it out for JoJo to inspect. 'Ten years, single malt.'

'How much is it?'

Barry's eyebrows rise ever so slightly – he has to turn back to the shelf and read the price tag, bending from the waist as he does so. He'd make a very good butler in a murder mystery, thinks JoJo. Knife in the back. Maybe two.

'The *Glen Cathan Gold Label* is sixty-four ninety-nine.'

JoJo grunts.

'And what's your most expensive bottle?'

Without a beat, Barry replies: 'That would be the *Royal Salute Tribute to Honour*.'

'How much is that?'

'£150,000.'

After JoJo has stopped laughing, Barry adds, slightly defensively: 'A total of twenty-one bottles have been produced in the world. It's so rare that only one person – the Master Blender – has ever tasted it.'

'If only one person has tasted it,' says JoJo, 'how do you know it's any good?'

Taking a deep breath, Barry gives an approximation of a smile (JoJo can see something bread-like stuck between his teeth) and asks: 'Is madam buying the whisky for herself or as a gift?'

'Both. I mean, no – it's a gift.' (*Or a bribe*, she thinks – *a tool to pacify and inebriate*.)

'Do you have a country in mind? There are some interesting malts coming out of Italy. And we have an exciting new ten-year-old from Japan…'

'Let's stick with Scotland,' JoJo says, aware she'll have to cook up a story about the whisky to keep Frank from getting suspicious, so best to keep the facts simple.

'Would you prefer one with a lighter, fresher palette, or smoky and peaty?'

'Smoky and peaty,' replies JoJo. She's had enough of lighter and fresher things in her life, thank you.

Barry walks to another cabinet and removes an amber bottle.

'*Dhonn Druim* is a rare eighteen-year-old single malt from Islay,' he gives a brief pause, 'which is two hundred pounds.'

JoJo takes the bottle. Deer antlers. Embossed gold lettering. Tartan.

'Done,' she says, passing the bottle back to him.

At the register, Barry asks JoJo how she would like to pay.

Blast, she hasn't thought of this – Frank will see the purchase on their monthly statement if she uses the joint account. JoJo rummages through her purse, but she can't use her credit cards for the same reason. The problem with marrying an accountant (or a former accountant – he had now peaked at managing director, having passed up the offer of CEO many times as he enjoyed working in the trenches too much) is that nothing goes unseen.

'I'll have to get cash out,' she tells Barry, who nods as if he predicted this would happen. Probably assumes I don't have the money, thinks JoJo as she rushes up the escalators and out onto Oxford Street to find a nearby bank – buying the whisky is a matter of principle now – but when she returns fifteen minutes later, a younger, scruffier assistant has replaced him.

'Where's Barry?' she asks.

The new assistant gives a sly grin, as if about to say something impolite, but thinks better of it. 'On a break,' he says.

His name tag reads 'Stuart', and JoJo decides she likes him.

'I need to pay for some whisky.'

'This one?' asks Stuart, lifting the bottle from beneath the counter. 'Why did you decide on this bottle?'

'Your colleague recommended it.'

Stuart makes a face. He has a hole in his left nostril, and three in each earlobe. He must have to take out the rings before his shift and put everything back again afterwards.

'I wouldn't.'

'You wouldn't what?'

'Buy this one.' He lowers his voice; beside them the Harry Gordon bar is opening for business. '*Dhonn Druim* tastes like crocodile piss.'

'And how would you know what crocodile piss tastes like?'

Stuart grins again. 'Six months in New South Wales. It's the local speciality, their version of a snakebite.'

JoJo doesn't know if she believes Stuart, but she admires his gall.

'I stand corrected.'

'Can't have one of our more discerning customers buying a complete dud.'

'How do you know I'm discerning?'

'I can tell.'

Is he flirting with me? thinks JoJo. Not out of the question, she supposes. It's happened in the past, usually with a combination of machismo and pity. *Give the old girl a bit of a thrill.* JoJo understands there are men who have a thing for much older women, but Stuart is all of twenty-five.

'Who are you buying the whisky for?' he asks.

'My husband.'

'Lucky man! What's the occasion?'

'I'm trying to make him leave his mistress permanently.'

Stuart takes this information in his stride.

'Fair enough,' he says, coming out from behind the register and walking into the middle alcove, scanning the glass cabinets. 'What's his regular tipple?'

'Ale mostly. Guinness.'

'Is he a sleeper?'

'A what?'

'Does he nod off after a couple of drinks?'

'Yes – sometimes.'

'You don't want anything too heavy in that case.'

He gets the nearby ladder and launches himself up it to access one of the higher cabinets (JoJo tries not to look at Stuart's pert backside, but it's directly in her eyeline).

'This one is filtered with coca leaves from Peru. Gives it a bit of a kick.'

'I don't want him climbing the walls.'

Stuart shakes his head.

'It's a mellow buzz – wears off in an hour. Or, if you want to spice things up, try this: Liquid Viagra. We only have one bottle left – a Russian guy comes in once a week and buys all our stock.'

'Do you have anything…?' JoJo wants to ask if he has anything that will make a man feel – what? regretful? nostalgic? But it's a bottle of whisky, she reminds herself, not a time machine. And nostalgia is not the right weapon here.

JoJo clears her throat. 'Do you have anything that will blow his socks off?'

Stuart moves the ladder right and climbs to the very top, opening the highest cabinet.

'This,' he says, passing a bottle to her from the ladder. 'This is the good shit. Smooth finish, but deadly. He won't know what's hit him.'

'Perfect,' JoJo says.

They head back to the register and as she takes the wad of notes from her purse, Barry reappears, back from his break. JoJo waves the cash around lavishly for him to see and slips a twenty to Stuart when no one's watching – it's not customary to leave a tip, but this morning he's more than earned it.

*

The dummy run into central London had not exactly gone well. After Dylan finally stopped vomiting, Chris tried to tie the handles of the plastic bag together, splashing blue coloured sick on their shoes. It was pretty gross. When the train arrived at Victoria station, Chris and Dylan visited the toilets to clean up (sadly, Chris's moccasins would never be the same), but afterwards Dylan was still feeling nauseous, so instead of heading into the West End, they'd boarded the first train back to Croydon. The trip was officially a bust.

Analysing the journey later, Dylan tried to pinpoint what had gone wrong. The energy drinks were a mistake – he could see that now; hindsight was always twenty-twenty. But was the motion of the train the trigger? Would it be different if he'd travelled by car? Should he have tried breathing exercises? And would everything have turned out better if he'd travelled with someone less infuriatingly Chris-like?

It was hopeless. How could Janelle possibly depend on him if he couldn't even make it out of Croydon? Dylan hears her voice in his head, berating him cheerfully: *It's only hopeless if you think it's hopeless. You have to visualise to prioritise. No slouching, no shirking.*

Over the past few days, Dylan has become increasingly worried about Janelle. She hasn't replied to any of his emails, even the one he'd titled: 'Important'. 'Just checking you're okay,' he'd written, but there was no response. What if her ex-boyfriend had hacked into her email, and was reading all her messages? Maybe that's why she wasn't replying…? Then later, Dylan was checking Janelle's Facebook for updates, when he discovered she'd closed down her account. If that wasn't a cry for help, what was?

Something else was worrying Dylan – the package Janelle said she was sending still hadn't shown up – and perhaps it would offer more clues? He'd rung all the delivery places he could think of, but none of them were helpful. What really concerned him was a recent article he'd read about depression. Apparently, when someone became very low, they started to tidy up and give away all their prized possessions – especially when they were contemplating suicide. Suicide. Janelle couldn't possibly be thinking about that, could she?

Dylan decides he has to send Janelle a message somehow and if she won't respond to her email, he'll have to communicate with her another way. This is easier said than done – her jealous ex might be monitoring his blog too, so the message needs to be disguised. Dylan decides to use codes and carefully writes a new post:

> Otis has this annoying habit of whining in his sleep. If I kick him with my foot to wake him up, he looks at me like I'm mad. And when I'm on the computer, he jumps onto my keyboard to see what I'm staring at and presses all the buttons. bsfzpvplbzkbofmmf? – see, he did it just now. Sometimes I wish dogs had those communicator devices from the film Up to decode what they're thinking. It would make life so much easier.
>
> ----- --.. --.. --..----. ...-- ....-- ...-- ---.. .----

Hopefully, Janelle will see the reference to decoding and dig deeper. With any luck she will find the cipher – bsfzpvplbzk-bofmmf? – translated into 'areyouokayjanelle?' (if you moved every letter back one step in the alphabet) and the line of dots and dashes are a phone number in Morse code (Dylan didn't use his own number – he isn't stupid – he ordered a free SIM card and activated it in an old unlocked phone).

Dylan looks at the live post for a very long time. Would Janelle really be able to figure out the codes? Were they too obscure? He didn't want to leave anything to chance...

Opening up another new post, Dylan writes:

> Janelle, call me.

He types his number and hits 'publish'.
It's done. Now all he can do is wait.

*

JoJo turns right out of Selfridges and walks the short distance to her next stop. *So, this is it*, she thinks as she enters Mothercare. The name has a sinister ring to it: *Mothercare is watching you.*

Mothercare cares. At the entrance, an assistant tries to give her a basket, but she declines the offer – she wants one hand free to protect herself from the torrent of pastel blues and pinks – but she's mistaken, the bibs and babygros are in this season's bright tropical colours: reds, oranges, yellows.

JoJo heads downstairs – thankfully, things are more muted here – and wanders the aisles, unsure of what to buy. She picks up something called a *Prenatal Listening System* – it comes with a 'heartbeat sensor' and 'two sets of earbuds'. *How cosy*, she thinks. Would it be too obvious to buy Belinda a surveillance system? Belinda was smart, Frank was right about that. JoJo's usual mode of *head first, guns blazing* wouldn't work this time – Belinda was too outwardly reasonable, she'd make JoJo seem hysterical, or worse – toxic. Her gambit had to be different. Although anything JoJo presents to Belinda will probably be received with the same disbelieving apprehension. To be fair, JoJo is not entirely sure of her own motivations – to protect against Belinda's potential allegations of cruelty to Frank, that was certain, but there was something deeper too. JoJo recalled an old quote she must have read once: 'Take this little gift,' it went, 'in the spirit I send it,' but, tellingly, she couldn't remember if it was the Buddha who'd said this, or Machiavelli. All she knew was her instincts were telling her to get close to this woman – ingratiating herself would eventually lead to acquiring something useful. Call it a hunch. She'd also be able to assess the truthfulness of Frank using this second information source (however trustworthy Belinda might be). JoJo had used up all her tactics with Frank – there were only so many heartfelt letters you could write, only so many declarations of love – hence these gifts. She needed a new way in, collateral to keep herself in the race. It would be easy for Frank to drift off with Belinda once the baby came – JoJo had to do everything in her power to stop this from happening. One last push, you could call it.

She watches a mother and her daughter browse the cots. The girl is seventeen, eighteen? What was JoJo doing when she was eighteen? Avoiding places like this, she thinks. There were christenings – later, birthdays, a few funerals. But really, when JoJo's friends started to have children, she'd left them to it, or that was how she appeared at least. She either made new friends or relegated herself to the few annual get-togethers (which JoJo made sure were extravagant feasts to prove who was *actually* missing out), and then, as soon as the children were teenagers, the marriages collapsed, while she and Frank seemed set to sail smoothly into their twilight years… (JoJo smiles. *How smug I was*). Deep down though, deeper than she normally liked to go – all those babies, all of those children, not every one of them was noisy, ugly and annoying, not all of them had been so easy to dismiss. JoJo had worked so hard over the years to wall-off any covetous emotions – the envy, the sadness, the fear she was missing out – that now those feelings had calcified, and she could no longer trust them. *Who will take care of you in your old age?* her mother had asked. *What will you leave in this world?* Nothing. JoJo hadn't planned to leave anything behind. No plaque on a bench. No legacy. The future had been none of her business. Did she still believe that now? Were the cracks finally beginning to show?

JoJo remembers Frank's niece, Shelly – a lovely girl with straw coloured hair – Frank had doted on her until the family emigrated to Australia in the early nineties. When they eventually did see Shelly again, years later, she was all grown up, and aloof – no sign of the capricious girl who had loved them, the bond gone. Frank had been crushed. But soon, he would have a capricious child of his own to love…

JoJo picks up a baby's rattle and gives it a terse shake, as if to ward off evil spirits. A woman, roughly her own age, browsing the toys nearby, smiles.

'Shopping for your grandchild?'

'No, a friend.'

The woman nods.

'I don't know why my daughter wants half of this stuff. She already has every gadget and widget and she's not even six months yet.'

JoJo grunts.

'Different in our day,' the woman continues. 'You were lucky if you got hand-me-downs. It's all so space-age looking. Half of this stuff, I have no idea what it's for.'

'You're telling me.'

'I've said to my Charlotte time and again, don't worry about the gizmos, dear. They won't help you at four in the morning, when you've been up two nights straight. You won't remember your own name, let alone how to turn on the bottle maker, or whatever it is. And no amount of potions and lotions can prevent stretch marks. But she won't listen, it's like we never had babies ourselves.'

'Isn't it?'

They both fall silent.

'I mean, what's this?' the woman asks, picking up a plastic tub.

'A wine cooler? Nana needs her drinky!'

They both laugh.

JoJo picks up a horn-like contraption. 'And what's this thing?' she asks.

'Oh,' says the woman, 'I think that's a breast pump.'

JoJo holds it to her breast. 'Honk, honk!', and they fall about laughing, weeping like schoolgirls.

*

As soon as Dylan's overall health improved, his father introduced a sit-down meal on Fridays – part of Operation: Normal Family – which meant no TV, phones or any other distractions. Tonight's menu is cannelloni. The pasta is rubbery and oozes a stodgy white sauce, so Dylan surreptitiously circles the plate, trying to find the least offensive mouthful to load onto his fork.

'We'll have to check if your trousers still fit,' his dad is saying, 'take down the seams if the legs are too short.'

Dylan nods, but he can't seem to muster up any excitement about returning to school. He stabs a cannelloni with his fork and it haemorrhages sauce.

'Anything you want me to buy at tomorrow's shop?'

Dylan shrugs. 'We're out of Coco Pops.'

Under the table, Otis yawns.

Resting his cutlery on the side of his plate, his father takes a swig of beer (he hasn't eaten much of the cannelloni either, Dylan notes), wiping the foam from his moustache.

'Dylan, I want to ask you something.'

'I'll clean Otis's bowl after dinner, I promise.'

'Good, but that's not what I meant. I noticed your Xbox has gone from your room. Have you packed it away?'

'Not exactly…'

'Where's it gone then?'

Dylan pokes at his plate.

'I wasn't using it much anymore,' he says, with a shrug, 'so I sold it on eBay.'

Dad drops his fork with a clatter.

'You begged me to buy that – it was all you could talk about *for months*.'

'I didn't like it *that* much.'

'You cried when you opened it. I videoed it on my phone.'

'That was years ago – I was a kid. You promised you'd delete that too!'

'Dylan – serious talk now – you should have asked me first.'

'I'm starting school in a couple of weeks,' Dylan says with a stoic expression. 'I thought it would help me focus.'

'That's very admirable… What about all your games though? We only got that one recently. Battlefield… Battleground whatsit. You were desperate for that.'

'I sold them too.'

'For how much?'

'With the money from the Pokémon cards – three hundred and fifty pound.'

'What? You sold your cards? Not your rare collectable ones? What about the one you were so happy about, which looked like a fancy fox?'

'Delphox. Sold it. Wasn't that rare anyway.'

'What about the one I had to drive over to Carshalton to pick up? With the holograms?'

'Sold it too.'

'Not the legendary card, I thought there's only five of its kind in the world? The one that boy in Japan rang up about in the middle of the night?'

'I want to give up all my kid stuff,' says Dylan with another shrug.

Dylan's dad picks up his cutlery again and turns his remaining cannelloni tube 180 degrees.

'What are you planning to spend the money on?' he asks quietly, cutting the pasta into pieces.

'I don't know yet,' replies Dylan, biting his bottom lip.

'Maybe you could put it towards a tutor to help you catch up at school?'

'Yeah, maybe…'

His father plonks his cutlery down and pushes his plate away.

'You know, when I was in the army I played a lot of poker, and you learned a lot about someone over a pack of cards. Most people have a "tell" when they're not being exactly forthcoming with the truth. They touch their nose or scratch their ear. Your tell is you bite your bottom lip.'

Dylan, currently chewing his lower lip, stops immediately.

His father crosses his arms. 'Normally, this is where I should give you a lecture about not buying something you'll regret – like that ninja sword I saw you looking at on the computer last week,' Dylan, who is about to argue, has a sip of his Vimto instead, 'but I won't. I just want to remind you to take things slowly. If you had a relapse now, where would we be? Your health is worth more than all the money in the world, remember that. When I think about you getting sick again – lying there, unable to move…' his voice starts to tremble.

'I won't, Dad. I'm taking good care of myself.'

His father balls up the sheet of kitchen towel and throws it on his plate.

'Good,' he says, 'so whatever you're planning, whatever scheme you've cooked up, I trust you, Dylan Moon. I trust you. Do you hear me?'

'Yes.'

'I. Trust. You.'

'Stop looking at me like that, it's creepy.'

'Trust, Dylan.'

'Okay, I get it, I get it,' Dylan says, realising he's chewing his lip again, and taking another big gulp of his glass of Vimto to hopefully disguise the fact.

*

JoJo is no prude. She had several lovers before Frank and although she never bought into the hippie trippy movement, she smoked enough weed in the seventies to disqualify her from ever joining the Mary Whitehouse Brigade – but standing at the threshold of Ann Summers, she feels daunted. The shop layout seems to follow the same structure as the Mothercare: tiny pieces of frilly fabric on the ground level (in satiny blacks this time, like a photo negative of the baby clothes) and contraptions in the basement, so she scuttles down the stairs into the 'Pleasure Emporium', glad to find it's empty of customers and only a female assistant in the far corner, unpacking boxes.

JoJo doesn't know where to start. At first viewing, they're more *abstract* than she was expecting: more like Alessi kitchen utensils than anything sordid. Someone's had fun naming them: one is called 'Average Joe', while another, a slanting purple device, is called the 'Learning Curve'. Others are modelled on Alice in Wonderland characters: the Pleasurepillar, the Kinkykat and the White Rabbit. It's an education.

The pornography is relegated to a small, slightly apologetic-looking display of DVDs. JoJo picks one up. It's called *Honolulu Honeys*, the women naked except for skimpy grass skirts. They remind her of the joke hula girls she and Frank buy on their anniversary and other important milestones, the only gifts they allow each other. As their honeymoon had been so grim (a stuffy weekend in nearby Brighton – all they could afford at the time), they'd celebrated their tenth anniversary in Hawaii, and the hula girls had become a running joke – the figurines were sold everywhere and were so dreadfully tacky. In a moment of weakness at the airport, JoJo had bought a few as mementos and when they'd returned to London, Frank would sometimes hide the hula girls around the house for JoJo to find unexpectedly: sitting, waiting to ambush her in the water closet or wrapped in her knickers. In revenge, JoJo had bought him a new hula girl as his next anniversary present – wrapped in an oversized box – and it had become an annual tradition, points scored for tastelessness.

She thinks of Frank now, sitting in his office at Mercer and Daggen (or *Purses and Daggers*, as he always called it). There was a time she might call by his office for lunch, but not now. They can't be seen together for fear of Belinda finding out. The girl still didn't know the full extent of hers and Frank's reconcilia-tion, and it was best to keep it that way. She and Belinda had obviously decided to keep Frank in the dark about their meeting. He would only overreact, and that was useful to neither woman. Outwardly, they would be civil and take things one step at a time, while inwardly, they were both plotting their counter-attack. Or JoJo was at least…

'Can I help you?'

JoJo nearly jumps out of her skin – the poor assistant, a curly haired Asian girl, is equally traumatised.

'You'll give me a myocardial!'

'I'm so sorry! I didn't mean to…'

JoJo realises she's still holding *Honolulu Honeys* so plonks it back on its shelf guiltily.

'Are you looking for anything in particular?' asks the assistant, now recovered.

JoJo considers how to reply. 'Just browsing' might make her sound like a pervert.

'Is there anything here for the more (she hates the expression, but uses it anyway) mature woman? Something that's not too… frenetic?'

The assistant – she has no name badge – walks over to one of the stands, picking up what appears to be a large nutcracker.

'The Viber is very popular.'

She switches it on and the thing starts to buck and writhe.

'It doesn't seem very happy,' JoJo says, taking it from her.

'It's for maximum clitoral stimulation.'

'Very good then.'

JoJo stares at the Viber, its undulations hypnotic.

'Is this more of a solitary thing?'

The assistant shakes her head.

'You can use it with a partner too.'

'And how would that work?'

The assistant goes into quite graphic and considerable detail about how that would work: the many permutations, while suggesting other products to support the first: lubricants, items to tickle, to probe, for her – and so it seems – for him.

'I don't think this one's for me,' says JoJo, handing it back.

'How about the SheLuxx?'

'No,' JoJo says, 'too shiny – it looks like something a gynae-cologist might use.'

The assistant suggests more mechanisms, but they're either too loud, too long or too strange. JoJo, it seems, is the Goldilocks of fake cocks.

'But what's *your* favourite?' she asks finally.

The assistant smiles. She walks to the far stand and picks up what looks like a garlic press.

'My girlfriend and I love this one.'

JoJo takes the mechanism, and turns it around in her hand. It's smooth and fits into her palm and has two – handles maybe? levers? – at the top. It starts to vibrate gently.

'How is it…?' asks JoJo, startled – but now she can see, the assistant is holding a wireless control.

'You can choose any speed and setting – or your partner can too.'

The device purrs in JoJo's hand, the levers pulsate.

'What's your girlfriend's name?'

'Talia.'

'Talia… That's a lovely name.'

The assistant turns the dial on the controller, and the device is nibbling JoJo's palm now. It reminds her of the baby animals she used to hold as a child: the chicks, the puppies, naked and translucent. Their bulbous eyes and tiny claws. How they would nestle into the warmth of her grasp.

'This one,' she says, cupping it with her other hand, as if it might escape.

The assistant smiles.

CHAPTER TEN

(To be read as a prayer):
O gentle presence, bless your lovers today // Feeble or strong, short or tall, seen or unseen. // May their toast land butter side up. // May their requests be accepted and their photos liked. // Give them 30p for the toilets, or help them change a fiver without too much hassle. // By your blessing, grant them a dry yoga mat, a last-minute cancellation, an umbrella in the rain. // Let them avoid all those with BO // Yea, the men and the women (and the unwashed youths). // Protect them from charity muggers, from rogue pigeons, from paper cuts. // Approve them for a Master's degree in endocrinology, and let them continue to live in a city with no wars, no plagues or natural hazards. // *[Together:] May we be early. May we be on time. May we not be late.* // Greatest of all, O blessed presence // bestow on them that rarest of gifts; //
Grant them a second chance.

*

'Hello.'
   'Hi.'
   'You look beautiful.'
   'Thank you. I like your suit, your hair's shorter.'
   'What would you like to drink?'
   'I don't mind, whatever you're having.'
   'Champagne?'

'Perfect.'

'Here you go.'

'Cheers.'

'So, how are you?'

'I'm okay, I'm good.'

'I'm glad you're here.'

'Me too. I want to apologise, properly.'

'There's no need.'

'But I want to explain…'

'It's in the past.'

'Please?'

'Sure.'

'I had a whole speech prepared in my head.'

'If it helps, just picture me naked…'

'…I'm sorry, I really am. I don't want to be that crazy emotional girl. I hate being that person. It's like – you know when you're a kid and you realise Santa Claus isn't real?'

'Santa Claus isn't real?!'

'You're joking, but I was fourteen when I found out the Easter bunny didn't exist.'

'Hang on, are we talking about Santa Claus or the Easter bunny here?'

'The Easter bunny. Big rabbit?'

'Do the face again. That's priceless.'

'What? It's my impression of a rabbit eating a carrot.'

'Ah, so that's what it's doing…'

'Anyway, I was fourteen, and I already knew Father Christmas and the tooth fairy weren't real. I mean – come on – Santa Claus has flying reindeer and the tooth fairy is, well, a fairy. But there *are* actual bunnies in the world. I just imagined one with a big bow around its neck and a basket full of eggs. In my mind, it was as real as baby Jesus or the Queen.'

'Some might question the realness of baby Jesus too, but I can see your logic.'

'So, I was at school and I asked my friend Emma how many chocolate eggs the Easter bunny had brought her, and she looked at me funny and said: "You know it's not real, don't you?" And I was floored, completely devastated. I knew the moment she looked at me there was no Easter bunny, but it was as if the last piece of my childhood had been ripped apart.'

'What did you say to Emma?'

'Nothing, I didn't speak to her for a week.'

'Children can be cruel.'

'But don't you see, that's exactly what happened in the car. I'm told something which changes the image in my head, and I fall to pieces.'

'So, I'm the Easter bunny?'

'In a way, yes.'

'Except I have opposable thumbs – much more efficient.'

'Aren't you angry with me?'

'Not anymore.'

'So, you were angry?'

'Not really.'

'I wouldn't blame you.'

'I have one question for you though.'

'Okay, sure.'

'You do know money doesn't make someone a different person despite popular opinion?'

'I know. I'm such an idiot. I think I'm still working through stuff from my childhood – some horrible stuck-up girls at school that made fun of my poxy tights. In the car, I was triggered, and I projected and reacted – all the things you're not supposed to do when someone lovely is trying to whisk you away on a romantic weekend. I'm so sorry. Can we forget it ever happened?'

'I think that's the worst thing we can do. Let's get everything out in the open instead. Come on, ask me something.'

'About what?'

'About my inheritance.'

'I can't!'

'Why not?'

'It's none of my business.'

'That's where you're wrong – if I'm your business, it's your business too.'

'It's too personal.'

'Money isn't personal, it's the opposite of personal. You here, sitting with me now – this is personal. Money is money. Go on, ask.'

'My mind's blank.'

'Don't you want to know how much it is?'

'No!'

'I get an allowance of £3,500 a month. Slightly more or less depending on inflation. You see, it's not a fortune. I'm luckier than most, I own my flat outright, but I live pretty frugally. Or more frugally than many people in my situation.'

'Why are you telling me this?'

'Because I don't want it hanging over us. I know I can trust you. And it's only money. Ask me something else.'

'I don't know – what's the most expensive thing you've ever bought?'

'A Maserati Spyder on my twenty-first birthday.'

'I thought you said you lived frugally?'

'That was frugal. I could have bought two.'

'But you don't have the car anymore?'

'No.'

'What happened?'

'Twenty-one-year-olds shouldn't be allowed to drive anything with a top speed of 177 miles per hour. Give me your hand.'

'Are you sure? You usually don't like me touching that shoulder.'

'It's okay this time. Can you feel the metal plate here?'

'I can – you're a cyborg. Were you in an accident?'

'I was – a bad one. A very bad one. I don't want to get too heavy, because tonight is a celebration after all, but I wanted to show you exactly what I carry round with me every day. Just here. Just under my skin… Do you want your hand back, by the way?'

'No, you can keep it, if you like… I do have a question though, but it's not about money. How did you know which studio I was shooting at, to send the card to?'

'That was easy. You mentioned working with a Samira, so I did some snooping and I found her on Twitter. She has, how can I put this kindly, the online equivalent of verbal diarrhoea – I've never seen someone tweet so much in my life! Samira not only named the studio you were at, but posted a lovely picture of you too – nice fanny pack and overalls, by the way.'

'What was I doing in the photo?'

'You seemed to be attacking a tree. I'd always picked you as a friend of Nature, but this one must have really ticked you off.'

'Oh my God, I'm going to kill—'

'Daisy?'

Hearing her name, Daisy swivels around on her stool, and sees – it can't be, but yes, balls and bollocks! – walking towards them is her ex-shag, ex-boyfriend, whatever you want to call him – Warren.

*

Voicemail received from Patrick at 7.44 p.m.:

Hey, mate, how's it going? Big news. One of the partners retired, and there's been a reshuffle and somehow I'm getting a promotion. It's more work, and not a whole lot more pay, but it means I'll be sticking round this side of the equator for a few more years! Are you around Friday for a celebratory drink? Bring your workmates, we can have a good old-fashioned piss-up – mad men vs. wanker bankers, last man standing. Also, Mrs J called. We had a long chat – she's worried she hasn't spoken to you in a while so I told her you were curing world peace or making cancer or something, but give your poor mum a call. Oh, and the landlord wants to send a guy over to fix the boiler – could you organise it with him? Thanks, mate. Longest phone message in the world, eh? Laterz.

*

'Warren!'

'I thought it was you. Not interrupting, am I?'

'Of course not!' says Daisy, her voice squeaky with panic. 'Chris, this is Warren. Warren, Chris.'

The men shake hands in the gruff, rigid way men have – and something in Warren's manner – the way he's sizing up Chris and glancing furtively at her – makes Daisy wonder whether perhaps he had liked her even more than she'd guessed.

'Good to meet you, mate.'

'You too.'

'What brings you out this evening?' Daisy asks, afraid if she doesn't lead the conversation it will stumble into awkward territory.

'My folks are down for the weekend,' says Warren, nodding towards an older couple reading menus by the bar. Beside them, a pretty but bored-looking blonde girl in her mid-twenties texts on a phone. 'Mum, come over here. I want you to meet someone.'

Warren's mother joins them, wearing a voluminous pink scarf and an appearance of weary indignation.

'He's doing it again,' she says, 'I told him we'll eat after the show.'

'Where's the food on this menu?' says Warren's dad as he approaches. 'Not bar snacks, proper food.'

'I'm Daisy, nice to meet you.'

'You too, love,' says Warren's mother, her Mancunian accent much stronger than her son's. 'Ooh, I'm jealous of your bubbly!' She nods in her husband's direction. 'He's had us pounding pavements all afternoon.'

'Five quid they want for olives! Five quid!'

'It's Mum's birthday today,' explains Warren.

'Wow!' says Daisy. 'Have you been anywhere nice?'

Warren's mother nods.

'We had a lovely afternoon tea at, what's the hotel again?'

'The Ritz.'

'That's right, like the song.'

'Hours ago,' chimes in Warren's father.

The blonde girl wanders closer, still texting. Daisy can't remember if Warren had a sister.

'Which show are you seeing?' asks Daisy.

'*Mamma Mia!*,' Warren's mother replies.

'Tiny cakes and tiny sandwiches. I say, leave the crusts on if it's going to make them more substantial.'

'I do love – whats-her-name, Meryl Streep – in the film. But how do you two know each other?'

'We work together on shoots,' Warren says to his mother. 'Daisy's the best in the biz.'

'I'm not sure about that…'

'If there's someone better, I've not met them.'

'I'm just a props maker, Warren's the real whizz kid.'

'You should see some of the things she's made, Mum. One time, she built an elephant for a safari shoot – this big it was. The trunk moved with switches and everything.'

At this exchange, the girl glances up from her phone with a look of – what? Intrigue? Jealousy perhaps? Definitely not a sister then.

'And what do you do – Chris, is it?' asks Warren.

Chris sits upright on his stool.

'Investments, mostly.'

Warren's dad sniffs. 'Hope you're not one of those criminals who ruined the country.'

'Don't listen to him. Clive, don't be rude. We're guests here.'

'I pay my taxes,' Clive replies.

'But you're enjoying London?' Daisy says, trying to change the subject.

'We are,' says the mother. 'There's so much going on, isn't there?'

'Too much, if you ask me.'

'No one did, Clive.'

'What type of investments?' asks Warren.

'The usual sort,' replies Chris. 'Developed equities. Corporate bonds.'

'Who do you work for?'

'Myself mostly.'

'Six pound fifty for a bowl of chips!'

'And where do you live, Daisy?' Warren's mother asks.

'I'm in Queensway, near Notting Hill. It's my friend's place though, I just rent a room – I wish I could afford somewhere near Notting Hill!'

'Clive, we've seen the film of that, haven't we? Whats-her-name with the teeth, the one you like…'

'Julia Roberts. She's a member of Mensa, did you know? A very intelligent woman.'

'Chris lives just around the corner.'

'Does he? Must be nice to live by all the shops. Very central.'

'Those investments must be doing well,' says Warren. 'Maybe I should ask you for some advice?'

'Feel free, any time.'

'She's an accomplished equestrienne,' continues Warren's father. 'Not a lot of people know that about Julia Roberts.'

'And isn't the Charlotte Street Hotel beautiful?' Warren's mother says to Daisy.

'It's one of my favourites. Where are you staying?'

'The Travelodge in Southwark.'

'Ah – that's nice too. How are you finding it?'

'The staff are very friendly.'

'But you can't get ice for love nor money,' Warren's father grumbles.

'Sorry, I don't think we've been introduced?' Daisy says to the girl.

'Cara,' she says, smiling wanly.

'Oh, you're American?'

'Canadian. I'm from Toronto originally.'

'I like your dress.'

'It's vintage.'

'I wish I had the patience for vintage. Rooting around all those second-hand shops. Doesn't it take a lot of energy?'

Cara shrugs. 'I bought this on eBay.'

'Oh, well, it's lovely on you. Do you work in fashion?'

'No, I'm a receptionist at the investment bank Mercer and Daggen.'

'But what about you, Daisy?' interrupts Warren. 'I don't think I've ever seen you in a dress. You scrub up nicely.'

'If there's one thing I hate,' announces his father, 'it's drinking tepid liquids.'

'Clive, really! I've had it up to here with you today! When you get back to the hotel, just have bottled water from the fridge.'

'It's never cold enough.'

'Anyway,' Warren says, 'we should let you get back to your evening.'

'I'm not going anywhere until I've eaten.'

'Let's get a table then, Dad.'

'Lovely to meet you,' Daisy says to Warren's mother.

'You too, love. Take care.'

'Enjoy the rest of your trip.'

'I'll try,' she says, rolling her eyes in the direction of her husband.

'They seemed nice,' Chris says when they've gone to the other side of the bar.

'Mmm hmm,' says Daisy, taking a big sip of champagne.

'I've never seen you like that.'

'Like what?' she asks nervously.

'All charming with the parents.'

'Yes,' Daisy says, relaxing a bit. 'Parents do tend to love me.'

'And Warren, he's…'

'Your glass is empty,' says Daisy, quickly standing up. 'My round this time. Same again?'

*

Voicemail received from Adam at 9.16 p.m.:

Heya, mate. Congratulations on the promotion! Do they know how much of a reprobate you are? I'm a bit nervous they're putting you in charge of million p-pound accounts, when you're still not confident taking down the clothes horse. Hang on, gotta—.

Voicemail received from Adam at 9.19 p.m.:

Sorry about that. Bit hectic here tonight. Seriously, well done. I've been given a sort of unofficial p-promotion myself, so we both have something to celebrate. The only thing is, I can't make Friday – I'm being sent on a last-minute business trip to Frankfurt and I'll be away most of the week. It also means I won't be able to let the boiler guy in either. Ap-p-pologies, it's chaotic here, but better than being unemployed though, right? Ha. I'll give Mum a call t… (Hushed whisper, barely audible) Oh no, someone's com—

Sorry again. Phone p-playing up. Owe you a drink or twenty. Bottle of duty-free plum schnapps? A

*

Before she heads to the bar, Daisy nips to the loo and afterwards, as she's washing her hands, Cara enters the bathroom.

'Hello,' Daisy says, cheerily.

'Oh, hi…' replies Cara, with a strained smile.

'I'm sorry about just now,' Daisy says, drying her hands with a paper towel.

'What do you mean?'

'My woman's intuition picked up on your woman's intuition.' Cara looks at Daisy blankly. 'With Warren. When he was introducing me to his mum.'

'I don't…'

'I could tell by your expression that you knew about Warren and me. And I don't want anyone to feel awkward. They're always weird, these situations, right?'

'What?'

'You seemed a bit off with me. And I totally get it. But I'm not a threat, I'm nothing you should be worried about. We didn't even have a proper thing. It wasn't even a thing really, it was nothing.'

'You were seeing Warren?'

'Not really seeing…'

'What were you doing then?'

'We just had a few… dates.'

'So, you were dating?'

'Not really even dating. Like I said, it was a thing, but it's nothing to worry about. Not even a thing!' Daisy says with a laugh, which is supposed to convey *savoir faire* but comes out as a manic cackle.

Cara folds her arms: 'So *when* were you dating?'

'I, er…' says Daisy, stumbling over her words, 'Like I said, we were never officially dating.'

'When were you *unofficially* dating?'

Daisy shakes her head.

'I'm sorry, I'm really confused – I thought you knew already. The look on your face? When we were being introduced?' Daisy lowers her voice. 'While Warren was praising my elephant.'

'I don't know what you're talking about, but if I had any look on my face, it was probably because I'm fed up with his parents. His dad never stops complaining, and his mum… She's all smiles on the surface, but she hasn't said one nice word about me since she got here!'

Cara starts to tear up.

'Oh, I'm sorry.'

'And now some mad ex-girlfriend is accosting me in the toilets. I told him it was too soon to meet his parents, we've only been going out a few months.'

'Here,' says Daisy, passing her a paper towel.

'Thanks,' Cara says, blotting the underneath of her eyes. 'Last night, his mother said I had a "healthy appetite" just because I ordered the garlic bread.'

'People can be cruel,' Daisy says gently.

'So, how long ago were you seeing Warren?' Cara says, still blotting.

'It – whatever "it" was – started over a year ago, and finished, I guess, a couple of months back.'

'When exactly?'

'I don't know – some time in July.'

Cara's mouth drops open.

'July this year?'

'Or maybe early August. But we hadn't seen each other for…'

'*We* met in *June*!'

Back at the table, Chris is playing with the salt and pepper shakers when Warren sits down opposite him.

'Hi,' says Chris uncertainly. 'Did you... order some food?'

'We did, we did. So, how long you known Daisy for?'

'A couple of months now.'

'She's a great girl.'

'She sure is.'

'I've been working with her for a couple of years,' Warren says, leaning forward. His breath has the slightly sour note of someone who hasn't drunk enough water. 'I guess you could say, we keep an eye out for each other. There are a lot of weirdos in the world, a lot of players, if you know what I mean.' Chris doesn't know what Warren means, but he assumes it has something to do with a hurt male ego, and so he nods anyway. 'I'm a bit protective of her, I suppose.'

'That's very good of you.'

'I want to make sure she's not going to be jerked around by anyone. Because if someone hurt Daisy, I'd be pretty upset.'

Chris feels that strange Spider-Man tingling which usually means someone is about to be punched. Warren is as tall as he is, and about the same weight. Chris wishes he hadn't worn his toecap Derby brogues – the soles are new and haven't been broken in yet – they'll be slippery in a scuffle. He also doesn't want to get blood on his suit. Chris has only ever been in two fights – once when he was eight at boarding school (which he lost), and the time he tried to stop a brawl between two drunken girls in Oxford, for which he received a black eye. He was definitely a lover, not a fighter – but something in Warren's body language says he might not have a choice in the matter.

'I think we're on the same page about Daisy,' says Chris, trying to buy some time. He looks around for a makeshift weapon, not to do any serious harm, just something to bop Warren over the head with and render him unconscious.

'I hope we are, mate. Because you know what they say about northern men?'

There's only the salt and pepper shakers – nothing good for clobbering in reaching distance. Why hadn't he bought a whole bottle of champagne instead of just two glasses?

Chris realises Warren is waiting for an answer.

'I don't know. Northern men are male and live at higher latitudes?'

'Are you getting smart with me, mate?'

Surreptitiously, Chris fists the pepper shaker in his left hand.

'*Friends with benefits*! How's that better than dating?'

Daisy is not making her point very effectively.

'Because it wasn't a relationship,' she says, 'There was just…'

'Benefits?'

'Yes. But not very often. And not in June. At least I don't think so.'

'Warren and I had a very long, very open conversation about our exes. I thought we were being honest with each other. And now his parents hate me!' Cara starts to cry again. 'I should break up with him!'

'No, you don't want to do that. Sleep on it, you'll feel very differently about things in the morning.'

'We're all going to breakfast at Balthazar in the morning!' wails Cara. 'I'll have to eat an egg white omelette while they all have sausages and chips. No, I'm going to break up with him now.'

'But Warren's such a lovely guy.'

'Why didn't you date him then?'

Daisy doesn't have an answer for this.

'He must like you a lot if he introduced you to your parents?'

'If he really cared about me, he'd stand up to his mum.'

'But you'll miss *Mamma Mia!*' says Daisy in a last-ditch effort to salvage Warren's relationship.

'I'll rent the movie,' Cara says, stomping into one of the cubicles and banging the door closed.

Chris has a plan. He's unscrewed the top of the pepper shaker under the table and as soon as things get hairy, he'll throw pepper into Warren's eyes and make a run for it. What about Daisy? He can't leave her here. New plan. He'll biff the pepper and yell for Daisy while Warren's blinded. When Daisy returns, he'll grab her hand and run – he can explain when they're somewhere safer.

'You think this is a joke?' Warren is saying.

'Not at all. I appreciate you only have the best interests for Daisy. It's admirable she has such a strong network of people looking out for her.'

'You're taking the mickey.'

'I mean it. But if we really care about Daisy, shouldn't we be less worried about each other and more concerned about how the system treats women? Pay parity, glass ceilings, unrealistic body expectations…'

'Right, mate. This is your last chance.'

'What are you boys talking about?' Daisy says, appearing slightly flushed.

'Daisy!' says Warren, all big smiles again. 'I was just getting to know Chris better.'

'Good, good! Chris, I think we should go otherwise we're going to be late for the thing.'

'Yes, the thing,' Chris says, jumping up. 'We better run.'

'Sorry, Warren. Must go, can't be late.' Daisy gives Warren a swift kiss on the cheek, and then she and Chris are out the door, lickety-split.

'I'm sorry,' Daisy says as they hurriedly try to put some distance between them and the bar. 'Warren and I had a bit of a thing.'

'I thought as much,' says Chris.

'We can call it a night if you like?' she says, downcast.

'What do you mean, the evening's only started!' Chris puts his arm around Daisy and kisses her on the side of her forehead. 'Takes more than an aggressive ex-boyfriend to put me off.'

Daisy nestles her head into his chest gratefully.

'Chris?'

'Ya-ha?'

'Why are you holding a pepper shaker?'

'No reason,' he says, kissing her head again.

*

Voicemail received from Patrick at 3.59 p.m.:

Hi, mate. Tried to call you a few times, but your phone is always off. Not sure if you've gone to Germany already? Had a bit of a funny conversation with the landlord – apparently our rent hasn't gone in this month. He said the standing order has been cancelled, which is weird. I put my half into your account like normal – maybe there was a mix-up at your bank?

One other thing. I called your reception and they said there was no record of an Adam Jiggins working there. You should get that sorted, mate – you don't want people to get the wrong impression. Speak soon.

CHAPTER ELEVEN

The delivery man struggles with the box down the hallway.

'What's in here?' he says, out of breath, resting one shoulder against the wall. 'Bricks or somefing?'

Dylan still has no idea what's inside the box, but his imagination has been working overtime.

'Where do you want it?' asks the delivery man, dumping it on the coffee table without waiting for an answer.

Otis sniffs the cardboard box suspiciously. It's sealed with thick black tape – there's no writing on the sides of the box, only a plastic delivery patch with Dylan's name and address.

The delivery man wipes his sweaty forehead on his bicep.

'Right, if you can sign…'

Dylan has a thought – what if there's something scary inside the box? An old-fashioned doll that says 'Mama' when he picks it up or a stuffed black cat with staring marble eyes? What if he finds a knotted ball of feathers and twigs? Or hair? Or *teeth*?

Otis sniffs the box again, steps back a pace and licks his chops.

'Can you wait till I've checked it – in case it's broken?'

'Got anyfing to cut the tape?' asks the delivery man. 'My van's double-parked.'

Dylan fetches a pair of scissors from the kitchen and tries to cut through the seal, but his hands are clumsy in front of an audience.

'Careful, you'll scratch what's inside.'

'Why don't you try?' Dylan says stroppily, passing over the scissors, but the delivery man seems nonplussed, slicing through the tape and opening up the cardboard flaps with ease.

Both peer inside.

'What is it?' asks Dylan.

The delivery man reaches into the box and with considerable effort, hoists out the contents, polychips raining onto the floor. Otis springs on these new curiosities and Dylan has to take two soggy packing chips out of the dog's mouth before the animal can swallow them.

'It's a typewriter,' announces the delivery man, plonking it next to the box with a thump. 'No wonder it was so bloody heavy! Vintage too.'

Dylan has never seen a real-life typewriter. It's massive – almost as big as televisions before they went flat screen – and black, and shiny. Along the top is written 'Imperial' and underneath this, in smaller writing, 'War Finish'. Why has Janelle sent him a typewriter? Is it some sort of coded message? She did like old-school things (the French films, for example), but the typewriter worried Dylan. It was so random – it felt like a bad omen.

The delivery man whistles.

'It's in good nick. Must be worth a bob or two. How'd you get it?'

For some reason, Dylan's impulse is to lie and say he's an antiques collector, but he shrugs instead.

'Someone special has given it to me as a present.'

'Worth a coupla hundred quid at least. You should take it on the *Antiques Roadshow* – get it valued. Or I've a mate in Carshalton who'll…'

'I'm not going to sell it,' Dylan says indignantly.

'I'm not saying sell it, but you need to know these fings for insurance purposes.' Dylan hasn't thought about that – he's never owned anything valuable. Where is he going to keep it?

Somewhere up high, otherwise Otis will chew off the keys. 'You got any paper? We should see if it works.'

Bristling at the delivery man's use of 'we', Dylan heads into the computer room to get some paper. He starts to feel dizzy – he must have stood up too quickly – so he takes a moment to compose himself. *River of calm*, he whispers to himself by the printer. *River of calm*. He tries to visualise the river – muddy banks, reeds in the water, the swift line of the current – but he sees his school uniform hanging up on a hanger, and his mind skips to school on Monday. Uniforms. Homework. *River of calm. River of calm.* GCSEs. Assemblies. The smell of old farts. Classrooms roasting from the central heating. The never-ending tide of boredom. *River of calm. River of calm.* How many humiliations await him, he wonders? What new combinations of old-fashioned bullying techniques and cutting-edge social media?

Distractedly, Dylan reaches for the 'Janelle phone' and checks it for messages. Still nothing. He logs into his email. Nothing. His blog. Nada.

Returning to the living room, he finds the delivery man squatting in front of the typewriter, his hand raised as if about to hit one of the keys.

'Don't!' Dylan shouts, and the delivery man looks up, surprised. 'I have to try it first.' The delivery man shrugs and stands up to let Dylan take his place.

Loading the sheet of paper into the typewriter gives Dylan a strange sense of *déjà vu*. He wonders what to write, so he starts with: J A N E L L E. The sound is amazing, the thwack of the keys as they hit the paper – the keys seem to spring from nowhere, yet always find their mark. Dylan starts to speed up: O W N E D T H I S T Y P E W R I T E R. At the end of the line, he's unsure how to make the bar go back again. He experiments with a few of the levers and finally, one releases the bar, sending it whizzing back to the start again with a 'ding!', making both Dylan and the delivery man chortle out loud. T H A N K Y O U. G O O D B Y E, he types. Dylan rolls the sheet of paper out of the machine and stares at it. The words are really there, physically on the page. He doesn't even have to press 'print'.

Dylan lets the delivery man have a go now – it seems only fair. On a clean sheet of paper, he in turn types: B O O B S A N D N I C K E R S – not hugely respectful, but Janelle would find it hilarious.

While the delivery man taps away, Dylan searches the box, sifting his hand through the polychips. He finds a small card, on it is written:

Dearest Dylan,
Don't forget there's a real world out there too.
Lots and lots of love, Janelle xxxxooooxxxx
P.S. Now go get 'em!

He slips the card in his pocket as the delivery man starts to wind down.

'Want to have a race to see who can type the fastest?' asks Dylan.

'Can't,' says the delivery man, getting to his feet. 'Got the van. Can you sign here?' He hands over a tablet, and Dylan writes his name on the screen with a stylus thingummy – although it doesn't really look like his signature, it's more of an illegible scrawl. *Technology*, he tuts to himself, as he lets out the delivery man, returning to wrangle up the loose packing chips before Otis can choke himself to death, and pondering the meaning of the note for the entire rest of the day.

*

Adam's incarceration happens on an evening that, at first, appears like any other. He spends most of the morning and an uneventful afternoon in his sixth-floor shack, working on his master presentation – a huge PowerPoint doc (at last count three hundred and forty-four pages, with graphs, pie charts and at least four types of fancy slide transitions) which was so large the document constantly crashed – moving down into the corner office by half seven. If he notices anything unusual – the sound of drilling or the increase in security guards – it's only peripherally. Perhaps he's become too complacent, or the mystery of the cleaners is drawing him in too fully (the question is no longer *what* the cleaners are doing – Adam has managed to overhear snippets of their phone conversations and discovered the cleaners are making scripted telemarketing calls for a printer cartridge company – but *how* Mr Maintenance is involved and when he might retaliate).

Later in the evening, after finishing for the night in the corner office, Adam turns off the desktop computer, washes his cup in the kitchenette and then rides the elevator down to the ground floor. As he approaches the foyer, he notices Cara the receptionist is sitting at her post behind the desk – lust and panic ripple through his body.

'You're still here?' he manages to say as the spasm passes.

Cara looks up wearily, but as soon as she makes eye contact with Adam, her face reactively warms with a smile (*Does she remember our conversation on the first floor?* he wonders).

'We're testing some new systems,' Cara explains. 'There's been a few hiccups.'

A walkie-talkie on the reception counter comes to life with a bird-like chirp and the crackly sound of a man's voice.

'What type of new systems?' asks Adam, bouncing his rucksack higher onto his shoulder.

'Security mostly. You probably haven't noticed but we've been a bit lax so everything's being upgraded – cameras, network protection – the works.'

Adam's stomach does a double backflip.

'Have there b-been any… s-security issues?' he asks, casually.

'No – it's only a precaution. And it shouldn't affect you much.'

'Good,' Adam says, adding with forced joviality, 'so no retina scans or strip searches?'

Cara's smile starts to fade.

'Hope they're p-paying you overtime for this,' he adds quickly. 'Have you been here all day?'

'For my sins,' she replies, picking up the walkie-talkie as it squawks again and holding it to her mouth. When she speaks into it, her accent is more clipped, with less of her usual Canadian twang. 'Yes, over.'

Sins. A pair of long black gloves. Cara pulling them off, finger by finger, and peeling them down her arms, revealing alabaster skin. The snap of latex. Good God, he was going to wet himself!

As Cara finishes her conversation on the walkie-talkie, Adam realises he's been staring at her the whole time.

'Is there anything else?' she asks.

'No. I m-mean – er, yes,' Adam stammers.

Cara waits patiently.

'I… I just wanted to say, I think you're doing a really good job. I mean, in general. A lot of people in your p-position would phone it in, but you seem to really care about this place. And it's appreciated.' Cara stares at him with a strange expression on her face. 'Like tonight, staying late, or yesterday, when you organised flowers for the g-guy on the third floor because he forgot his anniversary, or the way you put out a b-bowl of sweets on a Friday (*And all while you've been going through a breakup, if your recent emails are anything to go by*, Adam thinks, but doesn't say). It's the small things, but they add up, so… thank you.'

They stare each other for what feels like a hundred years, and then a tiny voice in Adam's head yells: *go!* and he walks towards the turnstiles. 'Yes, well – good night, hope you don't have to stay too…' Adam pushes his weight against the rung of the turnstile, but it doesn't budge.

Cara snaps out of her trance and stands up.

'I forgot to say, you have to swipe out with your card now too.'

She waits encouragingly, as Adam – almost in slow motion, or so it feels – takes the security card out of his pocket and swipes it on the scanner. Red light. And again. Red light.

Cara frowns. 'That's odd. Try it again, slower this time.'

Red light.

'Give me the card.'

Helplessly, Adam hands Cara the card (piano-player fingers, slender wrists, cream coloured skin) and she scans it on her computer.

'I'm sorry,' Cara says, still frowning, 'there's something strange here.'

Should he run? He could easily clear the turnstile before she had a chance to raise the alarm. What if she locked the main doors… perhaps he should double back and find a fire exit instead?

Cara studies her computer. Adam imagines his mug shot and a flashing red cross emblazoned on the screen. He's surprised he can't hear a siren.

'It's saying your card's been cancelled,' Cara says, sitting back in her chair.

'How… odd,' Adam manages to say.

'Very odd.'

Adam feels faint. Maybe he wouldn't make it over the turnstiles after all.

'Don't worry,' Cara says, shaking her head. 'It must be this switch-over. Leave it with me and I'll get a new one sorted out for you tomorrow. Just ask at the desk in the morning.'

The turnstile light turns green.

The walkie-talkie screeches again. Cara picks it up: 'Reception, over.'

Adam considers the green light. If he steps through the turnstile now, he'll never be able to return. Cara will check with the other receptionists and discover a replacement card has already been issued to the real owner, and in the morning, Adam will find a squad of policemen waiting to arrest him. They might even use plainclothes detectives to avoid making a scene: *Come this way, sir. Could we have a moment of your time?* Very discreet.

If he leaves now, what will he have? No job, no prospects. He'll be back where he started – worse now there's a sizeable gap on his CV. At least here he has a routine, a function – perhaps even a future once he's exposed the misdoings of the cleaners.

For a second, the mask slips. Adam isn't a hero – he's something much worse – a *parasite*. It's only a matter of time until he's caught, and even if he doesn't go to prison, he'll still be forced to move back to Hereford with his mum and sleep on the fold-out sofa. Eventually, he'll have to start taking antidepressants again, which will eradicate his sex drive and open him up to a whole host of possible side effects – dry mouth, dizziness, strange electric jolts that felt like being struck by pigmy lightning bolts – and he'll get a job in a local agency that prides itself on being as good as a London one, although it won't be. And his older brothers will have that look in their eye: *you thought you were better than us. You thought you could leave.*

Adam stares at the green light. He should take this opportunity before it all goes horribly wrong.

Then there's Cara. Beautiful, efficient Cara. Deep down, he knows she'll never be interested in him – she's only friendly because that's her job, she only ignores his stutter to be professionally polite. Not being able to see her every day though, to listen to her playlists or read her messages – to never again know what she was considering for lunch – it will crush him.

Adam pushes his knee against the turnstile and it starts to move. *Tick...*

'Actually,' he says, stepping back, 'I've just remembered, I have another report I need to p-print out.'

'Okay,' says Cara, still holding the walkie-talkie. 'I'm leaving shortly, so one of the security guards can let you out.'

And now something miraculous happens. Cara smiles at Adam, but this time it's not her generic 'Welcome to Mercer and Daggen' robo-smile, or the tight-lipped grin he's seen her use to resolve difficult situations, or even her *putting on a brave face* toothpaste commercial smile. Her eyes are engaged. *Her eyes are engaged!* There's a spark, a light, a twinkle even.

'Thanks, Cara,' Adam says, as he starts towards the elevators, endorphins surging through his body.

'No problem, Mark,' she replies, giving him a quick farewell wave as he goes.

*

JoJo is brushing her teeth, and contemplating a streak she must have missed while cleaning the bathroom mirror, when the top of the laundry basket starts to vibrate. She rinses her mouth and dries her hands, hoping it will stop of its own accord, but it's nothing if not persistent. Reluctantly, she sources the mobile phone from her pile of folded clothes, and glances at the caller ID. JoJo hits the mute button immediately. She opens the door carefully – Frank, who purportedly was watching the news, is already sound asleep, one leg out of the duvet, one arm over his head – and hurriedly skulks through the bedroom, down the hallway and onto the stairs.

'Yes?' JoJo says in a hoarse whisper, answering the phone in the dark bookshelf-lined study at the bottom of the staircase.

'Sorry to ring you so late.'

JoJo checks the stairs to make sure Frank hasn't followed her.

'I was washing my face,' JoJo says, and instantly regrets it. She doesn't want Belinda to know the ins and outs of her private life, and washing her face sounds too pedestrian. She should have said she was reclining in a bath of camel's milk and geranium oil while reading *The London Review of Books*. Not washing her ruddy face.

'I wanted to thank you for your present – it arrived today.'

'Oh that – it's nothing.' JoJo had actually forgotten all about posting the Mothercare gift. She'd finally decided on a 'Baby Einstein Nautical Friends Play Gym', which seemed to be some kind of garish interactive learning mat – the child on the packaging was smiling at least.

'It was very thoughtful.'

Belinda's voice sounds different tonight – thinner somehow, as if it's been stretched out and left to dry in the sun.

'You can't ring me in the evenings,' JoJo says, tersely. 'Frank might find out.' There's no response. 'Hello?'

'I'm still here,' says Belinda. 'I'm sorry, I know I shouldn't have called. I guess I wanted to hear a friendly voice.'

'Why did you phone me then?'

JoJo means this seriously, but Belinda only laughs.

'I wanted someone to tell me to snap out of it, I suppose.'

'Snap out of what?'

'Whatever this is.'

JoJo sighs. The girl was obviously maudlin. She changes the phone to her other ear.

'It's late. You're pregnant. Your body is infested with hormones. You just need a good night's sleep.'

'Maybe. I wish I could have a glass of red wine though.'

'Why not? One won't hurt. Two probably won't hurt.'

In a dark recess of her mind, JoJo realises the potential power she has over Belinda at this very second. She has an evil thought: what if she encouraged Belinda to drink a whole bottle of wine? Or two? What then? She admonishes herself instantly, feeling rightfully guilty.

'Have one glass of wine and go to bed, you'll be fine in the morning.'

There's another silence.

'Hello?' barks JoJo again.

'Sorry, I'm still here,' replies Belinda flatly.

Good lord, what was this, the Samaritans hotline? What disappoints JoJo the most is she assumed she'd found one of her brethren: a woman with a bit of spunk and mettle to her. Yes, Belinda was boffing her husband, but even that gave her a certain amount of *chutzpah*. Now the girl was being so wet, it was embarrassing.

'What's really the matter?' JoJo asks.

'It's nothing, I should…'

'Don't be a martyr.'

There's another long silence.

'I don't know if I can do this,' Belinda says at last.

'Do what?'

'All of this,' Belinda starts to sob.

'Come on,' reprimands JoJo, 'pull yourself together. You're a big girl, no crying.'

'I'm sorry,' sniffs Belinda.

'Is it Frank?'

'No.'

'This Duke business?'

'No, although I do wish that would stop. The papers are all making out Teddy and I are bloody engaged now.'

'Then what?'

Belinda gives a long drawn-out sigh.

'It's this stupid antenatal class. All these north London Stepford wives and their bland, boring husbands. You should see how much they pity me.'

'Why doesn't Frank go with you?'

'I haven't asked him to.'

JoJo grunts. She can't really see Frank doing breathing exercises with the other mummies and daddies. He was more of a cigar-in-the-waiting-room kind of man.

'I would go by myself,' says Belinda, 'but I'm scared I'll jinx everything. I'm convinced I'm doing it all wrong as it is.'

'Can't you take your mother?'

'She's not well. And anyway, she doesn't approve.'

'Of antenatal classes?'

'Of the baby. Of Frank too. Of anything really.'

JoJo thinks of Frank, tucked up serenely in their bed, and fights the impulse to go tip a pint glass of water over him. *He should be taking more responsibility*, she thinks angrily, *it was his duty*.

'I'll talk to Frank,' JoJo says, clearing her throat, although how she'd bring it up without blowing her cover, she had no idea. She was basically a double agent in her own life. 'Leave it with me.'

'Please don't,' says Belinda anxiously. 'It's fine, you're right – I'll sleep on it. Everything will be better in the morning…'

'What's the problem now?'

'You know what Frank's like. It's almost worse when he takes an interest. And really, he's doing his bit: he's buying vitamins and reading books.' This is news to JoJo, and she feels a tight pinch in her side. 'I needed to vent and now I feel better, so thank…'

'When's the class?' JoJo finds herself saying.

There's a slight pause.

'On Saturday.'

'What time?'

'One o'clock, but…'

'I don't think I'm doing anything on Saturday.'

'JoJo, I didn't mean…'

'Nonsense! If you give me the details, I can meet you there.'

'That's… really… are you sure?'

'Of course, but Belinda?'

'Yes?'

'You'll owe me one.'

*

Adam returns to the corner office in a daze. He checks the time on his phone: it's a few minutes past midnight – all the adrenaline from his encounter with Cara has drained from his body now and he feels sluggish and tired. Peeking through the blinds, he tries to spot the new cameras (he can't see any, but that's the point – there might be one trained on him this very minute) before recoiling from the window and nervously sitting down at the desk. Turning on the computer, Adam finds he can still access local files, but the intranet now has an ominous new security page (and his old login details don't work).

To calm himself, Adam opens one of the Excel spreadsheets from the pile of documents on the desktop. He scrolls down the long list of numbers and notes – he remembers this one, he'd changed 'Valution Pint' to 'Valuation Point' and 'Anal Management Charge' to the markedly more appropriate 'Annual Management Charge'. He'd also tweaked the font (Verdana was so uninviting, Arial worked much better on the page) and tidied up the alignment. The row numbers speed away – 5,645, 10,193, 15,022 – until he reaches the end of the data list. Here, he stops. At the bottom of the spreadsheet, on the last line of the column, someone has written: 'Hello?'

Adam stares at the innocuous word for a very long time, so long in fact, black spots start to blur his vision. He clicks the cell in the next column – the black spots in his eyes fading to a bruised purple. 'Hi' he types, saving the changes, closing the document and shutting down the computer.

He sits staring at the wall. What has he done? A grenade had been thrown at his feet, and instead of running for cover, he'd ignored it and lobbed another one back. Something was about to detonate. The only question was – when?

*

It happened most nights between three and four – the racing heart, the sweating, the tightening of her chest. Strangely, it was worse if Frank stayed. During the weeks when JoJo was alone, at least she could walk the length of the house, or turn on the World Service to distract herself until she was so drowsy, this new bout of sleep anaesthetised her completely. With Frank beside her, JoJo was forced to lie still – he was a deep sleeper, true, but the risk of accidentally waking him was too great. There could be no witnesses in this secret, shameful place...

Her father, of course. His death when JoJo was six. Her mother's grief and resentment; the farm slipping into disrepair. Leaving South Africa without saying goodbye to her family, not properly. Flying on an aeroplane for the first time: the adrenaline, the fear and the deep sense of *what now?* The rogue's gallery of men who hurt her – or tried to – before she developed tough, rubbery skin. The indifference of the doctor bearing news after JoJo's hysterectomy. Everyone who labelled her 'great fun' or 'feisty' at parties, but neglected to invite her again. And the people (almost always women) who called her 'insensitive' or 'heartless' to her face, when JoJo was only protecting herself from an *ocean* of emotions. 'You handled that so well,' others would say, more recently. 'I would have gone to pieces...' *Come and stand at the foot of my bed each night,* JoJo felt like screaming, *and then see!*

But mainly it was Frank. She'd been so careful not to fall apart, she'd never cried, not once – it wasn't seemly, her mother would not have approved, she didn't want to appear broken – but she was, oh she was, and it was only here, wilfully paralysed in the dark, that her truest anger appeared. It would build then, furiously – everything Frank had done to her, the betrayal! – and here she was, lying next to him as if none of it had happened. JoJo wanted to beat him with her fists, beat herself, tear at her chest and wail. How could she think so little of herself to try and win back this *liar*? Her blood boils! She seethes! Her feet arch and her fingernails almost cut the skin in the fists of her hands. JoJo wants to curl into a ball, and for her mother, and grandmother, and all of her female relatives going back generations, to coddle her in their arms. She imagines death. She imagines the ground swallowing her whole. This is how it goes, almost every night.

But now, a new image creeps in from JoJo's subconscious. It takes a few moments for her to figure out who the hell this man is. Some old flame perhaps, sent to torture her? But no – it's the *Duke*, she realises. Belinda's closeted Duke. JoJo's seen so many photos of him – always smiling, as if the viewer has stumbled upon some wondrous moment, the Duke clutching the hand of a pretty, well-dressed young woman – the images are burned into her brain. But why him? What demon does he represent? And then she understands – it's his eyes. The 'aren't-we-having-fun-ness' trying desperately to mask the deceit. Just like Frank, when he came home a little too jolly, a little too 'everything-is-fine' – his eyes giving him away before JoJo found the note in his wallet, before there was even an inkling of suspicion. In every photo, the Duke has this exact same expression. JoJo thinks of his lover then – the son of the Sheik – and what he must see in those photos; the defence and the apology all rolled into one. *It's not really happening. I'm sorry, it's not really happening.* But it was, it was! The foolish Duke, his poor secret lover! And JoJo knew how ridiculous it was to cry over strangers, especially ones who could afford to buy a Caribbean island – this was all a hysterical projection – but it's easier to cry over the tragedy of others, especially in the seething darkness. And so JoJo sobs for these two men playing out their games of deception, and finally, for herself, and sometimes even for Frank, the tears streaming down either side of her face, JoJo unable to move and wipe them, hoping against hope that her pillow will be dry by sunrise.

*

A foreign noise jerks Dylan awake. Illuminating the corner of his bedroom is an odd beam of light and his brain takes a few moments to register its meaning. *The Janelle phone*! He jumps out of bed and snatches it off his chest of drawers – he's shaking, he's so excited. The text message reads:

Oh, Dylan, why is this happening to me?

Dylan writes:

What's happening?

Five minutes go by. They are the longest five minutes Dylan has ever experienced in his life.

The phone beeps.

I'm scared.

Of what?

He sits on his bed, waiting for a response, but after twenty minutes he climbs back into bed to keep warm, and the next thing he knows, it's morning.

CHAPTER TWELVE

Not wanting to tempt fate twice, they make their journey by train this time, boarding at Marylebone station with coffees, pastries and an ecologically irresponsible number of the Saturday papers. Once on the carriage, they snag a table by a window and settle down, still wearing their coats and scarves to ward off the late November cold.

Neither has slept well, so as the train pulls away from the station, they huddle together, eyes closed, occasionally mustering up the strength to take sips of their coffees. Daisy imagines she'll sleep, but before she can nod off, they're disturbed by a gang of train-walkers roaming the aisles for better seats, laughing and banging the carriage door as they go. *Maybe just as well*, she thinks, sitting up. Last night, she'd been visited by a spectral Cara, her voice ringing in Daisy's ears like Marley's ghost: *'I told him it was too soon. We'd only been going out for a few months… too soon! Too sooooon!'* Dream Daisy had phoned Dream Chris in a panic, but he'd never picked up or returned any of her calls, and when she'd tried to message him instead, the buttons were wrong, the vowels all Egyptian hieroglyphs, only adding to her anxiety. *Why was he ignoring her?* she'd thought. *What if Cara was right? And could the cat sphinx symbol be an 'a' or possibly an 'i'?*

Chris is staring out the window, a dopey expression on his face. Daisy puts aside her unsettling dream and takes a moment to appreciate how lucky she is to have fallen for one of the *nice boys* finally. She wants to squeeze his ribs, or take a bite out of his freshly shaven jaw.

'We should've brought a hip flask,' Chris says in a hoarse voice, turning to meet her gaze.

'And arrive half-cut? No, thank you!'

Chris shrugs and faces the window again.

'What are they like?' asks Daisy.

'Don't want to ruin the surprise.'

She is quiet for a second, before asking coaxingly: 'Are you more like your mum or dad?'

'My dad, I guess.'

'I bet you look like him.'

This was only an assumption, as there were no family photos anywhere in his flat (not that Daisy had snooped – okay, yes, she'd snooped).

Chris doesn't respond – Daisy wants to grab his lovely jaw and give it a good yank. Instead, she tries a slightly different tack:

'When was the last time you visited them?'

'Hold on, you have an eyelash,' he says.

Daisy knows all of Chris's avoidance techniques by now, but she lets him gently scrape the inside of her eye with his finger and hold it out to her.

'Make a wish.'

She can't see anything, but Daisy dutifully blows on his finger.

I'm about to meet your parents, she screams in her head as the imaginary eyelash flutters away, *and you've not told me anything! Not one thing!*

The train chugs on through the outer boroughs. Chris takes a bite of his Chelsea bun and reads their horoscopes aloud from all the papers. Mystic Meg tells Daisy, a Taurus, to 'take a closer look at relationships and reassess them on both an emotional and practical level,' ('Gulp,' says Chris), while *The Telegraph* suggests it might be time to 'stop putting off difficult decisions.' Chris, an Aries, is 'going on a journey,' (full marks), but shouldn't 'set too many expectations,' or he'll 'find [himself] in dangerous water,' (ominous). And with 'Pluto at odds with Uranus' (unfortunate), 'things may not go to plan.'

'We should call for a live personal consultation,' Chris says. 'It's only seventy-seven pence per minute.'

Daisy snorts: 'And ask why their predictions are all so different?'

Chris folds the newspaper and places it on the table.

'The real art is figuring out which ones are genuine.'

'The horoscopes with good news, you mean?'

'Bingo,' he says, the 'O' developing into a long yawn.

The rest of the hour passes in a similar dozy fashion, interrupted only by the ticket inspector, and their bladders. Their arrival at their destination – Aylesbury (a market town an hour out of London) – catches them off guard, and they have to rush to make it off the train in time.

It's bitter outside. Three cars wait in the small car park, and from one especially shiny Mercedes steps a sandy-haired man in a dark blue shirt and pressed trousers.

'Here we go,' says Chris under his breath, squeezing Daisy's hand.

'Christopher!' the man calls.

'Dad!'

The two men hug and slap each other's backs (a good sign, thinks Daisy) and then Chris's father – introducing himself as Jack – sticks out his hand rather formally. Daisy's prediction was right – Chris does look like his father: taller, less crinkly, and without the frosting of dandruff, but otherwise a carbon copy. She shakes Jack's hand, but also opts for a simultaneous cheek-kiss, somehow managing, as she leans forward, to pull his clasped hand into her cleavage. *Classy*, she thinks, as Chris opens the rear door of the Mercedes for her, *good start.*

Inside the car, Daisy realises Chris is sitting up front with his father. *Of course*, she thinks, *probably doesn't want his dad to feel like the chauffeur* – but she can't help feeling like a wayward child abandoned in the rear of the saloon.

'This your first time to Aylesbury, Daisy?' asks Jack as they set off.

'It is,' she replies. 'Seems lovely,' she adds charitably, as they've barely left the station.

'Looks can be deceiving. We're having a huge problem with the gypsies at the moment.'

'Dad…'

'What? It's a fact.'

'We don't call them gypsies anymore.'

'Travellers then. Not that they do much of that. Stay-Putters would be closer to the mark.'

Rolling his eyes, Chris mouths the word 'sorry' to Daisy.

'It's pandemonium here on the weekends,' Jack says, tapping the driving wheel with his thumbs. 'The gypsies start fights with the chavs, and the skateboarders join in and beat up all the goths. It's like Romford High Street on a Saturday night.'

'When have *you* ever been to Romford?'

Jack ignores his son's question. 'Puke and blood all over the streets. Sorry, Daisy,' he says, 'I shouldn't be so vulgar with a lady in the car.'

'Let's talk about something else,' suggests Chris.

'The police are powerless,' continues Jack. 'They're too afraid of being sued by one of these louts for messing up their hair. It's mob rule, I tell you.' He shakes his head sadly. 'Mob rule.'

'I think it's a more complex issue, Dad…'

'I'd forgotten you were a human rights crusader. Daisy, did you know my son was going to run off and join the Peacekeeper Corps? – for all of about five minutes, until he realised he might catch a tropical disease or possibly be shot at. Personally, I think it was a ruse to meet Angelina Jolie – although you'd never have stood a chance with those terrible dreadlocks of yours…'

'*What?*' Daisy says, propelling her head between the gap of the front seats. 'Chris had *dreads?*'

'Glorious, they were. Flowing in the breeze like Botticelli's *Venus*. And a breeze was desirable because those things could get pretty whiffy!'

'I don't believe you,' says Daisy, laughing. 'I need to see pictures. Oh my God, do you have pictures?'

'They can be arranged,' Chris's dad replies jovially.

'It was a long time ago,' explains Chris, a strain to his voice. 'And dreads don't smell, that's a myth. Wash them once a week and they're fine.'

Daisy is still shaking her head in disbelief.

'What made *you* get *dreads*?'

'It was a cry for attention,' says Jack. 'A way to punish his weary parents.'

'I was twenty-three – I'd been travelling around Brazil. It was the thing to do.'

'There was also a dreadlocked *señorita* in the mix, if I recall correctly,' Jack says, raising an eyebrow in the rear-view mirror. 'Only a pretty woman can make a man do something *that* ridiculous. Your mother nearly had kittens, she was afraid you'd start tying yourself to trees or throwing red paint on her furs.'

They stop at a zebra crossing, abruptly, and wait for an elderly pedestrian to totter across the road.

'How is she?' Chris asks, turning down the heating as they drive on.

Daisy cranes forward a few inches.

'Your mother? Fine, fine. The same. Actually, no – she's had a rough week. The azaleas in the glasshouse all performed *hara-kiri*, en masse. They were rather festive one day and,' Jack blows a raspberry, 'gone the next.'

'How awful,' says Daisy, unsure what *hara-kiri* meant (but it sounded posh).

Jack glances at her in the rear-view mirror. 'So, Daisy, tell me everything. News. Gossip. Embarrassing stories. We never hear a peep from Christopher. Has he joined a cult?'

Daisy tries to think of something funny yet parent-friendly to share.

'No cults – but he does look a bit like Charles Manson in his new passport photo.'

'Terrifying,' says Jack, wiggling his eyebrows. 'So, how long have you lovebirds been dating?'

'Over three months now,' Daisy replies.

'Cripes, and he's brought you to meet us already! You're not pregnant, are you?'

Jack says this with a grin, but he also locks eyes with Daisy in the rear-view mirror as if waiting for an answer, so she shakes her head vigorously.

'Good-oh,' he says with a laugh that triggers a rattling smoker's cough. He winds down the window to let in some air.

They've left the town of Aylesbury now and are driving along a country road. The sky is dark grey, rain seems imminent. Somehow the muted light makes the fields appear more vivid and subdued at the same time.

'Must have been lovely to grow up in the countryside,' Daisy says, after a while.

'If you like mud and tractors,' Chris replies, 'and anyway, I didn't grow up here.'

'We shipped him off to boarding school when he was five and he still holds a grudge. Can you reason with him, Daisy? There was asbestos in the roofing, we probably saved his life by sending him to Sandicott.'

'You both seem alright.'

'Your mother is eighty per cent asbestos to start with. I, on the other hand…' Jack gives a few comedic coughs, triggering another coughing fit. He's still hacking away when they turn into a long driveway and start their approach towards a large stately home.

Daisy's cranes forward. Framed by dramatic clouds, manicured lawns and sprawling woodland, the Georgian house is like something out of *The Wolves of Willoughby Chase*. It's huge – three storeys tall – and set on a terrace with stone steps leading up to front doors with granite archways. Chimney stacks jut from either side of the slate roof, while ivy clambers across the sepia bricks. To the west of the house sits a walled garden, and beyond this – poking through the trees – the impressive dome of what must be the glasshouse with the hoity-toity azaleas. *Bloody hell*, thinks Daisy.

'It's not too late,' Jack says, clearing his throat. 'Give me a sign and I'll turn the car around. I can say your train was cancelled.' Getting no response, he floors the accelerator instead and they race along the final stretch of driveway, skidding onto the terrace with a disturbingly loud crunch of gravel.

A woman – grey-blonde, slender, dressed in tasteful neutral colours (not quite pearls and a twinset, but the Buckinghamshire equivalent) – appears from inside the house and, after scowling at the clouds of dust, makes her way down the steps, opening Daisy's door.

'Welcome to Farleford Manor,' she says, peering down at Daisy, who is trying to pull her dress over her knees.

As if on cue, a clap of thunder rumbles across the sky.

*

The gist of it was this: our body takes in food and water and converts them into a bounty of excretions: sweat, tears, mucus, saliva, semen, vaginal fluids, urine, pus – you name it, we produce it. A pregnant woman also begins to secrete a new edible substance – a cocktail of fatty acids, protein and antibodies – which, when fed to her newly-born offspring, is converted into other bodily fluids; predominantly, shit. This JoJo knows. She'd not grown up on a dairy farm in Johannesburg without learning a thing or two.

What she had never really considered, however, is that a mother's choice of foods can affect not only her own, but also her child's excrement. Citrus fruits might turn an infant's stomach and produce bouts of diarrhoea, bitter greens could keep the baby awake all night with cramps and wind, coffee was a scatological game of roulette. JoJo found herself marvelling at the digestive process – food filtered through not one, but two organisms, like human sieves, one atop the other.

Belinda is diligently writing everything down in her handsome leather notepad (she is, JoJo is realising, quite the girlie swot). JoJo, on the other hand, is not scribbling away with a pen, or tapping away on an iPad like everyone else in the classroom. She even refused the loan of a pencil offered to her by Mary, the heavy-set midwife leading today's session. Instead, JoJo sits on the mat with an air of quietude, silently willing her legs not to fall asleep.

A woman with a ponytail, seated at the front of the room, puts up her hand. JoJo knows exactly the type of person she is by her posture (her back so erect it's somehow aggressive) and the velocity with which the woman's hand shoots into the air.

'What about alcohol?' she asks in a tone that seems to convey concern, condescension and judgement all at once.

Mary sits taller herself, or as best she can on the mat.

'Anything you consume – including medications and alcohol – will be passed on through the breast milk, so…'

Ponytail woman's hand shoots up again. Her husband, beside her, rubs the small of her back.

'I meant light drinking,' she says, adding dismissively: 'Studies show two units a week is quite safe. My question is – should red wine be avoided because of the tannins? I've read somewhere that clear spirits are best.'

Mary frowns. 'I'm not sure we can say any amount of alcohol is one hundred per cent safe.'

The woman looks at her husband and back at Mary as if she can't believe her ears. 'I think it's pretty well established by *the medical industry* that two units a week is harmless.'

'To be honest, we don't really know what effect alcohol has on a growing baby.'

'But *studies show* that women who drink occasionally have very similar pregnancies to those who abstain.'

'Is she serious?' JoJo mutters to Belinda under her breath. 'I mean, have a drink, don't have a drink – but this woman's only talking because she likes the sound of her own voice.'

Mary shifts her weight forward and then sits back on her knees. 'Perhaps I can give you some extra reading after the class?'

The woman shrugs. 'Doesn't bother me. I've been teetotal for years, haven't I?' Her husband nods his head. 'I only assumed everyone here would want the *correct information*.'

'I need a drink just listening to her talk,' JoJo says more audibly, provoking titters from some of the other couples.

Ponytail woman snaps around with such a fierce expression, the titters stop immediately. JoJo feels the anger rise in her throat, but she doesn't want to retaliate and embarrass Belinda – and it's a new and puzzling sensation.

Another woman, with a belly the size of a Ford Fiesta, asks a question about spicy food, but before Mary can answer, Ponytail interrupts. 'Spicy food is out,' she says emphatically. 'It can give them *severe abdominal pain*.'

JoJo snorts. 'Rubbish!'

Ponytail whips round to face JoJo again. She's in her mid-thirties, and has a scrubbed, shiny complexion – like a piece of wax fruit.

'You can't tell me every baby in India is in pain after breast-feeding?' JoJo says.

Ponytail seems momentarily taken off guard.

'It's different in Asian countries – you have to factor in water quality…'

'JoJo's right,' Mary interjects, 'and if your breast milk sometimes tastes different, after eating a curry, for example, your baby might get more used to trying a range of foods when they go onto solids.'

'You wouldn't want to eat spicy food every day though,' Ponytail says defensively.

'Maybe not every day,' concedes Mary. 'Variation is important.'

Another woman, in a bright green shawl, puts up her hand.

'So, should you eat spicy food or not? I mean, is it something we should introduce, or should we only include it if we're eating it already?'

JoJo watches Belinda write down 'spicy food?' and underline it. *Nerd*, she thinks.

'Did you eat spicy food when you were pregnant?'

It takes JoJo a moment to realise the woman is directing the question at her.

'Things were different in my day,' she says, offhandedly. 'Spicy foods weren't as popular.'

There's nodding across the classroom.

'And what would you say are your tips?'

'Tips on what?' asks JoJo.

'On having a baby,' replies the woman in the green shawl.

There is what can only be described as a pregnant pause. JoJo glances at Mary, but she smiles encouragingly, obviously pleased to have someone else in the spotlight. Belinda looks as if she's about to say something, so JoJo starts:

'I'm no expert,' she begins – Belinda's eyes widening – 'but if you ask me, a nasty disease is taking hold and it's putting your unborn baby at risk.' JoJo pauses. *Yes*, she thinks, *that's sufficiently grabbed their attention*. 'And I'm not talking about antibiotic-resistant super-bugs either,' she continues. 'Although *we* had polio, diphtheria, whooping cough – and they were really something to worry about. Once you've seen a child in an iron-lung, it puts a few things into perspective.'

JoJo wiggles her toes, trying to keep the blood circulating.

'I was in Mothercare the other week and you couldn't move for kiddie-safe this and child-protector that. An entire industry, millions of pounds every year, built on paranoia. *What if something happens?* What if it does? In my day, we prescribed a healthy dose of ignorance. The Russians might have been ready to drop the bomb, but we were still hanging out the washing and grumbling about the weather. You couldn't sit about worrying *what if*. You had to carry on, despite everything. There was no twenty-four-hour news. None of this Googling every ache and pain and diagnosing yourself with leprosy. We pride ourselves on living in the Information Age, but knowledge is only powerful if it doesn't cripple you with fear.'

Ponytail's hand flies into the air. 'What are we supposed to do then?' she asks in a shrill voice. 'Bury our heads in the sand?'

In wet cement, more like, thinks JoJo.

'Of course not,' she says, her faux-grandmother smile at maximum wattage. 'That's not what I'm suggesting at all.' The smile is making her left cheek twitch. 'Have you heard of the nocebo effect?'

Ponytail is unsure.

'Is it like the *placebo* effect?' she asks.

'Close, my dear – it's the opposite. *No*cebo is something completely safe that creates a harmful effect because people *believe* it will hurt them. Mind over matter. You imagine eating a slice of bread or drinking a glass of milk will give you a migraine, so it does. It's completely psychogenic, but very powerful. And now it's affecting our unborn children.'

'What should we do?' asks green shawl woman nervously.

JoJo uncrosses and re-crosses her legs.

'It's easy,' she says. 'Worry less. All of our bodies are different. Take spicy food – maybe you can eat chillies, maybe they rip a hole right through you. But if you eat them thinking they might hurt you, *research shows*,' she nods pointedly at Ponytail woman, 'that yes, they're more likely to. I'm not saying don't use your common sense, but a certain level of cluelessness might actually be healthy for you *and* your baby.'

With some satisfaction, JoJo observes several of the women are furiously taking notes.

*

As Chris pulls out her chair, Daisy feels herself bob a curtsey. *Stop it*, she commands herself, *you are not in a Jane Austen novel. Behave normally.* The opulent dining room where they're about to have lunch isn't helping: the grand wall panelling, the fancy plasterwork, the silver candelabras (candlelight has never felt more baroque, especially with the rain pelting against the windows).

'The chicken's lovely, so juicy,' Daisy says, to break the silence after they've been eating for a few minutes.

Chris's mother, Evelyn – the woman who met them at the car – smiles weakly.

'It's guinea fowl,' she says.

'I don't think I've ever had guinea fowl.'

'It's not a proper meal unless you've throttled at least one exotic bird,' Chris says, taking a sip of his wine.

Evelyn contemplates her son for a moment.

'You've lost weight,' she says.

'I don't think so. If anything, I've put weight on.'

'No, you seem gaunt. Are you taking care of yourself?'

Chris takes another, larger sip of his wine.

'Daisy's from north London,' he says, as if introducing her for the first time.

'Were you born in London?' asks Evelyn.

'Yes,' Daisy replies, unsure if this is a good thing or not. 'I grew up in Dollis Hill.'

'A real Londoner, eh?' Jack says, raising his eyebrows.

Evelyn sits back in her chair, holding the stem of her wine glass.

'I do love London,' she says. 'Such a vibrant city. Much nicer than Paris or New York. New York is full of overly friendly Americans, and Paris – the French can be abrupt – but London… London lets you be.'

'I've never thought about it like that,' says Daisy.

'Only if you're wealthy,' Chris says, wiping his mouth with a napkin. 'London is basically controlled by a few wealthy old boys who all went to school together – everyone else is picking at scraps. And don't get me started on the Royal Family.'

'Every city has its problems,' says Evelyn coolly. 'And anyway, the monarchy is a carnival act these days.'

'One funded by millions of pounds of tax payers' money,' Chris says into his glass.

'The Parsons are moving away,' announces Jack, as he chomps on a guinea fowl bone.

Chris is shocked by this news.

'Really? Why?'

'Couldn't afford to keep their place up. They even went on one of those country house restoration TV shows where the lady comes over and makes you sell your furniture, and tries to charge people to traipse around the gardens on a weekend, but it didn't help.'

'Where are they moving to?'

'In with their daughter.'

'They're moving in with *Susie*?' Something about the way Chris says Susie makes Daisy's jealousy muscle tense up. 'Why don't they buy a smaller house?'

'Their business went bust, hit them pretty hard financially. Sold the land first, but had to let the house go too. Poor them!'

'Poor Susie, more like!' Chris says. He turns to Daisy. 'They're our neighbours on the east side,' he explains. 'Susie and I used to ride horses together.'

'She's a lawyer now, in Bath,' adds Evelyn.

'How nice,' Daisy replies, picturing Susie – bronzed and beautiful – riding side-saddle on a white stallion, her reins in one hand and a law degree in the other.

'And poor Theodore in all the papers,' Jack says. 'He can't seem to catch a break.'

'The Duke of Buckinghamshire,' Chris explains to Daisy. 'Our families are friends.' She raises her eyebrows, impressed.

'Doesn't seem to be able to find a nice girl,' Jack continues. 'They all seem to rat him out to the tabloids after one night of passion.'

'Not at the dining table,' rebukes Evelyn.

'Yes, Teddy's a real heartbreaker,' says Chris, covertly winking at Daisy. 'No woman can possibly tame him…'

Daisy has no idea what the wink means, but it feels like she's missing the joke, so after a short lull, she changes the subject.

'What was Chris like as a boy?' she asks brightly.

Evelyn considers this question.

'He was a lovely child, quite serious. I remember one time, we lost him – not completely, we knew he was in the house somewhere – this was before we had the renovations, years back. He must have been two. We spent an hour calling for him, and then we found him, asleep in a pile of clothing. It was like a Caravaggio painting of Cupid. I couldn't disturb him, I just had to sit and wait until he woke up.' She turns to her son. 'How quickly they grow up.'

'Whenever I watch Chris sleeping, it creeps him out,' Daisy says, helping herself to some more potato dauphinoise. 'To be fair, I do stand over him holding a kitchen knife.'

'Ho-ho!' says Jack, chuckling.

*

The couples are dispersed around the room to work on mindfulness breathing exercises, with partners instructed to hold the mothers in their laps, using a cushion for support. After some awkwardness, JoJo and Belinda shuffle into a physical approximation of the other couples, with Belinda's head more or less resting on JoJo's groin.

'So, that's your answer to child rearing?' Belinda's says once they're settled, quietly enough so no one else can hear. 'Keep calm and carry on?'

'These women are so highly strung,' scoffs JoJo, 'the biggest risk to their health is *spontaneous combustion*.'

Belinda throws her a withering look.

'And to think, you were very nearly a doctor.'

Speechless, JoJo stares at her.

'Frank told me you went to Imperial College,' she explains.

JoJo tries to move her legs, but she's pinned under the weight of Belinda's massive head.

'That was not Frank's information to give,' she says in a low voice.

'If it's any consolation, he took some persuading.'

'But that didn't stop you?'

'It's my job to ask questions,' replies Belinda, unfazed. 'And I was curious why you never had your own career. Also,' she says, breathing in through her nose and out through her mouth as per the exercise, 'when you have a baby resting on your internal organs, you tend to be less tactful.'

'What else did he tell you?'

'You were twenty-nine and finished the first year, but didn't go back for a second.' Belinda shuffles up so her head is pressed even further into JoJo's groin. 'I think you'd have been brilliant. Straight-talking. Shooting from the hip. My doctor's an absolute idiot, I can't get a sensible word out of him. They undergo a personality bypass to graduate these days.'

JoJo clenches and releases her jaw.

'What made you go?' asks Belinda.

'Why does anyone go?' she snaps.

'There can't have been many other women in your class?'

'No, I was quite the trailblazer – blazing a trail all the way from the admissions office, right back out onto the street again.'

Belinda's upside-down forehead frowns. 'Getting into Imperial is an achievement in itself.'

'*No pride in failure*, as my mother would have said.'

'But you passed the first year?'

'I would have been thirty-five by the time I had a degree. Another two years of foundation, three for specialty training – I'd be looking down the barrel of my forties by then. Medicine is a young person's game. It was hard enough sitting in a room full of hyperactive children in my twenties, watching them all jostle for attention. And they didn't exactly like the competition. I've a good brain for facts and figures. I'm not exactly squeamish. Some of those boys were afraid of their own shadows. They dropped like flies during our first dissection – you had to watch your feet.'

'I can't believe a room full of spotty boys would have made you leave,' Belinda says. 'You'd have eaten them for breakfast. And twenty-nine isn't that old.'

'It was a lot of things.'

'Was it Frank?'

'Frank? No, he couldn't wait to have a doctor for a wife.' JoJo takes a deep breath, releasing it in one long huff. 'When I started at Imperial, there wasn't even a women's toilet in the building – I had to cross over to the secretary's office and use theirs. It was a different time. We were told no self-respecting man was going to let a woman near him with a stethoscope – let alone a scalpel – and my classmates never let me forget it. I opened my bag once and found a severed penis inside. One of them must have visited the morgue. They thought it was hilarious.'

'Couldn't you have told the professors?'

'They were even worse. There was one – Patterson, his name was: horrible man, breath like turpentine – had a "reputation with the nurses". That's what they called it back in those days. He tried it on with me in his office, and I knocked back his advances – using the pointy end of my knee. But I knew if I told Frank, he would overreact. You know what he's like, all his bluff and blunder. And there was a slight chance he might actually try and kill the man. Patterson wasn't going to make things easy for me either. So, I left.'

Belinda is quiet for a moment. She's about to say something, when JoJo holds up her hand.

'It's in the past,' she says firmly, 'let's leave it there.'

From the other side of the classroom comes the voice of Mary locked in a heated debate with Ponytail woman.

'Someone should go and save her,' JoJo says, shaking her head.

Belinda chuckles in response.

JoJo surveys the couples around the room: 'You're much smaller than the other women here,' she notes, thoughtfully.

'Don't worry, I'll get bigger.' Belinda props herself up on one elbow. 'My doctor suggested I come to classes earlier as a precaution.' JoJo gives her a quizzical look and Belinda shakes her head. 'There's a slightly greater risk I might have complications. Everything's fine,' she adds quickly. 'The doctors are being overcautious. It's standard practice when...' She stops short. 'When you're having twins.'

JoJo lets out another long breath.

'I wanted to find the right time to tell you,' Belinda says, her eyes like saucers. 'You should have seen Frank at the ultrasound – slapping the doctor on the back, offering everyone cigars... Are you okay?'

'I'm fine,' JoJo says, getting jerkily to her feet. 'It's hot in here – I need some air.'

'Do you want me to...?'

'You've done enough,' hisses JoJo, as she bolts for the classroom door.

*

With lunch over, Jack enlists his son to help him in the shed, leaving the 'girls' to tidy up. Ignoring this slight, Daisy stacks the dirty dishes with Evelyn, and follows her through a narrow hallway. They arrive in a large eighties-style kitchen, considerably less impressive than the dining room.

'Shall I stack the dishwasher?' Daisy asks, after they've made a few trips.

'I'd rather not,' replies Evelyn. 'We'll do them ourselves.'

She runs a hot sink and, without donning gloves, starts to wash up, checking each dish carefully and passing it to Daisy to dry. They work together in silence, staring out onto the wet gardens. The rain has stopped and a wind has come up, sending the dark clouds racing overhead.

'Christopher tells me you work in fashion,' Evelyn says, passing Daisy a large soapy plate.

'I make props and things for photo shoots,' she replies, wiping the bubbles with her tea towel. 'It's not very glamorous. People always assume it must be glamorous if you work in fashion.'

'I imagine it's a business, like anything else.'

'Exactly. Everyone's very tight with money – no one gets to take home designer dresses anymore. I even had my bag searched once. Not just *my* bag, by the way – everyone's was searched. The designer was paranoid and it was all a misunderstanding. Anyway, they didn't find anything.'

You're rambling, Daisy, she thinks to herself.

'And where do you see yourself in, say, five years?' Evelyn asks, rinsing a wine glass and placing it on the drying rack.

'I don't know. Maybe working in New York? I'm not conventionally very ambitious – I sort of fell into this job. I helped out a friend one day, and it all went from there. I actually studied biology at Warwick.'

'Really? Now that is interesting.'

'I wanted to be a marine biologist, but I get seasick even looking at a picture of a boat.'

'Don't you want to do something with your degree?'

'Not right now – it's something I can always fall back on.'

'You're really very interesting, Daisy. You have a proper grasp on life. And so young.'

Daisy feels herself start to blush. She picks up a handful of washed cutlery without realising how hot they are from the sink, and almost drops them.

'Christopher was never ambitious,' Evelyn says, scrubbing one of the serving bowls. 'He was always distracted so easily. Music lessons, rugby, football, choir – he tried everything, but nothing would stick.'

'That's one of the reasons I like Chris. His energy is very…' Daisy searches for the right word: '*encompassing.*'

'It makes me sad to think of him wasting his skills. He has talent – he could become something, take part in the world for once. But Christopher's like his father – they're both big kids. They'll be in the greenhouse now, getting stoned together.'

Getting what? thinks Daisy, startled.

'Marijuana,' Evelyn says, reading her expression. 'Jack grows it for me. I have a bad hip and I'm too young for a replacement, so I have to wait for my operation until I can literally no longer walk. Unfortunately, the pain gets the better of me, so Jack started growing a few plants. He bought the seeds off one of the local boys in the village.'

Daisy doesn't know how to respond. 'I'm sorry about your hip,' she says finally.

'Thank you. It's hereditary. My mother would have had the same issue if she'd lived long enough. Chris will have it too, regrettably. Which is why I don't use the dishwasher any more. I can't bend down, you see?'

Daisy shakes her head, annoyed with herself: 'I should've come earlier and helped you make lunch.'

'What?' Evelyn says with a laugh. 'I didn't cook lunch, Daisy – I had it delivered. I've never enjoyed cooking – don't have the knack for it. The boys tease me about it mercilessly.'

They fall into a slightly awkward silence again.

'Christopher was always a lovely child,' Evelyn says at last, finishing the final serving bowl and pulling the plug, 'but he went astray when he was younger. I don't know how much he's told you, but he made some bad choices. We all do as teenagers, that goes without saying – but in his case, they had consequences.'

Daisy can't imagine her loveable goof with a dark past, but she remembers the metal plate in his shoulder, the haunted look in his eyes as she touched it, and the new image of Chris that forms in her mind scares her.

'Meeting you is a step in the right direction, Daisy. I can see how much he cares for you. He's hard on himself. And as a result, he can be very hard on us too. But Christopher is still missing something, and I'm afraid when the time comes…' Evelyn smiles again, a sad faraway smile. *Odette*, thinks Daisy, *cursed to become a swan each day, returning to human form at dusk.*

Outside, the clouds part for a brief second, exposing a pale beam of light before vanishing again for good.

*

JoJo throws open the front doors of the building with such force, they crash against the sides of the alcove, startling a group of pigeons. Her impulse is to flee, but she has to pause at the gate to get her bearings. Belinda had ended up driving them here and JoJo realises she hasn't paid enough attention to their route in the car. They're in north London, near Hampstead, but that could be anywhere. Chalk Farm? Golders Green? The road is mostly residential and none of the shops – a small French restaurant, a pizzeria and a dry cleaners – appear open. No bus stop either. If she starts walking in any old direction, there's no telling where she'll end up. She ferrets in her handbag, but her battered mini *A–Z* is missing. She could call a cab, but how long will that take? JoJo wants away this very second.

Twins! The word comes back to her like whiplash. Two little Franks running around. Twice the ignominy. And what is JoJo doing? Practising *breathing exercises* with the woman. *I'm an idiot*, she fumes – *no, worse than that: an idiot who thinks she's being shrewd.*

Crossing the road, she peers through the window of the dry cleaners. A note is stuck on the door: 'Back in ten minutes', so JoJo heads back over the road and takes out her phone.

'JoJo!' She glances up to see Belinda at the main doors. 'Do you want me to drive you home?'

'I'm fine. Go back inside.'

Belinda seems stricken, and for an instant JoJo regrets running out of the class. Pregnant women seem to elicit an involuntary sympathetic response, and JoJo doesn't like it.

'I want to thank you for coming today. If there's something I can do…'

'You don't owe me anything,' JoJo says, with a wave of her hand.

'Yes, but if I can…'

Something distracts Belinda, and JoJo turns to see a man walking towards them along the footpath, holding a camera with a long lens attached. In one swift movement, he lifts the camera to his eye and takes a succession of pictures with a whirring *click-click-click*.

'What's he doing?' asks JoJo, flabbergasted. 'Is he taking photos of the building?'

'He's a snapper for *The Sun*,' Belinda replies, stony-faced.

'A what?'

'A pap.' Nothing Belinda is saying has computed yet. 'It's this silly thing with Teddy, the Duke – that's in all the papers, and now I have one of these morons tailing me every time I leave the house. Hey, mate!' she yells at the man, 'why don't you do us both a favour and get a proper job?'

'In journalism? No such thing!' he calls back. 'Why don't you do me a favour and give us a smile, dahling?' Belinda gives him the finger and he snaps away happily. 'That's it, dahling.'

'Don't encourage him,' JoJo says, covering her hand. 'Where did you say he's going to publish these photos? In *The Sun*?'

'I doubt they'll actually print any.'

'But Frank could see them!'

'He won't,' Belinda says, but a seed of doubt creeps into her face.

JoJo starts to walk towards the man, prompting him to back off down the pavement.

'Can I have a word with you?' she calls to him.

'You can try, dahling.'

'What's your name?'

'What's yours?' he parrots back. The paparazzo is wearing a turquoise puffer jacket, black jeans and scuffed trainers, and he has dark rings under his eyes – he obviously hasn't had a good night's sleep in days.

'Leave him,' Belinda calls from behind JoJo. 'He's a bottom feeder. Not worth the hassle.'

'Cheers, love,' he responds.

'Listen here,' JoJo says angrily, 'you can't sell those pictures.'

'Just watch me.'

'Fine,' she says, stopping. 'I'll pay you a thousand pounds if you give me every roll of film. Right now.'

'Sorry, love. It's digital, *innit.*'

'A thousand pounds for the memory stick. Belinda says it's an open secret in your industry that this Duke is a homosexual.'

'Possibly…'

'She obviously can't have anything to do with him then.'

'What makes you so concerned? A grand's a lot of money…?'

JoJo preloads the next sentence in her mind, and winces at it.

'I'm her mother,' she says. 'It's my job to protect her. I'm sure even people in your line of work have mothers.'

The smarmy expression fades from the man's face.

'She's not well,' he says, and pauses. 'I don't take cheques.'

'You'll have to drive me to an ATM in that case.'

JoJo calls back to a puzzled Belinda: 'It's alright, he's going to give me a lift. I'll see you later!'

CHAPTER THIRTEEN

Welcome, at last, to the festive season, *the golden quarter…* when all good lovers fill their sacks to overflowing and London is bountiful, and bursting at the seams. Forget your woes and worries until the cold dark void of January – cast aside your thoughts of hangovers, high cholesterol and empty bank accounts – for now we shall drink! And be merry! But, most importantly, eat!

Chicken crouton lollipops and chocolate cherry cups. Sticky prawn twisters, mini kebab skewers and pulled pork stacks. Scorching mince pies, branding their mark on the roof of your mouth. Limited-edition sandwiches bursting with spurious festive fillings: tofu-turkey feast, artisanal polenta stuffing, some misguided brie. Oh, the cheese! Wagon wheels – no, tractor wheels – no, *Ferris wheels* of the stuff: Barkham Blue, Rothbury Red and a lovely Stinking Bishop. Great barrels of imported nuts – brazils, macadamia, a few gourd-like walnuts – which will sit untouched and unshelled for yet another year; or roasted chestnuts from a grubby cart behind the British Museum, slightly stale and out of season (but good enough to Instagram). Whipped winter squash, purple yam gnocchi and hot 'reindeer' pie. Braised turkey ramen, Thai ginger dumplings, Brussels sprouts with soy. Booze-soaked cakes, meats wrapped in meat, chocolate-covered everything! Eat, my friends – eat while you can! Fill your mouths and hearts with only the most tempting of morsels, pour mulled wine onto even the smallest of problems. Eat and eat again. Because, deep down, we all know that once it's gone, it's—

*

Gone. Adam stares at the empty table, crestfallen. All those vital calories – the refined sugars, the hydrogenated fats – not a single crumb of the Yule log has escaped the cleaners' purge. *Very thorough*, thinks Adam bitterly, *it's almost as if they know...*

He hovers near the closest bin, wary of the security cameras, and peers inside. Vigilance is key – he doesn't want to be discovered elbow-deep in a rubbish bag – but there's nothing in this one anyway: they've already been emptied. Stomach growling, he doubles back on himself and heads for the kitchenette.

It's been three weeks since he last stepped foot outside the building – 30,240 hermetically sealed, air-conditioned minutes. Adam knows the precise location of every edible item around the office: the packets of chewing gum, the canisters of mints, the chocolate bars, but there's not much he can eat safely – a Tic Tac here, a Rolo there – slim pickings. The communal kitchenette is the obvious destination, and boxes of long-forgotten cereal have become Adam's staple (luckily, fresh milk is plentiful and replaced daily), but the supplies of stale cornflakes and weevil-infested porridge oats are dwindling, forcing him to dip into the fresher, fancier mueslis with their flame raisins and yoghurt-coated almonds, skimming off a tablespoon at a time to avoid detection.

The refrigerator holds the greatest bounty of food, but it was also where people stored their lunch, and Adam knew from experience – people took notice if their lunch went missing. Some attrition would be blamed on the cleaners, but Adam couldn't tip the balance – it was all about stealth. His first step was to identify food that had been forgotten or abandoned (rather than simply saved for later). This was crucial. Next, came concealment – he might strategically move some chicken pasta salad behind a tub of margarine, or an apple onto another shelf – burying items in the vegetable drawers, Adam felt, would eventually arouse suspicion.

Finally, harnessing every last ounce of resolve, he would wait – if the article of food hadn't been claimed in two days, it was all his.

Adam opens the fridge now to see what's ready for harvest. A half-eaten Greggs' cheese and ham baguette, positioned behind a jar of mayonnaise, has been inching past its use-by-date for days. Shakily, he unwraps the baguette and takes a massive bite: the dough is tough, the cheese hard and the ham flavourless, but to Adam, it tastes Michelin-star good. After wolfing it down and licking his fingers, he pockets a few of the shrivelled grapes from a punnet on the second shelf and scours the fridge for anything else. Scurvy is a growing concern. Fruit is scarce, and vegetables – aside from limp brown lettuce leaves – are rare as hens' teeth. For the first time in his life, he craves broccoli, and some nights he can't sleep for visions of sautéed green beans or steamed cauliflower cooked al dente.

When Adam wasn't obsessing about his stomach, he fixated on grooming. Keeping clean was a never-ending challenge, especially because he only had the clothes he was standing up in. Using one of the disabled toilets as a makeshift laundry, Adam washed his socks on a Tuesday, his boxers on a Thursday and his shirt on Sundays to make sure everything wasn't wet at the same time. Fortunately, there was a heating vent in the toilet, but the results were crinkly at best and at worst, frustratingly slow – sometimes he had to quickly put on the damp item and wear it back to the corner office before the security guards resumed their rounds.

General hygiene was an issue too. Pirate baths left him vulnerable (what if someone knocked on the bathroom door while he was naked and dripping wet?) so he preferred to wash with a supply of cleaning wipes he'd found stashed in a cupboard. Razor blades were almost impossible to come by, so Adam had decided to let his beard grow out, keeping it trimmed. He kept his hair short too – by snipping some off every day, he could keep the shape relatively even (with only a couple of missteps – a bald patch on the first attempt, and a nicked ear on the second). The discovery of a discarded tube of toothpaste in a wastepaper basket meant Adam could brush his teeth (using a piece of paper towel wrapped around his index finger), and there was a good stock of mouthwash, and even dental floss, in the office. Despite all these efforts, he noticed a definite musky aroma emanating from his person – particularly his feet – and his suit was developing a kaleidoscope of stains that no amount of dabbing and sponging could remedy.

Still, at least it gave him something to do. Now that his access to the company Wi-Fi had been revoked after the security update, Adam had plenty of time on his hands. Books seemed the obvious answer, but they were in short supply – most were either stuffy business tomes or sports-star autobiographies (and occasionally both at once). He'd found a few works of fiction: *American Psycho*, *Infinite Jest*, *The Fountainhead*, but Adam longed for something fun and pulpy like a Grisham or a Stephen King.

Over the past twenty-one days, the biggest sacrifice hadn't been the Internet, or a hot bath, or even a good meal – it was not being able to see Cara. Adam has weighed up the pros and cons of taking a trip to the foyer to catch a glimpse of her, but he knew this was unwise, especially with Mr Maintenance still loose in the building. He had to stick to his own floor, and keep his head down. So, using the frustratingly erratic 3G on his mobile phone, Adam borrowed enough money from online payday lenders to cover rent and bills for the next couple of months. He sent a long text to Patrick, explaining he was on a business trip in Chicago and not to worry. He took meticulous notes on the activities of the cleaners. And he started to exercise again: press-ups and bench dips to work on his arms, squats for his legs. After finding a promotional yo-yo for a local gym under a desk, he practised every night until he had it mastered – walking the dog, rocking the baby, one he nicknamed 'the rat's nest' because it always tangled the string – sending it humming to the floor and back again with a flick of his wrist. He would sit for hours, in a trance-like state, not thinking about anyone or anything: not Cara, or Mr Maintenance, or his painfully empty stomach – but as soon as the rhythm of the yo-yo was broken, Adam would snap out of his daze and find himself on the fourth floor of a building overlooking St Paul's without fully understanding how he'd got there.

*

In his bedroom, Dylan rifles through his wardrobe, removing the black bomber jacket, buried deep within. When his fingers touch the leather, it's so cold and oily-feeling, it seems almost wet. The jacket had been an unexpected present from his mother two years ago, sent randomly it seemed, as it didn't coincide with his birthday and was too early for Christmas (there had been a note, which his dad offered to read out loud, and then left strategically around the flat, but Dylan had actively avoided it. What could it contain except disappointments?). When the jacket first arrived, it was comically big on him, but now Dylan tries it on in front of the wardrobe mirror. It doesn't exactly go with his *Adventure Time* pyjama bottoms, but yes – it's a good fit, the sleeves not too long at all. It was definitely an upgrade to his image – he could almost pass as a French film star from the sixties (possibly, Dylan still hadn't watched that film).

He wishes he'd remembered the jacket earlier and worn it to school the other day. Maybe it would have made him feel more confident. Dylan and his father had gone to see Mr Lacey, the Head of Year, to talk about sitting GCSEs. Mr Lacey had been very careful with his language, making sure to refer to Dylan's 'situation' and 'the circumstances we find ourselves in', never mentioning the word 'illness', and from anyone else, this might have been considered tact. From Mr Lacey, however, it meant only one thing: he still didn't believe them. The boy was making it up: his 'illness' was the result of downright laziness, bad parenting or a character flaw. Dylan had bit the inside of his mouth. *What about all the tests? The doctors, the specialists, the therapists. The weeks his father had to take off work? Why would they make that up?* After twenty-five minutes, the outcome of the meeting was this: even with his extra study, Dylan had missed too much coursework and would have to be put back a year – unless Mr Moon wanted to home-school? Mr Lacey had seemed unabashedly hopeful.

Afterwards, Dylan and his father walked through the H Block corridor, towards the car park. H Block was exactly the same: the crisp packets on the floor, the beat-up lockers, the smell of marker pens and Lynx deodorant.

'Might not be all bad,' Dylan's father had said, 'You've covered so much of the reading material, you'll be ahead of the game for once.'

Dylan had walked faster, mentally hurrying them both along. At any moment the bell might ring, and hundreds of his classmates would surge into the corridors, pushing and yelling, and either stare – or worse – completely blank him. To be invisible to your peers was to be practically worthless.

Touching the soft leather of the jacket one last time, Dylan takes off the jacket and returns it to the wardrobe, sits down at the computer desk, and launches his blog. He'd procrastinated for a week, but yesterday the words had finally started to flow:

<u>End of an Era</u>

Sorry I haven't been posting very much anymore. Truth is, I've decided to stop this blog. I still want to write, I even have a typewriter to help me now, but I want to focus on important things – not just random stuff in my life. Sometimes it feels like an echo chamber of my thoughts bouncing around my head. I know that was the point when I started the blog, to express myself, but now I need to be braver about how I communicate those thoughts. And to whom. That's the next challenge, I suppose.

Anyway, I'm going to delete everything tomorrow. Bye.
Moon over Croydon

Dylan is about to navigate away, when he notices two comments on the post:

Sorry to see you go :-) Crystal
Best of luck.. liked your blog - G

He can't believe it – actual people have left comments! Dylan feels a pang of regret, but he can't back down now. He needs to rid himself of all distractions and focus. He thinks of Janelle's note with the typewriter: 'now go get 'em'. His heart swells at the thought of her. *He was coming, Janelle!* Dylan hoped he was in time.

At the bottom of *Account Settings* is a big red 'Delete account' button. Dylan hovers the cursor over it. Should he keep the blog for posterity's sake? What if his kids wanted to see it one day? He imagines if his own father had kept a blog at his age, would he want to read it? Dylan clicks the red button and the browser churns, spitting him out onto the generic homepage.

He takes a deep breath. There's still a lot to organise. Transport, for one. The train isn't an option after his last disastrous journey (and anyway, Dylan wanted to travel in style). Whichever way he made the journey, it might be sensible to have someone with him, in case anything unexpected happened. And it obviously couldn't be his dad.

Picking up his phone, Dylan brings up his contact list. He scrolls down to C and pauses. If he opens this can of worms, there's no way to retroactively close it. Maybe he could make the trip by himself? A vision of bright blue vomit flashes into his mind…

Chris answers the call after only one ring: 'The Twilight Saga,' he trills, 'New *Moon* Rising in da house, what's up fo shizzle, my nizzle?'

Oh my God, thinks Dylan, *what have I done?*

*

JoJo puts down the phone and settles back in her armchair. She'd forgotten this feeling – the warm tingly afterglow, the buoyant hopefulness of it all. The last time she'd experienced anything like this was *decades* ago. Kicking off her shoes, JoJo rests her head so she's staring up at the ceiling, her bare feet wiggling. She's still not sure about his name though: Keith *Lepsis*. It sounded like an incurable disease.

After their altercation on the street a few weeks back, JoJo had followed Keith to his beat-up Nissan Micra, and squeezed into the front seat, kicking aside the empty fast food cartons. While he'd taken off his coat, Keith had popped his camera on the seat next to her, and JoJo considered snatching it up – and what? Sprinting off with it? Dashing it against the pavement? That wouldn't have helped anyone, not in the long run.

Once on the road, Keith had begun to quiz JoJo about her life, and two things became apparent: he was fishing to see if *Mr* JoJo was in the picture, and they had driven by at least three cash machines. Instead of finding this alarming or sleazy, JoJo began to enjoy the flirtation (making sure she didn't lower her guard too much – this was a paparazzo after all) so by the time they reached the West End she even consented to having a quick drink in a bar he knew well. And that was how JoJo, still in her antenatal class outfit, found herself drinking caipirinhas in a Salsa club until the early hours of Sunday morning (but not before JoJo made Keith fetch the camera memory stick and smash it under the foot of his bar stool). She'd eventually warmed to his looks too – yes, his eyes were deep-set, but there was a sparkle to them, and he appeared less weasely as the night wore on. At some point in their conversation, he must have mentioned he was forty-two; he never asked JoJo's age though, or mentioned her wedding ring, and she kept schtum about both.

When the evening was over, they parted without a kiss, but Keith asked for her number and surprised her a few days later by calling to arrange a second meeting (she couldn't bring herself to call it a *date*). JoJo wondered if she liked *him*, or the idea of being liked. Either way, there had been three such 'meetings' now, and the matter of her age still hadn't come up. Perhaps he was a granny chaser? She knew they existed. Or maybe he was after her money? He didn't *seem* to have an agenda when they were together. They talked about US politics, and the legalisation of prostitution, and hypocrisies in the government's stance on drugs (despite papping celebrities for the right-wing press, he was a diehard lefty), but most of all, they made each other laugh. It felt good to break free from the petty dramas of her life, to leave thoughts of Belinda and Frank far behind.

Obviously, JoJo hadn't told anyone about her *liaisons* (no, absolutely not, 'liaison' was more appalling than 'date'), but Frank, perhaps sensing a shift in their dynamic, had become uncharacteristically needy the past fortnight. She knew she was being a terrible hypocrite, but there were definite merits to having the ball in your court for a change. The small things no longer bothered her: when Frank arrived late for a meal, or if she caught the smell of perfume on his shirt, or whenever he slipped away to make a call. And really, there wasn't much to tell. JoJo had met someone interesting, and they were getting to know each other. They *had* eventually kissed, but as affairs went, it was all rather tame. And his surname was Keith *Lepsis*, for Christ's sake! It reminded JoJo of a boil that needed lancing.

She picks up her mobile – she should probably ring Belinda back at some point. After the class, Belinda left several messages – JoJo purposefully avoided her calls, sending her a text instead, explaining she was fine, just busy.

JoJo traces a crack along the plaster that runs from the light fitting all the way to the opposite corner of the room. She should really get it seen to. There was a time when Frank would have coveted a job like that, crashing around on a ladder, but not anymore – he didn't have the legs for it. Was the same true for her? If JoJo's relationship with Keith (Christ no, 'relationship' was even worse than 'liaison') evolved naturally, certain *things* would be expected. Why was she being coy? – sooner or later, they were going to *fuck*. The concept isn't completely terrifying, which comes as a sort of revelation. JoJo remembers something then – the trip to Ann Summers, her hard-won purchases – where had she put them? She never had found an ideal moment to introduce them to Frank (although he'd found the whisky and guzzled that down happily, so much for that being a pawn in her original scheme to get him drunk and jazz things up in the bedroom). Would she have put them at the back of her underwear drawer, or in a box under the bed? And did they come with their own batteries, she wonders drowsily. Talking to Keith in the afternoons (when it was safest to chat) always did this to JoJo – the conversation itself wasn't sleep-inducing, but the afterglow seemed to melt away any tension.

Yes, she'd hidden them in the drawer, she remembers now. And there were spare batteries in the kitchen. Maybe she'd have a nap first. Or then again, maybe she wouldn't.

*

At midnight, the building's heating system flipped onto standby, sending the temperature plummeting, so Adam made sure he was in his nest of coats, generating as much warmth as possible before the early morning chill. His makeshift mattress, created using foraged jumpers and cushions, didn't protect against the hard floor or getting a painful crick in his neck, and he'd often wake up shivering so much it felt like he was having a mini seizure.

Adam empties his pockets and finding the shrivelled grapes he'd taken from the fridge, throws them into his mouth as he strips down to his underwear and socks (it would be warmer to keep his clothes on, but he can't afford the wrinkles). He lies down, adjusting himself to make sure he's not visible from the doorway. Sleeping on his side, using a bundled-up leather jacket as his pillow and tucking his knees up into the foetal position works best, but tonight he can't get comfortable. It's his stomach. An almost exclusive diet of sugar and wheat (not to mention all the lactose!) is taking its toll: stomach cramps, constipation, bloating, and terrible, crippling gas.

Unable to sleep after an hour, Adam gives up, puts his clothes back on and turns on the computer. As the machine boots up, he arranges the leather jacket over both his head and the monitor (like the cape on an old-timey tripod camera) to stop the screen from leaking light and to help keep warm. When the computer's ready, he launches the master Excel document, and scrolls down to the discussion thread.

Hello?

Hi

What on earth had made Adam reply? It was an involuntary reaction, he'd told himself the following day: when someone waves, you instinctively wave back. But something else had occurred to him: what if, on some level, he'd *wanted* to get caught? He's definitely lonely and desperately craves human contact. Either way, there had been no one waiting in the office to apprehend him that evening. The security guards had continued their rounds as normal. The only follow-up from their interaction had been a new message in the Excel document:

Who is this, please?

Now Adam was caught. But something gave him pause. Adam knew the daytime owner of the office wasn't technically savvy. Maybe he didn't understand even the basics of IT security? There was only one way to find out. Under 'Who is this, please?' he had typed:

Computer support

When he'd nervously logged in the next night, a longer response was waiting:

Ah yes. Thanks for fixing mistakes. Old dog and all that.

Adam had written back:

No problem – it's my job!

And that's how it had begun.

At first, their discussions were simply operational: how to change the name of a document, or calculate a set of numbers, or remove an annoying function, and Adam was happy to oblige. But as the days progressed, they created new threads on different tabs, allowing them to have several conversations at once, and moving on to new topics: football, Formula One, the state of the economy, until they finally came round to the issue of women.

Don't get me started. Adam had written a few nights ago: There is someone, but it's complicated.

Ha. You don't know what complicated is. Came the reply the next day.

Why? Are you married? Have a girlfriend?

Yes. And yes. That's the complication. Especially as it appears I love them both.

Adam now clicks the box under this text and types:

Alright for some.

He saves this, and moves on to another discussion thread on a new tab. Yesterday, he'd found:

I never asked your name?

Adam had sweated over this for hours. Should he give a false name? Would the owner of the office not check the employee records? Finally, after running every possible scenario through his head, he'd typed:

Adam.

He scans to the bottom of the thread. Under his name, he can now see written:

Good to make your acquaintance, Adam. I'm Frank.

*

'Mister Moon?' comes the raspy voice on the other end of the phone, 'I'm outside your pick-up address.'

Dylan curses Chris. He's late and the driver is already here.

'I'm really sorry,' he says, 'I shouldn't be long, a couple of minutes…'

'Take your time. Whenever you're ready, sir.'

Dylan has never been called 'sir'. He's rarely been called 'mister'. One time, he'd received a letter addressed to 'Dylan Moon Esquire' which he'd liked so much he'd stored the envelope in his special memory box.

There's a jaunty knock on the door, sending Otis ballistic – he seems to know instinctively when it's Chris. Dylan grabs his new black rucksack, quickly checks he has everything (for the umpteenth time), and heads to the front door.

'Moon…!'

Dylan gives Chris his sternest look – they don't have time for any of his shenanigans.

'Can you take Otis' lead?'

Giving Chris something to do was always a good tactic: keep him busy. Dylan hands over the lead and Otis pants happily.

'There's something different about you?' Chris says, as Dylan locks the front door and starts down the front path. 'Have you had a haircut?'

'Come on,' Dylan calls over his shoulder, and dog and man start to follow.

'So, what's the plan, kiddo? You sounded mysterious on the phone. Are we walking or…?'

Just then, a man dressed in a smart navy suit steps out of the shiny town car, which is waiting on the side of the road, and walks around to meet them.

'Mr Moon?' he asks, opening the rear door expectantly.

'Ah, thank you,' Dylan turns to Chris. 'I thought we'd take a car this time,' he says, as nonchalantly as he can.

'This is *yours*?'

Dylan nods.

'What about Otis?' Chris stammers.

'He can come too, it's all arranged.'

Chris seems very unsure, so Dylan dives into the dark interior of the car, and a few seconds later, Otis springs inside too, followed by a sheepish Chris. The door closes and the driver walks to the front of the car, getting into the driver's seat. There's a sound of static, and a raspy voice comes over an intercom:

'Would you like to head straight to our destination, sir?'

'Yes, please,' Dylan says. 'Thank you,' he adds, into the air.

With that, they begin to glide down the street. The inside of the car is like a quilted cocoon – it makes Dylan's ears feel strange. Otis doesn't seem to like it much: he cowers at Chris's feet and whines plaintively. Sitting forward, Dylan feels for a panel under the glass divider. Sure enough, he finds one and slides it across, revealing a refrigerated hatch, which contains a row of small bottles.

'Do you want a drink?' he asks Chris, fetching himself a can of Coke. 'There's water, beer, champagne? You can help yourself, it's free.'

'Moon, what's going on?'

'We're just going for a ride,' Dylan replies, innocently.

'Going for a ride *where*? Who's paying for all this? And why are you dressed up like someone from *The Matrix*?'

'I haven't watched that movie.'

'You haven't seen *The Matrix*?' Chris shakes his head in utter disbelief. 'Moon, I'm reeling here.'

'I'll watch it online then.'

'Not about the film, about all this,' he gesticulates around his head wildly. 'The car, the champagne, the friggin' chauffeur. Has your dad won the lottery or something?'

For a moment, Dylan considers going along with this story, until Chris takes out his mobile.

'I'm going to call him…'

'Please don't!' yelps Dylan. He lets out a long sigh. 'Okay, I'll tell you. I've used the money I made from selling my Xbox. And remember the woman I told you about? We're going to visit her.'

'So, this is a *date*? Moon, I'm happy to chaperone, but I wish you'd told me first.'

'I thought you might stop me from going.'

'I won't stand in the way of true love, Moon. Where does she live?'

'North London. In Archway. Or Highgate.'

'You don't know?'

'I'm pretty sure it's Archway. I'll be able to work it out when we get there.'

Chris sits back in his seat, and stares out of the window as if lost in thought. It's disconcerting to have him so quiet. Dylan opens the can of Coke – the hiss as he pulls the tab seems to be absorbed by the car's interior.

'How's Daisy?' Dylan asks, and takes a long sip.

'She's good,' replies Chris distractedly. 'Today she's on a shoot for Vivienne Westwood.'

He falls silent again, and Dylan starts to feel about for any more secret compartments. Maybe there's a TV somewhere?

'Are you sure you don't want anything to drink?' he asks, about to close the hatch again.

'Dylan,' Chris starts in a small, serious voice that he's never used before, 'I don't know what's going on here, but you're not telling me the whole truth. And it's my job to take care of you. I could get into some very serious trouble if anything happens to you. I know what it's like, I was your age once. I got mixed up in things I shouldn't have – it's all part of growing up. But I try to treat you like an adult, and I don't think you're giving me the same respect. I want you to be straight with me, and tell me what's going on. Everything.'

Dylan stares at Chris for a moment.

'Alright,' he says, after an involuntarily burp from the fizzy Coke – and he starts the whole story, right from the top.

CHAPTER FOURTEEN

The intercom crackles.

'We're here,' announces the deadpan voice of the driver. 'Junction Road, Archway.'

Dylan peers through the window. The warmth of his breath fogs the glass and he wipes it with the sleeve of his coat, forgetting it's a nice leather jacket and probably shouldn't be used for wiping things.

Rifling through his bag, Dylan takes out a notebook stuffed with folded pieces of paper. As soon as he opens it, the sheets spill onto the floor unceremoniously.

'Where would you like me to park up, sir?'

'Can you keep driving, please?' Dylan asks into the air, as he scrambles to pick up the fallen sheets. 'As slowly as you can?'

There's no response, but the car continues at a crawl.

'Moon, which one is it?' says Chris.

'I'm looking!' snaps Dylan, winding down the window and letting in a blast of frosty air. He inspects one of his papers, which seems to be a printout of a Google Map screenshot, and, after carefully referencing it with some other of the sheets, shouts, 'Stop!' to the driver, and the car comes to an abrupt halt.

'Can you bring Otis?' Dylan asks Chris, as he swings his bag over his shoulder and opens his door.

It's a busy Saturday morning in the cafés and discount stores and Turkish minimarkets of Junction Road. The pavement bustles with December shoppers – their arms weighed down with grocery bags and early Christmas presents, the cold turning everyone's exhalations into vapour. A ridgeback dog, much larger than Otis, stops to sniff his haunch, and Otis shrinks back, tail between his legs. *Come on, boy*, thinks Chris, as he smiles at the dog's owner. *Pull yourself together.*

Dylan is engrossed in his notebook again, mumbling to himself, and Chris, moving out of the way of a tandem pushchair, is about to suggest they head somewhere less hectic – a football stadium, or Heathrow Airport perhaps – when Dylan shuts the book, points to a bakery, and starts across the road. As he steps out, he blindsides a cyclist, who narrowly swerves to miss him, swearing colourfully over his shoulder as he rides off. Otis yaps anxiously, wrapping his lead around Chris's leg, and the Number four bus thunders past, inches away.

'That's it!' cries Chris, bending down to untangle Otis, and grasping the dog to his chest with one arm. 'Take my hand.' Dylan stares at him blankly. 'I'm not joking, take my hand now.'

Very reluctantly, Dylan obeys, and together they wait, hand in hand, for a break in the traffic. The moment they reach the other side of the road, Dylan wriggles free of Chris's grip and sprints towards the bakery, but instead of heading inside, he darts into the doorway beside it.

'Which one does she live at?' asks Chris, when he and Otis catch up.

'I'm not sure,' Dylan replies, as he inspects the buzzers. None of them have names on.

'Let's ring all the buzzers and see if she answers,' Chris suggests, pressing each of the buttons in turn before Dylan can argue.

'Hello?' comes a man's voice through the speaker.

'Sorry, wrong number,' Dylan replies hurriedly.

'What now?' asks Chris. 'Moon, I'm all for grand gestures, but this isn't much of a plan, even if we have the right address. Maybe we cut our losses and head back?'

Dylan chews his lip.

'What if Janelle's being held against her will or something?' he says. 'She hasn't replied to any of my texts for days.'

Chris is about to say something glib, but Dylan has such a sincere expression on his face, he falters.

'Let's go and buy a big slice of cake,' he says instead. 'We'll sit down, have a regroup. With any luck, we might even see her walk by.'

'I've got a better idea,' Dylan says, pulling out one of the Google Map printouts from his notebook and starting down the road.

'What about the car?' Chris shouts after him.

'It'll wait for us,' Dylan yells back.

Chris and Otis follow him into a side street, and down an access road behind the shops.

'This is the back of the bakery,' Dylan says, pointing to a vent, 'so she must live in one of those flats. Can you give me a boost up? There's a window open.'

'Whoa! Stop right there,' says Chris. 'We're not breaking into someone's house, that was never part of the deal.'

'It's not her house, it's the communal stairwell.'

'There are laws against this sort of thing, Moon. What if someone thinks you're a burglar? Or worse. You're not a child anymore, this isn't a game. There could be serious repercussions.'

'What if Janelle's fallen and broken her leg? Or her ex-boyfriend has hurt her?'

'She could call an ambulance. Or the police.'

'What if she can't reach the telephone?'

'She could bang on her door until her neighbours hear.'

'What if she's unconscious?'

Chris gives a big sigh.

'I'll just see if she's there,' pleads Dylan. 'If not, I'll come straight back, I promise. You'd do the same if it were Daisy.'

Chris shakes his head, defeated.

'What am I supposed to do while I wait for you?' he asks. 'Stand here and look suspicious?'

'If anyone asks, you're walking your dog. That's why I brought Otis. Now, give me a boost.'

Resigned, Chris clasps his hands together so Dylan can get a foothold, and lifts him up.

'What's in your bag?' asks Chris. 'Bricks? You weigh a tonne!'

Dylan pulls himself onto the roof of the extension building and gets to his feet. 'Be careful!' Chris calls after him.

'I will.'

Otis jumps up, his paws against the wall, and lets out a long whine.

'I know how you feel,' says Chris, as he watches Dylan open the window and disappear inside the building.

*

It's dingy in the hallway, and smells of damp and yeast from the bakery. Two doors stand in front of Dylan, both painted magnolia white, with identical chrome handles. A quick scout up and down the staircase reveals another flat on the second floor, and one on the ground. Dylan starts downstairs, pressing his ear against the door. He hears a loud revving sound and, peeking through the keyhole, sees a massive television broadcasting motor racing to a room of black leather couches. Dylan moves on: it's too much of a man-cave to be Janelle's place – it must be the home of the guy who answered the buzzer.

Flat two appears empty and the keyhole in flat three reveals only a wall and either a small mechanical claw or an umbrella handle (but most likely an umbrella handle). Dylan heads up to the top flat, but the keyhole here is blocked.

At a loss, he walks over to the second-floor window – in the lane below Chris is busy texting on his phone, Otis is sniffing the cobblestones. He takes out his phone and checks it. No messages, no emails. Nothing.

Dylan walks back to the second-floor door. Getting to his knees, he inspects the keyhole. A key is blocking it, he realises now, which means someone must be home, and they didn't answer *their* buzzer. He tries peering underneath the door, but he can't see anything but floorboards. Remembering Otis on the cobblestones, he leans closer and gives the space under the door a tentative sniff. Immediately, he catches something – faintly – a smell he associates with Janelle, something sweet and feminine and safe. With his heart pounding, Dylan stands bolt upright and knocks on the door. He hears a creak – of furniture perhaps – and waits, but nothing happens. Even so, he has a sense that someone is on the other side of the door.

'Hello?' he ventures at last. There's no reply. 'My name's Dylan Moon. I wondered if…'

He hears a muffled voice through the door.

'There's no one here of that name.'

'No,' he clarifies, '*my* name's Dylan.'

'We're fine, thank you very much,' comes the muffled woman's voice.

'Please, I'm looking for someone. It's important.'

There's a silence.

'I'm Dylan,' he says again, as clearly as he can. 'I'm looking for Janelle Stevens…'

He hears the sound of locks being drawn, and the door opens a fraction, a fastened chain swinging on its latch.

'Dylan?'

'Janelle, is that you?'

There's the rattle of a chain being unfastened and the door swings open…

*

Chris is rewriting the text for what feels like the thousandth time:

Hey you, I'm hanging out with the kid today. Hope it's going well in fashion land. Can't wait to see you tonight xxxx Chris

The sign off was the easy part – they had settled on a standard four kisses, which seemed adequately demonstrative without being overdone – it's the 'Hey you' that worries him. It feels too blasé. 'Hey you' could mean anyone – *Hey you over there* – but 'Hey my love' feels too old-fashioned, and 'Hey' by itself too informal. He tries 'Hey my fashionista' (this makes him sound too gay), 'Hullo gorgeous' (ditto), 'Hey hey' ('we're The Monkees,' nope), and 'Hey sweetcheeks' (douchebaggy) with no success.

It's not only the text messages that have been off lately. Daisy hasn't been herself ever since returning from his parents (Chris knew his mother must have had something to do with the change) – it was subtle, but to him it is a seismic shift, like a river starting to flow upstream.

Looking at the screen again, he types 'Hey Daisy'. Weirdly, this is the worst of the bunch so far.

The phone starts to ring and Chris nearly drops it.

'Hey you,' he says, when he answers.

'What do they say about never meeting your idols?'

'Is it not going well?'

'Vivienne Westwood is lovely, like some super-cool, dotty old aunt. Her assistants are a pain in the neck though. They keep calling me Debbie and getting fingerprints on the Perspex. Sorry, First World problems. It's nice to have someone to rant to.'

'That's what I'm here for. Rant away.'

'Are you alright?' asks Daisy. 'Your voice sounds… odd?'

'Everything's fine.'

'How's Dylan?'

Chris glances up at the window.

'He's good, he's great.'

'What are you guys up to?'

'Not much. We're on a bit of an expedition.'

'Sounds like fun. Wish I didn't have to work on a Saturday.'

'Say the word, and I'll come get you,' says Chris.

'Don't tempt me. Where are you?'

'What?'

'Where have you gone on this expedition of yours?'

'Near Archway…'

'That's a long way for you two. I thought Dylan didn't like to travel?'

'I know, isn't it great?'

'And where is he now?'

'What?'

'I was expecting to leave a voicemail. When you're with Dylan, you usually don't pick up your phone.'

'He's off meeting a… friend.'

'Aren't you supposed to stay with him in case he has another dizzy spell?'

'Well, yeah… he's not far. I'm giving him a bit of… because he's… you know he's…'

Daisy doesn't speak for a moment.

'Are you sure everything's fine?' she says at last. 'Because it feels like you're not telling me something.'

Chris sighs – he isn't winning any battles today. And so, in the fastest and least incriminating way possible, he explains to Daisy all about Janelle and their journey to find her house.

'So,' Daisy says, when he's done, 'you've taken a teenager on a day trip to break into someone's house?'

'I better go and get him, shouldn't I?'

'Yes, I would.'

'Daisy, I'm usually pretty good at this.'

'I know you are,' she replies gently. 'And I shouldn't judge. I'm probably about to be fired. I better get back to the madhouse – see you tonight.'

'Love you.'

There's a muffled noise, the sound of another voice and the line goes dead.

*

'What are you doing here?'

Janelle is standing at the doorway in a mint green bathrobe, clutching the robe to her chest, a white towel wrapped around her head, her exposed hair damp, as if she's recently taken a shower. Her face looks different – her skin doesn't have its typical glow, her cheeks are less rosy, her eyes seem smaller – and Dylan realises it's because she's not wearing her usual makeup. But maybe that's not it either, not completely – has Janelle lost weight? Dylan tries not to stare.

'I… I came to see you,' he manages eventually, nervousness outweighing his excitement.

'But… how did you get here? Was that *you* buzzing before? I thought it was those Mormons again…'

'Yeah, I…'

'Actually, let's not stand around in the hallway – come inside, Dylan. Come in. We're letting all the heat out.'

Janelle quickly shuts the door after him.

'I'm sorry about the state of the place,' she says, as she beckons him through the short hallway, into a living room. 'You've caught me off guard – I wasn't expecting anyone.'

The living room would be crowded enough with the sofa, two armchairs, the plastic Christmas tree in the corner blinking, and the television (the muted screen filled with flying monkeys – Dylan recognises the film, but can't remember its name), but there are cardboard boxes everywhere, their contents spilling out onto the floor and the coffee table and the window ledges – books and old binders and stacks of papers, jewellery, cables, wires, shoes and piles and piles of clothes. There are clothes on the sofa too, and when Janelle moves to one of the armchairs, Dylan pushes a pile to one side, so he can sit.

'Now tell me,' she says, leaning forward, still clasping the robe together, 'how did you even know where I lived?'

Dylan bites the side of his mouth.

'You said your place always smelt like croissants,' he explains, 'because there was a bakery next door. And you mentioned once there was a post office box right outside your flat. I already knew you lived somewhere in Highgate or Archway, so I searched Google Maps until I found a match. It wasn't difficult.'

'But why did you come?'

'To help you,' he replies. 'To make sure you were alright.'

Janelle turns away as if she's thinking. When she faces him again, Dylan can see her eyes are wet.

'Why wouldn't I be alright?' she asks, her mouth tight.

'Something's wrong, I can tell.'

'Oh, Dylan,' Janelle says softly, her eyes beginning to fill with tears. 'This is so surreal. I haven't seen anyone for days, and then you turn up out of the blue.' Sniffing, she arranges her bathrobe to better cover her knees. 'I feel like I'm imagining this…'

'No, I'm real,' replies Dylan. 'You can pinch me if you like?'

'I've been cooped up here all week. I'm going stir crazy.'

'Because of your ex-boyfriend?'

'What?' Janelle frowns. 'No… why? I haven't spoken to Justin in months.'

'I thought he was threatening you or something?' Dylan says quickly. 'Because of the way he was before, when he grabbed your wrists. And you left Facebook, and you didn't reply to my emails. And then I got your text message…'

'I know – I'm sorry I sent you that. It wasn't fair. When I saw the post on your blog… Oh, Dylan, I've let you down. I've let everyone down.'

Janelle starts to cry, big gasping sobs.

Dylan doesn't know she means – how could she possibly have let anyone down? She's Janelle...? He sits with his hands tucked under his legs, trying to think what to say next.

'I've failed everyone,' Janelle says through her tears.

'No, you haven't.'

'I have.' Janelle wipes her face with her hands – Dylan considers getting some toilet paper, but remembers he doesn't know where the bathroom is yet. 'I'm just not strong enough,' she says, rubbing her wet hands together as if to dry them. 'I've tried to be, but I'm not.' Janelle gives a sad chuckle. 'I can't even say it out loud,' she says, rolling her wet eyes.

'Say what?'

'It's come back.' Janelle exhales deeply. 'The cancer.'

Several muscles in Dylan's stomach contract all at once.

'Oh,' he says, as if he's been kicked very hard in the gut. His fingers grip the sofa cushion, and he puts his weight on his toes to brace himself against the wave of sadness coursing through his body.

'*It*. This *thing*. This *other* thing. Do you know what cancer really is, though?'

Dylan can barely muster a shake of his head.

'It's your own cells,' Janelle says. 'They don't want to hurt you. They don't mean to be abnormal and multiply, they're only trying to help. But you're supposed to *fight* cancer – every step of the way. The first time it happened, oh, I did – I fought,' she wipes her eyes, 'I fought so hard there was skin under my fingernails, and blood in my mouth and everyone was right there with me. It was almost a relief after my ME, to have a disease people could get behind. You must know what that's like when people don't believe you,' Dylan nods, he does. 'All my friends and family kept sending inspirational quotes on Facebook, and offering to come to doctor's appointments, or making sure I was eating right – a couple even went on charity runs to raise money – everyone says *we are going to beat this. We'll make it pay. Kick its butt.* That's how people talk, as if you're going to jump cancer in some alley. But I did, I beat it. Dylan, I was so happy too. Strangers would send emails congratulating me, my dad took me out for dinner – my feet didn't touch the ground. I told myself the remission was a sign from God. I might not have the grades to go to medical school, but I could help people like me – children and teenagers with chronic fatigue – so I signed up for the training. I didn't have any money, but I knew I'd find a way, and then: tax rebate, holiday pay, money from my grandmother, just like that it all fell into place.'

Janelle wipes her mouth with the back of her hand.

'Do you mind if I have a cigarette?' she asks Dylan.

'*You* smoke?' he replies, shocked.

'Only sometimes,' she replies, sniffing. 'Don't tell anyone.' Janelle hunts around on the cluttered coffee table until she finds a crumpled cigarette packet, a small black lighter and a used ashtray, hidden under a magazine. 'Actually,' she says, taking out a cigarette, 'more than sometimes now. Most times. My flatmate is going to hit the roof when she gets back from her trip.'

'But smoking is so bad for you!'

Janelle shrugs.

'It's not like it's going to kill me. Won't get the chance…'

Dylan does not like this joke.

Janelle lights the cigarette and inhales deeply.

'I wanted to become a practitioner to help people.'

'You have. You did. You helped me.'

She smiles, genuinely now it seems, and it's the first glimmer of the normal Janelle he's seen.

'Thank you. I appreciate that.'

'I would still be in bed if it wasn't for you.'

'I know… and that's wonderful, but what if I was only trying to pay back a debt I felt I owed? If I was only helping people so

I wouldn't get sick again? What if God, or the Universe, could tell I was being selfish? The cancer came back because there's something malignant in me? Something that was only pretending to be nurturing and kind?'

She rubs her eyes with one hand, the cigarette in her other hand sending up a plume of smoke.

'I spent so many years being sick – not knowing if I'd ever get better again, stuck in my house with chronic fatigue, while my friends were off getting driving licences and going on dates, or choosing their universities. The cancer was my wake-up call, I knew I had to make a change. This was my chance. I mastered the course, reprogrammed my thinking, and I did get better, step by step. I focused everything on becoming a better person, being a role model, leading by example. I know I've told you some things about my childhood and growing up, but it was really tough. My mum was always working, she did her best, but I was alone a lot of the time. I was awkward at school, extremely shy, and being the only brown kid in my class didn't help. I don't look like anyone else in my family – for a long time I thought I was adopted. So, when I was fourteen, and the ME started, I wasn't in the best place. This shadow had formed already: "I'm not good enough. I deserve to be sick. I'm ugly. Useless".' She starts crying again, and after putting the cigarette in the ashtray, covers her face with both hands. 'No one would ever love me.'

She sits back in the armchair, still covering her face, and sobs.

Dylan doesn't know what to do. He's impinged on something he's totally unskilled for. *Above my paygrade*, as his dad would say. The pain and sadness of this beautiful woman, who meant so much to Dylan, who he admired so much, who had helped him more than anyone else – it was almost too much to bear. He could feel the emotion building in his chest, but he didn't know how to express it.

'This is why I've been hiding myself away,' Janelle says finally, 'I'm so miserable.' She chuckles again, sniffing. 'You should have to wear a biohazard suit to come in here, my despair is probably contagious.'

'I don't mind,' Dylan lied. 'Emotions aren't scary to me.'

'You're so sweet. Not everyone is so understanding. That's why I left Facebook, I just couldn't handle it anymore. All the people with their opinions. Have you tried this? Have you done that? Worse is the deafening silences. No one offers to go on a charity run for you a second time. There's no rousing calls to "beat it" again. Because maybe, you're just sickly? Maybe you brought this on yourself? Or perhaps you're not really a survivor after all?'

'No,' Dylan says, sitting up straight. 'That's the sort of negative stuff you taught me about. I don't think you have to beat up cancer, but I do think you should stop hurting yourself. Because that's what you're doing.'

'I know, I've tried to, but I can't.'

'You must have felt low before – and you overcame it then.'

'My cancer is back a second time, they're not even sure if it's operable, or if the chemo would work. They don't know how far it's spread.'

'Which means it might not be as bad as you think…'

'Or it might be worse.' She shakes her head. 'I know what you're doing, because it's what I would say. I can play all those confidence tricks in my mind, but I don't believe them anymore. They have no power. There's nothing behind the curtain, Dylan. Nothing. It's hopeless.

'I wanted to write books,' she continues, almost wailing, 'and go to university, and maybe get my law degree eventually – I don't know, fall in love, have a family. I wanted so much to help people, I really did. I was trying to help the world.

'Now I can't even sort out my flat. Look at this place… I keep trying to get rid of stuff, but then something triggers a memory, and I can't touch it. I'm not making any progress. I made you sit on my clean clothes. I should have folded that laundry days ago, and the pile keeps growing…'

'I can fold them,' Dylan says suddenly. 'I'm good at folding laundry.' He springs up and takes the item from the top – a cream cardigan – and starts to fold it.

'No, Dylan, it's fine. You don't have to.'

'I want to,' he says, still folding. A blue t-shirt now.

'Dylan,' Janelle grabs his arm gently, sending a tingle through his body, 'just leave it.'

'Please,' says Dylan in a firm voice, avoiding her eyes, his own brimming with tears. 'I want to do this. Please.'

They stand like this for what seems like a very long time.

'Okay,' she says, at last, letting his arm go.

'Thank you.'

He puts the t-shirt on the folded pile and starts on a green Puma jumper.

'Can I help?' Janelle asks after a few seconds.

Dylan shrugs, keeping his attention on the process of folding, and Janelle joins him, making a pile next to his. They work in silence.

'Do you need some assistance with that one?' Janelle asks, eventually, when Dylan has an issue with a wraparound top with long ties, 'I suppose you don't have women around your place, do you? You're not used to all our weird clothing?'

'No,' Dylan replies flatly. He does his best and places it on the pile.

'I'm sorry,' Janelle says quietly. 'That was too much before.'

Dylan doesn't say anything, as he folds a jumper that reads, 'Out of Office,' but tears begin to stream down his cheeks.

'I'm sorry too,' he says, and wraps his arms around her waist, and now they're hugging – Janelle still holding the t-shirt she was folding in one hand – a deep embrace, both sobbing together, *into* each other, as if the other person is a vessel for their tears, their shoulders and necks and the sides of their faces soaked wet, as the Christmas lights blink on and off, on and off.

'Shall we stop now?' Janelle asks, once the tears have run dry, and they're mostly sniffling, and rocking together, side to side. Dylan chuckles, nodding. 'Are you sure,' she teases, 'there's more washing?'

'I don't know how to fold the bras anyway,' Dylan says, wiping his face and sitting again.

'They are tricky,' Janelle agrees, laughing as she sits too. And then they're both giggling through the tears and snot. And crying again. It's like a weird game of Simon Says. One starts, and the other follows – but it feels good, this flow of spontaneous tears and laughter.

'I don't want you to give up,' Dylan says, wiping his eyes with the palms of his hands and wishing he'd brought a tissue. As if reading his mind, Janelle gets up, returning with a large wad of tissue paper.

'I don't want to give up either,' she says, back in the armchair, giving him several tissues and then blowing her nose. 'I won't, I promise.'

'And you don't have to hide away like this. There are people that really care about you.'

'I know.'

'What about your family – your mum, your step-sister?'

'They're doing everything they can. They're amazing really, I have incredible people around me. But they have jobs and lives. No one can be with you in the darkness, in the dread. I think that's why I lost it a bit, I went too deep down the well. That's the reason you showed up.' Janelle smiles again. 'You're my Guardian Angel.'

'I don't know about that,' he replies, cheeks flushing.

'You've come all this way, it's a long trip from your house…'

He shrugs, still wiping his nose with a tissue.

'I guess.'

'And you're so much taller than the last time I saw you. Stand up.'

They both stand up again.

'Look,' Janelle says, 'you're taller than me now. Shooting up.'

Dylan stares at his feet and gives an embarrassed grin, before they both sit down again.

'Thank you for the typewriter,' he says.

'Oh, it arrived? Good! I really wanted you to have it. That typewriter's been in my family for years. It belonged to my great grandmother – she was a Wren during the Second World War, and she wanted to write a book about her experiences, but then she had a family, and life got busy. She passed it on to my mother – I was never allowed to play with it as a kid – but when Mum gave it to me, I hardly ever used it. Don't make the same mistake, Dylan. Your writing's really good. You must keep it up.'

Dylan smiles sheepishly again, feeling guilty for stopping his blog.

'Do you want a drink?' Janelle asks. 'I haven't offered you anything…'

'I'm okay,' Dylan replies. He already had three Cokes in the limousine on the way over.

Janelle watches him for a moment.

'One thing I've always wanted to ask,' she says. 'You don't ever mention your mum?'

Dylan looks away.

'There's not much to say,' he says.

'I understand what it's like when your parents split up – but you were so ill for so long. Your mum didn't come to visit once?'

'She has her other family now. Other children.'

'So, you have brothers and sisters?'

'Sort of. A half-brother and half-sister in Trinidad.'

'Are they older or younger than you?'

'They're eight and five.'

'What are they like?'

Dylan squirms in his seat.

'I haven't met them.'

Janelle opens her eyes wide. 'Never? Why not?'

'When I was a baby, my mother had clinical depression. She went to Trinidad for a visit and didn't come back.'

'But you've been so ill? I'm surprised your mum didn't visit at all.'

'Dad said we'd tell her if they found something serious.'

'But you were in bed for months and months…?' Dylan can't explain the rationale to Janelle – it would have been too jarring to have his mother in the same room while he was grappling with his illness, too stressful after all that time.

'You're getting better now though. I mean, you came all this way from Croydon!'

'Everyone keeps saying I am.' Dylan stares at the floor.

'But you're not sure?'

He shakes his head. 'If I tell them, I'll only have to do more tests. Dad can't take any more time off work anyway. And I'm starting school on Monday.'

'That might be good – you'll get to see your friends again?'

Dylan doesn't reply.

'You're getting so tall, I bet you'll be breaking hearts when you go back, what with those babyface good looks.'

'There's someone I like already…' Dylan is surprised by his own words.

'Oh really? Who?'

Dylan shrugs nervously.

'Just someone.'

He gives Janelle an awkward look. It's taking his energy to try and hide his emotions, but they're written all over his face.

'Oh,' Janelle says, understanding. 'I wasn't sure you even liked girls…' she changes tack. 'Well, I can honestly say, you are the best man in my life right now, Dylan. I'm very close to marrying you, watch out.' He smiles and stares at his feet again. 'It's true, I'll marry you if you're not careful. Then you'll be stuck with me.'

'That doesn't sound too bad,' he says.

'No? You don't know the half of it. What you saw today was just the taster. You ready for the full-on crazy Janelle experience?'

She nudges him.

'Sure.'

'Sure?' Janelle smiles at him. 'You're going to make someone very happy one day, Dylan. Once you develop better folding skills.'

'Ha-ha,' he replies, deadpan. 'Funny.'

'Seriously, where did you learn your technique from? You just rolled that t-shirt into a ball.'

'All your clothes are too small, there's not enough fabric to fold them prop—'

He's interrupted by a noise he recognises. *Otis. Otis is barking.* Dylan waits to see if he stops, but the barking only gets more insistent.

'Sorry,' Dylan says. 'I have to check something. Is there a window out to the back?'

'In the kitchen,' Janelle says, pointing.

He gets up from the sofa, and hurries into the kitchen. From the kitchen window, he can make out the small brown body of Otis, tied by his leash to a post on the opposite side of the lane. Chris is nowhere to be seen.

Janelle enters the kitchen, a worried expression on her face.

'Is everything okay?'

'It's Otis,' Dylan explains. 'I'll just go and make sure he's alright. He's probably seen a cat or something. He's scared of cats.'

'You left him out there alone?'

'I'll be really quick,' he says, ignoring her question and heading to the front door, bolting into the hallway and down the flight of stairs, cursing Chris at each step. *Where is he?* Dylan wonders angrily. Probably next door at the bakery, stuffing his face with cream buns.

Opening the first-floor window again (it's quicker than exiting the front door and running all the way around), he climbs out onto the tin roof. Otis is still barking manically.

'Quiet!' he yells, but the stupid dog takes no notice.

It's slippery on the roof – the downward angle making it much trickier on the return journey. Dylan takes small careful steps towards the edge, using his hands to steady himself, and when he reaches the verge, he peers over.

His first thought is, *Why is Chris lying on the ground?* And then he notices the way Chris's torso is twisted across the gutter, and the peculiar angle of his arm, and the growing puddle of Ribena someone has spilt by his head.

CHAPTER FIFTEEN

Here is one of life's great injustices – although it may take many years to find a lover, they can be whisked away again in the blink of an eye. They might simply step out at the wrong moment and get smooshed by a UPS delivery truck. There's no way to avoid this possibility either – even if you track them with GPS (the lover, not the truck), or make them wear one of those blow-up sumo wrestler costumes, or tell them before they leave the house: *be so very careful, my love. You grew up on the Continent. Remember the traffic moves in the opposite direction here, look both ways.* They will smile, and say, *of course*, but how can you be certain? What if they shake hands with the wrong person, fresh off a transatlantic flight and get some new, insofar unknown tropical disease? What if they go sightseeing on The Shard and lean over too far? What if a metal beam drops from a crane in Canary Wharf? What if, what if, what if…? Love will always be tested, and unfortunately, nothing is more certain in life than *trial by fire…*

*

'Wake up sleepy, sleepy!'

Adam bats away the hand. *Two more minutes*, he thinks groggily. He's having a lovely dream – he and Cara are on a desert island made of actual dessert, and they're about to skinny-dip in a lagoon filled with vanilla custard.

'Time to wake up!'

Opening his eyes, Adam finds himself only inches away from the smiling face of Mr Maintenance. He sits bolt upright, giving his head a good smack on the underside of the desk.

Mr Maintenance makes a soothing noise, as if trying to calm a jittery horse.

'Careful,' he says, 'Go slow, slow.'

Rubbing his head, Adam stares at the man.

'What are you doing here?' he asks, disorientated.

'Builders find your house on the sixth floor,' Mr Maintenance replies. 'They're watching the security tape. You have ten minutes.'

Adam scrambles out from under the desk.

'What should I d-d-do?'

Mr Maintenance raises his palms to the sky – the international sign for *not my problem*. 'What else,' he says. 'Run.'

Adam doesn't need to be told twice. After hastily dressing, he crouches by the window and parts the blinds with his fingers. Mr Maintenance has gone (slipping away while Adam tied his shoelaces) and the rest of the office is empty, almost eerily so. Adam checks his phone – it's 9.26 a.m. The cleaners would have usually woken him up with their vacuuming by now – they were so reliable, he didn't even set an alarm anymore. On Saturdays, a couple of M&D early risers – dressed in tight-fitting running gear and clutching huge coffees – came in to check the weekly stats, but there's no sign of them at their desks this morning either. *Could the security guards be watching through the cameras right now?* Adam wonders. One thing's for certain, he can't stay here.

Summoning all his courage, Adam picks up his bag and makes a direct course for the elevators, acutely aware of any movement in his periphery. He's about to push the button to call the elevator, when he hears a voice from behind him.

'No lift!'

Adam jumps a full three inches into the air, and turns to find Mr Maintenance grinning like a Cheshire cat. 'In emergency, please use stairs,' he says, pointing to the fire exit.

'Why are you helping m-me?' Adam practically shouts, trying to regain his composure.

Mr Maintenance winks.

'The enemy of my enemy is my friend.'

Adam's eyes light up.

'So, the cleaners *are* s-stealing sugar for you!'

The man's toothy smile disappears.

'Stealing, no, no. Stealing is a very bad word.'

'I've seen the cleaners p-putting sugar cubes in their aprons.'

'They are cleaning, it's their job.'

'But they take sugar out of the packets, sugar that hasn't been used yet.'

'Yes.'

'What would you call that then?' asks Adam, baffled.

Mr Maintenance's smile returns, bigger and brighter.

'We call this *recycling*.'

'And what happens to the sugar they... recycle?'

'It goes back to the supplier. Office equipment. Paper. Anything not in use.'

'So, you're selling b-back supplies to the supplier?'

'Yes – *recycling*!'

'And what about the phone calls?' Adam asks.

Mr Maintenance's brow furrows.

'The cleaners do not make much money,' he says solemnly. 'They have families in England, families overseas. All they do is borrow phones. Like you do.' He beams again. 'Borrow food, borrow water, borrow electricity, nice white man, *you* borrow *everything*. Now they come,' he pushes open the fire door and slaps Adam on on the shoulder, 'you must go.'

Tentatively, Adam enters the stairwell and the door immediately closes behind him. He doesn't know if he should trust Mr Maintenance – *what if he's leading him into a trap?* – but despite his misgivings, he starts down the stairs. He only manages to make it down one flight of steps, however, when he hears the *cheeps* of a walkie-talkie coming from below, and turning on his heels, Adam leaps up the stairs, three at a time. His impulse is to run all the way to the top, but the builders have started work on the sixth floor, he remembers, and so he rushes into the fifth floor instead.

'*Hide!*' every molecule in his being screams. He sprints down the corridor of meeting rooms, but everything here is too open and exposed. Finally, in the last meeting room, Adam finds a storage cupboard. He flings open the door; inside it's stuffed with chair cushions, a projector and a nest of cables – there's barely room to squeeze a child in, much less a fully-grown man – but he's running out of options. Piling the cupboard contents onto the floor, he climbs into the space – it requires him to squat and twist his body, but with the help of a couple of cushions, he manages to squeeze in.

Adam has only just closed the cupboard door again when his phone beeps. He shifts the weight off his right hand, so he can take the phone from out of his pocket – in his crouched position, this takes some doing. When he eventually retrieves the phone, he finds a message from Patrick:

> *Hi mate, didn't want to do this by text, but heads-up I'm moving out in a month. Didn't count on living on my own so much – I'm going nutty! Found a place in Angel with two Kiwi girls I know through work. Thought you could probably take on the whole place by yourself now you're such a high-flyer. Sorry about the shitty early text. Would have preferred to do this face to face. Laterz.*

Remembering to switch the phone onto sleep mode, Adam returns it to his pocket and contemplates the series of unfortunate events that have led to him being wedged in a supply cupboard with not even a flatmate to call his own. An idea dawns on him, seductively: *surrender is an option*. He imagines hot running water, a proper mattress, a cooked meal – even the most basic of police cells would feel like the Shangri-La.

Adam realises he needs to pee. Shifting most of his weight to his left leg, he tries to alleviate some of the pressure on his bladder, but this only makes the cupboard lurch worryingly, and he stops. *How long should he stay hidden?* he wonders. The security guards are probably doing a rigorous sweep of the building, checking every floor. They're bound to examine any potential hiding place. Thinking logically, the cupboard is much too obvious – it's the sort of place the youngest child would choose in their first game of hide and seek. Perhaps he should try the stairwell again and make a break for it before…?

Two men approach, talking loudly and jovially – one is quite posh, the other has an Italian accent. *Don't come in here, don't come in here*, Adam pleads silently, as he holds his breath.

'Let's go in here,' suggests the one with the posh voice. 'This room has bottled water.'

Adam hears the chink of glasses and general chit-chat about the weather – they're not security guards at least, but this does nothing to calm his nerves.

'Apologies for getting you in on a Saturday,' the posh voice says once they've settled, 'but I thought it was time for a proper sit-down.'

'It's no problem,' says the Italian.

'Things are still highly sensitive round here – especially after what happened last time. But with the new project off the ground, it's an opportunity we can't miss.'

'I agree – the timing couldn't be better. I don't want to say, er… "smokescreen" – but yes, we have a smokescreen.' The Italian clears his throat. 'In terms of size, what are we talking here?'

'Everything.'

'All fifty thousand?'

'Can your guys handle it?'

'This is more than I was expecting,' the Italian says, 'but I'm sure we can make this work, yes.'

'Good,' posh voice says. 'Because my balls are literally on the line here. No one should realise what's happening until it's practically in the bag.'

'Don't worry,' says the Italian. 'We can strip the place down with careful phasing, they won't notice a thing.'

'And timescales?'

'A large transaction like this – six weeks, from start to finish? Mostly during evenings and weekends, for obvious reasons. But, er – what about Frank?'

Adam's ears prick up.

'You know what it's like with these old boys… Frank considers himself a champion of the people, but he has his priorities all wrong. He's been stalling me for months.'

'Won't he be concerned we haven't followed due process?'

'By the time we have all the templates and cost models to make him happy, the opportunity will have passed. It's a small amount of pain for a lot of gain. We'd be stupid not to bend the rules.'

Adam's right leg is starting to cramp. And now he *really* needs a wee.

'We'll move forward with other parts of the business,' posh voice continues. 'By the time it's on Frank's doorstep, he won't be able to stop a thing.'

And then it happens – Adam's phone begins to ring. Not vibrate silently – *ring*. In the enclosed space of the cupboard, the noise is deafening. *How can this be happening?* he thinks hysterically. *I turned it onto silent!* Wrenching the phone from his pocket, he sees the name on the screen reads 'Patrick' – and Adam remembers: Patrick is on his favourites list, which means his calls are set to automatically override the sleep mode settings: the jig is officially up.

Adam nudges open the cupboard door, and peers up at the two astonished men.

'What the...?' begins the posh one, and Adam scrambles out of the cupboard. As he runs past the table, Adam's foot clips a chair leg, and he smashes shoulder first into the wall. Except it's not really a wall, it's more of a semi-loose partition dividing the meeting rooms, and as he makes contact, it produces an incredible banging noise, shaking several ceiling tiles onto the incredulous men.

'Whoops,' Adam says, picking himself up. 'Sorry!'

He races into the corridor, past the reception area, and into the stairwell again, barrelling down the stairs. This time, he makes it all the way to the ground floor, but he's careful to tread lightly as he approaches the last flight, and listens attentively at the fire door at the bottom. It's lucky he does – in the foyer he can hear at least two security guards, waiting in ambush outside the elevators. *So, this is it*, he thinks. The inevitability of what's to come is almost reassuring.

Brushing the ceiling plaster off his shoulders and shaking the dust from his hair, Adam considers his options. If he has to give himself up, he wants to bow out with grace and quiet dignity – like Nelson Mandela, Gandhi or Martha Stewart. Adam recalls one of the zanier job interviews he went to, shortly before his Mercer and Daggen days, where an interviewer asked which superpower he'd rather have – flight or invisibility? *Flight*, he'd said, without hesitation. *Didn't everyone choose that?* The memory feels like a long, long time ago now.

Bracing himself for whatever might happen next, Adam is about to pull open the fire door when he realises there is another option – one that could make everything worthwhile, a final act of valour. *Why hadn't he thought of it earlier?*

He dashes back up the stairwell, running all the way to the fourth floor and into the corner office again, switching on the computer at the desk.

'Come on, come on,' he says, still catching his breath, as the machine powers up. When the computer's ready, Adam brings up Frank's Excel spreadsheet and clicks on their shared tab, frantically scrolling to the bottom of the page. He finds their most recent exchange:

Good to make your acquaintance, Adam. I'm Frank.

Likewise.

So, what's your advice for a foolish old man with love problems?

You're asking the wrong guy. The girl I like doesn't even know I exist. My only recommendation is don't wait to tell them how you feel. You might not get another chance.

Selecting 'bold' and the colour red, Adam begins to type:

Frank. There are enemies inside your gates. Don't trust the man with the posh voice and short brown hair. I know that probably doesn't narrow it down round here, but it's all I have to go on. He means to undermine you – I'm not sure how, but it sounds like it will have a major impact on Mercer and Daggen. Acquisition? Merger? Or shadier dealings?
   Have eyes in the back of your head.
   Good luck.
   Adam.

As he saves the changes and closes the Excel doc, Adam has one more thing to do. Hearing an approaching noise from the main office, he launches Frank's email service – he doesn't like intruding into Frank's email, but desperate times call for desperate measures.

Creating a new email, he types:

Cara, my name's Adam. We've talked a few times at reception and once on the first floor – I'm the evil twin guy – but you probably don't remember me. I'm sorry we didn't have a proper chance to get to know each other, sometimes lives connect and sometimes they only…

The door flies open with a crash. Frenziedly, Adam clicks the empty address box as two security guards bear over him.

'Step away from the computer!' booms the biggest of the pair.

'I'll b-be with you in a second,' yelps Adam as he types: 'cara. wilson@'.

'Sir, I'm going to ask you again to step away from the device.'

'Nearly d-done!' he trills, manically typing: 'mercerandda…'

He's about to hit the 'send' button when one of the security guards launches himself at Adam. As things start to move in slow motion, Adam is surprised to find it's the *smaller* of the two security guards – the older, shaggier man, one of the daytime Jekylls – who's made such an aggressive tackle. Pens and pencils scatter into the air, the computer crashes to the floor, and Adam is slammed against the wall, not once, but twice. The guard's not finished with him yet though – he picks up Adam again, and flings him down onto the desk. There's an almighty cracking sound as the table gives way, and everything goes dark.

When Adam comes to, he's lying on his stomach on what appears to be a stretcher, with a male paramedic hovering over him.

'Good, you're awake,' says the paramedic, cheerfully. 'I can give you something for the pain.'

What pain? Adam wonders. *And what happened?* It's as if a tornado has ripped through the corner office. He feels it then – a sharp searing sensation that starts below his left calf and goes all the way up the side of his body. He tries to turn over onto his back, but the paramedic – his name badge reads 'Terry' – shakes his head.

'I wouldn't if I was you. Not until we extract the objects.'

Terry wipes Adam's arm with a cotton bud, and jabs him with a syringe.

'Extract the what?' Adam asks fuzzily.

'You have half a pencil sticking out of your right buttock. A few pieces of desk. Some pretty deep staples embedded in your back. But apart from some slight concussion and a few other abrasions, you'll be fine. Better than the chap I had this morning who drove into that lorry! Bet he wishes he could swap with you!'

'I have a p-pencil in my buttock?' Adam repeats slowly.

'One of the best places for it, if you ask me,' says Terry. 'No vital organs. No important nerves. Nothing serious to skewer. If I was going to have a pencil inserted somewhere, it would definitely be in the buttock area.'

'And why am I wet?'

'You seem to have urinated yourself. Quite a normal response. I've had to cut away your trousers and shirt to get to the wounds, so you might feel a slight draft in your nether regions when we move you.'

Adam tries to process all this information.

'Am I going home?' he asks.

'Maybe eventually, but we're taking you for a ride in the ambulance first.'

A warm sensation starts to fill Adam's body. He wonders if he's weeing again, but he's not sure. Another paramedic approaches, and together he and Terry lift up the stretcher and Adam feels like he's a reverse Superman, flying backwards. *Goodbye, corner office,* he thinks as he soars away, *goodbye, kitchenette, goodbye, angry security guards, goodbye, shifty cleaners*. The stretcher won't go in the elevator – it doesn't fit! – so they'll have to use the stairs, but it's okay, they've already strapped him in, even handcuffing his wrist to the stretcher so he won't fall off. Adam flies down the stairs in reverse, saying goodbye to all the floors, and now he's in the foyer. *Where it all started*, he thinks proudly. He says goodbye to all the ferns in their pots, and then he wonders how they'll get through the turnstiles, but they must have opened a gate because they don't stop, they keep going right on through. Adam props himself up onto his elbow to get a better view, and who should he see standing in front of the reception desk, but Cara? Beautiful Cara! But she doesn't work on Saturdays? It's definitely her though – she's in clothes he's never seen before: jeans, a pink sweater, Converse shoes. Her hair is down, and she's wearing much less makeup too. Cara is standing beside a man who looks like a builder because he's wearing a high-visibility jacket and holding a hard hat. Both of them are staring at him, so Adam gives them a wave.

Goodbye, Cara, he thinks, or maybe says.

Hesitantly, she waves back. Beautiful Cara.

The doors of M&D open. The paramedic was right, Adam does feel a slight draft on the lower part of his body.

Goodbye, Mercer and Daggen! he thinks, as the small crowd of onlookers part way to allow the stretcher through.

*

A few miles away, JoJo is learning the joys of a languorous morning. Celebrities, like vampires, don't venture out until dusk, so Keith is free during the days, unless he's staking out the occasional plastic surgery clinic.

'I won't do children,' he'd explained to JoJo. 'It's not a moral thing, I just can't be assed to get out of bed to snap some sticky-faced toddler arriving at playschool.'

'Aren't there laws about that sort of thing?' JoJo had replied.

'There should be. Half eight some of them start.'

She kicks off the duvet with her foot – it's almost come out of its cover again. Around the bed lie an array of empty fast-food cartons. JoJo is also being educated on the delights of modern home delivery. You can order almost anything, at any time of the day – sushi, barbeque grill, a Chinese banquet (last week they'd ordered an entire whole crispy duck that stunk the place out for days).

At first, JoJo had assumed she'd be time-sharing the flat with other women – an arrangement, although never discussed, she was perfectly fine with. But over the last few days, Keith has made it abundantly clear he wants them to be 'exclusive'. JoJo finds this alarming. She's not ready to start another relationship – she's still very much in her previous one. And without being unkind to Keith, there are other things she wants to do, other *people*. Sleeping with a woman for the first time had occurred to her, and she quite fancies the idea. She'd considered suggesting this to Keith, but his recent neediness has made her reassess: he might not be ready for something so radical.

JoJo reaches for the dressing gown slung over the back of the chair, and puts it on. Keith is snoring beside her; it still feels strange to be on this side of the bed – at home, Frank always commandeered the left.

Plodding her way to the bathroom, JoJo shuts the door behind her. A frayed bath towel is draped haphazardly over the radiator, there's mould around some of the shower tiles, and the toilet roll holder is broken, but the least charming aspect of the bathroom is the full-length mirror directly opposite the toilet seat. She sits down heavily and does everything she can to avoid eye contact with herself. Letting out a long breath, as if she's being deflated, she begins to wee. Forgetting the mirror for a second, she glances up, but it's too late – the image of herself meets her unfortunate eyes: robe open, her exposed breasts hanging off her body in a particularly unflattering way. There is one good point about the bathroom though – the lighting fixture's so dirty it creates a pleasantly diffused light. Still peeing, JoJo sits taller and sucks in her stomach. Not too bad, especially considering all the takeout she's eaten (and the booze – good God, they can put it away!). She cups one breast, and lets it go, then the next, then both together. If she were to make some tweaks to her body, where would she start? The upper arms definitely, two bulldog clips should sort those out. Polyfilla on the varicose veins. Her hands could do with some hydrochloric acid. And the lines around her mouth? She experiments with her reflection – they disappear whenever she opens her mouth, so maybe a large ball gag? Laughing to herself, JoJo wipes, flushes, and washes her hands in the sink.

Keith is lying on his side when she returns to bed, exposing a leg and muscular buttock. He seems considerably younger from behind. Tearing her gaze from his delicious glutes, JoJo realises she hasn't seen her phone for a long time, and pokes around the food packages on the floor, until she finds it under the bed. There are four messages: one from the dry-cleaning place, a missed call from the travel agent about the potential trip to South America (Keith doesn't know about this either), a message from Frank and one from Belinda.

Frank's text is typically brief and to the point:

We need to talk.

Hadn't they talked enough? They'd talked and talked and talked and talked.

She opens Belinda's message, which is equally abrupt:

JoJo. There's a problem with the babies.

And just like that, her languorous morning is over.

CHAPTER SIXTEEN

Samira appears at the foot of the ladder.

'This is impossible,' huffs Daisy on the top step. 'Tell them the chandelier's not going to hold.' She bangs the craft knife down on the ladder, the sound echoing around the ballroom. 'I knew these stupid crystals were a fucking terrible idea!'

'Daisy…'

'They weren't designed to "float in space" or whatever the fuck! If they fall off and skewer one of the models, it's not my fault. Although they'll probably love that – very fashion forward, a model with a massive great Perspex crystal sticking out of her skull! Give them all fashion boners, those cigarillo smoking, pasty-faced…'

'It's not about the shoot.'

Daisy looks down at Samira. Something seems very different about her, she realises now. Samira seems *older* somehow. All the flyaway energy has gone, as if the electrostatic generator behind her has been turned off.

'Maybe you should come down from the ladder?' Samira says, not in her usual tone at all.

'What's going on?' Daisy asks apprehensively.

'I really think you should come down here.'

'Samira, I don't have time…'

'It's Chris.'

Later, Daisy will remember Samira's eyes – her unnaturally large dilated pupils staring up at her, almost ghoul-like.

'What's happened?'

'He's been in an accident.'

Daisy feels light-headed, and begins to wish she wasn't ten feet off the ground. She starts down the ladder, but her knees are wobbly. Fortunately, Samira is there, guiding her feet down each step, and once she's on the ground, she takes Daisy's hand.

'Is he alright?'

Samira grips her fingers.

'He's been involved in a fall,' she says, carefully.

'*Involved*? Why are you talking like someone on *Downton Abbey*?'

'He was on a roof.'

'What was he doing on a blinking roof?' Daisy asks. And now she remembers her phone call with Chris, an hour and a half ago, and her blood runs cold.

'Samira, he's okay though?'

She grips Daisy's hand tighter.

'He has a fractured wrist…'

'But he's alright? Generally?'

'They're not sure,' Samira says. 'He might have broken his back.'

All the air gets sucked out of the room.

'Broken his back,' repeats Daisy.

'He's in surgery now, so they'll find out more soon. Someone named Dylan called – your phone was on silent but it kept ringing and ringing, so I answered.'

'Broken his back or broken his spine?' Daisy asks in a small voice.

'I'm not sure,' Samira replies. 'Casper's already booked an Uber, and I'll come with you to the hospital.'

'No, it's okay. They'll need you here – I'll get my things.'

She starts up the ladder, but Samira catches her on the second step.

'Don't worry about all that now, I'll take care of it.'

'Of course,' Daisy says, in a daze, stepping down. 'What am I doing again?'

'Waiting for the taxi.'

'Yes. Thank you.'

Samira threads her arms around her neck and gives her a squeeze.

'Will everything be okay?' Daisy asks into Samira's bony shoulder.

There's another squeeze, harder this time.

'I don't know,' Samira replies.

*

Keith drives JoJo to the hospital in the Nissan Micra, zipping around traffic and running two red lights in the process. Once parked, they race into the main entrance – a brightly lit atrium with a reception desk island at the far end.

A sour-faced woman in her fifties greets them – or more precisely, doesn't. Avoiding all eye contact, she taps at her computer, ruffles through a stack of papers, makes a call – and when JoJo finally gets her attention, practically waving a hand in front of her face, there's no record of Belinda in the hospital's computer system.

'I'm sorry,' says the receptionist, not sorry in the slightest.

JoJo tries Belinda's phone again, but it goes straight to voicemail.

'She definitely said here?' asks Keith.

'St Thomas's Hospital,' JoJo says, brandishing the text message at him.

Keith turns to the receptionist.

'Can you try searching for, first name: Belinda?'

'That's not how the system works,' replies the woman unhelpfully.

'It's an *emergency*,' JoJo hisses, but before she can launch herself at the woman and throttle her, Keith pulls her to one side.

'I think I know what's going on,' he says. 'Belinda is using a different name.'

'Why the heck would she do that?'

'Because of people like me.'

JoJo realises what he means – this silly Duke thing was still in the papers. It would make sense for Belinda to use an alias.

'How are we supposed to find her then?' she asks.

'Leave it to me.'

Keith thanks the receptionist politely (far too politely in JoJo's opinion), and they head back through the entrance. Outside, they hurry right, around the perimeter of the building, until they reach the Accident and Emergency bay area.

'Wait here,' says Keith. He wanders past the ambulance bay, and stops at a young curly-haired man in a blue hospital tunic who is texting on his phone (JoJo is momentarily distracted as a man on a stretcher – singing 'Rock-a-hula Baby' – is unloaded from an ambulance, with what looks like half a pencil sticking out from his buttock). Keith makes the 'cigarette' gesture, but the man shakes his head. This doesn't deter Keith however, and the two men have a brief but intense conversation, which concludes in a brisk handshake.

'All sorted,' Keith says, on his return. 'This bloke's a junior porter, he'll help us find Belinda.'

'How did you make that happen so quickly?' asks JoJo.

'Impressed?' he replies, with a wink.

Once the junior porter has finished with his phone, he gives them a nod, and Keith and JoJo follow him back around the building, standing at an appropriate distance while he opens a side door with a security card.

'Take my hand,' says Keith, as they follow him inside. 'Look as if we know where we're going.'

They trail the porter – a few steps behind – down a series of corridors, outside again and into the Northern Wing, up an elevator, and towards the Maternity ward. As they enter, the nurse on duty looks up from her desk and is about to say something, when the junior porter ducks into the alcove to speak to her, and a few moments later, he beckons Keith and JoJo through, unchallenged. Moving through the ward, they check each bed and examine the chart of anyone absent, the porter poking his head into all the private rooms too – he gets a few quizzical stares from their occupants – but they can't find any trace of Belinda. JoJo is starting to lose hope, when she spots a familiar-looking face sitting by an empty bed.

'Frank?' she says, as they approach.

The man turns, and for a moment JoJo thinks maybe she's been mistaken – he's too small and deflated to be her Frank, surely?

'What are you doing here?' he asks.

'Can you give us a few minutes?' JoJo says to Keith, and he nods and wanders further along the ward with the porter.

JoJo sits down in the empty seat beside Frank.

'How is she?' JoJo asks.

'Not great,' replies Frank. 'The specialist's seen her, but she needs more tests.'

'What happened?'

Frank massages the top of his nose with his finger and thumb.

'There was some bleeding,' he says. 'She's in quite a lot of pain.'

'Do they know what caused it?'

'Something called *placental abruption*.'

'If my memory serves, that's not too bad. The placenta detaches from the uterus.'

'They're saying they might have to induce labour.'

'Premature labour is almost run-of-the-mill with twins.'

Frank brushes his left knee with his hand.

'She looks so ill,' he says, his voice breaking.

JoJo takes Frank's big craggy hand in hers. She finds his right pinkie, the fingernail lost years ago moving a piano, and rubs the groove with her thumb.

Frank clears his throat.

'So, that's him, is it?' he says, nodding in the direction of the departed Keith.

JoJo nods.

'What's his name?'

'Keith.'

Frank repeats the name to himself.

'I'm sorry,' says JoJo – she didn't want him finding out like this.

'No, *I'm* sorry,' Frank says, squeezing her hand.

They sit silently again. A nurse walks by, pushing a trolley, and smiles at them, the touching picture they make.

'I thought you were bored of me,' says Frank, when the nurse is gone.

'What? When?'

'Before all this started. Before Belinda.'

'Why would I be bored of you?' asks JoJo, dumbfounded.

A baby starts to cry, the indignant raspy wail of a newborn filling the ward.

Frank shakes his head.

'How could you not be?' he replies, quietly.

*

He's lying upright in the bed, supported by pillows – a metal splint attached to his left wrist, a brace on his neck and a thick bandage around his head, but it's his hair she finds most alarming. It's so fluffy, sticking up through the top of the bandage like a troll doll. *He'll* hate *it*, she thinks. She wishes she'd brought her bag of tricks now – there was definitely a comb in there, maybe even some hair putty. She could run and buy some eighties-style gel from a local shop, but then what would she do? Mould the fluffiness into a walnut whip? She wants so badly to do *something* though – if only to stop herself from crying – but she steadies herself, watching the rise and fall of his chest instead, remembering the story his mother had told, about finding him as a child, asleep on a pile of washing.

His eyes begin to flicker open.

'Hey, you,' Chris says, in a hoarse whisper, when he sees her.

'Did I wake you?'

He shakes his head, or tries to – the neck brace makes it impossible.

'Are you thirsty?' asks Daisy. 'I can go and get you some juice?'

'No, stay,' he says, taking her hand in his good one.

'I didn't know you'd be able to lie on your back so soon after the surgery. I thought you'd be in some fancy brace, suspended from the rafters.'

'Like a sex swing?'

She rolls her eyes extravagantly, grateful for the joke.

'I'm not sure they provide those on the NHS,' she replies.

'We could ask. They might throw in a nurse's uniform.'

'You'd never get it on over your neck brace.'

'If I've learnt anything today,' he intones sombrely, 'it's that dreams *can* come true.'

Daisy smiles, squeezing his hand, but not too tightly.

'How are you?' she asks, gently.

'Fine. I only did this to give you an excuse to leave work early.'

'Well, it worked,' she replies. 'But how are you really?'

'Tired,' Chris says, sounding appropriately exhausted. 'Glad it's all over. We went to the University College Hospital first, but the best spine guy is here so they brought me down. I knew it was serious when they wheeled me straight into the operating theatre. I don't want to brag, but I've had quite a few emergency surgeries, and usually there's a lot of waiting – you see the registrar guy, they give you pre-med drugs, they take you to the anaesthetic room. This time, everything was *whoosh*! There were fifteen people in the theatre, and one of them was hammering something metal – and I couldn't understand what they were doing until I realised – *rods*! They're making the metal rods to go into my spine. So that was neat.'

On the bedside table, his phone chimes an alarm. He lets go of her hand, turns off the alarm, and picks up a small plastic remote with one green button that administers the morphine.

'Free drugs,' he explains, waving the remote. 'I can take them every ten minutes. Want some?'

'I think you need them more than I do.'

'Suit yourself.'

He pushes the button.

'Are you in a lot of pain?' she asks.

'Only when you're not in the room.'

'You big goof!' she says, blinking back tears. 'I was really scared.'

He reaches out and takes her hand again, closing his eyes. She thinks maybe he's falling asleep again, but he starts to speak, his eyes still shut.

'My wrist actually hurts more than my back. There's this tiny vein that supplies your hand with blood, and if they don't reconnect it, the bone can die. I'll get the cast tomorrow. I've also fractured my T12 and L1 vertebrate. Or maybe it was my L2 – one of them. They're both compression fractures, because of the way I landed. And they managed to find the piece of bone lodged in my spine. They were worried about that for a while.' His eyes jolt open. 'Oh God!' Chris says, 'I'm never going to hear the end of it, am I?'

'What do you mean?'

'Dad. The fact I *literally* fell on my ass. He's going to be unbearable.'

'I think he'll just be pleased his son's still able to walk.'

'That's what you think. You've seen what he's like, he won't leave anything alone. It'll be torture. Maybe it would have been better if I *had* become a paraplegic.'

'Don't say that,' she reprimands him.

'Sorry.' He strokes her hand with his thumb. 'I'm glad you're here.'

'So am I.'

'How's Dylan?'

'Desperate to see you, but the nurse said only one visitor at a time. His dad came to pick him up hours ago, but Dylan doesn't want to leave.'

'Is Mike angry at me?'

'Angry isn't the right word. Concerned and relieved, mostly. I can tell how much they both care about you. Dylan especially.'

'Did he find Janelle's flat?'

'Yes, she was the one who rang the ambulance when they found you.'

'Is Janelle okay? Dylan was so worried.'

Daisy hesitates slightly.

'I'll tell you all about it when you've had some better rest. Oh, and Dylan really wanted you to know – Otis is safe. Apparently, you kept saying his name over and over in the ambulance?'

'I was scared I'd fallen on him.'

'He's fine. The driver of that fancy car took him back to stay with a neighbour.'

'Chauffeur-driven all around town. He's going to be a nightmare the next time we have to take a bus.' He smiles, but for the first time it seems slightly forced. *I mustn't tire him out*, Daisy thinks. *He's using up a lot of energy, talking to me.*

'Shall I let you get some sleep?' she says.

'Don't leave. How far away are my parents?'

'They were leaving Heathrow, so forty minutes?'

'Good, we still have some time.'

He threads his fingers through hers.

'I need to tell you something,' he says.

'Of course, anything.'

'Something happened to me when I fell.'

'I know, that's why you're in the hospital,' Daisy says kindly.

'No – I mean, something *good* happened.'

She stares at him, confused.

'I'd pulled myself up onto the roof thingy to go after Dylan,' says Chris, 'and I was wearing those leather Chukka boots – you know, my new ones – I haven't had time to score the soles on them yet, so really they were an accident waiting to happen. And Otis is yapping away like mad, because he doesn't want to be left alone, and so I turn around to tell him to "shush" and my feet keep moving. Just like that. *Swoosh*! So, I'm falling backwards, which isn't great, and I remember worrying about crushing Otis, of course, and not wanting to hurt myself, or let Dylan down, but I also notice all this crazy background noise in my head. It's like,' he makes a high-pitched mosquito sound, 'and it's made up of all these worries I have, and some of them are really small – is that a pimple on my neck? Where should we go for dinner? Am I putting on weight? What if you don't like me if I get fat? But there's bigger stuff in there too, and all these thoughts are making this angry hum in my mind, taking up so much space, and none of them are *real*. In those few split seconds, I can see them, separate from myself for the first time, and I remember thinking, *Huh. How stupid?*'

He closes his eyes again.

'Daisy, there are so many things I've avoided in my life, because I didn't feel like I deserved them. A job, a purpose, someone to love. I've been waiting and waiting – *for what*? But in that moment, before I hit the ground, everything changed. I was fearless.' Chris's eyes snap open again. 'I'm going to forget that sensation soon – I can feel the window closing already – and I want to tell you something before it's gone.'

'You can tell me anything,' she replies nervously.

'But that's the point...' he looks up at the ceiling. 'It's fading, so I'm just going to tell you, alright?' He puffs out his cheeks, releasing a long breath through his lips. 'Do you remember I told you about the sportscar, the one I bought for my twenty-first birthday?'

'The Maserati Spyder?'

He nods, or tries to.

'I was staying with my parents and I had to go pick it up at the dealership in London, so my mate Nicky came down with me on the train. He was a good guy, Nicky. We'd met at my cousin's stag do years ago, we were best mates even though we grew up in pretty different worlds – he would come over and we'd smoke pot and shoot clay pigeons or use pellet guns to scare the pheasants, any of that "to the manor born" stuff really tickled him. Nicky worked at the local garage, a proper petrolhead, and I'll never forget his face when he saw the Maserati. I mean, I was excited too, but Nicky was *reverential*. He knew all the specs of the car right down to the paint job – I'd had it painted this ridiculous Lamborghini orange colour – and he kept getting pissed at me for smudging the polish or pulling the clutch too hard. We left the dealership and cruised around central London for a couple of hours, but eventually we wanted to see how it would handle on the open road. And it went *zoom*! *Zoom zoom zoom*! I think we made it back to Aylesbury in under an hour – I still can't believe we didn't get a ticket. All the adrenaline had worn off by the time I dropped Nicky back at his house and we were flagging and grating on each other's nerves, so I was pleased to head off by myself. I wasn't driving for long, when I saw Nicky's sister walking along the footpath. Now, Michelle was beautiful – not as pretty as you, of course, but a lovely girl. A couple of years older than me, she was training to become a veterinary nurse. To be honest, Michelle had never given me the time of day, but then I pull up beside her in this shiny new beast of a car. We were five minutes away from her house, but I wanted to impress her, so when I finally convinced her to get in, I take this massive detour. And up until this point, I'd only ever driven my dad's

Saab, or one of the tractors, but here I am, with this woman I've had a crush on for years, the smell of her perfume, the sun setting over the horizon – everything so perfect. I'm flying along these country lanes, Michelle was telling me about this old lady who brought in her cat which they thought was pregnant, but actually had a stomach full of maggots – she was funny too, Michelle, you know? – and I was manoeuvring around these tight bends, trying to give the impression I did this type of thing all the time.'

He stops, and closes his eyes again, composing himself for what's about to come.

'I lost control. The police report said I clipped a fence, the impact causing us to spin around before going down a ravine at the side of the road. They did tests afterwards, there was nothing wrong with the car, everything was working perfectly – it was all my fault. I remember feeling Michelle's hair brush the side of my cheek as the car started spinning. It was like a hand stroking my face, and I turned to look at her. As I did, something hit me, her elbow maybe, or her forehead, breaking my nose. The pain helped. At least with the taste of blood, I knew everything was real. We were really being thrown around in our seats, those were really shards of glass, that really was the squeal of crushing metal.' He takes a breath. 'We hit a tree going down the ravine. Michelle died on impact, the coroner said, as if somehow that made it better.'

'Oh my God,' Daisy says, covering her mouth.

He swallows twice.

'They put a metal plate in my neck and shoulder.' Daisy recalls the moment she first accidentally touched his shoulder, how he'd recoiled. 'I had about six months of rehabilitation, and I was on painkillers for a long time. I didn't care how physically messed up I was, I deserved it. I was arrested too, of course, charged with reckless driving and manslaughter, but my parents were friends with the judge, and so I only lost my licence for two years and received some community service. I wanted to apologise to Nicky as soon as I was out of hospital, but he wouldn't speak to me, and his family tried to sue me in civil court. They obviously had a strong case, and I didn't want to go to jail, so I let my parents hire a big London law firm. I regret that decision every day of my life. The lawyer made their family out to be money-grabbing opportunists. He really raked them through the mud, it was disgusting – Nicky's dad had a bit of a gambling problem, his mother drank – but it worked, and I walked away scot-free in the eyes of the law. But I never forgave myself – I had taken a life, stolen their daughter away and destroyed Nicky's family.'

Daisy takes her hand away from her mouth.

'What happened to Nicky?' she asks.

'He was fired from his apprenticeship, started drinking. There was a fight. He's in prison now, gets out in a couple of years.'

'Oh my God,' Daisy says again. 'You were all so young.' She shakes her head. 'How did you even begin to cope?'

'I didn't really. I drank a lot. I woke up each day with the darkness heavier than before. I almost did something really stupid a couple of times – I don't know what stopped me. Cowardice. Being an only child. The look on my mum's face.'

'But it was an accident.'

'I bought a racing car. I begged Michelle to get in. It was my foot on the accelerator.'

'And it went terribly, tragically wrong, but we…'

'…all make mistakes?' He smiles blankly. 'That's what everyone said to me. That's the only thing they said.'

They're silent for a long time.

'You should be resting,' Daisy says at last. 'You've had major surgery. We can talk about all this when you're feeling better.'

'I'm fine,' Chris says, picking up the remote from his bedside table and firmly pushing the green button.

'I'll let you get some sleep. I'll be waiting outside, I promise.'

'Daisy, there's something else.' Chris licks his lips. 'Do you remember my dad telling you about how I tried to join the UN Peacekeeping Corps?'

She nods. 'Was that pre or post dreadlocks?'

He smiles again, more convincingly this time.

'Post dreads. It was pie in the sky back then. I wasn't really serious, but it's something I'd like to try now.'

'Of course, once you're better we can find out all about it. I can do some Internet research later if you like?'

'It means I would have to go away.'

Daisy's forehead furrows. This hadn't occurred to her.

'For how long?'

'A couple of years.'

She falls silent.

'Daisy?' he prompts, at last.

'Are you breaking up with me?' she asks in a low voice.

'No. I don't know,' his face is crumpled in pain. 'You're amazing, Daisy – you deserve to be with someone who's a whole person. I'm missing something, you must see that.'

'*I'm* missing something, we all are. That's the whole point of finding someone to be with,' she says. 'You probably have concussion, you're hopped up on painkillers. We can talk about this later.'

'I want to be honest with you, Daisy.'

'So, what, you're going to run away and join the UN Peacekeepers? That's not really a thing, it's like running away to join the circus. People don't *actually* do it. And you can't just walk in and pick up a blue helmet. If you don't want to be with me, fine, but don't make up a crazy story about it.'

'I'm doing this *because* of you. What happened today was only the – I don't want to say final push, but…'

'Go in five years then,' she says, blinking back tears. 'I already thought I'd lost you once today.' She takes out a tissue from her pocket. 'I've just got you the way I like you.'

'But *I* don't like me. That's the problem.'

How did they get here? Daisy wants to put it down to the accident – Chris will wake up tomorrow, and of course everything will be the same. But there's something different in his eyes. Something that rings true, however painful.

Daisy thinks of the time she'd walked away from Chris. The moment she could have ended it on her terms. He'd tricked her into caring for him again, robbed her of her agency, and now he was abandoning her. She was a fool.

'Why couldn't you have sorted this all out before you met me?' she says, wiping her eyes. 'Why didn't you fall on your ass years ago?'

'I wish I had, I really do.'

He takes her hand again.

'But I love you,' she says, sobbing.

*

A few hours later, JoJo is stalking the hospital corridors, searching for something to eat. All the cafés have closed, and she doesn't feel ready to venture from the building yet – Belinda still isn't completely out of the woods, although she's nearly stable enough to induce labour, which they'll do as soon as they can. Keith had left a few hours earlier – he'd been a real trouper, giving JoJo space, but hovering close enough in case she needed him (considering his day job, he was exceptionally sensitive when it came to personal space). Frank was in with Belinda, so JoJo should go home and get some sleep, but she can't seem to tear herself away. She'd sat with Frank for a long time in silence this afternoon, and it was as if some important truth had been communicated between them, and now she needed time to digest, to recalibrate. JoJo can feel her mind ticking over.

This was getting her nowhere. She's walked the entire length of the place, and there's nothing. Her stomach growls angrily. But then JoJo sees what might be a vending machine about fifteen yards away. She doesn't care what atrocities masquerading as food it contains – as long as they have calories. And yes, as she approaches, she can see it's full of the usual crap: chocolate bars, biscuits, crisps, pot noodles, but it will have to do. She considers the chicken and mushroom pot noodle: it would be nice to have something warm, but she's not sure where to source boiling water at this late hour. There was the smell too – Styrofoam, coagulants and chemical flavourings – it would stink out the place. No fork either. JoJo decides on a large Twix – the wrapper says 'sharing size' rather optimistically – and she takes coins out of her purse to pay.

'It doesn't work,' comes a voice from behind her.

JoJo turns to see a young man in a smart leather jacket, sitting next to a slumped older man, who is fast asleep.

'Typical,' JoJo tuts. 'Is there another one close by?'

The young man shrugs.

'I'm not sure.'

'Probably for the best, what with all the junk they put in everything.'

She turns to go.

'Here,' the young man says, opening his backpack. 'You can have these if you like?' He reaches into the bag and takes out a packet of expensive-looking biscuits and holds them out to JoJo.

'Those are fancy. Fortnum & Mason… Golly!'

'Take them.'

'No, I couldn't.'

'Really, it's no problem.'

'Let me buy them off you at least. They're too nice to give away.'

'I've got other stuff.' He opens the bag wider, and it's true, there are all sorts of things in the bag: a bottle of champagne, truffles, a jar of olives. 'You'd be helping anyway – it's making my bag really heavy.'

'Did you win a Christmas hamper in a raffle?'

The young man shrugs again.

'I sort of bought them for someone, but I forgot to give them to her.'

He holds out the biscuits.

'Are you sure?' JoJo asks.

'Yeah, it's fine.'

She takes the packet.

'Thank you,' she says. 'I appreciate it.'

'My pleasure.'

'I'm JoJo, by the way.'

'Dylan.'

'Good to meet you.'

'If you want anything else,' Dylan says, 'let me know. I have brandy snaps too. And some pâté in a tin. But I already ate the crackers.'

'I'll start with these and see how I get on. Thanks again.'

She's about to leave when she stops.

'I could bring him a blanket, if you like?' She gestures towards the sleeping man. 'I know of one going spare…'

'Okay.'

'I'll bring it then?'

'That would be great, thanks.'

'Excellent. I'll see you in a minute.'

JoJo smiles, and then makes her way back down the corridor, wondering where the heck she's going to steal a blanket from at this time of night. She turns into the first storage room she comes to, searching for the light switch, when she hears the sound of crying.

'Hello?' JoJo says into the darkness.

'I'm sorry,' comes a female voice, sniffing. 'I shouldn't be in here.'

'Don't apologise,' replies JoJo, holding the door ajar with her foot. 'If you can't have a good cry in a hospital cupboard, where can you?' The voice laughs, sniffs, and returns to a gentle sob. 'I'll leave you alone…' says JoJo, but she hesitates. 'Unless you want someone to talk to. As my mother used to say: "a problem shared is a problem halved".'

'Oh, it's too insane to say out loud.'

'Try me.'

There's a long, wet sigh.

'My boyfriend fell off a roof, and now he wants to break up with me and move to Africa. And there are people in here with actual problems – people in comas and on ventilators and things – but I can't stop crying because it's late, and I'm tired – and I don't know if I can do this – lose him again, I mean. I don't think I can do it.'

JoJo feels very tired herself all of a sudden.

'It's surprising what we're capable of,' she says, drawing energy from somewhere deep within.

'I'm sorry. Have you…? Did you lose someone recently?'

'In a way, yes,' JoJo says. 'Although, he's not dead. Just adulterous,' she clarifies. 'But I'm slowly realising the ability to start over is one of life's small luxuries.'

'I wish I felt that way.'

'You will, eventually. I promise. The shape of everything changes over time. Things you thought were absolutes start to ebb and flow. The knack is to let them – without causing yourself too much pain and suffering in the process. If you can, they often turn into something better.'

They're both silent for a moment.

'Right, now – cry, stamp your feet, gnash your teeth,' says JoJo, 'get it all out. But unless I can interest you in a fancy biscuit, I'll let you be.'

'I'm okay,' says the voice. 'Thank you.'

'My pleasure,' replies JoJo as she leaves – only to return a few seconds later to ask about the blanket she's supposed to find…

CHAPTER SEVENTEEN

'London,' they say, lips quivering. 'London is a breeding ground for sadists and masochism!' Peer tentatively down the arteries of Oxford or King's, and you'll see them, jaws clenched, shoulders hunched, shuffling towards their irrevocable deaths. On the Number seven bus, they'll stand on your toes, or shove past you, crutches 'n' all, just to grab the last tattered copy of the *Metro*. His clammy armpits will reach new malodorous heights, while she'll talk constantly on her phone, and sniff and file her nails, before screaming at the driver that she's missed her stop.

No, London is for fantasists, goons and the morally bankrupt. With house prices rising at £6 million an hour, the constant threat of terror (and the terror of constant threats) – you're a chump to have ever stepped foot here.

That is, until one afternoon, when a stranger offers something so preternaturally kind – a shared joke, a spare seat, help carrying some especially heavy groceries – that we find ourselves in a vibrant city once more, one of endless possibilities, both familiar and yet not the same.

But until then, *mein freund* (grumble, grumble), until then!

*

The borrowed suit is pinching. Adam misses his old, more comfortable one, but of course it had to go in the bin after it was returned by the police – so covered in food stains and dry blood was the poor suit not even the most indifferent of charity shops would have accepted it… *and* there were massive slashes across the seat of the trousers. Adam's left buttock twinges at the memory, and he eases more weight onto the right one by tilting his hips. Over the past six months, he's put on weight, which is good, but it makes Patrick's trousers very snug on him. Adam pulls at the groin area, trying to stretch the fabric.

Glancing up, he catches the receptionist eyeing him carefully. She continues to monitor him, even after he stops pawing at his crotch, as if he might bolt from the room, or strip naked at any moment. It's a reaction Adam has become used to over the last six months, even after the psychiatric assessments had pronounced him (relatively) sane. It was in the eyes of the nurse who'd brought his meals, on the faces of his parents when they'd finally come to visit, and in the judge's expression, during his first brief appearance in court.

Only Patrick seemed unfazed.

'Don't sweat it, mate,' he'd said at the hospital, after Adam had woken from the operation to remove a pencil from his butt cheek. 'We all make mistakes.'

And with those words, Adam had started a very public journey of redemption. The newspapers had mocked and vilified him at first (*The Sun* having particular fun with 'bum' wordplay juxtaposed with pictures of his straggly beard or pink, naked ass), but then a new story developed – Adam was a champion of sorts. He'd even provoked a spate of copycats: a twenty-five-year-old biology student broke into the AXA building and was found living in the ventilation space; a young couple camped out in a disused supply room at the Clintons head office for eight weeks before they were discovered. There was talk that the newly coined phrase 'corporate squatting' might even enter the Oxford Dictionary. Adam had become, if not a celebrity, then a *cause célèbre*, making the rounds on the breakfast TV circuit (he'd chatted with Lorraine about the housing crisis before helping to make a pecan tart), with rumours he was to appear on the upcoming season of reality show *The Apprentice* (untrue).

The glitz and glamour were fleeting, however, and the threat of prosecution loomed heavy. Fortunately, Patrick had organised a good lawyer on his behalf, a fellow Australian who was willing to work for mate's rates, but there was still the issue of money coming in. Adam was borderline penniless – his credit cards were all maxed out, he was being harassed by payday loan companies and he had even fewer options for employment now he was an infamous corporate renegade. His family had been little help and there was only so much he could borrow from Patrick with a clear conscience. Prison might be the cheaper option, he'd joked.

'It could happen,' the lawyer had said unequivocally (and with no apparent sense of humour). 'Mercer and Daggen may decide to make an example of you. You embarrassed them, and they'll want to discourage anyone else from pulling a similar stunt.'

'What about their use of excessive force?' Patrick had asked.

'It's a consideration, but they'll say Adam provoked it.'

'Provoked it? They'd piledriven him onto a desk, they smashed it in two.'

'The security team had reason to believe he was a cyber terrorist. They'd been monitoring him for a week. He was trespassing on private property. They'd verbally warned him before making their approach – you can hear it all on the CCTV footage.'

'What about the stuff he overheard in the boardroom cupboard?'

'It checks out – the Italian is a well-known interior designer, they were talking about an office refurbishment. There's no leverage there.'

'There must be something else, Adam, something we can use?'

Patrick and the lawyer had looked at him expectantly.

Mr Maintenance had popped into Adam's mind then. The sugar scam. The phone call racket. That broad, Cheshire-cat grin during those last fated hours in the building.

'I can't think of anything,' Adam had replied, mentally crossing his fingers.

He crosses his legs and regrets it instantly. *Too tight.* The receptionist arches one disapproving eyebrow in his direction, so he uncrosses them again as casually as he can, like any normal non-crazy person.

Adam thinks of Cara. Beautiful Cara. He can't help himself.

When the charges against him were dropped – much to everyone's surprise – Adam had felt an overwhelming impulse to call the M&D switchboard to hear Cara's lovely voice, but his lawyer had warned him point-blank: any contact would lead to incarceration. So instead, Adam sat on his bed and read *On Her Majesty's Secret Service*, his favourite Bond novel, quietly pining each time Mary Goodnight, the beautiful secretary to the 00s, appeared.

His room had become a strange place after so long away. All the clothes, sitting neatly folded in their drawers, so many pairs of shoes – it seemed perversely decadent somehow. A pile of letters had accumulated on his dresser, most were final demands for credit card payments, but several were from 'fans', and a couple were sent by women professing their love for him. Adam had no idea how they'd found his address, but the love letters were a meditation in both sweetness and sadness.

I know we have never met, read one, which smelt a bit of gin, *but we have a connection. Something cosmic. Something real.*

But of course they didn't. And in the end, it was those letters, acting as a mirror to his own creepiness and desperation, that finally cured him of his love-sickness for Cara – well, almost. Several weeks after his court date, Adam was amazed to receive a friend request from none other than Cara herself, but remembering his lawyer's warning, he'd hesitated for a second – a nanosecond, really – before accepting. An hour later, a message window had popped up:

Cara: You're famous round here
Adam: Am I?
Cara: I think it's hilarious

Adam hadn't been sure how to respond – did Cara think *he* was hilarious? Or the resulting fallout? Fortunately, she'd followed up with another message:

Cara: How are your injuries?
Adam: The physical ones are healing
Adam: Still feel pretty foolish though
Cara: I bet
Cara: They told us you went through everyone's emails
Cara: Did you read mine?

He'd paused again.

Adam: Yes
Cara: That was a bit of a jerk move
Adam: I know
Adam: I'm sorry

Adam had waited for Cara to reply. It seemed to take an eternity:

Cara: There's a lot of douche bags in this city
Cara: Don't lower yourself to their standards
Cara: You seem too nice
Adam: I'll remember that
Adam: Thanks
Cara: No problem
Cara: Goodbye, Mark
Cara: Kidding
Cara: Bye, Adam

And with that, she'd logged off. Adam conjures her image now. No sharp pang, only slight crippling shame. Progress.

A phone rings and the receptionist snaps to attention.

'They're ready for you,' she informs Adam, and he follows her into the hallway, adrenaline pumping. The décor is very different from Mercer and Daggen he's noticed: chrome and glass, rather than wood and plaster, like a fancy eighties airport. The trip out to Osterley on the train had taken almost an hour, but everyone agreed, it was a necessary precaution. Neutral ground. Less chance of anyone snapping a difficult-to-explain photo. 'We can't give everyone who breaks into our office a job,' the Human Resources person had quipped, 'otherwise they'll all be at it!'

The receptionist knocks twice on the meeting room door before opening it. Inside, two men are leaning back in their chairs, chatting together. It's the very picture of corporate conviviality, but it showed their status too – such extravagant chair leaning only came with a certain amount of power.

The more senior-looking of the two jumps up. He's spritely for his age, and grabs Adam's hand.

'Great to finally meet you,' he says, shaking his hand vigorously.

Now in closer proximity, Adam catches the scent of cologne and shaving foam – the exact combination is instantly familiar.

'You too, Mr…'

'Please,' the man says, slapping Adam on the shoulder, 'after everything we've been through?' His face crumples in mock hurt. 'Call me Frank.'

*

JoJo spreads out her bare legs. It's good to have sun on the old girls – varicose veins be damned! It's been a long cold winter after all, and the early summer heat feels hard-won and glorious.

Beside her, on the picnic blanket, Ava wobbles slightly before righting herself; sitting is an act of total concentration for her small person. JoJo leans over and repositions the umbrella so its shade fully covers her – Ava's delicate baby skin is almost translucent, like a layer of filo pastry wrapped across pink marble.

Down by the pond, Belinda is showing Millie – Ava's sister – the ducks. Millie loves birds of all kinds, but Ava has no time for them. It's not that she's scared, per se, it's more that she can't see the point. JoJo can empathise: what *is* the point of ducks anyway? To shit all over the place and demand bread? (Although you weren't supposed to feed them bread anymore, lest they become fat and even more obnoxious.) Besides, Ava is courageous in her own way. Surviving, for one. She'd been so small when she was born that her entire body would have fitted right inside the palm of your hand, with room for change.

Ava holds up her fist and JoJo nods encouragingly, so Ava pops it in her mouth and sucks hungrily. *Smart girl*, thinks JoJo, closing her eyes again, and drinking in the sunlight.

A shrill voice interrupts her reverie.

'Look, Anabelle, a baby!'

Standing over them now is a ruddy-faced woman, with an equally ruddy toddler on her hip. The child is pointing a pudgy finger at Ava, but she, in turn, is giving them no truck.

'How old is she?' the woman asks.

Mind your own bloody business, thinks JoJo. She's discovered that having a baby (and worse – twins!) gave anybody the licence to come and talk to you. It practically made you public property.

'Six months,' replies JoJo, squinting up with her best *please leave us alone now* smile.

'Isn't she tiny!'

Ava turns, still sucking her fist, and gives mother and child a dismissive look. *Good girl*, thinks JoJo.

Anabelle whacks her mother on the side of her neck.

'I want to go!' she whines.

'Yes, in a minute, petal, we're just saying goodbye to our new friends. Don't you want to say goodbye?'

Anabelle shakes her head and hits her mother again.

'She's tired,' her mother explains apologetically.

'Needs a good smack, if you ask me.'

The woman stares at JoJo wide-eyed for a second, and laughs. Kneeling down, she leans forward and whispers conspiratorially:

'Do you know, sometimes I want to. I want to slap her right on her tush. Does that make me a monster?'

JoJo waves the question away, but she pictures Ava, her wonderful buttocks, and her own wrath if anyone dared touch those juicy little thighs. Other people's children, JoJo could whack until the cows came home. She'd give this Anabelle kid a good smack right now and not think twice. But Ava... It was strange how the sense of proprietorship worked.

'Is she your granddaughter?' the woman asks, as Anabelle wrenches her earlobe.

'No, she's my husband's mistress's child,' replies JoJo, without missing a beat.

'Oh really?' The woman's eyes widen again. Taking a quick glance around, she leans in even closer and places a hand over Anabelle's ear. 'I'm not one hundred per cent sure who the father is,' she whispers. 'John or his brother! Luckily, they look the same!'

Just then, Gregory appears, holding two 99s.

'They were out of Magnums,' he announces to JoJo in his wonderful gravelly baritone.

'I guess this will do,' JoJo replies, taking the ice cream and giving it a good lick. 'Meet my new friend,' she says, indicating the woman with her cone.

'I was just saying what a cutie-pie you have here,' the woman says brightly.

'She's alright, I suppose,' replies Gregory, winking at JoJo. 'When she's not giving me grief.'

JoJo clocks the woman's gaze as she stares up at Gregory. At six foot three, and with long dreadlocks, he does strike a commanding figure. Gregory was both bisexual and polyamorous, which meant he wasn't traditionally jealous, but you had to be extra vigilant about STDs. There were plenty of perks though – many more than outweighed the risks. (Unfortunately, JoJo had to let Keith go a few months back as he was getting too clingy, but she still drops by to see him occasionally, when he isn't busy sulking.)

'We'd better be off,' the woman says, standing again. 'Come on, Anabelle,' she bounces the child on her hip, 'shall we try to find Daddy?'

'Yes, good luck with that,' says JoJo, still licking her ice cream.

The woman appears confused for a moment, and then laughs, slightly manically.

'Wave, Anabelle! Wave!' she cries to the unresponsive child.

JoJo closes her eyes again, wiggling her toes and luxuriating in the eventual blissful silence.

*

Dylan inserts a fresh piece of paper into the typewriter. He's only just getting the hang of typing, and still makes plenty of mistakes, but even the errors seemed charming and olde worlde (to a point). On closer inspection, the '@' and the '#' keys had confused him. What was their use *before* email and social media? Was writing 'at' so common in the old days, they needed to abbreviate it with a symbol? And did people send hashtags in telegrams?

He could go online, of course, and find all the answers in a few clicks, but ever since he'd been grounded over Christmas, and his computer privileges taken away, Dylan has spent considerably less time on the Internet. He was shocked at how much he enjoyed living an 'analogue' life. He read more books, took Otis on longer walks, and had even learnt to cook (properly – the other day he'd made an apple strudel from scratch). Dylan also discovered the world became slightly more mysterious when you didn't have an instant answer for any minor question your brain randomly generated.

Spending less time on the Internet did make choosing the next film for Janelle's movie nights more difficult, but Dylan had visited the local library and found a couple of useful books on French cinema instead. Referencing a book (rather than a blog post or an online article) also had the added benefit of making you sound much smarter, he'd discovered. Now Janelle was starting chemo again, Dylan also wanted to make sure the movies weren't especially sad – although it had to be said that most French films were a little bit miserable, even the supposed comedies. He also tried to avoid any ones with accidents, deaths, extended scenes in hospitals or anything else unnecessarily bleak – so that ruled out most. Dylan's dad had been wary about his son's burgeoning relationship – especially the movie nights at Janelle's flat (she was too unwell to travel to Croydon) – but he'd relented because, at the end of the day, Dylan was an adult, visiting Janelle seemed to be helping him get better, and it was almost impossible to go against the wishes of someone struggling with cancer. Therefore, calls to Janelle and trips to see her were excluded from the terms of the grounding.

With fingers poised above the keypad, Dylan starts to type his address. From one of the bedrooms, Otis responds to the *click-clack* of the typewriter by barking his head off.

'Every time!' yells Dylan. 'It's not going to hurt you!'

He stops typing, and the barking ceases, but there's a charged quality to the silence – Otis is waiting for his encore. Sure enough, as soon as Dylan commences typing, so too does the barking.

Ignoring the noise, Dylan finishes his address, adds the date and presses the return key.

He stares at the paper.

A warm breeze ruffles the curtains at the open window.

It was much harder to procrastinate on a typewriter. You couldn't just open up another browser window. He needed to get this finished soon. Dave and Shelly, friends from school, would be here in twenty minutes – they were spending their sunny Saturday afternoon revising for a test on Monday because life was unfair, blah blah… but secretly, Dylan didn't mind too much. *Purpose is happiness*, Janelle had told him. And now he was no longer the youngest (or skinniest) kid in class, school was almost bearable.

He wonders what Chris is doing now. Dylan was surprised to find how much he missed him. A postcard had arrived only today, a picture of a giraffe wearing a comically long tie – classic Chris. It read: 'Meet my neighbour.'

Come on, Dylan thinks, *focus*.

He starts to type 'Dear' (Otis starts up his chorus again), but misspells it 'Deat'. *Don't stop,* he thinks. *You can change it with some correction fluid afterwards.*

But what if the stress of writing the letter caused him to get sick again? Dylan hasn't had an attack in months, but the shadow of his illness still hung in the air. *Didn't something always, though?* he thinks. *Illness, exams, injury, death…?* Janelle caged in her flat, smoking cigarettes. Chris in a pool of blood…

'Deat Mum,' Dylan continues, 'Sorry I haven't written before…' – the sound of typing eventually masking the cacophony of barking, until Otis finally gives in, defeated.

*

And at Heathrow Airport, Terminal Five, almost seven weeks since Chris left from the very same terminal, Daisy's fellow passengers are already starting to line up at the gate. *It's ticketed seating,* she thinks exasperatedly, *why not wait comfortably in our seats until we're called, guys?* But no, there's a rush to join a queue to get on the plane and be first to… sit down again. *Oh well*, she thinks, standing and picking up her things, *people are fucking idiots*.

Daisy joins the queue, and checks she has her boarding pass for the umpteenth time. It's her first ever trip to New York and she's nervous. Her friend Bryony, the one who helped Daisy get into fashion in the first place, moved there three years ago and was constantly inviting her to go over for a holiday – Daisy definitely needed one, but what if it was too overwhelming? What if someone tried to make her buy a pretzel and she didn't want a pretzel, but they were so American and insistent about everything that she bought them all? What would she do with so many pretzels? Or worse, what if she liked New York so much that she never wanted to leave again, and realised she'd been living in the wrong city all this time?

Her rational mind knows she's over-analysing everything, but Daisy can't help it. Enduring one of the world's slowest-burn break-ups will do that…

Oh, Chris.

For someone with so many injuries, Chris managed to heal at a remarkable rate (like a wolverine, he kept saying, although Daisy couldn't recall why wolverines were so especially fast-healing). By day two, he was sitting up by himself, and on the fifth day, he was hobbling around the hospital with a walker, racing a kid in a wheelchair down the corridor and getting them both in trouble with the nurses. Daisy knew he was in a lot of pain – Chris self-administered so much morphine it made him chronically constipated – but he never complained and systematically charmed everyone in a half-mile radius, whether they liked it or not.

After a fortnight, Chris was discharged from hospital, and spent a month convalescing at his parents' house, Daisy travelling up each Friday to stay the weekend. It was an intensely emotional time – often they'd spend hours just *holding* each other, like soppy characters in a Nicholas Sparks novel. One afternoon, Daisy found herself standing by the kitchen sink with a full glass of water, and no idea how she'd got there, her brain was so wistfully ticking over. *Would Chris still leave? Should she end things pre-emptively?* But then Daisy would return to the bedroom to find Chris grinning up at her, a halo of empty chocolate wrappers around his head, and all those thoughts would dissolve…

It was on his return to London that life began to accelerate. At first, Chris wanted to share his findings with Daisy – the programmes he liked, facts about Maasai or Mombasa, pictures of poor malnourished children and potbellied babies – but it was all too painful, and she begged him to stop. *Better to be in the dark*, she'd thought, naively. *And it might never happen?* Daisy's own covert research revealed most of the volunteer programmes wanted skilled workers – teachers, doctors, builders – and competition was fierce. She'd taken comfort in the fact that Chris turned down an offer from his father to introduce him to a diplomat who could pull some strings – *surely that meant he wasn't serious?* And anyway, it would be hot, unglamorous, physically punishing work – not exactly Chris's forte. Daisy had to admit though, there was something steely about him now, a focus and tenacity missing before – it had made her nervous.

A male flight attendant makes an announcement over the intercom: business class and families with small children first, and the queue starts to bunch forward impatiently. Daisy digs through the contents of her bag – she's misplaced her boarding pass already – but finds the unopened envelope from Chris instead. She takes it out gingerly, as if it contains uranium or something explosive. The edges of the envelope are dog-eared and grubby. He had delivered it in person, moments before she had to leave for a last-minute shoot in Paris – their goodbye dinner cancelled. Standing at her front door, they'd kissed, but the farewell had felt rushed and unsatisfying. The taxi driver was watching. She was late for the Eurostar. She'd worried about morning breath. Things went unsaid. Ever since, Daisy has been carrying the envelope around – for weeks now – without finding the courage to open it, and who could blame her? Those final few months with Chris had been… fraught. One moment, Daisy wanted to chain herself to his ankle; the next, she just wanted him to *leave already*. Even now, she still felt a gnawing fear that this whole 'going to Africa for a minimum of two years' thing was only an excuse to break up. That Chris had never really cared for her.

Daisy finds her boarding pass again and hurriedly stashes the envelope back in her bag, as another announcement starts the line moving. When she's through the gate with her boarding stub, she joins another queue on the gangway of thirty or so people, slowly trudging forward. Taking out her phone, Daisy makes a final sweep of messages, checking texts, her emails, Facebook, WhatsApp, Instagram and PingBubbl. Nothing juicy, and of course nothing from Chris, who is completely off-grid – the nearest telephone over an hour's drive away. She remembers their pact when they first met: no social media. Pick up the phone. Proper communication. How ironic then that their relationship should end with such a comprehensive media blackout.

Stop it, she says to herself. *You're on holiday. No more thinking about him.* What she wants most is a break from her mind – the churning over every small detail, the waking in the middle of the night with new damning evidence or missed opportunities – but as Daisy turns the corner and sees the entrance to the aircraft for the first time, she's seized with panic. *If I don't open the envelope before I get on the plane*, she thinks frantically, *all this sad energy will follow me to New York. I have to do it now, or it'll be too late!*

Flinging open her bag, Daisy gropes through its contents until she locates the envelope again. She holds it for a second, muscles tense. *Why am I so scared?* she thinks. *Maybe I should throw it away? Or borrow someone's lighter and burn it?* She chides herself for her own melodramatics, and slips a finger under the seal to open it.

Inside, she finds a card. On the front is a drawing of the Underground logo in red and blue pencil, except the red circle part of the logo is heart-shaped. The blue pencil has been smudged, and next to the smudge, in black ballpoint, there's an arrow with the word 'whoops!' beside it in block letters. *Cute.*

Closing her eyes, Daisy takes a deep breath and opens the card. Looking down again, she reads:

For Daisy
x Chris

Daisy stares at the card. *That's it?* 'x Chris'? Not to be ungrateful, it was a lovely card – as cards go – but *X BLOODY CHRIS…?* After all that?!

'Excuse me,' a woman with an American accent says behind Daisy, 'I think you dropped something.'

Confused, Daisy turns.

The woman is wearing a carnation pink jumper with a 'Save our Spaniels' badge pinned to her chest. 'I thought it might be your ticket,' she adds helpfully.

'Er… thank you,' says Daisy, peering at the mottled eggshell linoleum – but she can't see anything and she's still holding her boarding stub in her hand.

'I saw it too,' pipes up another American woman, obviously a friend or maybe a sister of the first one, wearing a matching sweater in yellow. 'Seemed to me like a piece of paper, flew all the way down there.'

She points to a spot on the ground, but when Daisy investigates, she can't see anything.

'Strange,' says the first woman. 'It's disappeared. Maybe I need to get my eyes checked?'

'No, I definitely saw it,' the other woman says. 'It can't have vanished.'

Soon, all three are searching the floor. The line ahead of them moves forward a few paces, causing some annoyed grumblings from the passengers behind them, but the American women seem oblivious to the fact that they are transgressing British queue etiquette, asking people to lift up their bags and check under their shoes until it's a concerted group effort.

Daisy is about to suggest they give up – it can't have been anything important, and they're getting dirty looks – when the first woman gives an excited yelp.

'Found it!' she cries victoriously, pulling herself up stiffly from the hips and waving a piece of paper above her head. 'I'm not going crazy.'

'Where was it hiding?' the other woman asks.

'Over here. It was camouflaged on the floor – practically invisible.'

And so it is; the folded piece of paper she gives Daisy is the exact same colour as the linoleum – it even has a similar dappled pattern.

The people behind them are fed up of this nonsense now, and start to barge past. Daisy thanks the two women profusely, and steps to one side, letting the queue swarm by her.

Carefully, she opens the sheet of paper. Written in Chris's big loopy handwriting is the following:

- You, held aloft by two muscled men during the breakdown of that 'Lola's Theme' remix, as everyone else in the club whooped and hollered.

- The time you called me on the phone to say goodnight after our second date. The nervousness in your voice. I could have squeezed you.

- Your fury at the District line. 'Seriously, it's the OAP of Tube lines! It might as well be going *backwards!'*

- Your horror when I asked the cab driver to check that weird-looking mole on my back for me.

- Empirical evidence proved you do like sitting at the front of the cinema (*Lawrence of Arabia*, the Prince Charles). You don't get a crick in your neck, your eyes will adjust, and it is more immersive. And better than being stuck behind a tall person. Or your nemesis: *hat guy*.

- Receiving my first ever telegram (if I'm being completely honest, I thought it was a court summons).
- The way you decline the offer of cream on top, but then always ask for a cheeky squirt at the end (I'm talking about coffee, by the way, in case you were wondering).
- New favourite green spaces you introduced me to – the Phoenix Garden and the Geffrye Museum Gardens. You're right, Regent's Park is overrated.
- Your alternating look of terror and polite enthusiasm as Dad showed you his horrible gun collection.
- That Japanese restaurant we could never remember the name of is called Ten Ten Tei (and it's closed most of Saturday and all Sunday because no one wants sushi on the weekend, right?).
- The way you stopped at every person with a pushchair, any tourist with a suitcase. It didn't matter what you were carrying, you'd help haul their things up the stairs.
- Your face when I woke up in hospital, those eyes.
- Goodbyes aren't my strong suit, and I probably made too many stupid jokes at ours. So I wanted you to know this: whichever road you're on, whatever path, I love you, Daisy. With all my heart. Every ounce of it. I love you.

    xxxx Chris

    p.s. Remind me I still have that weird-looking mole I need you to check.

Daisy folds the letter, wipes her face with her sleeve, and continues down the walkway onto the plane.

EPILOGUE

JoJo is loitering (or was she? Weren't all universities public spaces?). No, *lurking* was a better description.

The buildings of the Imperial College were very different to the ones she remembered – they loomed above her, unnecessarily modern and ugly – and everyone seemed all of fifteen years old, of course. These students appeared hectored too, as if the weight on the world was on their heavy shoulders.

JoJo had cruised past the building at least twice, trying to figure out her motivation for being there. Was she really wandering by, after meeting Frank for lunch, simply because she was in nearby South Kensington? Or, had she ensured today's restaurant would be in close proximity? Either way, JoJo was getting dangerously close to entering the place, and she felt a strong sense of imposter syndrome – a couple more steps and she'd be over the threshold. She rattles the key chain in her pocket as if to summon a protective hex. When Frank moved in with Belinda for good, JoJo had finally taken off the mystery keys from their metal ring and thrown them in the bin. She obviously didn't need them, or by now, she'd have found what they were for. The lightness of the key chain felt liberating.

Why was her heart beating? She was inside the building now – her mouth felt dry, maybe they had a water fountain somewh—?

'Can I help you?'

Rumbled.

JoJo straightens up and turns to meet a young man who is wearing a style of glasses she remembers from the eighties: blocky, plastic, electric blue.

'I used to go here,' she announces, surprising herself with her candour. The young man's manner changes slightly, his expression less interrogatory, more interested. 'But I'm not a doctor,' JoJo clarifies quickly. 'I never finished.'

'It's a pleasure to meet a former student,' the young man says – genuinely? JoJo can't tell. Maybe they wanted more Alumni money; she still received letters from them every year, begging cash for something preposterous – the latest was for 'sleep pods' (*why don't they just nod off in the library like we did?* she'd thought).

'I'm not sure where you are in your education cycle,' he continues, 'but we have quite a few short courses you might be interested in?'

'In case I don't live through the longer ones?'

The chap tactfully ducks this question – or maybe he doesn't hear – and nips behind the desk, taking out a stack of expensively produced-looking, brightly coloured brochures and plopping them on the counter between them.

Ah, so he's pumping me for the upsell, thinks JoJo, but secretly she's pleased. She's been deemed a worthy enough mark.

'Food allergy?' he says, holding up one of the brochures.

'Don't know if I'd have the stomach for it,' JoJo replies.

He ignores this too – the chap is a master of the polite ignore. 'Diabetes and obesity?'

JoJo struggles for a witty rejoinder. Gregory, who as well as being a bisexual and polyamorous, was also a holistic therapist, had raised the notion that JoJo used humour as a distancing defence mechanism, but she'd only laughed it off, thereby annoyingly proving his point. When she'd mentioned his observation to Frank, he'd raised his eyebrows as if to say: *Gregory is a brave man.*

'He's on his own,' Frank had said with a smirk, 'I'm not touching that one.'

'Pass,' JoJo says to the uni chap – a witticism eluding her. Maybe something about the course not having enough meat on the bone to interest her? Ah, it was too late, the moment had gone.

'Now this one is excellent – medical ethics. And it begins in just a few weeks too.'

JoJo opens the brochure. It's several moments before she realises she's been quietly reading, engrossed in its contents: *the examination of the concepts, assumptions, beliefs, emotions and arguments that underpin decision making in medicine.*

'Hmmm,' she says to herself.

'Take it, have a think. I'm here until three o'clock, I can have you enrolled in a flash.'

Mumbling her thanks, JoJo still has her nose in the brochure as she emerges outside, full of sunshine and anxious young people, all busily trying to get somewhere with their lives.

*

'Dad!' Dylan yells from his bedroom, still surprised at how deep his voice sounds now, 'do we have any candles?'

Dylan's father appears at the doorway, eating a ham and cheese sandwich.

'What do you want a candle for?' he replies, between chews. 'You nearly burnt down the place making those pancakes this morning.'

'You said you liked them!'

'I did, they were crispy. But the whole house still smells of smoke. And there's batter on the kitchen ceiling.'

'That was Otis' fault. He gives me very judgemental looks when I'm cooking.'

'He's only hoping you drop something.'

'Do we have any candles?'

'What for?'

Dylan looks sheepish.

'Today is the six-month anniversary of Janelle's…' he trails off. 'I wanted to light a candle. In remembrance.'

Dylan's dad has just taken a big bite of his sandwich, so he chews furiously until he's able to speak again.

'You should have said something – we could have taken flowers to the cemetery if you wanted…'

'No!' Dylan says quickly. No more graveyards. He'd had to summon all his courage to put aside his irrational fears during Janelle's funeral: the ancient cobwebs on the ceiling of the church, the strange archaic language used by the vicar, the ghoulish crypt near Janelle's final resting place, only momentarily distracting him from the knowledge her body was being lowered into the ground. Creepiness was no match for the real horror, though. Janelle was gone. *Gone.* The tears didn't flow until he was in a toilet cubicle by himself, and then he'd cried so much he was afraid he was going to puke. And then he *did* vomit – normal coloured sick this time – but the purge somehow helped him to the truth. Yes, there was a corpse in a box in a hole, but the real Janelle was still with him. There was nothing he should be scared of, except forgetting this fact.

'There's a pack of tea candles under the sink – I'll get you one.' His dad hesitates. 'Do you want some company while you light it?'

'I think I'd like to be on my own, if that's okay?'

Dylan's father nods.

When his dad returns with the candle, Dylan locks Otis out of the bedroom (Otis claws at the door but will calm down eventually), sits on the rug by his bed and places the candle next to a box of matches in front of him. He's found an old photo of Janelle from the Firebolt Process website and printed it out in black and white. The image is grainy, but you can still make out how beautiful she is. Was. He's mounted the picture onto card –

the back of an old Weetabix box – and propped it up in a bent paperclip so it stands by itself. Dylan strikes a match – it flames nosily and as he lights the candle, he breathes in the sulphurous smoke. He's not sure what he's supposed to do now. His impulse is to say a few words, but he feels silly speaking to himself in an empty room. Instead, he closes his eyes, and tries to think of Janelle. Maybe not the Janelle in those last few days – her face gaunt, eyes dull, the spark only returning when she managed to smile, which at the end, was rare but radiantly wonderful, like mid-winter sun – that image was still too raw. Even through all the pain, she radiated goodness. Not always – sometimes she was extremely fed up and grumpy. Fed up with the hospital food, her neighbour's loud TV and especially with the cancer. After that fateful Saturday in Archway, their relationship had become much more intimate, but apart from holding hands, and sleeping in the same bed, it never became truly physical. He'd tried to explain the dynamic of his relationship to his mum in one of his fortnightly letters, but it never sounded right. *Janelle helped me get better*, he typed at last, *she was my best friend. She died too soon.*

Dylan can hear Otis clawing at his bedroom door, so he brushes the stray tear out of his eye and goes to free the dog. As Dylan gives the black and white picture of Janelle a final kiss – he has writing to do, University applications to finish – Otis gives a panicked yelp. The idiot dog has discovered the candle and managed to get hot wax all over his nose.

*

Adam rubs his neck. His body is sore from being forced to stare at his computer so long – it still felt so constricting to work like this, always sitting at the same desk, on a chair, facing the same way. He often longed to kick off his shoes and slide underneath the desk, but that would definitely result in funny looks, and he didn't want to draw any more attention to himself. Adam was already the butt (groan) of many office jokes.

'Have a good week,' his line manager had said one team meeting recently. 'And remember, you can always ask Adam if you have any questions about bottom lines.' The requisite sniggers ensued.

When Frank had fast-tracked him a job in Mercer and Daggen's offsite marketing arm, Adam had secretly hoped that he might become his private mentor, or at least keep in contact, but that had not become a reality. Frank was too far up the food chain; he was an apex predator, Adam was practically a newt in comparison – their relationship had no grounds to be. Several of Adam's colleagues had pressed him on what Frank was like, but he could never think of anything impressive to say. What they'd shared via Excel spreadsheet was ultimately too personal, and there had also been that final crippling handshake from Frank, along with the look: *let's never mention* that *stuff again, shall we?* Adam's job was perhaps a case of keeping, if not your enemies close, then 'the people hiding under your desk who know a few of your inner secrets' even closer.

No, Adam was being ungrateful – he was gainfully employed, after all – but a big part of him missed those halcyon days on the top floor and his corner office (he now worked firmly at ground level), with all the time in the world, no deadlines, no meetings, no reports – when he truly believed in what he was doing. His work now was adequate, fine, but it was so hampered by corporate standards and protocols and branding guidelines, the result was stripped of any real chance to make change.

'Your girlfriend's here,' one of his colleagues says, his voice dripping envy.

Adam looks up, and seeing Cara standing in the reception, his palms start sweating immediately. When Adam had moved from the offices in Osterley, back into The City, he'd dropped

Cara a message to see if she'd like to go for a coffee, and they started going to lunch together once a week. Initially, Adam very much wanted to suggest a proper date, but he also didn't want to spook the horses. Cara had seemed (understandably) wary of him – he knew he needed to prove himself before she could be more intimate. But she was worth the wait, he'd decided. And as Adam had learned, it was best to enjoy the journey, because who knew where you'd end up…

Cara smiles as he walks into the reception area – and Adam feels that topsy-turvy sensation in his stomach which he's learnt is the result of getting something you desperately want, but still subconsciously believe not to be true.

'Hey, Adam,' she says, and hearing Cara speak his name dispels some of the anxiety. 'Where shall we eat today?' she asks, taking hold of his hand.

'Hmmm… a place with soup?' replies Adam.

Cara's forehead furrows.

'Your stomach not feeling well again?' she asks.

He squeezes her hand. Lovely Cara. He's never been able to adequately explain the real reason for all his nervy tummies, but moments like this – their fingers interlaced, her thumb stroking his – they were worth all the easily digestible lunches in the world.

*

As he waited for the bus (which was scheduled to arrive in half an hour, but he knew from experience might be anywhere from one to six hours late), Chris considered his hands. They'd never been so tanned in his life. There were a radical amount of new sun spots and freckles on the backs, and a mole on his wrist – all joking aside – that he should really be keeping an eye on. The sun had bleached his arm hair white, and turned the hair on his head the same colour as photos of him as a toddler. Chris was less enamoured by the wrinkles which had appeared around his eyes and on his forehead, but maybe it wasn't such a bad thing to look your age… Would Daisy think he seemed older – *weathered*, as his mother would say – or worldly?

Chris opens his backpack and takes out a tin flask of water and gulps some down. Inside the bag, there were presents for everyone back home – a carved wooden dog for Dylan, a woven blanket for his mother, a joke generic fertility statue (made in bulk for gullible tourists) to tickle his father, a beautiful Maasai necklace for Daisy. Chris again worried it was too early to go back after just a year, but he filed away this concern. The well project had been completed three weeks ago. He'd achieved what he'd come here to do. It was time.

Surprisingly, Chris has been celibate the entire year. He hadn't planned it exactly, and initially there was no one to be non-celibate with (unless he'd wanted a fling with the sweaty French male engineer who'd shared his hut), but then a bigger group of volunteers had arrived in the spring, with three attractive women in the mix. Chris had decided, however, not to act on any of his flirty impulses. It was strange, without the possibility of sex, he'd made some great female friendships. Stranger too, he couldn't wait to tell Daisy all about this experience (Chris had only recently come back to social media – he'd noticed Daisy was spending more and more time in New York on shoots, but luckily there seemed to be no new boyfriend…). He was also looking forward to telling her about the wonderful people he'd met – especially the kids! Lemasolai, with the world's cheekiest smile, and shy Neserian and her tiny sister Esiankiki, and all the boys who played football, Roinet, Leshan, Norlari – or the Flash, as he become known to Chris, because of the way he chased the ball, legs a blur.

An old villager, who was sitting on a basket, grins at him and chuckles. Chris is used to this reaction by now. When he arrived, he'd been militant never to slip into *white saviour* thinking, but he hadn't expected to be greeted by the locals as so… farcical. This tall, white weirdo walking around – Chris was basically the local birthday clown.

'Where you go?' the old man asks, toothlessly, the 'wh' sound whistling.

'Home,' replies Chris.

'Where home?'

'London,' and what follows would have sounded corny to a native English speaker, but here in South Kenya (where the only universally known phrases were 'fish and chips' and 'David Beckham'), none of that mattered. This was the great thing about being miles away from your own culture, the old clichés were washed anew. Chris sits up, the memory of Daisy playing on his face. He can't wait to see her. To smell her. To be with her again.

'There's a girl I have to go see,' he says, gazing towards the horizon, wistfully.

And the old man laughs, as if it's the funniest thing he's heard in his life.

*

Daisy wipes the beads of sweat from her forehead with the back of her wrist. Today has been a nightmare. First, the air conditioning on set broke (not her fault). Then the glue holding the synthetic icicles had come unstuck in the heat (not her fault either). Then, a few minutes ago, she'd dropped a glass sculpture, smashing tiny shards all over the floor, so everyone was scrambling to sweep them up, except the models (barefoot, of course), who were acting as if the ground was made of razor blades. So yes, that was very explicitly her fault.

Daisy glances up. For the second time in her life, a wild gorilla is ambling towards her.

'Careful,' she says, holding up the hand, not clutching a broom handle, but the gorilla ignores her warning.

'Ah buk!' it says, as something crunches underfoot, and Daisy rushes over.

'Sit here,' she tells the beast, helping it onto a nearby stool. Seated, the animal lifts its right foot onto its left knee and starts to search for something on its sole – it reminds Daisy of the nature programmes, where apes groom themselves for fleas.

'We've got to take those off,' she says, but the ape is already one step ahead of her and shucks off the gorilla foot. Bare human feet are revealed. Men's feet. And yes, she can see a puncture wound now, but it's nothing. No glass, and barely any blood. *Such tanned feet though*, thinks Daisy. Odd, she feels she knows them. The long toes. That arch. She's about to say something to this effect when the animal finally manages to take off its mask.

'Oh,' says Daisy, looking up in surprise.

The day is no longer ruined. In fact, it's one she'll want to remember for ever.

'It's you,' she says.

A NOTE FROM DREW

Thank you for reading *The Shape of Us*, my quirky little love letter to London, and well, love. I had so much fun weaving together these characters and their stories, and I'm so excited they're out there in the real world, so you can enjoy them too.

Actually, that's presumptuous – I *hope* you enjoyed them. But if you did, please consider leaving me a short review. Something along the lines of: *Drew's great. He has all his teeth.* Or even a review of my book? Whatever suits, I'll leave it up to you.

You might have some outstanding questions (such as, what exactly is Pingbubbl?) or want to know when my next book is out (very soon, I promise!), so click on the link below to sign up to my newsletter. I'll only contact you when I have a new book out and I'll never share your email with anyone else.

www.bookouture.com/drew-davies

So, thanks again. And remember, as of the date of this message – I still have all my own teeth.

Cheers,
Drew

@Drew_Davies

drewdavieswriter

drew.davies.75873

ACKNOWLEDGEMENTS

Thank you to my earliest readers: Lizzie Catt, Christopher Kinsey (also for your help on unfortunate injuries), Sam Harvey, Toby Futter, Sam Piper, Felicity Monk, Alexandra Silber and Peter Farmer. Nothing is more foreboding than a friend asking you to 'take a look at this', but you bravely did nonetheless and gave reassurance. Leo Richardson, of course – thank you. Writer Sue Guiney for her sage advice to sit down and just finish the rest. In the later stages: Diana Seifert for being my patient, ultimate reader, Amelia Cranfield, not only for her friendship, but for giving me a place to write that one heartbroken Christmas, Joseph Marriott for his continual support and advice, and Joshua St Johnston for his generosity and encouragement. Thanks as well to readers Emma Leeper, Jenny Southan, Mernie Gilmore, Judy Heminsley, Stefan Kyriazis and my Uncle Dave, I really appreciate it. My brother, Alex Birmingham, for his fact-checking and vital feedback – thanks, kiddo. To my endlessly supportive grandmother, Mary Davies, for her constant grilling about when the book would be ready. Hopefully, you can order it from the library now, Nanna!

Of course, none of this might have happened if it wasn't for my exceptional agent Hattie Grunewald, who so wonderfully plucked me from unsurety – and all the team at Blake Friedmann. And it definitely would not have happened if it wasn't for my incredible editor Christina Demosthenous – and all the team at

Bookouture. Thank you, thank you – it has been such a pleasure working with you all.

Thanks also to Maggie Wicks for her initial proofreading and encouragement, and The British Library Reading Rooms and the Barbican Library for being excellent (and free) places to write.

Special thanks to author Emma Jane Unsworth, who in the penultimate stage of this book, swooped in with some valuable words that really gave me a final boost. Mr Saunders, my primary school teacher, for encouraging me to keep writing (yes, we're going there). My late grandfather, Tom Davies, for so effortlessly showing me how to blend humour with charm. My mother, Sarah Davies, for reading to my sisters and I as children, and afterwards, popping on the audiobooks, and to Marios, for his love and support, calmly putting up with me blocking out weeks at a time for writing and edits, a hysterical look in my eyes.